Poisoned Ground

Books by Sandra Parshall

The Rachel Goddard Mysteries
The Heat of the Moon
Disturbing the Dead
Broken Places
Under the Dog Star
Bleeding Through
Poisoned Ground

Poisoned Ground

A Rachel Goddard Mystery

Sandra Parshall

Poisoned Pen Press

Copyright © 2014 by Sandra Parshall

First Edition 2014

10 9 8 7 6 5 4 3 2 1

Library of Congress Catalog Card Number: 2013941231

ISBN: 9781464202247   Hardcover
        9781464202261   Trade Paperback

Poisoned Pen Press
6962 E. First Ave., Ste. 103
Scottsdale, AZ 85251
www.poisonedpenpress.com
info@poisonedpenpress.com

Printed in the United States of America

For Jerry

Acknowledgments

As always, I owe my thanks to many people who made the writing and publication of this book possible:

My husband, Jerry Parshall, and my friends Carol Baier and Cathrine Dubie for reading and critiquing the manuscript;

My editor, Barbara Peters, for her perspective and guidance;

Jessica Tribble, Nan Beams, Suzan Baroni, and the rest of the crew at Poisoned Pen Press;

My friends in Sisters in Crime and Mystery Writers of America, who freely share their expertise in many professional fields and on a staggering range of topics;

And, most of all, my readers, whose notes of appreciation and encouragement make me believe the effort is worthwhile.

Chapter One

Rachel Goddard drove up to Joanna McKendrick's brick farm-house to make a routine veterinary call and discovered her friend standing on the porch, pointing a shotgun at a man in a business suit.

What on earth? Rachel pulled her Range Rover to a stop on the narrow farm lane and jumped out. A wicked cold wind whipped her auburn hair across her eyes and she had to hold it back with both hands to take a closer look at the surreal scene before her.

The man at the end of Joanna's shotgun barrel was unmistakable, with his beaky nose and rooster comb of reddish brown hair: Robert McClure, president of Mason County's oldest and largest bank. Holding up one hand as if to fend off an attack and clutching a briefcase with the other, he backed toward the steps.

Rachel couldn't catch most of the words pouring out of Joanna, but her fury came through loud and clear.

"Joanna," Rachel called. "What's going on?"

"Stay out of this," Joanna yelled back.

Under a glowering November sky, the wind rattled bare tree branches and sent a few dead leaves tumbling down the driveway. Rachel glanced up the road to a cluster of small houses where the farm employees lived, and beyond to the horse paddocks and the rolling hills. Where was everybody? Hadn't anybody else noticed what was happening here?

When Rachel swung her gaze back to the porch, Joanna had advanced on McClure, forcing him to the edge of the steps. Another few inches and he would tumble backward.

Rachel jogged across the lawn to the bottom of the steps. From behind the glass storm door, Joanna's two dogs barked to get Rachel's attention. Nan, a golden retriever, wagged her tail, and the mutt Riley stood up against the glass, scratching and whining for release. Rachel had come over this afternoon to vaccinate the dogs and the barn cats, but it might be a while before she fetched her medical case from her vehicle.

His right hand still raised, McClure half-turned toward Rachel. "I'm glad to see you, Dr. Goddard." He sounded calm. In his pinstriped suit and tie he might have been greeting her at his office under normal conditions, not at a horse farm while its owner held a gun on him. But his tall, bony body looked rigid with tension and he held his briefcase in a white-knuckled grip.

"Joanna," Rachel repeated, "what's going on?"

"Honey, you know I love you like a daughter, but I have to ask you to please shut up and butt out. And if Robert knows what's good for him, he'll get off my property and he won't come back."

A fit and still youthful woman in late middle age, Joanna normally tackled problems with an unflustered, practical attitude. Rachel had never seen her like this, her cheeks flaming, strawberry blond hair tangled by the wind, hands trembling so violently that the gun barrel jerked up and down. She kept a finger on the trigger.

"But—" Rachel waved a hand, indicating both Joanna and McClure. "This is...bizarre."

"I just want him to *leave*." Joanna feinted with the shotgun.

McClure took a quick step back into empty air. Arms flailing, fighting for balance, he dropped his briefcase and lurched backward down the steps.

Rachel jumped onto the bottom step and caught his arm to break his fall. "Are you okay?"

"I'm fine, thank you." McClure's face flushed crimson. He pulled his arm from Rachel's grasp, straightened his suit jacket, and snatched his briefcase from the steps. "I came here to offer Joanna the deal of a lifetime, and I expected a civilized response. I got a gun in my face instead."

"Civilized?" Joanna cried. "After what you said to me? You *threatened* me."

McClure snorted. "Oh, Joanna, don't be so melodramatic."

"Threatened you how?" Rachel climbed the steps to stand beside Joanna.

"I did not threaten her," McClure said. "I simply pointed out—"

"He told me I'd be sorry if everybody else sells their land to Packard and I'm the only holdout. The whole county will blame me if Packard backs out. He said they'll come after me, they'll make me pay one way or another. If that's not a threat, I don't know what is."

McClure shook his head, making his cockscomb of hair bounce. "You're misconstruing—"

"Those statements are pretty hard to misconstrue," Rachel said. "Who are you talking about, anyway? Who's agreed to sell?"

"Nobody," Joanna cut in, before McClure had a chance to answer.

McClure's lips twitched in a faint, condescending smile that made Rachel want to kick him in the shin. "Actually, we've already reached agreements with Jake Hollinger and Tavia Richardson. I've been authorized as Packard's agent to offer very generous payments, and they couldn't turn down a windfall like this. I think the Jones sisters and the Kellys will come around—"

"Lincoln and Marie Kelly will never sell their farm," Joanna protested. "If Packard wants to build one of their fancy resorts in Mason County, they can do it on somebody else's land. I don't want their money. I want to be left alone to raise my horses and run my business."

"You know the whole county is depending on this development to create a lot of new jobs." A pained expression creased his brow. "Each sale is dependent on *every* sale going through. If you hold out, the project won't go forward."

"Fine," Joanna snapped. "That's exactly what I want."

McClure extended a hand palm-up as if entreating her to come to her senses. "As I told you, a lot of people will be very angry if you block this project."

"And I told you not to threaten me."

"I'm not—"

"Why do they have to have Joanna's farm?" Rachel asked.

McClure hesitated and seemed to debate with himself before answering. "I probably shouldn't tell you this, but I want to be honest. They've determined that this is the only suitable place in the county for what they propose. We're standing on the spot where they want to build the lodge. They want to offer horseback riding, so it's an advantage to buy a property already equipped to keep horses. Joanna, you're in a position to make a very lucrative deal, if you—"

"Are you saying they've already designed it?" Joanna demanded.

"Without knowing whether they can get the property they need?" Rachel added.

"That's the way these things are done."

These things. As if McClure, a small-town banker in the Blue Ridge Mountains of southwestern Virginia, had a wealth of experience with high-end development. Rachel almost laughed. "How could an architect draw up a plan without knowing what the land is like? Oh, wait a minute. They did know. They've been out here, haven't they? Without Joanna's permission. Or did they fly over?"

McClure, clearly losing patience with Rachel's interference, threw an irritated look her way. He directed his words at Joanna. "Does it really matter? Nobody trespassed, if that's what you're worried about."

Joanna had her gun up all the way again. "I've never seen such arrogance in my life. You tell them to take their damned design and stuff it. Now I want you to get—"

The crack of a gunshot in the distance cut her off. The three of them swiveled their heads west, toward the sound.

Rachel felt suspended, waiting for something more.

"It's just a hunter," McClure suggested with an indifferent shrug. "They've been out in the woods all week looking for wild turkeys for Thanksgiving."

A second shot rang out. Rachel's heart broke into a gallop, the way it always did when she heard a gun fired.

Joanna lowered her weapon. "That came from the Kelly farm."

"Maybe they're trying to bag a turkey, too," McClure suggested. "Or thinning out the rabbits."

Rachel shook her head. "They wouldn't shoot animals."

"Robert," Joanna said, "I don't see how you could work with Lincoln at the bank all those years and still not know a damn thing about him and Marie. They keep pet rabbits in the house, for God's sake, and Marie puts out food for the wild animals. They don't even own a gun. And they don't allow anybody to hunt on their land."

A third shot made them all flinch.

"I don't like this." Rachel pulled her cell phone from her jacket pocket. "If something's wrong over there, we can't stand here wasting time."

She punched the speed-dial number to call her husband, Sheriff Tom Bridger.

Chapter Two

"But it could be bad, couldn't it, Sheriff?" Brandon Connolly, the young sandy haired deputy riding with Tom Bridger, yanked on his seat belt to loosen it across his chest. After a few minutes of quiet, he'd picked up the conversation where they'd dropped it. "I mean, gunshots on private property."

"It'll probably turn out to be nothing." With more than a decade in law enforcement behind him, Tom sometimes had to remind himself what it was like to be as young and eager as Brandon. "You getting bored? Hoping for a little excitement?"

"Well, Sheriff, it sure seems like a long time since we had much to do."

Tom kept the pressure on the accelerator, holding the cruiser's speed at fifteen miles above the limit. The two-lane road wound past fallow cornfields where crows scavenged, and skirted hills carpeted with fallen leaves—deceptively peaceful scenes in a rural Virginia county that had known its share of violence.

"It'll suit me fine if this is just somebody trespassing and shooting at squirrels or wild turkeys on the Kelly property." Silently, Tom challenged his own statement. If the Kellys had a trespasser, why hadn't they called it in themselves? And why weren't they answering their telephone?

"But, Sheriff—"

"You know, you don't have to call me Sheriff every time you speak to me."

Brandon laughed. "Hey, I like the sound of it, *Sheriff.* You getting elected was the best thing that's happened to Mason County in years. Too bad we don't have a newspaper anymore. I can see the headline." He framed the imaginary words between his hands. 'Bridger Wins in a Landslide.'"

"That wasn't hard to do with no opposition." Tom spoke absently, his mind fixed on the Kellys. "None to speak of anyway."

"Yeah, I almost felt sorry for the guy. I don't think anybody voted for him except his relatives, and probably not all of them did. Must've been downright embarrassing."

"He'll survive. He makes more money selling cars than he would in this job."

The Kelly place came into view up ahead on the left.

Their dog, a collie mix, paced in the driveway, looking like she was about to jump out of her skin. Tom's grip tightened on the steering wheel.

Brandon sat forward, peering at the dog. "Uh oh. Something's wrong, all right."

Tom swung the car in a U-turn and braked beside the silver mailbox with KELLY spelled out on its side in black stick-on letters. Opening the car door, he told Brandon, "Wait here."

The shaggy brown and white dog ran toward Tom. He held out a hand. He'd encountered her before, at Joanna's place. What was her name? Bonnie? "Hey, Bonnie. What's up, girl?"

She halted before she reached him. Backing up, she barked once, a high-pitched yelp. She ran a few feet up the driveway, turned and barked again.

Tom got into the cruiser, turned onto the driveway and followed the dog at a crawl. "You know the drill," he told Brandon. *Keep your hand on your gun. Go in slow and stay alert.*

The farmhouse, a two-story box covered with faded brown siding, sat a hundred feet off the road. The only vehicles in the driveway were Marie Kelly's blue Chevy sedan and Lincoln's mud-splattered pickup. The patchy lawn between the house and road had been raked clean of leaves shed by the two oaks that framed the house. Along the front of the porch, coneflower seed heads bobbed under the weight of foraging goldfinches. Nothing looked out of the ordinary—except the dog, now pacing in the grass where the driveway ended and barking as if begging the men to follow her to the backyard.

After killing the engine, Tom sat behind the wheel for a moment, scanning the house and the area around it. The dog's barking escalated to a nonstop plea that made his skin prickle and his breath come a little faster. Disturbed by the racket, the goldfinch flock rose in a flutter of yellow and green and disappeared into a nearby spruce.

"I'll try the front door first," Tom said. "Just in case. You keep an eye out."

Brandon waited by the cruiser, one hand on the butt of his holstered pistol, while Tom knocked on the door.

He got no response.

"Lincoln? Marie? Anybody home?"

Again, nothing. The dog barked, spun in a circle, edged toward the backyard.

When Tom and Brandon started for the rear of the house, the dog broke into a run ahead of them. A cluster of hens, some white and some red, were pecking at the ground in the side yard but scurried out of the way as the dog streaked past.

As Tom rounded the side of the house, he spotted the couple. Lincoln, a rangy man in his sixties, lay in the yard with his arms flung outward, his eyes staring at the sky. A wet red stain soaked the front of his flannel jacket. Marie sprawled facedown on the back steps, head toward the ground and the toes of her shoes still touching the porch, as if she'd been standing there and pitched forward when she was shot. The exit wound had blown a ragged hole in her green sweater, and the wool had wicked enough blood from the opening to cover her back.

"Jesus Christ," Tom said. "Keep the dog out of the way."

While the dog whined and yipped and strained against Brandon's hold on her collar, Tom pressed two fingertips to Lincoln's temple. The man's skin still felt warm, but Tom didn't find a pulse. He repeated the fruitless exercise with Marie, brushing her hair back from her face. Like Tom himself, Marie was Melungeon, a mix of several races, with olive skin and thick black hair that had been beautiful before it turned gray.

Straightening, Tom blew out a breath and stood for a moment thinking of his late mother, letting memories of her and Marie Kelly crowd into his mind. The two friends had spent long hours together, spinning wool from the Bridger farm's sheep, coloring it with vegetable dyes Marie had concocted, winding it into skeins. Tom had known Lincoln and Marie all his life.

He shook off the memories and told Brandon, "Call it in. We need Dr. Lauter, and Dennis with his camera, and four more deputies."

"What am I gonna do about her?" Brandon nodded at the dog.

"I'll take charge of her, I guess. I'll see if I can find a tie-out or a leash."

Brandon patted the dog's head as Tom took hold of her collar.

While Brandon headed back to the car, Tom swept his gaze over the yard and surrounding fields, alert for movement, anything that shouldn't be there. The Kellys had about twenty acres where they maintained a small apple orchard and grew corn, tomatoes, and other kitchen crops to sell at the local farmers' market. They also had a miniature greenhouse for growing vegetables in winter and a big chicken coop for egg-layers. The coop, where the hens were shut up at night to protect them from foxes, sat next to the greenhouse about a hundred yards back from the residence. A couple dozen chickens pecked and scratched the ground in front of the coop and drank from a low, wide trough.

On a flagstone patio beside the back steps where Marie Kelly lay, a table and chairs were already covered with a tarp for the winter. Other than the two dead bodies, Tom spotted nothing unusual in the yard, nothing disturbed or out of place. But he caught a whiff of an acrid odor—something burning. Following the smell, he noticed that the back door of the house stood open, with only the storm door guarding the entrance.

Letting go of the dog's collar, Tom moved around Marie's body and mounted the steps. Through the screen door he saw a burner on the electric range glowing red hot beneath a saucepan. A plume of dark smoke rose from the pan.

Tom yanked open the door and crossed to the range in five strides. He grabbed a pot holder from the counter and slid the saucepan away from the heat with one hand as he switched off the burner with the other.

The liquid in the pan had evaporated, and heat had welded chunks of vegetables to the bottom. Assembled on the counter next to the stove were a loaf of homemade bread, a head of leaf lettuce, and two knives. Marie must have been starting preparations for an early dinner when the killer showed up. Did she hear shots from the yard, run out to help her husband, and get hit before she could reach him? Was she murdered only because she could identify the attacker, or had the killer come here intending to shoot both the Kellys?

And why? Why in God's name would anybody kill these people?

Tom set the pan in the sink and found a plate in a cupboard to cover the top and contain the smoke and odor.

He yanked a dog leash off a hook by the back door, but before he took it outside he glanced around for signs of a disturbance that would point to a robbery. The kitchen had an old-fashioned, homey look, a perfectly preserved artifact of the mid-twentieth century. The only thing that caught Tom's attention was a file folder open on the table, exposing a printed document. In the center of the document, a butcher knife stood straight up, its tip penetrating the paper and the red gingham oilcloth, and anchored in the wooden tabletop.

Tom stepped over to examine the document. The first page bore the logo of Packard Resorts, stylized type bordered by graphics of a bikini-clad woman on water skis and a man skiing down a snow-covered slope. Skimming the boilerplate language that laid out Packard's plans for an elaborate rural resort in Mason County, he found a clause stating that all offers were contingent on the company obtaining every plot of land necessary for completion of the project.

Without disturbing the knife, Tom used the tip of one gloved finger to lift the first sheet. On the second page, he found the amount of Packard's offer for the Kellys' land. He gave a low whistle. Almost two million for twenty acres of pasture, apple trees, and cornfields. The company must badly want the land to offer this kind of money.

He caught a movement from the corner of his eye and jerked away from the table, a hand going to his pistol. The intruder, a black-and-white rabbit, bigger and plumper than any wild rabbit he'd ever seen, hopped past Tom as if indifferent to his presence. It made its way to a feeding station in a corner of the kitchen and settled into crunching green pellets heaped in a bowl. A second rabbit, pure white, hopped into the room, freezing for a second when it saw Tom. Then it took a wide detour around him on its way to the food.

Great. He had to do something about these rabbits as well as the dog and a yard full of chickens. As long as they had food and water, the chickens could stay where they were until the Kellys' son and daughter decided what to do with them. But the rabbits and dog couldn't be left here.

In the yard, the dog began to howl, a mournful, bewildered cry.

"Sheriff?" Brandon called. "You inside?"

Stepping over to the screened door, Tom said, "I'm going to do a walk-through, then I'll be out." He tossed the dog leash to Brandon, who caught it before it could land on Marie Kelly's back.

Nothing appeared amiss in any of the downstairs rooms. Every piece of furniture and every rug looked old, not shabby so much as well-used. Upstairs, Tom found all three bedrooms neat and undisturbed. The son's and daughter's rooms looked as if they were still occupied by teenagers, with Redskins pennants and posters of motorcycles on Ronan Kelly's walls, and framed photos of landscapes and wildlife decorating Sheila's. Like her father, Sheila was, or had been when she was younger, an amateur photographer. The brother and sister were in their thirties now, living elsewhere.

Before this day ended, Tom would have to call them and tell them over the phone that their parents were both dead.

Chapter Three

Rachel felt like a gawker, a crime groupie, standing in the weeds beside the road with Robert McClure and Joanna.

A couple hundred yards of yellow police tape strung along the front boundary of the Kelly property snapped and trembled in the wind. The only people Tom had allowed in were his chief deputy, Captain Dennis Murray, several other deputies, and Dr. Gretchen Lauter, Mason County's medical examiner. Joanna had ridden down the road with Rachel, and McClure had followed in his car, to find out about the gunshots they'd heard. Rachel would have left by now if Tom hadn't asked her to wait and take temporary custody of the Kellys' dog and two pet rabbits.

Trying to ignore the contentious chatter between McClure and Joanna, Rachel stuffed her hands into her jacket pockets to keep them warm and glanced up at the towering dark clouds. She wanted to go home, to get away from this quiet little farm that had been transformed in seconds into a place of violent death.

"I can't get over this," McClure murmured, shaking his head. "I actually heard the shots that killed them. And I brushed it off. I was sure it was just a hunter—"

"If you knew Lincoln and Marie at all," Joanna said, "you wouldn't have been so quick to shrug off gunshots over here." Tears glistened in her eyes, and her face flushed with the effort of clamping down on her emotions.

"Yes, Joanna." McClure sighed. "I'm woefully ignorant, and of course you were right to be worried. I talked to them earlier today, incidentally. About the land sale."

"Oh?" Rachel looked at him with new interest. "They weren't going to sell to Packard, were they?"

"Never." Joanna cut off McClure's response. "It was not going to happen. You were wasting your breath, Robert."

"Well, now you're the one who's mistaken." McClure spoke with the smugness that Rachel had always detested. "Marie called me yesterday and told me to have a contract drawn up for them to look over. She was thinking about Lincoln's future needs, as his condition worsened. I brought it over this morning, and I feel sure Marie was favorably inclined."

"No." Joanna shook her head. "I don't believe it for a minute. That's wishful thinking."

McClure issued another sigh, this one heavy with disappointment. "It's all beside the point now, unfortunately. I'll have to start over with their heirs."

"What's *unfortunate* is that two decent, kind people are dead. I'm so sorry it's creating extra work for you, Robert."

McClure pressed his thin lips together and didn't answer.

Rachel was surprised he'd gotten anywhere with the Kellys. She'd known them only because she was their veterinarian, but she was aware of their reputations as ardent environmental crusaders. They campaigned against anything that threatened the natural beauty of their rural mountain community. Rachel couldn't see the Kellys surrendering their land to a developer who wanted to make it part of a luxury resort. But she kept her thoughts to herself, having no interest in arguing with McClure.

"Here comes Tom." Joanna pointed up the driveway.

With a canvas tote slung over a shoulder, and holding a cat carrier with one hand, Tom tugged the reluctant dog toward them on a leash. Several times Bonnie stopped, looked back at the house, and whined. Poor girl, Rachel thought. The dog had just lost her whole world, but would anybody care about her broken heart?

When Tom reached Rachel he set down the carrier and handed her the canvas tote that held a couple of bags of rabbit pellets and some canned dog food. "I believe you know these three critters."

"This is Betty and Patch." Rachel leaned down to look in at the rabbits. They huddled together at the back of the carrier, bodies trembling, noses twitching. Taking the leash from Tom, Rachel stroked the dog's head and murmured, "Hey, Bonnie. It's okay, sweetheart. We'll take care of you."

The dog looked up at her with mournful eyes. Rachel saw red stains between the toes on both of the dog's paws. Bonnie had stepped in blood.

"Are you going to tell us what happened here?" Joanna demanded of Tom. "Were they really murdered? It just doesn't seem possible. Who would want to kill them?"

"Could it have been murder-suicide?" McClure asked.

"What?" Joanna rounded on him. "Have you lost your mind?"

"You just said nobody would want to kill them, so what else—"

"Can you tell us anything at all?" Rachel's question silenced McClure.

Tom ran a hand through his thick black hair, his gaze flicking from Rachel to Joanna to McClure. "No reason you shouldn't know, I guess. Yes, it was murder. They were both shot—by a third party, no doubt about that. We'll need statements from all three of you to pin down the time the shots were fired. We'll take care of that later, after I'm done here." To McClure, he added, "Were you here to see the Kellys earlier today? Did you bring a contract with you?"

"Yes, and of course I'll answer any questions you have. Just call my office and make an appointment."

Yeah, as if that's going to happen, Rachel thought.

"You'll have to come to headquarters," Tom told McClure. "I'll let you know when I expect you to be there." He turned back to Rachel. "You need any help getting them in the car?"

"No, I'm fine. Go back to work. I hope you can make it home for dinner."

Tom gave her a quick kiss and started up the driveway toward the house. Bonnie whimpered and strained at her leash, trying to follow him.

"No, girl." Rachel stroked her head. "You're coming with me."

"I also have work to do," McClure said to no one in particular. "I can't stand around here all day." He turned to leave.

"Robert?" Joanna called after him.

He looked back.

"My shotgun wasn't loaded."

"Well, isn't it nice to know that *now*." His spine rigid, he strode to his black BMW a few feet away. When he made a U-turn on the two-lane road and sped off toward town, he almost sideswiped an ancient brown station wagon that was pulling up.

"Oh, Lord." Joanna eyed the three women in the station wagon. "Here come the Jones sisters. Why didn't I leave when I had the chance?"

"I have an excuse to go." Rachel nodded at the animals. "I need to take care of them. They're scared to death." She wished, too late, that she'd avoided that phrase.

"Look, honey, I want to talk to you about a few things. Would you drive me back to my place so I can get my car and follow you home?"

Rachel didn't want to rehash the land controversy or speculate about the murders, but she couldn't say no to her best friend in Mason County if she needed someone to talk to. She handed Joanna the dog's leash. "Sure. Help me with the animals."

The three older women climbed out of their vehicle and hurried toward them, blocking their path to Rachel's Range Rover.

"Oh, my goodness, what do you have there?" Summer, the youngest of the sisters, leaned close to peer into the carrier. The others, Winter and Spring, looked over her shoulders. The sisters shared the same finely cut features and large dark eyes, but in other ways they seemed as different as the seasons they were named for. Spring, the second oldest—Rachel guessed she was approaching seventy—defied age with shoulder-length hair dyed bright gold, ample makeup, and brilliantly hued clothes that would have better suited her forty years ago. Summer, younger than Spring by at least ten years, was probably in her late fifties. Her rosy skin had few wrinkles, and only faint streaks of gray here and there dulled her dark brown hair. Something about Summer, a soft childlike quality, always made Rachel want to speak soothingly to her.

The oldest sister, Winter Jones, squared her shoulders and took in the crime scene tape, the four Sheriff's Department cruisers parked by the road, and finally the dog. Although she wasn't as tall as Rachel, she seemed an imposing presence with her white hair pinned back into a knot and a long black coat draping her body to mid-calves. "Why are all these police cars here? And where are you taking Lincoln and Marie's pets?"

Winter sounded affronted, as if someone owed her an explanation for this rip in the fabric of her day.

"I'll put the animals in the car," Joanna said as she took the carrier from Rachel. She edged past the sisters, pulling the dog with her, and left Rachel to handle their questions.

From experience Rachel knew they would keep her here for an hour if she let them. When one of their cats had an appointment at the vet clinic, however routine the visit, Rachel had a standing arrangement with the staff that after twenty minutes someone would knock on the door and summon her to a non-existent emergency or a phone call that couldn't wait.

"Has something happened to the Kellys?" Spring asked.

"I'm afraid so." Up the road, Joanna waited beside the Range Rover, trying to restrain the dog. Rachel realized the vehicle was locked and Joanna couldn't get the animals into it.

Summer stood with eyes downcast and one fist bunching the fabric of her blue coat. Her hands showed only a touch of the arthritis that had swollen her sisters' knuckles into knobs.

Rachel answered Winter's question. "Mr. and Mrs. Kelly have been shot. I'm afraid they were both killed."

Spring gasped. Winter stared at Rachel, grimacing as if she'd blurted a string of obscenities. Summer ducked her head.

"Was it a hunting accident?" Winter asked. "We heard gunshots earlier, before we went into Mountainview, but that's not unusual at this time of year. Or any other season, for that matter, but it certainly is worse with Thanksgiving coming up next week. Some idiot man is out and about every day, shooting at those harmless wild turkeys."

"I don't know anything for certain. I'm sorry, but I have to leave. I need to take these animals someplace where they can calm down and feel safe."

Rachel took a step toward the Range Rover, but the Jones sisters weren't finished yet.

"Perhaps it was a robbery," Spring speculated. "Is anything missing?"

"Oh, dear." Winter pressed a hand to her cheek. "This is frightening. We live so close, and we don't have guns in the house to protect ourselves."

Summer sniffled and touched a handkerchief to her nose.

"Oh, stop blubbering," Winter told her.

"I don't know exactly what happened." Rachel spoke more forcefully this time. "And I have to go now."

Winter wouldn't give up. "Hasn't Tom told you anything?" Gesturing toward the Range Rover, where Joanna waited with the dog, she added, "And what about Joanna? She has a gun, but she's still a woman living alone. If some maniac is running around shooting people—"

"There's no reason to panic." But Rachel couldn't be sure of that. Maybe they all had reason to panic but didn't realize it yet. Why was she bothering to reassure them?

Spring shook her head. "We're too close for comfort."

"Keep your doors locked, just to be on the safe side." Lame advice, but Rachel wanted to get away from them before they freaked her out too. "I'm sure Tom will find the person who did this. Take care."

As she clicked her remote to open the Range Rover's doors, the Jones sisters began a conversation among themselves. Rachel pulled open the rear hatch and slid the carrier holding the rabbits into the back of the vehicle while Joanna coaxed the reluctant dog to jump in. Just before she climbed into the driver's seat, Rachel heard Winter say, "I hope this doesn't have anything to do with Jake Hollinger and that absurd fight over his property line."

What was that about? Rachel was almost curious enough to ask, but she reminded herself she had other things to do. Police work was Tom's job.

Chapter Four

Tom leaned over the steps where Marie Kelly sprawled facedown, steeled himself for what felt like a violation of his mother's old friend, and slid his hands under her chest and hips. He tried not to breathe in the rank odor of the blood that saturated her blouse and sweater around the exit wound.

On the other side of the steps, Dr. Gretchen Lauter leaned over and spread her gloved hands, ready to catch Marie and ease her onto her back. Lincoln Kelly's body waited in the hearse that would take the couple to the state medical examiner's regional headquarters in Roanoke for autopsy.

Tom hefted Marie's body, a surprisingly heavy dead weight for such a slender woman, and rolled her over. When she dropped onto Dr. Lauter's waiting hands, her right arm swung wide and struck the doctor on the chest. She gasped and for a second her eyes shone with tears. The county's part-time medical examiner, a small woman in her late fifties with salt-and-pepper curls, had rushed to the Kelly farm without removing the white coat she wore at the public clinic, and when she'd crouched on the ground to examine Lincoln's body the coat's hem had picked up dirt, bits of dried leaves, and streaks of chicken manure.

"You okay?" Tom asked.

"Of course. Just—startled." Blinking away her tears, Dr. Lauter tucked both of Marie's arms across her midsection. With a tenderness Tom had seldom witnessed from the doctor on the job, she smoothed the dead woman's gray hair off her face and drew the lids closed over eyes that already looked dry and clouded. "Oh, Marie, you broke your pretty nose," she whispered, touching a fingertip to a gash and a bulge where the dead woman's nose had slammed against the edge of a step.

Tom had to look away, his throat tight. For once he was glad his mother was gone, because she had been spared the grief of her friend's murder. Forcing down a surge of irrational anger at Dr. Lauter's emotional display, he drew a deep breath and got his own feelings under control before he turned back to the body.

The front of Marie's blouse bore a small circle of blood around a neat entrance wound in her left chest. A single shot had blasted through her chest and out her back. In their search for the slug, Keith Blackwood had spotted a hole in the brown aluminum siding next to the front door, and now the young blond deputy was using a pocketknife to dig out what was left of the bullet.

Tom and Dr. Lauter stepped back to let Dennis Murray photograph the body. Pushing his glasses up onto his brown hair so he could use the viewfinder, the lanky captain moved around the steps, snapping pictures of Marie face-up, her head pointed toward the ground.

"She would hate this," Dr. Lauter murmured. "She would be humiliated."

"Hey, Boss," Keith Blackwood called from the porch. With a gloved hand he held up the small, misshapen slug he'd pried from the wall of the house. "Got it."

"Good job. After you log it, see if you can help your brother and Brandon find the slug from Mr. Kelly."

Instead of trying to go down the steps past Marie, Keith swung his long legs over the porch railing and jumped into the yard.

Dr. Lauter pulled a handkerchief from the pocket of her white coat and blew her nose. Regaining a brisk, businesslike tone, she said, "I believe Marie was killed by a shot through her heart, or possibly the aorta. If that's the case, it would have been quick. Instant, or nearly so."

A small mercy, Tom thought. "Looks like Lincoln took a little more effort."

Dr. Lauter moved farther into the yard, between the steps where Marie lay and the bloody patch of ground where her husband had fallen. "I'm having trouble visualizing what happened here. Lincoln was hit once from the front, once from behind, but which shot came first? Was he on his feet for both? And who was moving, Lincoln or the shooter?"

Tom scanned the murder scene and stepped sideways a few feet until he thought he had the right position. "My guess is that Lincoln was hit first, in the back, from this angle." With his hand he indicated the path of the bullet, then the fresh scuff marks on the ground. "I don't think the first shot knocked him down. I'd say he stumbled but didn't fall."

"Do you suppose he never saw the killer coming?"

"Either that or they argued and Linc cut it short and started to walk away."

"So the shooter was enraged at being dismissed and shot him in the back?"

"Could be." Tom nodded as he watched the attack play out in his mind. The only thing he didn't see was the killer's face.

"I think the weapon was a hunting rifle. Marie was in the kitchen cooking, she came out when she heard the commotion, and she probably got hit before she could take it all in. The shooter stood between Marie and Linc, and Linc was trying to reach his wife when he took another round in the chest."

"And the second bullet was the one that exited through his back." Dr. Lauter gestured at the dark stain left behind in the dirt when Lincoln's body was removed. "The one that killed him."

"The slug's not in the ground there. It exited before he went down, so he was standing when he was hit, and he fell backward." Thirty feet beyond the spot where Lincoln had collapsed, Brandon and the other Blackwood twin were searching the walls of the chicken house for bullet holes.

"Then the son of a bitch looked Marie right in the face and murdered her," Dr. Lauter said. "Can you imagine what that split-second was like for her?"

Tom didn't want to imagine it. The sight of his mother's friend lying dead on her back steps was enough of a memory to carry around. "Any thoughts on who might have had a reason to do this? Any enemies you know of?"

Dr. Lauter shook her head. "I know Lincoln in particular rankled some people, but you don't murder anybody because they lectured you about recycling."

"You know it was more than that with him. Marie soft-pedaled it, but Linc was a fanatic about all kinds of things, and his behavior was getting more and more erratic in the last year. The Alzheimer's, I guess."

Dr. Lauter nodded. "Yes, he was deteriorating rapidly. He wasn't diagnosed until a few months after he retired from the bank, but I think his mental confusion was the reason he stopped working. It took Marie a while to make him see a specialist for evaluation."

"I think that explains him raising hell over Jake Hollinger's fence." Tom recalled a string of similar incidents with the two neighbors in their early seventies yelling at each other over a section of dismantled post-and-rail fencing. "Hollinger called me out here half a dozen times because Linc kept tearing it down."

"I know." Dr. Lauter pulled her white coat closer around her against the wind's assault. "Linc got hold of the idea that Jake was trying to steal some of his land. Marie couldn't reason with him."

"He wouldn't listen to me either. I think Jake was running out of patience. You know, that kind of petty fight grinds away at people. If it keeps up long enough, it starts to seem like the most important thing happening to you."

"I hope you're not suggesting—" Dr. Lauter broke off when Dennis Murray approached.

Slinging his camera strap over his shoulder, Dennis said, "I'm done here. Want me to get the guys to move her now?"

Tom nodded and Dennis headed around the house to the driveway, where two funeral home employees waited with the hearse. A deputy would ride with them to Roanoke to deliver the bodies.

Dr. Lauter picked up her interrupted thought. "You can't be thinking Jake Hollinger did this, not over a few feet of fence?"

"That kind of thing matters, Gretchen. And Jake had a legitimate grievance." Some primal instinct stirred the blood when property was threatened and boundaries disregarded. "How many No Trespassing signs did you pass on your way out here? And how many of them said trespassers would be shot?"

Dr. Lauter gave a humorless laugh. "Good point. I saw one that was hand-painted, with 'That means your damned dog too' added at the bottom."

Frowning, Tom swept his gaze over the stand of evergreens along one section of the fence between the two properties. Jake Hollinger could have come through the trees to avoid being seen near the Kelly farm in his truck.

Dr. Lauter walked over to retrieve her medical bag from the bottom step. "I don't want to think Jake Hollinger's capable of doing something like this. I'd rather believe some random nut job came through here and killed these people."

"If that's the case, we'll probably never catch the shooter. Unless this turns out to be part of a killing spree. You know as well as I do what the odds are against that. It's a lot more likely the Kellys were murdered by somebody they knew. Somebody with a personal motive."

Tom's thoughts returned to the unsigned Packard Resorts contract on the kitchen table, pinned down by a knife. Had Lincoln stabbed the papers in a fit of rage at the people who were trying to take his land? Where did the contract place the disputed property line? Tom wanted the prosecutor's legal opinion on it. He wanted to question Jake Hollinger too. But first he had to find phone numbers for the Kellys' son and daughter and notify them that their parents had been murdered.

Chapter Five

All the way home to the farm where she and Tom lived, Rachel listened to the dog in the backseat whine and paw the window glass. Letting Bonnie stick her head out might distract her, but Rachel didn't dare lower the window and risk the dog making a break for freedom.

"It's okay, Bonnie," Rachel crooned over and over. "Everything's going to be all right."

For God's sake, I'm lying to a dog, she thought. Bonnie ignored her and scrambled back and forth between the windows, her whines escalating. Rachel hoped the Kellys' son or daughter would take all their parents' pets, but she doubted either would provide the doting care that Bonnie was used to. An older dog, deeply bonded with her owners, Bonnie was also a victim of today's monstrous act.

In her rearview mirror Rachel saw Joanna's Jeep Cherokee keeping a steady pace three car-lengths behind. Now that the Kellys were gone, with their property presumably willed to their absent offspring, how would the situation change? Joanna was probably thinking about the possibilities already and wanted to enlist Rachel's help in some way.

A fight over the Packard project had been brewing in the county for weeks, and Rachel sensed it was about to erupt into a nasty public battle. On Saturday afternoon, in a little over twenty-four hours, a Packard representative would speak at an open community meeting, and after that the lines would be clearly drawn between proponents and opponents. Rachel was determined to stay out of it, at least publicly. Privately, she would offer Joanna moral support, but any active opposition to the resort would cause trouble for Tom, who had been elected sheriff less than three weeks before and now had a double murder to worry about.

She wished her friend Ben Hern were here to take up Joanna's cause. Ben was a well-known artist and cartoonist, a big land-owner and taxpayer in Mason County who wasn't afraid to stand up to local politicians or big companies. But he happened to be in Europe and wouldn't return for more than a week.

The dog stuck her head between the seats and yelped. Rachel scratched her ears and murmured, "I know, I know. I'm so sorry, sweetie."

Looking up at the hills flanking the two-lane road, Rachel wondered how Packard Resorts would market Mason County as a vacation spot. True, the mountainside trees formed a breath-taking palette of red, orange, and yellow in early fall, but now all the leaves lay rotting on the ground, packed down by recent rain, their colors faded. The bare branches along the ridges had their own bleak beauty, dark spears aimed at the scudding gray clouds. But this was not a welcoming place in winter. Did Packard Resorts want to create a mountain retreat that would be open only in warm weather months? Or did they have a grand plan for transforming this small rural county in southwestern Virginia into a winter wonderland?

Their plans didn't matter. The project would probably die if Joanna stood in the way. The only question was what kind of penalty Joanna would pay for killing a lot of people's hopes for jobs and profit.

Back home at the farm, Rachel pulled into the driveway ahead of Joanna and opened the back door of the Range Rover. Bonnie shot out and slammed into Rachel. Reeling, Rachel grabbed at the leash but it slid through her fingers. The dog bolted across the yard, heading for the sheep meadow. Heading toward home.

"Bonnie, come back here!" Rachel yelled.

Joanna jumped out of her Jeep and the two of them sprinted after the dog. Joanna couldn't keep up with Rachel and quickly fell behind. When Bonnie charged across the meadow, the two dozen sheep scattered in every direction, uttering a chorus of frantic *baa-aas*. The dog swung to the right, then the left, as confused as the terrified sheep.

Rachel caught up, lunged at the dog and threw both arms around her. Bonnie surrendered, panting, her tongue lolling.

"You silly old girl." Rachel sank to her knees, gasping for breath. "I'll bet your arthritis is giving you fits right now."

The dog laid her head on Rachel's shoulder and whined.

"I know, sweetie. You're scared and you don't understand what's happening. Come on, let's go see Billy Bob." Rachel pushed herself up, the leash firmly in hand, and led the dispirited dog back to the house.

Joanna hauled the carrier holding the two rabbits out of the Range Rover, along with the bag of their food.

When they entered the house with the animals in tow, Tom's brown-and-white bulldog, Billy Bob, emerged from the kitchen at the end of the center hall. He barked with excitement when he saw Bonnie and trotted toward her, his nails clicking on the oak floor. Rachel unhooked Bonnie's leash and let her go to meet Billy Bob.

Frank, Rachel's black-and-white cat with one and a half ears, made a brief appearance in the hallway. He took a look at Bonnie, growled and hissed, then shot through an open doorway into the den.

"Okay, where's Cicero?" Joanna asked. "We might as well get his opinion, too, while we're at it."

Right on cue, Rachel's African gray parrot called "Hello, Rachel, hello" from the den.

"He's going to stay where he is," Rachel said. "He's one animal more than I can deal with right now."

"I'll take the dog home with me, if you want me to. She gets along with my dogs, and if she gets loose and runs back home I won't have far to go after her."

"Oh, God, yes, thank you," Rachel said. "Now what the heck am I going to do with these rabbits? They're used to running around loose in the house, but that's not going to happen here. Do you think the Kellys' son or daughter will take them?"

"Lord, I don't know." Joanna, holding the bag of supplies, used the fingers of her free hand to comb her reddish blond hair, smoothing the mess her short run had made of it. "I couldn't predict what those two will do about anything. Ronan and Sheila are both very different from their parents. And that worries me."

"Come on, I'll put the rabbits in the office for now." On their way down the hall, Rachel asked, "You think they'll sell the land to Packard?"

Joanna nodded and opened the door to the home office to let Rachel carry the rabbits in. "I feel so selfish for even thinking about it at a time like this, with Lincoln and Marie—" She shook her head. "But I can't help it. If Ronan and Sheila decide to sell, I'll probably be the only holdout, and I'll never have another minute's peace as long as I live."

While Rachel tried to find words that would calm Joanna's anxiety, she set down the carrier next to the desk and peered in at the rabbits. The white female had burrowed under the towel in the bottom of the carrier, facing the back, so that only her puff of a tail showed. Her male companion crouched, frozen in terror, next to the lump she created. Rachel took the bag from Joanna and removed two bowls and the rabbit kibble. "But what about the Jones sisters? They don't want to uproot themselves at this stage of their lives, do they?"

Joanna hugged her waist and bounced on her toes, her whole body thrumming with tension. "Who knows what those flakes might do? I can't get a straight answer out of them." Joanna launched into an imitation of Winter's stern schoolmarm tone. "We prefer to keep our own counsel for the time being. We won't be rushed into a commitment one way or the other."

Rachel had to smile at the pitch-perfect rendering, but she didn't find anything about this situation amusing. Two good people, a couple Tom had known all his life, had been gunned down in their own yard in broad daylight, the person who did it was walking around loose, and their deaths would pit neighbor against neighbor in a nasty fight over the resort development. Rachel crouched to pour kibble into the rabbits' bowls and place the food inside the carrier. "What about your other neighbors? Won't anybody stand with you?"

"Oh, Tavia Richardson's hell-bent on selling to Packard and getting her hands on all that money, and that means Jake Hollinger's in favor of it too. Tavia's got him dreaming about the two of them living the good life someplace where it never gets cold."

Rachel stood, frowning. "Hold on, you've lost me. Mrs. Richardson and Jake Hollinger are an item? Since when?"

"Oh, they'll admit they've been seeing each other since Sue Ellen Hollinger died last year. But the truth is, it started months before that. All the time Sue Ellen was going through torture with chemo and radiation, her shit of a husband—" Joanna's voice choked up. "I can't even think about it without getting mad enough to strangle him. Sue Ellen was my friend. And so were Lincoln and Marie."

Joanna didn't cry easily, and she was fighting the tears now, but her pain escaped in tremors and gulped-back sobs. At a loss for words or actions that could make a difference, Rachel placed an arm around her shoulders. This basket case was not the strong woman Rachel knew. In Joanna's distress Rachel saw something more than grief for lost friends, something darker than anger over events she couldn't control.

A half-formed fear had been niggling at the back of Rachel's mind for the last hour, and now she couldn't stop it from pushing forward, full-blown. Joanna seemed positive the Kellys would not have sold their land to Packard, that they would have stood firm with her to block the company's plan for a luxurious mountain resort in Mason County. Now the Kellys were dead.

Although she feared the answer, Rachel voiced the question. "Do you think the Kellys were murdered because they refused to sell their land?"

"You bet I do. Nothing else makes sense." Joanna's shoulders felt rigid in Rachel's embrace, and her expression was hardening, the sorrow and agitation giving way to a grim determination. "Well, nobody's going to get me. The next time I point my shotgun, you can bet it'll be loaded."

Chapter Six

"This is kind of a Hatfields and McCoys thing, huh?" Brandon asked when they were in Tom's cruiser, headed over to Jake Hollinger's farm. Tom had left Dennis Murray in charge of the murder scene.

"That's an exaggeration. I wouldn't call it a feud, just a running disagreement."

"We need to take precautions? I mean, what're the chances Hollinger's the shooter? What state of mind is he going to be in when he sees us coming?"

"I can't even guess," Tom admitted. "Just stay alert." A sick little knot had formed in his gut. He hoped this would be a routine visit, to give Hollinger a chance to provide a solid alibi for the time the Kellys were shot. He didn't want to discover that Marie and Linc had died because of a petty dispute over a property line. But if Linc had torn the fence down in the last day or two, that might have pushed Hollinger to the breaking point. And Tom and Brandon could be walking into a confrontation with a man who had already killed two people today.

Barely ten feet ahead of the car, three chocolate-brown sheep hopped over the narrow drainage ditch and landed in the road. Tom slammed on his brakes. When he tapped his horn, the ewes turned to regard the car with mild curiosity.

"Are sheep as stupid as they look?" Brandon frowned in disgust at the animals blocking their way. "I never could figure out why anybody wants to bother with them. And what kind of sheep is brown, anyway?"

"They're Merinos. They must be from Jake Hollinger's flock. He's the only one around here who keeps Merinos. And yeah, sheep are a little dense. Dogs intimidate them, but they're not afraid of people. Or cars, obviously."

"Why are they running around loose? They don't have the good sense to look out for themselves. And they could cause an accident."

"Jake's fence must be down," Tom said.

"You think Kelly and Hollinger might have had a fight about it this morning?"

Tom didn't answer as he inched the cruiser forward, encouraging the ewes to get out of the way. How long had they been loose? Why hadn't Hollinger rounded them up yet?

The three sheep, bunched together, seemed to have no plans to move. Tom shifted the car into park and got out to shoo them away. After balking long enough to make the point that they couldn't be hurried, they turned in a leisurely fashion and ambled back to the side of the road, their hooves clacking on the pavement. One by one they jumped the ditch into the field.

The Hollinger gate was another half-mile on. Both the Hollinger and Kelly farms, side by side, bordered the McKendrick horse farm. Joanna's property dwarfed all of its neighbors. If this was the prime location for the proposed resort, Joanna's land was the critical piece and would bring the biggest offer, but if the contract Tom had seen in the Kelly house was typical, the owners of adjacent properties could also sell for more money than they'd ever dreamed of having.

Tom pulled into Hollinger's driveway and parked behind his red pickup truck. The small brown-shingled house, with a screened porch on one side and an extra room tacked onto the other, looked neglected. Weeds choked the flowerbeds along the foundation, moss colored a patch of the roof dark green, and dead leaves had piled up in the gutters. Hollinger had apparently lost interest in keeping the place up after his wife died of cancer.

"Back me up," Tom said as he got out of the cruiser.

Brandon stood in the yard while Tom mounted the front steps and knocked on the door. He got no response, and after three tries he gave up and rejoined Brandon.

"He has to be here somewhere. Let's walk."

They rounded the house into the backyard, where unraked leaves from a massive oak tree covered a scruffy patch of lawn. At the edge of the yard sat a large chicken coop with a fenced space for a flock of brown hens. A big vegetable garden, surrounded by high wire fencing to keep deer out, took up a broad clearing, and beyond the garden the land turned to rolling meadows.

Tom and Brandon found Hollinger on his fence line, lifting rails and shoving them back into slots in the posts. The contested fence between the Hollinger and Kelly properties was a simple post-and-rail that was easy to take apart and just as easy to put back together, but either chore would be time-consuming. Each section had three thick rails made of pine branches, six feet long between posts. About a hundred yards of rails, stretching down a slope, lay in the grass. A mixed flock of about forty brown and white sheep grazed nearby, ignoring the call of the wild that had led a few of their sisters to wander when the fence went down.

Hollinger looked up as Tom and Brandon approached. Pausing in his work, he wiped sweat from his face with a handkerchief. Despite the chilly November day, he had hung his denim barn jacket on a fence post and rolled up his shirt sleeves. A tall man in his sixties with thick white hair, he looked fit and strong. And not the least bit rattled by the appearance of two cops on his property.

Tom relaxed a little. "Hey, Jake."

"Hey, Tom. And you're Brandon, right? The Connollys' boy?"

"Yes, sir," Brandon said.

"Haven't seen you since the election, Sheriff." Hollinger stuffed the handkerchief into the back pocket of his jeans and offered a hand. "Congratulations. The best man won."

"Thanks." Tom shook his hand, feeling the strength of the older man's grip and the calluses on his palms. "By the way, we saw some of your ewes in the road on our way over. I ran them back into a field."

Hollinger blew out a sigh. "Those girls never pass up a chance to go exploring. Usually they come back on their own. If they don't show up soon I'll go find them and give them a ride home in the truck."

"They're over on the Kelly property." Tom glanced to his left, but the stand of evergreens hid the Kelly house from view. "How long have you been working out here?"

"Just came out. I've been at the mill, and when I got home and started making my rounds, I found this." Hands on hips, Hollinger scowled at the dismantled fence. "Fourth time this month. He even managed to get one of the posts out of the ground. I thought I was securing them when I sunk them in concrete."

"He?"

"You know who I mean." Hollinger flung a hand toward the Kelly land. "You here to take my complaint?"

"No, I came by to find out if you heard any gunshots in the last hour or two."

Hollinger displayed no surprise or interest. He turned away from Tom and hefted one of the pine rails off the ground. "Nope. Like I said, I was at the mill. Somebody going over their limit for turkeys?"

"I'm afraid not," Tom said. "Somebody shot Lincoln and Marie Kelly in their backyard."

The rail dropped from Hollinger's hands and landed on the ground with a thud that Tom felt as a vibration under his feet. "God damn," Hollinger said. "Are they all right?"

"No." Tom watched the man's face for his reaction. "They're both dead."

Hollinger stared slack-jawed at Tom for a moment. He raised a hand, scratched his head. "God damn," he repeated. "Who did it?"

His shock appeared genuine, but if he was the shooter he'd had time to prepare for Tom's inevitable visit. "We don't know yet. Have you seen or heard anything out of the ordinary today? Any voices, shouts? Any strange vehicles passing by?"

"No. My God. This is unbelievable." Hollinger pulled the handkerchief from his pocket and swiped his face again. "Was it a burglary or what?"

Tom ignored the question and asked another. "Why were you at the lumber mill today? I thought you retired and turned it over to your son."

"Yeah, I thought so too." Hollinger seemed distracted, his gaze fixed on the trees in the distance that shielded the Kelly house. "But every time he screws up an order I have to go straighten it out for him."

"Was Mark there when you were? Can he vouch for you— what time you got there, when you left?"

Hollinger snapped his head around, anger flaring in his eyes. "Oh now, hold on. You can't be thinking I shot Linc and Marie."

"You've been fighting with Lincoln Kelly for a while now."

"About a fence, for God's sake, a property line. I wouldn't kill a man over something like that. Much less him *and* his wife."

"People are murdered every day over a lot less," Tom said. "How much land were you and Linc fighting about? How many feet?"

Hollinger threw up his arms in exasperation. "Who the hell knows? He kept changing his mind. He'd say six feet one week and twenty the next. Look, I knew the man had Alzheimer's, and I tried to make allowances. But the survey shows I put this new fence right smack on the property line. The old one was six feet inside the line. I just took back what's mine."

"Does it make any difference?" Brandon asked. "A six-foot strip on one boundary?"

"Hell, yes, it makes a difference. I've been thinking for a while about selling, even before Packard came looking for land to buy. That's why I wanted a fence right on the property line, so there wouldn't be any confusion when I found a buyer."

"I hear Packard's already been handing out purchase agreements," Tom said. "Have they made you a firm offer in writing? One that you like?"

"You bet I like it. They'll give me top dollar—a lot more than my acreage is worth, to tell you the truth, but they've got it to spend and they want the land. That was just one more reason for Linc to raise hell about the property line. He swore he'd do everything he could to stop me from selling."

"Do you expect things to change now that Lincoln and Marie are dead? Will Ronan and Sheila be easier to deal with than their father was?"

"Aw, God." Hollinger winced as if he'd forgotten about the killings for a moment and Tom's question had brought it all back with a jolt. "Who knows what'll happen? Their kids haven't lived here since they graduated college. They're professionals, they've got careers. I can't see either one of them wanting to come back here to live on the land."

"So you think they'll go against their dad's wishes and sell?" Brandon put in.

"Now don't put words in my mouth, son. I don't have the least idea what they might do. I'll just have to wait and see."

Hollinger lifted a rail and shoved one end into a slot in a post. Tom grabbed the other end and maneuvered it into the opposite post. "Why are you so gung-ho about selling?"

Straightening, Hollinger flexed his back as if loosening stiff muscles. Sweat rolled down his face, and half-moons of perspiration darkened the armpits of his shirt. He scrubbed the handkerchief over his face again before answering. "I don't want to live here alone anymore. That's the plain truth. It's not the same with Sue Ellen gone. Anyway, I'm almost seventy years old. I want some of that retirement leisure everybody talks about. If I sell to Packard, I'll be comfortable the rest of my life. More than comfortable."

Tom nodded. "Especially if you and Tavia Richardson combine your assets. The two of you together would have quite a nest egg."

"I don't know about that," Hollinger muttered, avoiding Tom's eyes.

Tom was surprised to see a deep flush rise in the man's cheeks. Was he embarrassed by his relationship with Tavia? They didn't flaunt it, but they hadn't hidden it either. Plenty of people knew about it.

"I guess you realize," Tom said, "that Joanna's not going to sell. Packard's probably going to scuttle the whole project if they can't get her land."

Hollinger waved off Tom's remark with an impatient gesture. "I'm not going to stand here talking about selling land when Linc and Marie…good God, I still can't take it in. Shot to death. Who could have—"

"Can you think of anybody who had a grudge against either of them?" Aside from yourself, Tom added silently.

Hollinger looked at Tom, his eyes widening as if something startling had occurred to him. "The drugs. It could have had something to do with the drugs. I know they had the best intentions, trying to help sick people, but I was always afraid it might turn dangerous."

"Wait a minute." Tom held up a hand. "What are you talking about? What drugs?"

"Not the hard stuff, I don't mean that. Pot. Marijuana. The Kellys have been growing the stuff and selling it for years."

Chapter Seven

Rachel was about to give Billy Bob a boost into her Range Rover when she spotted the strangers.

A black SUV sat on the road. Three men in suits and ties stood at the end of the driveway and seemed to be studying the property, the man in the middle throwing his arms wide in expansive gestures.

"What the heck?" Rachel muttered.

At her feet, Billy Bob gave a low growl from deep in his throat.

"Well, that's definitely not an endorsement." The bulldog had impeccable judgment when it came to people. Rachel wanted to get back to the vet clinic to check on a dog and a cat she had neutered that morning, but she couldn't go anywhere as long as the strangers stood in her driveway. In any case, she wouldn't leave and let them continue whatever they were doing. "Come on, boy. Let's check this out."

Billy Bob kept up a low rumble in his throat as they walked down the driveway together. The gesturing man dropped his hands to his sides, and all three watched Rachel approach with bland expressions that gave away nothing.

She stopped a dozen feet from them. "Can I help you with something?"

The man in the middle, tall with close-cropped dark hair, flashed a broad smile that transformed his face from pleasant to handsome. He looked to be in his early thirties, barely older than Rachel. He said, "And you are?"

Rachel stared at him for a moment. "You're asking *me* to identify myself? I live here. You're standing on our property, my husband's and mine."

"Oh, sorry about that." The man's smile widened still more. He glanced at the growling bulldog, and when they made eye contact Billy Bob turned up the volume and bared his teeth. The other two men decided to play it safe and backed off the driveway into the road, but the guy with the smile stayed put.

"My husband, by the way, is the sheriff of Mason County."

"Ah." The man nodded as if he'd achieved clarity on a thorny issue. "I see. Does he happen to be at home?"

Rachel folded her arms. "You haven't answered my question. Who are *you*? And what do you want?"

"We're with Packard Development." He extracted a business card from an inside pocket of his suit coat and handed it to Rachel.

The card identified him as Lawrence Archer, Property Acquisition and Management, Packard Resorts & Development. Frowning, Rachel regarded him warily, but his smile never faltered.

"We're taking a look around at potential locations for development," he added.

"This farm isn't for sale."

He went on as if she hadn't spoken. "It's always best to work with the existing landscape instead of trying to remake it. For some purposes, a fairly level expanse of land is preferable, and plots of that description are few and far between in Mason County. This property isn't ideal, but with a minimal amount of work it could accommodate a small airport and a heliport."

Rachel raised her voice as she took a couple of steps forward. "Either you didn't hear me, or you misunderstood. This land is not for sale."

Her sharp tone triggered a fresh round of growls from Billy Bob.

Now Archer took a step back, and his two associates moved farther away, edging toward the safety of the black SUV. Archer's smile remained fixed as if it were an object plastered to his face.

"We'd like to sit down with you and your husband—I didn't get your name. You're Mrs....?"

"I didn't tell you my name. I'm Rachel Goddard. Dr. Goddard. My husband is Sheriff Bridger."

"Well, then, Dr. Goddard, we'd like to sit down with you and Sheriff Bridger and talk about the opportunity—"

"No."

"We're prepared to offer you—"

"I said no." Sometimes the only remaining option was rudeness. "And I meant no. We have nothing to discuss. I have to get back to work, and I'd like you to leave now."

"I hope I'll have a chance to speak to Sheriff Bridger at the meeting tomorrow."

"I don't know if he can make it. He's working a double murder case." Two murders, Rachel thought, that might have been triggered by Packard's presence in this community.

Oblivious, Archer continued, "I hope we'll see both of you there, so you'll have a chance to learn exactly how our project can benefit Mason County."

Rachel wanted to slap that smile off his face.

When she didn't respond, Archer nodded and said, "Nice meeting you, Dr. Goddard, and I look forward to seeing you again." All three men turned at once toward their vehicle.

Billy Bob issued one sharp bark at their retreating backs.

Fuming, Rachel headed back up the driveway to her Range Rover. Billy Bob, satisfied that he'd driven away the intruders, trotted beside her on his short legs.

"Who the hell do they think they are, huh?" Rachel demanded of the dog. "Have you ever seen such arrogance? I wouldn't blame Joanna if she wanted to shoot them all."

Billy Bob answered with a low *ruff* that rose from deep in his throat.

Rachel had rarely heard Billy Bob bark before, and now he'd done it twice in a couple of minutes. "Wow, you really didn't like them, did you? Well, I'll try to make sure you never see them again."

Although she wanted to give Joanna moral support, she hadn't planned to attend the Saturday afternoon meeting because it would probably involve a lot of shouting between different factions. But now nothing would keep her away. She couldn't bear the thought that Lincoln and Marie Kelly might have been killed because of divisions created by her slimy visitors and their bosses.

Would the Kellys' killer be at the meeting, she wondered, looking as ordinary as everybody else while he made mental notes of which side people were on?

Chapter Eight

"Wow," Brandon said.

"Yeah, wow." Standing at the bottom of Marie and Lincoln Kelly's basement stairs, Tom surveyed a thriving crop of marijuana plants growing in pots. They sat on tables that lined the walls and crowded the space in the middle of the basement. In one corner a thick layer of flower buds lay drying on a screen. The fruity aroma in the air made Tom think of pineapple and cherries.

Black plastic taped over the half-windows blocked the view from outside. Tom raised a hand to partially shield his eyes while they adjusted to the glare of the fluorescent lights hanging above the tables.

Dennis angled his camera to get a wide shot of the plants. "What would you say, maybe fifty altogether?"

"We'll need a truck to get them all out of here."

"And plenty of muscle to move them," Brandon said. "These pots look like they weigh a ton. Man, this is wild. Who would've thought?"

Tom stepped over to the nearest table and brushed a hand along the bright green, fern-like leaves. "I hope Jake Hollinger was right about them growing this stuff for medical use."

"It hasn't got that skunk smell I'm used to when we confiscate pot," Dennis said. "I've read about these really mild varieties for cancer patients on chemo who have trouble with nausea."

"Let's hope that's what we've got here. If they were selling it to a dealer, that puts a whole new slant on the murders."

"Hollinger said there's more out in one of the fields," Brandon reminded him.

"I doubt anything's growing outdoors this late in the season. But let's see if we can find anything else before we get somebody out here to move it all."

Before leaving the house, Tom turned out the lights over the plants and the three of them sealed the basement door with crime-scene tape. They did the same with the front and back doors. The Kellys' son and daughter had both told Tom they wanted to stay in the house while they were in Mason County, but they would have to make other arrangements. This was a crime scene in more ways than one.

Taking Brandon and Dennis along, Tom drove out into the fields toward the center of the small farm. Hollinger had described a spot away from the road, where tall corn disguised the marijuana plants growing between rows. Now, in mid-November, nothing remained of the corn except dried stalks, but when Tom and the deputies walked the field they found a few small marijuana seedlings struggling to survive in the chilly weather.

"How many people do you suppose know about this?" Dennis laughed as he snapped a picture of one marijuana plant. "Everybody in the county but us?"

"And why didn't Hollinger report it?" Brandon added. "He sure didn't get along with Mr. Kelly."

Tom kicked a rock out of the way and tugged on one of the cannabis plants. It offered a little resistance, but when he yanked with both hands it came free with clumps of clay soil clinging to the roots. "I think we'll find out Marie and Lincoln helped Sue Ellen Hollinger when her cancer was terminal. They would have been happy to help ease her pain. And Jake wouldn't stand in the way of his wife getting some relief just because it came from the Kellys."

They pulled up five more small plants, carried them to the cruiser and tossed them into the trunk.

◇◇◇

Rachel braked in the middle of Main Street and stared at the building across from Mountainview Animal Hospital. When she'd left earlier in the day the storefront space had been vacant and dark. Now a small moving van sat at the curb, the door into the building stood open, and two men in coveralls worked inside, positioning three desks and chairs in a semicircle. A sign taped to the plate-glass window read PACKARD RESORTS.

"They're really moving in, aren't they?" No one was around to hear her except Billy Bob, and he lay snoring on the back seat.

When she pulled into her parking space in the vet clinic's lot, she realized half a dozen clients with dogs on leashes had gathered outside the door, all of them focused on the activities across the street. A couple of women called out questions as she opened her car door. She ignored them for the moment, while she roused Billy Bob and helped him down from the Range Rover.

The women repeated their questions when Rachel approached with the bulldog.

"Do you have any news about the Kellys?"

"Does the sheriff know who did it?"

The other dogs, big and little, swarmed Billy Bob in a flurry of sniffing and tail-wagging.

Rachel held up a hand. "Please don't ask me anything, because I don't have any answers. I haven't even had a chance to talk to Tom. Marie and Lincoln Kelly were killed today. That's all I know about it."

"Well, I can tell you what I think." This came from Mrs. Wilson, an elderly woman with snowy hair and a sharp little nose in a pinched face. Her spotted mutt strained at his leash to get closer to Billy Bob.

"We can always count on you to tell us what you think, Oline," said another woman of about the same age, rolling her eyes heavenward as she spoke.

Ignoring her, Mrs. Wilson pointed across the street. "There's the cause, right there."

All the women started speaking at once, their words tumbling together. The woman who had chided Mrs. Wilson raised her voice above the others. "That company's the best thing that's happened to Mason County in a hundred years. Nobody's got a right to stand in the way of all those jobs coming in here. We need to think about what's best for everybody."

"I can't believe somebody killed the Kellys because they didn't want to give up their land," another woman said. "I refuse to believe anybody's that evil."

Rachel didn't want to listen to their gossip and speculation. She started edging through the clump of women to the entrance.

Rachel's young assistant, Holly Turner, appeared on the other side of the glass door and pushed it open to let her and Billy Bob in. The last thing Rachel heard from the group behind her was, "It's going to get a whole lot worse before it's over, you can count on that."

With the door closed and the babble of voices shut out, Holly blurted, "It's all anybody's talkin' about, that nice couple gettin' shot." She leaned to pet Billy Bob, her long black hair falling forward over her cheeks. "And you were out that way when it happened, weren't you?"

Rachel sighed. Shannon, the plump blond receptionist behind the front desk, had also turned her way, wide-eyed and expectant. "Yes, I was out there, but I can't tell you anything. Now I need to check on my surgery patients—they'll need to be ready to go home when their owners come in."

She walked past the front desk and down the short hall to her office, where she planned to leave Billy Bob while she examined her patients. She was pulling on a white lab coat when Holly came in and shut the door behind her.

"I don't mean to pester you," Holly said, "but my grandma's been good friends with Miz Kelly as long as I can remember, and she's already called me, all upset, askin' if I know anything about what happened." Holly was a beautiful young woman with the dark olive skin that marked her as Melungeon, like Tom. Like

Marie Kelly. Unlike either of them, Holly had brilliant blue eyes that made a startling contrast to her hair and skin coloring.

"Oh, I'm sorry. I didn't realize they were friends. But I really don't know anything you could pass on to your grandmother. I'll let you know if I hear anything." Rachel stepped around Holly to open the door.

Holly stopped her with a hand on her arm. "I think Grandma might be the one that's got somethin' to pass on. I think Tom ought to talk to her about what she knows."

Chapter Nine

Tom wanted to question the rest of the Kellys' neighbors before the day ended—and while the shock of the murders was fresh enough to prompt honest emotions and unguarded statements.

"The two oldest Jones sisters are the worst snoops I've ever come across," he told Brandon as they headed over to the women's home. Their property lay between the Hollinger farm and the land belonging to Tavia Richardson, and it was twice the size of either. "Summer's not so bad, but Winter and Spring probably know more about their neighbors than anybody else does."

"When I was a little kid," Brandon said, "we all thought they were witches. If you got on their wrong side, they'd put a curse on you. Turn you into a frog or something. If we saw them downtown, we'd cross the street, pronto."

Tom laughed, as appalled as he was amused. "What made you think they were witches?"

"Oh, you know. All living together, none of them ever got married, keeping to themselves. Who knows what they're up to? They could be holding black masses and sacrificing babies for all we know." Brandon chuckled as if dismissing an absurd idea, but he didn't sound as dismissive as he probably thought.

"I'm pretty sure they're harmless. Winter and Spring were both good teachers. I had Winter for English and Spring for history in high school. Summer was a nurse at the hospital until a few years ago. She worked with my mom. But she didn't take to Dr. Hall when he bought the place, and she started doing private duty nursing. I'm not sure she works at all now."

"They had another sister, didn't they?"

"Yeah." Tom had never known her, but he'd heard occasional references to her through the years. "Autumn. She was a year or two younger than Summer. She was in nursing school, then their mother got cancer and she dropped out to take care of her."

"Their dad was a doctor or something?"

"A dentist. He had a big practice, with an office in town. Very successful, made a lot of money."

"Didn't he die in somebody's barn?"

"Yeah. Jake Hollinger's barn, in fact." Tom tried to summon the full story, but the details wouldn't come. "All that happened before I was born. For some reason Jones was in the loft, something to do with getting a sack of grain for their horse, I think, and he lost his balance and fell out the door of the loft, into thin air. Broke his neck when he hit the ground."

"Jeez." After a moment of silence, Brandon asked, "And Autumn, wasn't she the one who—"

"Yeah." Tom let the subject drop. He didn't know that story in detail either, and in any case the tragedy of Autumn Jones had no bearing on their job today.

He swung into the Jones driveway, passing a pretty post-mounted mailbox in the shape of a Swiss chalet. The sisters lived in a Colonial-style farmhouse, spacious and handsome, painted a creamy white with blue shutters and fronted by a broad porch. Every detail spoke of meticulous upkeep. Late-blooming asters and chrysanthemums filled flower beds in front of the foundation shrubs, and not a single fallen leaf marred the still-green lawn. A blue jay drank from a pedestal birdbath under a bare-limbed maple.

Winter answered the doorbell, wiping her hands on an apron tied round her waist. Before Tom could tell her why they were there, she pushed open the storm door and said, "Hello, Thomas, Brandon. Come right in. We've been expecting you."

She led them into the living room, where the mossy green walls and green and cream leaf-patterned fabrics made Tom feel like he was walking into a shaded garden. Spring and Summer stood by the sofa as if they'd been rooted there for a while, awaiting the arrival of the police. The aroma of warm chocolate wafting from the kitchen made Tom's mouth water.

"I'm not sure we have anything of value to tell you," Winter said, "but of course we want to help. I don't mind admitting this situation scares me out of my wits, a killer being loose among us."

"Can we bring you something?" Spring asked, her hands clasped under her chin in an oddly girlish manner. The youthful touch of long nails painted to match her red sweater only served to emphasize her gnarled, arthritic fingers. "Summer made a batch of brownies, and they're still warm. Would the two of you like some?"

Brandon threw a hopeful glance Tom's way. Tom didn't want to conduct an interview while licking chocolate goo off his fingers, but he was suddenly ravenous and guessed that Brandon was too. "Yeah, thanks. That'd be great."

As Summer scurried off to fetch the treats, Winter gestured at the armchairs facing the sofa. "Make yourselves comfortable, please. Let's wait until Summer rejoins us, why don't we? So you won't have to repeat any of your questions."

Winter and Spring settled at the two ends of the sofa and regarded Tom and Brandon with sorrow-tinged expressions. Tom found their silence interesting. Patient restraint wasn't what he'd expected from these inveterate gossips. While Brandon grew fidgety, bouncing a knee up and down, Tom glanced around the room. His gaze settled briefly on the photos that lined the mantel. The sisters' parents stood stiff and solemn in an old studio shot. The pretty young Autumn Jones smiling from what looked like a high school picture. All the pictures looked decades old.

Although it felt longer, the wait lasted three or four minutes until Summer bustled in with a tray and placed it on the coffee table. She'd brought two tall glasses of milk to go with the brownies. "There you go. Enjoy."

Brandon grabbed a plate that held two big, thick brownies studded with pecans. "Thanks." He took a bite from one, swallowed and nodded. "Mmm. This is great."

Settling into the space between her sisters, Summer beamed. "That's quite a compliment coming from someone whose parents own such a wonderful bakery."

The women sat in identical postures, their spines straight without touching the back of the couch, their hands folded in their laps. Although they had different haircuts—Tom wouldn't say any of them had a style—and Spring's vivid clothes and dyed blond hair stood out, the Jones sisters made a set which would be broken up only by death.

Tom took a bite from a brownie but resisted the temptation to devour the whole thing. Wiping his fingers with a napkin Summer had provided, he got down to business. "I heard that you stopped by the Kelly place earlier, so you know what happened."

"We know that Lincoln and Marie have both been murdered," Winter said.

A sound that could have been a gasp or a sob escaped from Summer, but she stifled the surge of emotion and ducked her head. In her lap, her folded hands shifted and the fingers locked in a grip tight enough to turn her knuckles white.

Winter ignored her sister and continued in a brisk tone. "But we don't know any details. Do you have any idea who could have done it?"

"We're just beginning our investigation."

Brandon reached for one of the glasses on the tray and swallowed a third of the milk in one gulp.

Spring shook her head. "Guns are an abomination. I'm so glad we got rid of all our father's weapons after his death. When somebody has a gun, it's too easy to use it to do harm. Think of all the people who are killed with guns every single day. If nobody had a firearm, that wouldn't happen."

No, Tom thought, but people had plenty of other ways to commit murder. He didn't hold out much hope that the human impulse to kill one's own kind would vanish if guns disappeared.

"Where were all of you when it happened? You might have heard or seen something that could help us."

"Spring and I were here in the house," Winter said. "Summer was out collecting the last of our blueberries, but she came running back to the house after the shots were fired. We assumed a hunter was in the area, and we know better than to be outside when we hear gunshots. We drove into Mountainview to do some shopping, and we stopped on our way home because we saw the Sheriff's Department cars on the road. That was the first we knew of what really happened."

"Such a sad thing," Summer murmured.

"Did you hear or see anything out of the ordinary before you left? Or any other time this week?"

The sisters exchanged looks, and Tom had the sensation of witnessing a three-way silent consultation as they compared notes. Why were they so reticent? He'd expected them to be brimming with speculation and opinion about the Kelly murders.

Summer gave him an apologetic smile. "It's not likely we would hear anything while we're inside the house. Hearing problems run in our family. I'm the only one who doesn't use a hearing aid."

"You need one, though," Winter said. "I'm growing weary of having to repeat everything I say."

Summer's face betrayed a flash of irritation, promptly squelched and replaced with a tight little smile. "My sisters don't like wearing theirs, and most of the time the hearing aids are on their dressers, not in their ears."

"Well, it's uncomfortable." Spring touched a finger to her left ear, and for the first time Tom noticed the small plastic device that was partially obscured by her hair. "You'll find out for yourself soon enough, Summer."

Winter cast a raised-eyebrow glance at her sisters. "I can hear what I need to hear. And I can tune out the useless chatter."

Tom felt like he was getting lost in a thicket. What were they like with each other, he wondered, when they were alone? He tried to drag them back on topic. "Have you noticed anything unusual going on around here in the last few days?"

"No, not a thing," Winter said.

"Have you seen any strangers in the area?"

The women's eyes darted from their hands to the wall beyond Tom's head, and sideways at the yard framed in the window. Then, at the same instant, they all focused on Tom and shook their heads no.

Their synchronized movements struck him as creepy. He was beginning to see why kids concocted weird stories about them.

"But that's not necessarily meaningful," Spring said. "If someone approached the Kelly farm from the opposite direction, he wouldn't have passed our place, and we wouldn't have seen him."

Tom glanced at the window. He could see the roof of Hollinger's house in the distance. Beyond that lay the Kelly farm. "With the leaves down, can you see Lincoln and Marie's house from your second floor windows?"

Winter's eyebrows went up. "We don't spend our time spying on the neighbors."

Like hell you don't. Come on, spill it. "What's been going on over there lately?"

"Well…" Winter patted the knot of white hair at the back of her head and pushed a stray strand into place. "I did happen to glance that way this morning. Not at the Kelly house, but at the fence between the properties. Lincoln and Jacob Hollinger were standing there, and they were gesticulating vigorously. I could only assume they were yelling at each other over that blessed fence. I noticed that Lincoln had knocked it down again."

Brandon sat forward in his chair, and Tom told him with a nod to jump in.

"What time was that?" Brandon asked.

"Oh, it was early. Nine o'clock, ten o'clock."

Summer sighed. "Our father should never have sold either of them a square inch of his land all those years ago. If he'd known it would come to this…" Her voice trailed off.

"And things have been considerably worse between those two since the Packard company started waving money around,"

Spring said. "Figuratively speaking. I guess they're waving contracts around, with promises of big money."

"Did any of you see which of them ended the argument
today?" Tom asked. "Which man walked away first?"

They all appeared reluctant, but after a hesitation Winter
answered, "Jake did. In fact, Lincoln appeared to continue
shouting at him as he walked off, but Jake wasn't drawn back
into the argument."

Tom wasn't impressed. If the sisters were telling the truth,
Hollinger had lied about being at his lumber mill all morning.
He might have returned home after the argument, stewed over
it for a while, then grabbed a gun and gone back to finish his
fight with Lincoln once and for all. "Has Hollinger been pressuring the Kellys to sell their farm to Packard?"

For a second none of the women spoke. Winter slid a sidelong
glance at her sisters before she answered. "Apparently so. We
only know what Marie told us. It was upsetting Lincoln terribly, she said. In his mental state—you must know he suffered
from Alzheimer's—he simply couldn't cope with the thought
of leaving his home."

"How do you feel about your neighbors selling land that used
to belong to your family? The Kelly farm, Hollinger's place, the
Richardson land, that all used to belong to your parents, right?
Are you planning to sell your own place to Packard?"

All three took on identical expressions of distress—furrowed
brows, faces screwed up as if they were in pain.

"That's such a contentious issue," Spring said. "I wish it had
never come up. Who could ever have imagined that a huge
development company would want to put a luxury resort here?
In Mason County, of all places."

"We're not even handy to the interstate," Summer added.

Winter's lips twisted in a cold smile. "That's the point, I
suppose. It would be a retreat from the rest of the world. But
with all the conveniences of that world, of course. For wealthy
people who can't imagine living a day without their e-mail and
smartphones and cable television."

"They want to put the lodge where Joanna McKendrick's house is," Tom said.

"Oh, we know," Spring said. "Isn't it awful? Poor Joanna is just beside herself, and who can blame her? Especially with Robert McClure badgering her. He can be such a vile man sometimes."

The other women murmured agreement.

"I guess you're not considering selling, then," Tom said.

"Well…" Winter glanced at her sisters.

"You *are* selling?" Tom had expected the Joneses to be Joanna's allies in blocking the project.

"Now slow down, Thomas," Winter said. "We are uncommitted at this point. This is our home, we've lived here all our lives, and we're naturally reluctant to leave it. On the other hand, we have been offered a princely sum for the land, and frankly, that money would make us quite comfortable in our declining years, especially when we develop the inevitable health problems. So, we are not committed one way or the other, but we are considering the offer—keeping in mind the changes the development would bring to the county."

"Changes for the worse," Summer said, a hard note in her soft voice. "This is the countryside. Bringing in a lot of outsiders would destroy its essential character."

Winter snapped, "Its essential character is that of a depressed place where unemployment is twice the national average."

"Some of us see the beauty of the hills," Summer said.

"Yes, and those beautiful hills tower over people so poor they're hardly surviving."

Summer emitted a barely audible sigh, and her lips formed a humorless smile. "Of course my sister is correct, as always."

Winter acknowledged her sister's acquiescence with a little nod and her own tight smile, then fixed her gaze on Tom. "A man I taught when he was a teenager came to me not long ago and asked if I knew how he could go about selling an organ. At first I thought he was talking about a musical instrument. But no. He'd heard that people could get by with one kidney and that only a fraction of the liver has to be transplanted. He believed he could make enough money by selling his internal organs to keep his family fed and housed for a year."

Tom didn't doubt this account. He'd heard worse. "What did you tell him?"

"The truth, of course. I told him that organ donation programs won't pay for body parts. They have to be donated. I didn't mention the black market. I didn't want to see him go on a quest for a broker. In any case, you know as well as I do that Mason County is in dire need of jobs and an overall economic boost."

"So you're in favor of selling your land." Tom gestured at Winter, then at Summer. "And you're not."

"I didn't say I wanted to sell," Winter said. "I haven't made up my mind. In any case, the three of us will make a joint decision, because we own the land equally. We may have our differences from time to time, but we stand together."

"Tom," Spring said, "I'm sure you've considered that Lincoln and Marie might have been killed because they wouldn't sell their land. That would be a very strong motive, wouldn't it?"

"Yes, it would. But it's also possible somebody had a personal motive to kill them. Aside from Jake Hollinger, do you know anybody who was holding a grudge or had a major problem with the Kellys?"

Summer spoke up, her voice tentative. "What about… Have you been in their house yet? Throughout it, I mean. Have you—"

"My sister," Winter broke in, "is trying to ask if you've found the marijuana yet."

Now it was Tom and Brandon's turn to exchange a glance. Maybe, Tom thought, Dennis was right about the police being the only people in the county who didn't know about the pot. "Yes, we've found the marijuana. Was it common knowledge that they were growing it?"

"Oh, not *common* knowledge," Spring said. "Semi-common, perhaps."

"All right." Tom's impatience was getting the better of him, turning his voice brusque. "You brought it up, so what about it? You think the murders are drug-related? Do you know who they sold the stuff to?"

"Oh, my goodness." Spring gave a little laugh and fluttered a hand. "How would we know anything about drug-dealing?"

"You need to tell me everything you know, and tell me now."

Another silent three-way consultation followed. After a moment, Winter cleared her throat and spoke. "They grew it for medicinal purposes only. Lincoln used to drive it out of the county to sell it. I don't know where. But his health was deteriorating, his memory and coordination were impaired, and he stopped driving months ago. Since then, we've seen an unusual number of vehicles coming and going over there. When we happen to be driving past."

Or looking out your upstairs windows, Tom thought. "You just said you haven't seen any strange people or cars over there."

"You wanted to know if we've seen them in the last few days," Spring pointed out, as if correcting a student's misstatement. "And we haven't. Not this week."

Tom felt like growling at them. "Describe the vehicles you've seen."

In a perfectly synchronized movement, the three women all shrugged. "I'm afraid we can't tell the difference between one vehicle and another," Winter said.

"I do remember a black one," Summer offered. "And perhaps a blue one? I can't really be sure. I believe they had Virginia license plates. The plates were white, in any case."

"Can you describe any strangers you saw over there? The drivers of the vehicles?"

"They were all men," Winter said, her tone decisive.

The other sisters nodded.

"As to their ages or appearance," Winter went on, "I'm afraid we can't be of any help. We saw them from a distance, after all."

"Oh, wait." Summer looked suddenly animated. "There was a woman who visited the Kellys frequently, and she usually left with something in a bag or box. I believe you know her. She's a Melungeon woman. Her granddaughter works for Dr. Goddard."

"Holly?" Brandon exclaimed. "You're saying Holly's grand-mother—"

Tom held up a hand to stop the deputy. Brandon and Holly were engaged, planning a Christmas wedding, and he couldn't be objective about Holly's grandmother. "Are you sure it was Mrs. Turner you saw? And she left with packages?"

Winter waved away the questions. "Oh, for heaven's sake, the woman wasn't buying marijuana. She's an old friend of Marie's. Marie always sent her home with some fresh eggs, and fresh corn too when it was in season. That's all it was."

Brandon slumped back in his chair in obvious relief.

Further questioning led nowhere. The Joneses insisted they had nothing more to tell the police.

Back in the car, Brandon dug into the bag of brownies Summer had given him and Tom to take with them.

"Don't eat all of those," Tom said. "Rachel likes brownies. I want to save one or two for her."

"I'm hungry." Brandon talked around the lump in one cheek. "If I don't eat some of these I'm gonna start gnawing on the car's upholstery."

"What did you think of the sisters?"

Brandon swallowed before he spoke. "They just rambled all over the place, didn't they? Like little old ladies that're getting fuzzy in the head. Except they're just as sharp as you and me. My guess is, they know something they don't want to tell us about."

"Yeah, I got that feeling, too." Frustration beat like a drum in Tom's chest. The sisters had steered them every which way except toward the truth. But he had no idea what the truth was or how to get to it.

Chapter Ten

Last stop: Tavia Richardson's place. Tom pulled his cruiser into the asphalt driveway, and he and Brandon bounced in their seats as the tires hit holes and cracks in the pavement. Killing the engine, Tom frowned at the sad mess of a house.

"Looks abandoned," Brandon said.

"I doubt she's done anything to it since her husband died." White siding had dulled to gray. The front gutter hung lose, at an angle guaranteed to allow rain cascading from the roof to fall behind it rather than into it. At the edge of the weedy front yard garden, a red finch pecked at a coneflower seed head. The plant stalk bounced up and down with the nervous movements of the little bird.

Before long, Tom thought, Jake Hollinger's house would look like this. Both of them were more than ready to move on.

Tavia Richardson pushed open the screen door and stepped onto the porch. As Tom and Brandon approached, she stuck her hands into her jeans pockets and cocked her head. A widow in her early sixties with four adult children, she looked many years younger. Her hair, dark without a single gray strand, formed a tousled cap that emphasized her delicate features, long neck, and high cheekbones. Her jeans and long-sleeved t-shirt hugged the curves of a slender body that could have belonged to a woman in her thirties.

"Let me guess," she said in a voice that always surprised Tom with its deep huskiness. "You boys want to know if I heard the shots and if I saw anything suspicious. The answer's no, and no."

Everything she said in that voice sounded teasing, seductive. Clearing his throat, Tom glanced around. Her property was separated from the Kellys' by many acres and a few rolling hills that would have blocked the sound of the gunshots. "How are you doing, Mrs. Richardson?"

"Oops, I skipped the social niceties and went straight to the bloodshed, didn't I? I'm very well, thank you, Sheriff. And congratulations, by the way, on both your election and your marriage. How are you and Dr. Goddard liking married life?"

"Thanks. We're very happy."

Her smile had a mocking quirk to it. "That's so sweet."

Tom doubted she was trying to be offensive. She had plenty to be bitter about in the marriage department and probably didn't give a damn if others knew it. "Have you talked to either of the Kellys lately?"

"Just to say hello at the bakery…" She nodded at Brandon. "The Connollys' bakery, and the supermarket. I can't offer you any clues that will solve the case for you, I'm afraid. I assume they were murdered by somebody who lives around here." She hunched her slight shoulders and gave a mock shiver. "We have a killer among us. Ouch."

"You think it's a joke?" Tom said.

Now her smile twisted into a condescending smirk. "Life is a joke, Sheriff. God knows what the punch line will turn out to be." She laughed. "God knows. And he's not telling."

Tom was beginning to wonder if she'd been drinking. "I've heard that Jake Hollinger was pressuring them to sell their land to Packard. Have you talked to them about it?"

"What would be the point? They're adamant. *Were* adamant. They wouldn't leave their scrubby little farm unless it was feet first. I guess somebody decided to call their bluff."

"You couldn't have been happy about them standing in the way of your plans."

"My plans?" Tavia gave a halfhearted little laugh, followed by a sigh. "I learned long ago not to make a lot of plans for the future. Especially not the kind that depend on other people cooperating. Yes, I'd love to unload this place. I've been trying to find a buyer since Ron died, but what use would anybody have for it? Nobody farms for a living anymore, and even if they wanted to, there's not enough land here to make a profit. The money Packard's offering… That money would be a real windfall. But I'm not counting on it."

"Because they won't buy your place unless they can get everybody else's, too."

"Exactly." Tavia leaned against one of the posts at the top of the steps and pushed her fingers through her head of curls. "I've just been watching and waiting. But I always figured it would fall through because Joanna won't sell. Why should she? She's probably the only person left in this county who's making a living on her own property."

"Have you talked to her about it? Tried to persuade her to sell?"

"Who am I to tell her what to do with her land? I know plenty of other people have been after her about it, though."

"Were people after the Kellys to sell, too?"

She shrugged, her shoulder bones showing in sharp relief under the t-shirt fabric. "I'm sure they were. There's a lot of money involved. At least people think so. I've been hearing crazy talk that makes Packard's plans sound like the Second Coming."

"You don't think it would work out?" Brandon asked. "The jobs and everything?"

"What if they build it and it's a bust?" Tavia spoke in a speculative tone that didn't demand an answer. "They might never attract all those rich vacationers they're counting on. If I had a lot of money, this backwater sure as hell wouldn't be my idea of a fun getaway."

"But that wouldn't matter, would it," Tom said, "if you and Jake got your money and got out? You could leave Mason County behind forever."

For the first time Tavia looked cagey, withdrawing behind a wary expression. "I don't speak for Jake. He doesn't speak for me."

"I thought you two were pretty close. I got the impression you want to cash in your land so you can move away and start over together."

One corner of her mouth lifted in amusement. "Oh, that's your impression, is it?"

"Are you saying it's not true?"

She pushed away from the post. "I'm not saying anything. I wish I could help you, Tom, but I don't see any way I can."

"All right. By the way, are you going to the community meeting with the Packard people tomorrow?"

"Oh, you bet. I wouldn't miss that show for the world."

Chapter Eleven

A chorus of barks and yelps erupted from the dog pens behind the house when Holly and Rachel parked their cars at the end of the driveway and slammed the doors behind them. In this quiet country setting, the residents of the Blue Ridge Animal Sanctuary picked up every sound, and they always reacted to the arrival of vehicles. Rachel had dropped Billy Bob off at home before following Holly out here. His time with the Kellys' overwrought dog was enough excitement for one day.

Holly and her grandmother, who once lived in the county's poorest district, now occupied a stately brick house on property Holly had inherited from a murdered aunt. That aunt had been married to Robert McClure's brother, and this house had been built by Robert McClure's grandfather. Rachel doubted the banker had ever accepted the idea of Holly owning it. She and her grandmother had transformed the property into an animal shelter, and its first beneficiaries were abandoned dogs Rachel had rescued and abused animals Tom had saved from a dog fighting operation.

On their way to the front door, Holly whispered to Rachel, "She's gonna be real mad at me for draggin' her into this."

"She may not be involved at all." Rachel kept her own voice low, although she wasn't sure why. Holly's grandmother couldn't hear them from inside if they spoke in normal tones. "If she knows something that could help Tom's investigation, I'm going to try to persuade her to go see him."

"Then she might be mad at you, too."

"Let her. She'll get over it." Rachel had tangled with Sarelda Turner more than once, starting the day Rachel had literally helped Holly escape her family's smothering grasp. They had developed a respect for each other since then, and Rachel knew the cranky old woman would usually do the right thing if somebody prodded her.

When Holly and Rachel walked into the living room, three mongrel dogs greeted them with wagging tails. Mrs. Turner lifted an orange tabby cat off her lap and used the arm of the couch for support to push herself to her feet. She looked as if she'd been crying for hours and had a reservoir of tears yet to shed. Her short hair, dyed black as boot polish, stuck out at angles, as if she'd been tearing at it.

Holly rushed to throw her arms around her. "Oh, Grandma, I'm so sorry about your friends."

After giving Holly a couple of pats on the back, Mrs. Turner pushed her away. "Rachel, you come to see the dogs? Did I forget an appointment?"

"No, I came to see you." Rachel placed a hand on Mrs. Turner's shoulder, intending it as a gesture of consolation, but removed it when she felt the older woman stiffen under her touch. "Holly told me you and Marie Kelly were friends."

Instantly Mrs. Turner's expression hardened, and she shot a peeved glance at Holly. "There's not any need for you to be tellin' people about my personal business."

"Now don't be that way, Grandma. I know you're hurtin' because of what happened to your friends. You don't have to act mean when somebody shows they care about how you feel."

Mrs. Turner pressed her lips into a hard line that wouldn't hold. One corner twitched upward in a rueful smile as she told Rachel, "This girl's done nothin' but talk back to me since the day she took up with you."

Rachel laughed. "Sorry about that."

The tension broken, Mrs. Turner sank onto the couch again. The tabby cat reclaimed its place on her lap and the smallest dog, a terrier mix, jumped up beside her. The other two settled at her feet. "Lord, that was awful news about Marie and her husband. It's just been eatin' away at my heart since I heard. Look at the time, and I've not even started dinner yet."

She began to rise, giving the cat a gentle push that prompted a yowl of protest.

"No, Grandma," Holly said. "You stay right where you are and talk to Rachel. I'll take care of dinner." She threw Rachel a look that mixed apprehension, hope, and a plea for tact, and headed off to the kitchen.

Rachel hoped she would be in her own kitchen preparing dinner sometime soon, although she doubted Tom would be able to join her. If this day seemed endless to her, she could imagine what a grind it had been for him. And his workday was probably nowhere close to being over.

Two more cats occupied the room's armchairs, so Rachel sat on an upholstered hassock. Although they lived in a house that many called a mansion, Holly and her grandmother were using the furniture from their old house and leaving many rooms empty or filled with supplies for their charges. New furnishings cost too much, they said, and the money was better spent on caring for the animals they took in and expanding the space to house them. Upstairs in the master suite, though, Holly was creating a freshly decorated apartment for herself and Brandon in preparation for their upcoming marriage.

"I didn't know the Kellys well," Rachel said, taking a cautious first step toward her goal, "but I thought they were good people. I can't imagine who would do such a thing to them."

She watched with dismay as Mrs. Turner's face crumpled and tears spilled down her cheeks. "I hope they burn in hell, the ones that did it," she choked out.

"I'm sorry. I didn't mean to—" Rachel cut off her apology. She had come here to get information, after all. She refocused. "Do you have any idea who it could be?"

Mrs. Turner extracted a fresh tissue from the pocket of her dress, mopped her eyes and blew her nose. "I'd like to load up my shotgun and go after them. Cut them down in cold blood, like they did poor Marie and Lincoln."

Rachel believed she was capable of doing exactly what she said. "The person who did it won't get away with it. Tom will make sure of that."

"He'd better, or I'll do it myself. You tell him I said so."

Oh, he'd love hearing that, Rachel thought. But she nodded to placate Mrs. Turner. "When was the last time you saw the Kellys?"

"Couple days ago."

"How were they? Did they seem worried about anything?"

"Marie was. Lincoln was worked up about their neighbor's fence, like he always was. His mind was goin' and he'd get so wound up and mad—I think he was scared, you know? He couldn't understand what was happenin' to him."

Rachel murmured agreement, although she'd heard none of this before. "What was Marie worried about?"

"Well, for one thing, that s.o.b. Robert McClure was on their doorstep all the time, tryin' to get them to sign away their land. All that talk just confused Lincoln. He thought the bank was gonna throw them off their land. But all the other stuff was even worse."

"The other stuff? Such as what?"

Mrs. Turner fixed a canny gaze on Rachel. "I know what you're up to. Don't think I don't. You want to find out what I know, so you can tell your husband."

Rachel shrugged, trying to look abashed. "Guilty as charged. You don't have to tell me anything. I'm not the one who needs to know. But if you can tell Tom something that might help, you really should talk to him. He has to find out who did this and put him behind bars."

"But that's the thing, you see." Mrs. Turner stroked the cat absentmindedly. "I don't know if it'll help. Even when Marie was tellin' me—and I trusted Marie, I thought she was a sensible woman—but it all sounded so crazy."

"Crazy in what way?" Despite what she'd said, Rachel couldn't stifle her curiosity. She wanted Mrs. Turner to tell her everything.

"Funny noises outside at night. Something, or somebody, knockin' on the side of the house. Scary sounds out in the apple trees, like a baby or a woman cryin'. Snakes in the house, three different times. One time in the middle of the night, she heard somebody up on the roof. Lincoln didn't wake up, thank the lord. Marie thought at first it was just a coon, but she said she never saw one big enough to make that much racket just walkin' around. She was too scared to go out and look. Next mornin' she found a dead crow in the fireplace, like it was dropped down the chimney."

"My God." Despite her jacket and the warm room, Rachel suddenly felt cold.

"Well, anyway, you can just imagine the toll it all took on Lincoln, with his mind already in a bad state."

"Did Mrs. Kelly report any of this? Did she call Tom?"

Mrs. Turner shook her head. "How was she gonna prove any of it? We all hear funny noises at night sometimes, don't we? And a bird down the chimney, that happens sometimes, too. I've had it happen to me. What could the police do?"

She was right, Rachel knew. Tom would have cared because Mrs. Kelly was his mother's friend, but he wouldn't have been able to help.

"I guess they got tired of waitin' for Marie and Lincoln to give up and leave. They decided murder was quicker."

For the first time, Rachel realized Mrs. Turner had repeatedly used the word *they*, not *he* or *she*. Colloquial grammar? Probably. Rachel did it often enough herself. But she wanted to make sure. "When you say *they* and *them*, is that just a figure of speech, or do you mean more than—"

"I mean exactly what I say." Mrs. Turner's knife-edged voice cut off Rachel's tentative question. "I mean *them*."

Chapter Twelve

Back at Sheriff's Department headquarters in Mountainview, Dennis Murray and Gretchen Lauter were sitting at one end of the long conference table, drinking coffee, when Tom and Brandon walked in. Eight-by-ten photos of the murdered couple filled the cork board on one wall. Tom closed the door so their discussion wouldn't be overheard by anyone passing in the hallway.

Dr. Lauter rose, straightened the jacket of her navy blue pants suit, and moved to the photo display. The three men gathered around. She drew a deep breath, let it out, and focused on the pictures. "I don't think we'll learn anything from the autopsies that we don't already know. I didn't see any evidence that they'd been assaulted. Struck, I mean. No bruises, no obvious broken bones, no bleeding anywhere except the bullet wounds."

"And no sign that they tried to save themselves," Tom said.

"No, none."

"Somebody just walked into their yard with a rifle and shot them."

"Exactly."

"Had to be somebody they knew," Brandon said. "Somebody they wouldn't be afraid of if he showed up in their yard carrying a gun."

"Dennis told me about the marijuana," Dr. Lauter said. "I don't mind admitting that completely floored me. But now that I think about it, it's not out of character, not if they were growing it for people who needed pain relief. Do you think that points to a motive? Some dealer who didn't like them cutting into his business?"

"I don't know," Tom said. "The plants weren't taken. We found leaves and buds drying in the shed. It didn't look like anything had been removed."

"Hollinger's the one acting like he's got something to hide," Brandon said.

"But everybody knows they were feuding," Tom pointed out. "Hollinger would be a fool to kill both the Kellys. He'd know he'd be the first suspect. He *was* our first suspect."

"If he did it during an argument, while he was angry," Dr. Lauter said, "he wouldn't have been thinking about consequences. Get a person mad enough and—"

The door flew open and a tall, dark-haired man in a business suit burst in. "I got here as fast as I could."

"Ronan, let's go in my office." Tom stepped in front of him, trying to get between the Kellys' son and the pictures before he saw them.

Too late. Ronan Kelly's eyes had found the photos of his dead parents and fixed on them, his face contorting in horror, his breath coming in shallow gulps. "My God— Mom, Dad—"

"This way." Tom locked a hand on his arm and forced him to swivel toward the door.

Ronan twisted his neck to keep the photos in view, as if he were still trying to make sense of what he saw. Tom had to shove him out the door. Keeping a firm grip on Ronan's arm, Tom led him across the hall and into the office.

Ronan collapsed into a chair facing the desk, leaned over and buried his face in his hands. His broad shoulders shook with sobs. A few years older than Tom, he was a former high school and college football player, now an engineer who had maintained his athletic physique, but at the moment he was a kid who had lost both parents under horrific circumstances.

Tom sat behind his desk, waited for Ronan to cry himself out, and struggled to keep the barricade up against the memory of his own parents' deaths and the grief that had overwhelmed him. He forced himself to mentally check through the questions he had to ask. And he reminded himself that until he was cleared, the Kellys' son was as much a suspect as anybody else.

At last Ronan quieted, pulled a handkerchief from his pants pocket and wiped his face. He ran his fingers through his thick hair, which left it looking worse rather than better. Like Tom, he had inherited coal-black hair and olive skin from a Melungeon parent. "I still can't believe this has happened." Ronan's voice broke on the last word. He paused a moment, took a breath, and went on, sounding a little calmer. "Driving out here, it was surreal, trying to get my mind around it."

"Can I get you anything? Coffee?"

Ronan shook his head. "I've had so much caffeine already I'm about to jump out of my skin." He sat forward, his face beseeching. "Tell me you know who did this. Tell me you've got him in custody."

"I wish I could. But right now…" Tom shook his head.

Ronan slumped back in his chair and leaned his forehead in his palm.

"When will Sheila be here?" Tom asked.

"Tomorrow. She's flying to Charlotte from Chicago, and I talked her into taking a hotel room and getting some sleep before she drives up here. I don't want her driving through the mountains at night when she's…God, I don't even know what to call it, the way we're both feeling. Shocked. Stunned."

"When was the last time you talked to your parents?"

"Last Sunday. I try to call them once a week."

"Did they say anything to indicate they were having problems with anybody?"

"Besides Jake Hollinger, you mean? That's all I ever heard from Dad lately, when he got on the line. But Mom, no, she never complained about anything or anybody. She got along with everybody."

"How serious would you say the trouble between your dad and Hollinger was?"

"Are you thinking—"

"I'm not thinking anything at this point. Just gathering information."

"All right. Let me try to remember." Ronan blew out a long breath and shifted his gaze toward the darkening sky outside the window while he gathered his thoughts.

Night was falling, Tom realized, and the wind had picked up, swirling a few fallen leaves across the parking lot. A couple of fat raindrops splattered the window glass.

"Hollinger…" Ronan began, then paused. "He's right about that fence, you know. If he'd taken it to court, Dad would have lost. I surveyed it myself, but Dad wouldn't listen to me, wouldn't accept my conclusion. I'm an engineer, for God's sake, and he wouldn't take my word. But he wasn't well, and he was getting worse, so I gave up trying to get through to him."

"Were you ever afraid the tension between him and Hollinger might escalate?"

Ronan looked at Tom in surprise. "Escalate into Hollinger shooting Dad and Mom both? No. Never."

"And they weren't having trouble with anybody else?"

"If they were, Mom would've made sure Sheila and I never heard about it. She never wanted to worry us. They kept things from us, health problems and stuff like that. Dad was having trouble for a long time before it finally got so bad, just recently, that Mom couldn't hide it from us anymore."

"When was the last time you actually saw them?"

"Well…" Ronan shifted in his seat. "You know how it is. I've got a wife, kids, it's not easy…"

"I understand," Tom said, keeping any hint of judgment out of his voice. "I just need to know the last time you saw them."

"I guess it was… Yeah, it was. Right after Christmas last year. We came out for a couple of days." He added, as if reinforcing an argument, "All of us, the whole family."

And here it was getting close to Christmas again, and Ronan lived within driving distance of his parents, one of whom had been suffering from Alzheimer's, yet he hadn't come to visit. All that was beside the point, though, if it had no bearing on the murders. "Do you have somewhere to stay while you're here? I can't let you stay in your parents' house, at least not tonight."

"What? Why not?"

"Did you know they were growing marijuana? And selling it?"

Ronan's expression wavered between astonishment and amusement. "Is that supposed to be a joke?"

"No. They were growing pot in their cornfield, and they had a lot of plants under lights in the basement. We have to get them out before we can give you and your sister access to the house. I've got men over there now, but I'm not sure when they'll be done."

Ronan's mouth hung open as the knowledge settled in. At last he expelled a short laugh that sounded like a grunt following a punch to the stomach. "Well, I'll be damned. They were *selling* it? My parents were drug dealers?"

"In the strictest sense, I guess. But my information is that they weren't selling it for recreational use. They grew it for people with terminal illnesses who need relief from pain. They probably gave away a lot of it."

Ronan considered that for a moment. "Okay. All right. Yeah, I can see them doing that. That's the kind of people they were."

"You know about the Packard development, don't you? The offer for their land?"

"Well, sure. I told them they ought to sell and move to one of those assisted living places where Mom could get some help with Dad. But they wanted to live out their lives on the farm."

"There was a lot of money on the table."

"I know. But…" Ronan shrugged. "It was their decision."

"It'll be your decision now. Yours and your sister's."

"I've got more important things to take care of. I can't even think about selling the land right now."

But plenty of other people, Tom knew, would be thinking about little else.

◇◇◇

Wearing only boxer shorts and a t-shirt, his usual sleep attire, Tom sat on his side of the bed but didn't lie down or turn off the lamp. Rachel had kept quiet while he ate his late dinner, letting him decompress a little after his long and stressful day. She'd been sitting up in bed trying to read while he took a shower.

Now she reached over to rub his back and felt muscles tight as ropes under the shirt's fabric. "You might want to talk to Holly's grandmother tomorrow. She was friendly with the Kellys, and Mrs. Kelly might have told her something that would help you in the investigation."

Tom looked around at Rachel. "Like what? Have you talked to Mrs. Turner today?"

"For a few minutes, but she'll tell you more than she told me. She hinted that she knew who killed them, but I couldn't pry it out of her."

"All right, I'll talk to her."

"By the way," Rachel said, trying to sound casual, "some men from Packard stopped by here today. They said this farm would be a perfect location for a private airport to serve the resort."

She expected him to be annoyed, but instead he laughed. "Did they say how much they'll pay us for it?"

"I'll take that as a joke."

Tom shifted to face Rachel. "Forget about it. Don't let them get under your skin. Listen, I'm worried about Joanna. Would you talk to her in the morning and ask her not to go to that meeting with the Packard people? She's more likely to listen to you than me."

Rachel shook her head. "She won't stay away. It's too important to her."

"She's the most visible and vocal opponent of the development. She's becoming a target. The more noise she makes, the more trouble she's going to stir up for herself."

Rachel raised her eyebrows. "*Noise*? Is that what you call—"

He held up both hands to stop her. "Poor choice of words. And I don't want you to go either, so I won't have to worry about you."

"But—"

"Just stay out of it. Can you do that for me? Please?"

"I'll try."

"Do more than try. Stay out of it. It's none of your business."

She hated to argue with him when it was late, he was exhausted, and they both needed sleep. But she had to protest, however mildly. "I live here, Tom, I'm putting down roots here. I invested every cent I had in buying that animal hospital. Anything that's going to affect the whole county—and a good friend of mine—is my business."

"Just wait it out. And tell Joanna to wait it out. That development is never going to happen. Nobody's going to force her to sell her land."

No, Rachel thought, they might do something far worse. She didn't understand how Tom could speak with such certainty of a happy outcome to the trouble brewing in the county. Sure, staying out of it would be easy. All Rachel had to do was radically alter her basic nature and abandon her friend.

Chapter Thirteen

Mark Hollinger wouldn't shed his brown leather jacket and he wouldn't sit down. Like a skittish dog, he patrolled Tom's office, halting as if to take the scent in one spot before jerking away toward another.

Tom leaned back in his desk chair, watching Jake Hollinger's son and waiting for an answer.

"I don't remember exact times. I wasn't looking at the clock." Mark paused at the window, his distracted gaze directed at the parking lot outside, his broad shoulders rising and falling in a shrug. He looked like a younger version of his father, with thick dark brown hair and a square jaw, his features drawn in bold strokes where age had blurred the lines on Jake's face. Only those odd pale blue eyes had come from Mark's mother. When the early morning sun caught them, their color faded and they gleamed like silver disks.

Tom fingered a pencil, tapped the eraser on the desktop. "Why was your father at the lumber mill? Did you have some kind of problem you couldn't deal with? He told me you're having a little trouble handling the business side of things."

Mark swung around, an angry flush riding up his neck into his cheeks. "I handle the business just fine when I've got the right paperwork. But I keep hearing from customers about orders I didn't know about and don't have any paperwork on. It's a mess sometimes."

"A mess your dad created, so you have to get him to come in and straighten it out."

Mark opened his mouth, closed it again, and seemed to be debating with himself before he answered. "Your words, not mine."

"Was your father at the mill yesterday for an hour, two hours? Longer? Did he stay all morning? Past lunchtime? You noticed that much, didn't you?"

"He was in the office. I was working with the men. I didn't even see him leave."

"Ah." Tom dropped the pencil on the desk and sat forward. "So you can't say for sure where your father was when Lincoln and Marie Kelly were shot."

"That's not what I—" Mark broke off, shoved his fists into his jeans pockets. "If he said he was at the mill, then he was."

Tom didn't respond to that. "How much do you know about your father's relations with the Kellys?"

Moving to a wall of photos, Mark studied a head and shoulders shot of Tom's late father, John Bridger, as if he were memorizing details of the face that looked so much like Tom's. "They were good to my mother when she was sick. They gave her something for the pain that worked better than the pills. It helped her get some rest."

"They gave her marijuana."

Mark pivoted, hands raised. "Now wait a minute. I don't know anything about—"

"Forget it. I'm not interested in the Kellys' pharmaceutical business unless it's connected with the murders."

A spark of something like hope bloomed on Mark's face. "You think it could? They ticked off some drug dealer, maybe?"

"I'm looking at every possibility."

Mark's expression collapsed into anxiety again. "Including my father. You actually think he would go over there with a gun and kill both of them just because they were fighting over that damned fence."

"They had more important differences. You know that. The Packard deal is all or nothing. Your father stood to lose a fortune if the Kellys—and Joanna McKendrick—refused to sell. I'm trying to establish your father's whereabouts at the time of the murders, but obviously you can't help me."

Fists in his pockets, his mouth clamped shut in a stubborn line, Mark tried staring a hole in the wall. If Jake Hollinger was counting on his son to give him a solid alibi—to lie for him, if necessary—he'd put his trust in the wrong person.

"All right." Tom stood. "Thanks for coming in. Come see me again if you decide to tell the truth."

That stirred a flash of indignation, but Mark didn't issue a rebuttal. Without speaking, he yanked open the door and stalked out of the office.

Tom followed, and he entered the squad room in time to witness Mark's encounter with Sheila Kelly Hayes, Marie and Lincoln's daughter.

She rose from a chair beside Dennis Murray's desk, clutching a black leather shoulder bag against her chest, its strap dangling. She'd scraped her long black hair back into a clip, but messy strands had escaped and hung around her face and down her neck. "Mark," she said. "Hello."

Mark Hollinger stopped in his tracks, then backed up a couple of steps to put more distance between them. Tom caught the deputy's eye and shook his head to keep Dennis silent.

"Sheila." Mark croaked as if he had something stuck in his throat. "Hey. I, uh, I'm sorry. You know, about your folks."

"Thank you."

"Well… I have to get going." Mark gestured toward the doorway.

"I'll see you again while I'm here, I hope."

Mark nodded and hustled toward the exit.

Tom walked over. "Hey, Sheila."

She pulled her gaze from the doorway where Mark Hollinger had vanished and tried to refocus, frowning at Tom as if he were an acquaintance she vaguely remembered but couldn't quite place, instead of someone she'd known most of her life.

Tom laid a hand on her shoulder. "How are you doing? I wasn't expecting you this early. I thought you were going to get some rest before you drove up here."

"Oh…" An absentminded flick of one slender hand waved away his concern. "I couldn't sleep. I gave up trying. I decided I might as well be driving." Her olive complexion, which Tom remembered as warm and vibrant, appeared bloodless now, and she wore that stunned expression he had seen too many times. Bad news poorly received, not yet fully absorbed.

"Let's talk in my office." Tom took her elbow to steer her down the hall. They passed by Sheriff Willingham's old office, which had stood empty since illness forced him to retire, and walked on to the smaller space Tom occupied. The name plate on the door still read Captain Thomas J. Bridger, although Dennis, formerly a sergeant, now held the rank of captain. When the new plate identifying Tom as sheriff arrived, he would tackle the hassle of moving offices.

He closed the door behind them.

Sitting in the chair facing his desk, Sheila hunched forward over the purse on her lap, rubbing her upper arms.

"Don't you have a coat with you?" Tom asked.

"My coat…" She frowned. "I guess I left it in the car."

"Have some coffee to warm up." Taking his seat, Tom grabbed a thermos from the desktop and unscrewed the cap. He poured coffee into his own mug, which he hadn't used yet that morning. "Here. This is good stuff, not the swill from the coffeemaker. I brought it from home."

Sheila reached for the mug, took a sip, and held it in both hands. "I think I'm in shock. I keep hearing what you said when you called me yesterday, it's playing over and over in my head, but I still can't take this in. Murdered? My mom and dad *murdered?*"

"I know. I'm sorry I had to give you the news on the phone. Your parents were good people. They'll be missed by a lot of us."

"Where are they now?" Her voice trembled. "Will I have to—you know—identify them?"

"No, you don't. They're already in Roanoke for the autopsies."

Sheila's face crumpled and sudden tears dropped from her eyes and splattered her purse. Bending over, she clamped one hand across her mouth, and for a second Tom thought she was about to vomit. He watched the carelessly held mug, now resting on her purse, tip almost far enough to spill its contents. Her voice muffled, Sheila asked, "Did Dad do it? Did he shoot Mom and then himself?"

Startled by the question, Tom took a moment to answer. "No, it wasn't like that. They were both murdered by someone else. We don't know who yet, but we're positive about that much."

She slumped in the chair as if relieved, letting go of a possibility she had considered worse than the reality. Tom rounded the desk, took the coffee mug from her and set it on the desk. Covering her face with both hands, she burst into sobs.

Tom returned to his chair and let her cry herself out. Sheila's raw emotion, like Ronan's, touched a chord in him, a grief of his own so enormous that it still threatened to overcome him when he allowed himself to look squarely at it. With an effort, he turned his mind back to Mark Hollinger's behavior, his unwillingness to lie for his father even as he refused to contradict Jake's alibi. And why had Mark reacted so strangely when he encountered Sheila? Guilt? Did he suspect his father of killing her parents?

At last Sheila pulled herself together and dug a tissue from her purse to wipe her face and blow her nose. "I'm sorry," she said in a voice still thick with tears. "I'm okay now, I promise. I want to help if I can. Is there anything you need to know that I can tell you?"

"Sheila…" Tom hesitated, wondering if he was about to set off another round of tears. But he had to ask. "What made you think your father might have done this?"

"He's not him— He wasn't himself anymore. I thought you probably knew that."

"I know about the Alzheimer's," Tom said. "I can't say I knew how bad it was. I hadn't seen him in a while. The last few times Jake Hollinger called about their argument over the fence, other deputies handled it."

Sheila grimaced. "It was mortifying for Mom, to have Dad behaving that way. I tried to talk to him about it. I begged him and begged him to let it go, forget about the goddamned fence."

"And what did he say?"

She gave a short laugh. "He told me not to swear when I talked to my father. I was worried that he might get confused and lash out at Mom. But she insisted she could handle him, she had ways to calm him down." Casting a speculative glance at Tom, Sheila added, "I talked to my brother on the phone late last night. He told me he was staying at Joanna's place and we can't go into the house yet because you found...something unusual."

"You mean the marijuana nursery in the basement? Yeah, that was a little out of the ordinary, although pot farms aren't really unusual around here. We've removed it all, so you and Ronan can use the house if you want to."

Sheila looked as if she were about to speak, but apparently decided silence was her best option.

"Look," Tom said, "I don't care if you knew and didn't report it. I realize they were trying to help sick people. But anytime there's a murder and the victims are involved with drugs in any way, we have to ask whether there's a connection."

"My parents were just hippies who outgrew their era. I mean, Dad was a loan officer at a bank. How much less of a hippie can you be? But they both believed medical marijuana should be legalized. They weren't drug dealers in any conventional sense."

"No, they didn't sell dime and nickel bags to school kids. But the people who do sell drugs that way might not take kindly to a couple setting up an independent operation."

"Oh my God." Sheila leaned her forehead into her palm. "I was worried about them being arrested, but I didn't pressure them because Mom said the pot helped her manage Dad. She put it in his meals when he was getting wound up, and it mellowed him out. It never occurred to me they might be making dangerous enemies. Do you know who it could be? You must know who's selling drugs locally."

"We've cleaned up the local drug business twice in the last couple of years, but it's the kind of crime we'll never be rid of. There's too much demand for the products." Tom hated to admit he hadn't been able to pin down who was running it now, but he knew somebody was. Business that lucrative didn't die because its CEO did. Plenty of people were eager to step over the corpse and take charge. "Anyway, it gives us one possible motive to look at. Can you think of anybody else they'd been having trouble with?"

Sheila shook her head. Tears filled her eyes again, but she blinked them away and held onto her composure.

"What do you know about the resort development?" Tom asked. "A lot of people are angry at the holdouts. Your parents and Joanna McKendrick were standing in the way of the development. Now you and your brother are going to be pressured to sell."

She shook her head, her lips twisting in a humorless smile. "No, that's going to be my decision."

"Oh? I thought you two would split everything equally."

"My brother probably thinks he has an equal share, but he's going to find out that he doesn't. Our parents put everything in a trust for us. I'm getting three-quarters of it and he gets a quarter. They've given him so much money already that they thought that was a fair division. I doubt Ronan will see it that way."

Chapter Fourteen

Tom paused at Dennis Murray's desk on his way out and recapped the conversation with Sheila, including what she'd told him about her brother.

"Whoa." The deputy's eyebrows rose behind his wire-rimmed glasses. "Three failed business ventures—that means a ton of debt. Now there's a motive for you. If Ronan doesn't know his sister's getting most of the estate, he's probably counting on a windfall from a sale to Packard."

"But any kind of inheritance depended on both his parents being dead. I'll let you work your magic on the Internet and see what you can dig up while I'm gone. I need to go see Sarelda Turner before I head out for the Packard meeting."

"You really think she's got something useful to tell us?"

"Don't be so skeptical. I've learned not to shrug off anything she says. In this case, she was close to the victims. If anybody knows what was going on with the Kellys, it's Mrs. Turner. She wouldn't tell Rachel much, though, and she wouldn't tell me anything on the phone this morning. It has to be face to face."

"What do you want to do about Ronan?"

"Let him be for now. I'll track him down after the meeting. When he finds out about the change in his parents' trust, he's going to blame his sister for it."

Tom knew Mrs. Turner wouldn't hear him above the barking and baying of the dogs, so he didn't try to get her attention as he approached the huge fenced-in exercise yard. About three dozen dogs of every size and description raced around in the yard, while Mrs. Turner stood outside the chain link fence, smiling and laughing at the animals' antics. Tom paused twenty feet away, enjoying the uninhibited delight on her face, something he rarely saw.

She caught sight of him, though, and he glimpsed a flash of apprehension before she snapped into the stiff, reserved persona she usually presented when he was around.

Tom stepped closer and raised his voice to compete with the racket the dogs created. "They all look healthy. You think you'll be able to find homes for any of them?"

Before she could answer, a white dog with black eye patches sprinted over to the fence and stood up against it, tail working in a furious rhythm. Tom stooped and stuck his fingers through the links to scratch the animal's head. This was one of the ferals he'd helped Rachel and the animal warden catch, on a brisk fall day more than a year ago. They had waited out of sight across the road as the dogs crept from the cave where they'd been hiding, lured by the aroma of canned dog food used as bait in cage traps. All the dogs had been near starvation and covered with ticks and fleas when they arrived at the sanctuary.

"They've got a home, right here," Mrs. Turner said. "Anybody that wants one is gonna have to prove they'll treat it right and keep it the rest of its life. After everything they've been through, they don't need to be shunted around anymore."

She motioned toward the house, where they could talk without having to shout. Tom gave the dog a last scratch and rose to follow Mrs. Turner through the back door into the kitchen.

"Take a seat," she said. "I'll get us some coffee."

Three mutts of different sizes and colors charged into the kitchen and surrounded Tom, sniffing his shoes and pants legs before lifting their heads to be patted. These were Mrs. Turner's personal pets, two of them aging dogs she'd had all their lives. The smallest, a young terrier mix, was the last feral rescued from the cave, the one Rachel had crawled into the low, narrow space to find. Tom pulled out a chair and sat at the kitchen table. The dogs settled in a row next to him, watching him with expectant eyes. If he was the morning's entertainment, they were probably going to be disappointed.

Mrs. Turner took her time pulling a couple of mugs from a cabinet and filling them from the fresh pot on the coffee maker. Stalling, Tom thought. Mentally rehearsing her answers to the questions she expected.

She placed a mug in front of him and took a chair across the table. Sipping the dark, fragrant brew, Tom wondered what Mrs. Turner did that was special. She made the best coffee he'd ever tasted. Eyeing her death grip on her own mug, sensing the anxiety that radiated off her, he decided to let her relax a little before he tackled the reason for his visit. "Are you and Holly planning to keep every animal you take in?"

She jutted her chin. "What's gonna stop us? We've got plenty more land here. Holly's got all that money Pauline left behind. We'll just keep right on expandin' as long as we need to."

"There's no reason you can't, if you're willing to cut down a few trees here and there."

"Trees can be built around." A little smile played on Mrs. Turner's lips, and her eyes took on an almost mischievous glint. "I keep expectin' Robert McClure to come around, tryin' to get Holly to sell this land to that big company. I know it just about drives him crazy to see what we're doin' to his granddaddy's place. First his brother married my scandalous Melungeon daughter and set her up here like a queen, and now there's Holly and me and all these dogs. I bet it keeps him awake at night. I almost feel sorry for the poor man."

Tom laughed. "Yeah, I'm sure you do."

They drank their coffee in silence, and Mrs. Turner's amusement faded to melancholy. Tom wondered if she was thinking about the Kellys or her own family, torn apart by murder and lies and mental illness. She never spoke of her lost daughters, one of them Holly's mother and the other the former resident of this house. As far as Tom knew, Mrs. Turner had no contact with her one surviving daughter, now locked up in an institution for the criminally insane, nor with the granddaughter serving a prison term. Holly was the only family Sarelda Turner had left. With Marie Kelly's death, she had also lost a good friend.

"I'm sorry you had to lose Mrs. Kelly," Tom said. "Especially this way,"

"Well, now." Mrs. Turner set her mug on the table and straightened in her chair. "I guess we ought to get down to business. Can't sit here the rest of the day. We've both got other things to do."

Tom sat forward, pulled his notebook from his shirt pocket. "Anything you can tell me might help me find the person who killed Marie and Lincoln."

Pursing her lips, Mrs. Turner regarded the notebook with wary eyes. "I'm not scared to talk because of myself, you know. Anybody comes after me, they'll get more than they bargained for."

"You have plenty of watchdogs inside and out to sound the alert if a stranger comes around." He glanced down at the three dogs next to him, and the runt gave a soft yip. Tom scratched his head, then had to do the same for the other two when they pressed forward for attention.

"I don't think it's strangers I need to look out for," Mrs. Turner said. "But as long as I stay right here, I'm safe as I can be. Holly, now, she's out and about, drivin' around by herself. It's her I worry about."

"I'll have a talk with her and Brandon. We won't let anything happen to her. You know Rachel and I both care a lot about your granddaughter."

Mrs. Turner acknowledged that with a nod. But still she hesitated. Tom waited out her silence.

At last she cleared her throat and spoke. "I guess Rachel told you that all kinds of little things was happenin' at Marie and Lincoln's house. Lincoln, his mind wasn't clear enough so he could understand what all was goin' on. But Marie was scared. I tried to get her to talk to you about it, but she said there wasn't anything real solid she could point to, like so-and-so did this or that. It wasn't stuff you could arrest somebody for unless you caught them in the act. But she was afraid it was leadin' up to something real bad. And she sure was right about that."

Tom saw the grief welling up in Mrs. Turner's eyes again, and he pushed on before she gave in to it. "Did she have any idea who was trying to intimidate them? Was she afraid of somebody in particular?"

Ronan, Tom thought, could have bought a few acts of vandalism for relatively little money. Arranging something like that long distance would be risky, though, with too many chances for discovery. Still, he almost expected Mrs. Turner to say Marie had been afraid of her own son. Although it would be hearsay, it might help Tom build a case for an arrest—if Ronan was, in fact, behind his parents' murders.

Mrs. Turner surprised him. "She was scared of their neighbors. People they lived close to all these years. People they helped out, anytime it was needed."

"Which neighbors?"

She seemed hesitant to speak names aloud, although the number of possibilities was limited: Jake, Tavia, the Jones sisters—and Tom doubted she was talking about the elderly Joneses. He allowed Mrs. Turner time to summon her courage.

"Jake Hollinger, for one," she said at last. "But Marie was a whole lot more worried about that woman he took up with."

"Octavia Richardson? What made her think Jake and Tavia were a threat to her and Linc?"

"They just wouldn't let up about Lincoln and Marie sellin' their farm. Marie said they'd come by together a couple times a week, regular as clockwork. Lincoln got all upset about it, every time. It was too much for him, on top of Robert McClure pesterin' them. He didn't understand exactly what it meant, but he could tell they all wanted to take his home away from him. And that woman, she'd come around by herself, too, real sly and nasty, a whole lot worse than she acted when Hollinger was there to see it." Mrs. Turner sniffed, her expression soured with contempt. "She's not from around here, you know. She's from down in Florida somewheres."

Right, Tom thought. Tavia had only lived here for the last forty years or so of her life. About as long as Joanna had been in Mason County. Both were still newcomers in the eyes of many natives.

Leaning forward, Mrs. Turner lowered her voice as if they weren't the only two people within miles. "You know she killed her husband."

"What?" The word erupted from Tom, jarringly loud in the quiet room. "Tavia Richardson?"

The largest of the dogs, a shaggy brown animal of indeterminate heritage, laid a paw on Tom's knee and issued a little whine. He didn't know whether the animal was offering reassurance or seeking it. Either way, she didn't like his raised voice. He patted her head.

"Now don't tell me you never heard the story," Mrs. Turner said. "Everybody knows about her and her husband."

"I know he abused her for years. I think she's probably lucky she didn't end up dead. But her husband died in an accident."

Mrs. Turner pursed her lips and looked at him as if she found his ignorance pitiable.

Tom wondered about the source of her tale. "Are you repeating things Marie Kelly told you? Did she think Tavia killed her husband?"

"She didn't think it, she *knew* it. That woman went runnin' to Marie and Lincoln every time her man got drunk and started knockin' her around. Her kids, too, they'd all show up on the doorstep. Her with a bloody mouth and black eyes and God knows what else. She could count on Lincoln to keep her husband away from them while he sobered up. And Marie got her ice packs and Tylenol and fed the kids."

Tom wasn't surprised by any of this. The Richardsons had never been part of his parents' circle, but he had been aware of the violence in the family because he went to school with a couple of their daughters. Scandalized whispers and murmurs of pity had always surrounded the girls, who kept to themselves and never invited other kids to the house. The boys had also been friendless, as far as Tom knew. The four Richardson offspring had fled, one by one, as soon as they were old enough, and Tom had never heard of them coming back to visit.

Still, all that misery didn't add up to murder. "Ron Richardson died in a tractor accident. What made Marie think Tavia killed him?"

"You're a lawman. You know how something can be fixed so it looks like an accident."

Tom paused, remembering. "My mother told me about it. She was one of the nurses who treated him at the hospital. She said he was so far gone by the time he was brought in that nothing could be done."

Mrs. Turner nodded as if he'd made her point for her. "How long did he lay out in that field with a turned-over tractor on top of him before his wife called for help? A couple hours?"

"Yeah, I know, but—"

"She told Marie she was gonna kill him someday. Said it every single time she showed up lookin' like a kicked puppy. She said she was gonna kill him, and she finally did it."

Tom held up his hands in surrender. "Okay. All right, let's put aside the question of whether Tavia killed her husband. Even if she did, what does that have to do with the Kelly murders?"

"Don't you see?" Mrs. Turner shook her head, clearly impatient with him for being so dense. "She got away with murder once. She let Marie know she'd do it again if she had to. Didn't come right out and say it, now. Never put it in words anybody could use against her. But she sure did get her message across. She planned it, just like she planned how she'd kill her husband."

"But gunning down two people in their back yard is a long way from tinkering with a tractor to make it turn over." Tom shook his head. "I can't believe Tavia would plan something as blatant as those shootings and think she could get away with it. She's not stupid."

Mrs. Turner sat back, nodding, with a satisfied little smile on her lips. "No, she's not a bit stupid. She knows exactly what she's doin'. And she's got the county sheriff himself sittin' here in my kitchen swearin' up and down that she's innocent."

Chapter Fifteen

Rachel threaded through the noisy, milling crowd in the high school parking lot, working her way toward the door into the gymnasium. Bright sunshine warmed the midday air, and the gathering of hard-faced people had an eerily festive atmosphere. As if they were collecting in the community square to watch a hanging, she thought.

Rachel found Holly near the door, where Deputy Brandon Connolly, her fiancé, scrutinized people as they entered the auditorium one by one.

"Tom's inside," Holly told her. "Joanna is too. She got here early so she could get a seat in the front row, and she's savin' room for you and me."

Rachel wasn't surprised that Joanna wanted to be right in the faces of the Packard people, but she was a little leery of putting herself there. Too much temptation to voice her own opinion. She had to practice self-restraint today, for Tom's sake.

"Do you know if Tom has talked to your grandmother yet?" she asked Holly. Rachel hadn't seen or spoken with Tom since he'd left for work early that morning.

"He was gonna stop by before he came out here. But I don't know if she told him anything. She wants the killer to get caught, but she's worried it might be dangerous to help the police. You know how she is."

Rachel knew all too well how stubborn and secretive Mrs. Turner could be. "It's more dangerous to keep things to herself. Come on, let's go in."

Rachel wanted to bypass the chaotic line and slip into the gym, but Brandon blocked everybody by stepping in front of the open doorway. He held up a hand to stop a young man with a shaved head who wore a camouflage jacket with his cargo pants. "Just a minute, sir."

The man, who looked about twenty-five, directed his affronted gaze at the palm raised in his face. "What?"

"I believe you've got a weapon there in your pocket."

Rachel peered over shoulders to get a better look. The man's jacket, hanging open, revealed the black butt of a handgun protruding from his pants pocket. A shiver of alarm made Rachel take a step back. In her three years in Mason County, she'd learned a lot about quick tempers and casual violence among people who usually had their guns nearby, if not on them. Holly moved with her.

"I got my permits," the man said. "Concealed carry and open carry both. I got a right."

"I can't let you take a weapon into the school building, sir. Sheriff's orders."

The man thrust his face into Brandon's. The two were close in age, but Brandon was taller and more muscular in addition to wearing a deputy's uniform. The other man, however, clearly felt he held all the authority in this encounter. "You don't have a goddamned thing to say about it, and you can tell the sheriff to go to hell."

Brandon visibly stiffened. Rachel had to admire his steely tone when he answered. "The Sheriff's Department put out the word ahead of time that weapons wouldn't be allowed inside the school and people should leave them at home. Now, sir, if you want to go in, you'll have to turn your pistol over to me for safekeeping, or lock it in your vehicle, or empty it and give me the ammunition. Your choice."

The man's face looked like a pan of water coming to a boil. "My gun goes where I go. I don't hand it over to nobody. And it stays loaded. You accusin' me of goin' in there to shoot somebody?"

"No, sir." Brandon kept his voice level. "But you know people are going to get all worked up. If somebody gets mad and decides to do something about it, we don't want a gun in easy reach. They could grab your pistol out of your pocket and use it. I doubt you'd want that to happen."

Bravo, Rachel thought. Tom himself couldn't have been more reasonable or steadfast.

Every thought streaming through the man's head revealed itself on his face. Rachel saw him waver, saw him debate whether giving in to this fresh-faced deputy would make him look weak in front of the suddenly attentive crowd.

A white-haired woman poked the young man's back with her cane, making him flinch and swivel to face her. "Oh, come on, Lamar," the woman said. "Do what the deputy tells you. You're holding up everybody behind you."

The middle-aged woman with her added, "Your grandma here needs to sit down. Step aside and let the rest of us get by, then you can stand out here and run your mouth all day if you feel like it."

Now that his mother and grandmother had scolded him, a dozen more women added their voices, calling Lamar by name and demanding that he show some consideration for others. Embarrassment overtook him, and he flushed a deep red that turned a blue eagle tattoo on his neck a lurid purple.

Interesting, Rachel thought. The women didn't hesitate to chide him for inconveniencing them, but the males in the crowd stayed silent rather than argue with a man who had a gun on him.

"Aw, hell," the young man grumbled. "I'll lock it in my truck." Calling on his dwindling supply of gruff defiance, he warned Brandon, "My gun better not disappear, or you're gonna be in a shitload of trouble. You understand me?"

"I understand you, sir."

As the gun owner shoved through the crowd, Holly whispered to Rachel, "I'm just so proud of Brandon sometimes. Heck, I'm proud of him all the time."

Rachel smiled, watching Holly touch a finger to the tiny diamond chip in her engagement ring. Although Holly's inheritance from her aunt had made her rich, she would always be a girl with down-to-earth dreams. She had everything she needed to make her happy: an animal sanctuary she had created with her grandmother's help, a job as an aide at Rachel's vet clinic, and plans to marry Brandon.

Brandon waved Rachel and Holly past the people in line, and they stepped through the doorway into the gymnasium.

The bleachers already overflowed, with more people filing in. The crowd's chatter echoed off the high ceiling. A speaker's podium bearing the Packard Resorts logo stood under the backboard at one end of the basketball court. In the center of the floor there was a long steel table covered with a green drape. From the dips and rises in the cloth, Rachel assumed it concealed a mockup of the proposed resort facilities, ready to dazzle all of them. She had to admit to herself that she was curious to see what it looked like.

Tom stood beside the podium, hands on hips, ostensibly listening to Lawrence Archer, the young Packard representative, but his vigilant gaze roamed the room and kept tabs on the crowd.

Joanna waved to Rachel and Holly, beckoning them to join her in the front row of the bleachers near the podium. By the time they made their way to her, Tom was there waiting. He took Rachel's arm and steered her far enough from Joanna that she wouldn't hear them over the general racket.

"I wish you'd stayed home," he said. "I've got a bad feeling about this. I called in almost the whole crew, but I don't know if it'll be enough." He gestured, indicating more than a dozen deputies spread along the top of the bleachers on both sides.

"I had to come for Joanna." Before he could respond to that, Rachel added, "The man you were talking to is the one who came by our place yesterday."

One corner of Tom's mouth lifted in a hint of a grin. "Well, he's still alive and doesn't have any visible wounds, so I guess you weren't too harsh with him."

"Very funny. Has he said anything to you about selling the farm to Packard?" Lawrence Archer was watching them, she noticed. Rachel's gaze connected with his, and he gave her a little wave and flashed the smile that transformed his face from pleasant to handsome. She acknowledged his greeting with a nod but didn't return the smile.

"Not yet," Tom said. "We've both been a little busy here. Don't worry about it. If he brings it up, I'll set him straight. I'll tell him our land's not for sale."

Our land. Although Rachel might refer to the farm that way, she knew it didn't belong to her. Tom had grown up there, and he'd inherited the property when his parents both died in an accident. He had told her he intended to add her name to the deed, but he hadn't done it yet. The land, and the house they lived in, were Tom's. He could sell it all and Rachel wouldn't be able to stop him.

Ridiculous. Tom had just told her he would reject Packard's offer, if one was made. Why was she inventing things to worry about?

Tom had turned his attention back to the crowd, scanning the bleachers on one side, then the other. "Try to keep Joanna quiet and in her seat. And the same goes for you." His eyes met hers. "*Please.*" With that, he strode back to his position near the podium where he could watch the entire room.

As she rejoined Joanna and Holly, Rachel realized the crowd had divided the way fans of home and away teams usually did. They had further sorted themselves by social class, a tendency she'd noticed at the few local sports events she'd attended with Tom. On the opposite side of the room, several county supervisors clustered in front of the bleachers, deep in conversation with Robert McClure. Doctors, lawyers, and small business owners, most of them men, took up the first three rows. Behind them, less prosperous county residents crowded the benches at the top.

At least two dozen people held signs with the single word JOBS handwritten on cardboard or white poster board.

Jake Hollinger, looking stiff and uneasy, and Tavia Richardson, detached and faintly amused, occupied a transitional zone with other owners of small farms, between the people in business attire and those whose clothing and general demeanor marked them as working poor or unemployed.

That was the pro-development side of the gym, and it was crammed.

Shifting to look behind her, Rachel saw an open space here and there but not as many as she'd feared. Most of the anti-development crowd was middle class, some were small farm owners, and she knew many of them as clients of her animal hospital and its vets. Tom's aunts and uncles hadn't shown up. They were better at following his wishes than she was. A sprinkling of signs, some hand-lettered and others printed, read NO TO PACKARD and HANDS OFF OUR LAND.

Rachel had publicly allied herself with the anti-development people, simply by sitting on this side of the room. And a lot of her clients were on the other side. Too late now to pretend neutrality. She wouldn't desert Joanna.

Joanna poked her with an elbow. "Just look at that son of a bitch. So damned proud of himself for bringing this on us."

For a second Rachel thought Joanna meant the Packard representative, then she realized the daggers shooting from her friend's eyes were aimed at Robert McClure. He had joined the Packard man at the podium and took in the crowd with a smile of satisfaction. On the pro-development side, latecomers who couldn't find seats jostled each other for space along the wall at the top of the bleachers or parked themselves on the steps in the aisles. Some people who had grabbed open seats on the anti side, apparently seeing they'd wandered into hostile territory, rose and stomped on a few feet in their haste to get out. They hustled across the gym to seek refuge with those of like mind.

When Brandon entered and closed the door to the gym behind him, the crowd quickly settled down. But even as the voices quieted, Rachel sensed a hum of tension and expectation in the air. Tom was right. This was going to be nasty.

Ellis O'Toole, the seventy-five-year-old chairman of the Mason County Board of Supervisors, stepped up to the microphone. The room went dead silent. O'Toole, a slight man with a rim of gray hair on an otherwise bald scalp, picked up the microphone and fussed with it. He flipped the on/off switch up and down. Tapping the head of the microphone, he set off a piercing feedback squeal that made him flinch.

Oh, for pity's sake. Rachel wanted to yell at the man. *Get on with it!*

"Ladies and gentleman," O'Toole began, his voice echoing, "thank you for coming out today. Our guest is vice president of Packard Development. As most of you know, Packard is a national company, and they're interested in bringing a major project to Mason County. A project that could revitalize our county's economy by creating a lot of new jobs."

Somebody on the other side of the gym let out a shrill whistle, and a few people, including Jake Hollinger and Tavia Richardson, clapped. The anti-development side remained stonily silent. Beside Rachel, Joanna sat rigid, hands balled into tight fists and pressed together in her lap.

"I know you're anxious to hear from our guest," O'Toole continued, "but first I just want to thank Mr. Robert McClure, from Mason County's oldest financial institution, for taking the lead in attracting development to our county. The Board of Supervisors is ready to work hand in hand with Packard to clear the way and make this happen."

That was code, Rachel assumed, for the county board's willingness to disregard zoning laws, permit requirements, environmental degradation, and other such pesky concerns. The developers would be given a green light to do anything they pleased.

"Now without any further ado, please welcome our guest, Mr. Lawrence Archer."

The pro half of the crowd broke into applause, and many in the upper tiers of the bleachers stamped their feet and whistled.

Glancing over her shoulder, Rachel saw that nobody on the anti-development side was applauding.

Archer smiled and patted the air to quiet the crowd. He took the microphone—he clearly felt more comfortable with the equipment than O'Toole did—and walked into the middle of the gym as he spoke.

"I know you've heard a lot of rumors about what Packard Resorts and Development plans to do in your county. I'm here to answer all your questions. By the time this meeting is over, I believe everybody here will agree that Packard is offering the citizens of Mason County an unprecedented opportunity for growth and prosperity."

Archer waited for the reward of applause and cheers from one side of the room. Rachel glanced at Joanna to see her face pinched into a grim expression and her glare following Archer's casual stroll around the draped table.

"What we plan to build," he went on, "will be one of the nation's premier mountain resorts, a destination that will attract an elite clientele looking for a restful place to get away from their busy lives. We'll also offer conference facilities for corporations that want to combine business with a retreat for their executives." He paused for a pregnant beat. "All of those people will be spending their money here in Mason County."

Another round of applause exploded.

"Yeah, right." Joanna leaned into Rachel, speaking into her ear. "They'll spend it here, but it won't stay here."

As if he'd heard her, Archer went on, "I know you're wondering how much of that money will stay in your community and benefit you and your families. Let me start at the beginning, with the construction. We'll need workers, a lot of workers, and we'll hire as many of them locally as we possibly can."

Wild applause, hoots, and yells bounced off the high ceiling. Smiling, Archer basked in the approval for a moment before raising his hand to signal for quiet. "It could take as long as two years to complete all components of the plan, and in a minute I'll show you exactly what we want to build here." He gestured at the cloth-covered exhibit on the table. "Once the resort is open, we'll need people to staff it and maintain it. Housekeepers, porters, cooks, wait staff in the dining rooms, gardeners and other grounds maintenance personnel."

Minimum wage jobs, Rachel noted, with no opportunity for advancement.

"We want to build a small airport," Archer continued, "and that will create jobs, too."

Not on our land, Rachel thought. She reminded herself that none of this would happen if Joanna stood firm. Yet Archer's confidence that the project would materialize stirred a deep unease in her.

After pausing when more handclapping interrupted him, Archer added, "But you won't have to work at the resort to profit from it. We'll buy vegetables, fruit, meat, and dairy products from local farmers. We'll serve your homemade jams and jellies in our dining room, and we'll sell them by the jar in the gift shop. We'll sell the work of local craftspeople in the gift shop— handmade quilts, knitted items made from locally grown wool, wood carvings. If you have something of value to offer, we'll help you reach customers willing to pay premium prices for it."

A change had come over the crowd. Quieter but more attentive, they seemed completely caught up in Archer's sales pitch. He was good, Rachel had to admit. He was handsome, he had a charming smile, and he painted a nice picture. A lot of people in the room were buying it. But Rachel didn't believe a word of it.

"He makes it sound like a feudal society," she murmured to Joanna.

"Exactly. He wants the whole county to work for Packard. They'd all be catering to a bunch of rich people at that fancy resort."

Archer grasped the hem of the green cloth draping the display. "What I'm going to show you is a model, made to scale, of the facilities we'll build if we're able to secure the land we need. If you're too far back to see clearly, please remain in your seats for now, and you'll have all the time you want to take a close look after the meeting."

With a flourish, he whipped off the green cloth and let it drop in a heap of folds onto the floor, revealing an elaborate cluster of buildings, parking lots, and what appeared to be two bodies of water. A smattering of applause rose from the other side of the gym, but it died down in seconds as people craned their necks to see the model and waited for Archer to continue.

"We'll have swimming pools here and here." Archer pointed to the two blue patches behind the buildings. He reeled off a list of other components: tennis courts, a children's playground, a ballroom for weddings and other special events, a spacious center for business conferences, a sports club with its own cafe, a spa, a bistro, a bar, and a full-size restaurant. "Adjacent to the sports club," he added, "we'll have stables for people who enjoy horseback riding, and an eighteen-hole professional level golf course. We might even start our own annual tournament eventually. That would put Mason County on the map and bring in a lot of visitors with money to spend. Not to mention creating additional jobs for county residents."

He was hitting the jobs button every two minutes, and Rachel felt sure that was all some people heard.

Beside her, Joanna choked out her words. "That's my property. He wants to put all that right smack in the middle of my farm. He even wants my *horses*."

"Just remember that they can't force you to—" Rachel broke off to hear what Archer was telling the crowd.

"We have signed letters of intent to sell from several property owners in the part of the county we feel is optimal for development. We can't move ahead until we have all the land we need. We're offering top dollar. We hope you can all see the unprecedented opportunity that's right in front of you." Archer turned his back on his supporters and directly addressed the anti-development crowd. "You can choose to move forward and grab this chance to bring new growth and prosperity to Mason County, or you can choose to let your community sink deeper into poverty, and watch all your young people leave home to find work. I hope you'll choose to revitalize your county, and that you'll persuade your neighbors to do the same."

The pro-development crowd rose as one, clapping and cheering. Rachel knew how they felt. Packard offered a rural, high-unemployment county the holy grail of jobs, jobs, jobs. Of course they wanted it.

Joanna jumped to her feet.

Rachel grabbed her arm. "Don't, Joanna, please. Just wait it out."

Joanna shook off Rachel's hand and started speaking over the applause. Rachel could barely hear her, so she was sure no one else could. Joanna raised her voice to a shout that stretched across the room. "You're not getting my land. I've put my heart and soul into that business, and I won't sell it so it can be turned into," she flung an arm toward the model on the table, "into *that.*"

"You ever been out of work, lady?" a man shouted from across the room. "You ever had to worry about feedin' your kids?"

That set off a chorus of jeers directed at Joanna. "You ain't even from here," a woman screamed. "And you'll get rich from sellin' your land. Hell, you're rich already. Take the money and go back where you come from."

Joanna wouldn't be silenced. Ignoring the whooping crowd, she focused on Archer. "Where do you get the right to tell me I have to give up my land and my business just because your company wants it?"

People around her rose in solidarity, and Rachel, then Holly, rose with them. Tom stepped forward into the center of the gym and raised a hand in a signal to the deputies at the rear of the bleachers. On both sides, the uniformed men began moving down into the aisles between sections, ready to act if the crowd got out of control. Archer looked on with a little smile, showing no inclination to help calm things down.

A woman yelled, "All you think about is keepin' what's yours. You don't give a damn if the rest of us can't find decent jobs."

Decent jobs? Keep your mouth shut, Rachel told herself. Stay out of it. But these people had no idea what a predatory company they were inviting into their midst. Rachel knew. She'd done hours of research on Packard. Somebody had to force the citizens of Mason County to look at reality. But it couldn't be her. She owed it to Tom to stay quiet.

To Rachel's surprise, Holly spoke up. "If this place gets built here, nothing's ever goin' to be the same again. We'll lose our peace and quiet. We'll get a lot of traffic and all those strangers comin' in. It'll destroy our way of life."

"What way of life?" a gravelly male voice shouted. "Bein' dirt poor? Easy for you to talk, missy, after gettin' all that money from your dead aunt."

Holly seemed ready to shoot back a reply, but Rachel gripped her arm hard enough to stop her. "Don't get into a fight with them. It's pointless."

A jumble of curses and accusations flew across the gym between the two groups, voices rising, fingers pointing, fists shaking.

Joanna had gone pale, her breathing rapid and shallow, and Rachel worried that she might faint. Placing an arm around her friend's shoulders, Rachel felt Joanna trembling.

Tom grabbed the microphone from Archer. "Settle down," he ordered the crowd, his deep, firm voice cutting through the racket, "or we'll clear the room. If you can't sit down and be quiet, you'll have to leave."

"She's gonna keep this from goin' through," a red-haired woman protested. "Somebody needs to make her do what's right."

"I don't owe you anything," Joanna cried. "You can't tell me what to do with my own property."

That provoked another storm of jeers.

Seeing Archer's smug expression, Rachel realized this was exactly what he had hoped for: division in the community that would be strong enough to intimidate the holdouts into selling their land. He, or someone working for him, had made sure everyone knew Joanna was the primary enemy. The Packard representative had a job to do here, and when he'd achieved his objectives he would move on to disrupt some other community and never look back. He never had to stay and live with the animosity he'd stirred up.

When Tom succeeded in lowering the uproar to an angry mutter, Archer reclaimed the microphone and held up a hand like an evangelist exhorting the faithful. He was slick enough to justify the comparison, Rachel thought. A salesman, through and through.

"We've made firm offers for our initial land purchases," Archer told the crowd, "and we hope we'll be signing contracts soon. As I told you, whether we move ahead or not depends on our being able to purchase the acreage we need. The future of this project rests with the people of Mason County. Whether you choose progress or stagnation—the decision is in your hands."

That was too much. Rachel had to say something. "Mr. Archer, would you mind answering a few questions about the way your company treats people?"

Without altering his smile, Archer opened his mouth to respond.

Rachel didn't give him the chance. "Is it true that you hire half your employees as part-time workers so you won't have to give them any benefits? And do you pay most of your employees minimum wage? Do you make them work on holidays without overtime pay? Is it true that if somebody gets sick, you fire them? If a woman gets pregnant, do you fire her as soon as her pregnancy starts to show? Is it true that more than two dozen major lawsuits by former employees are pending against Packard all over the country?"

The crowd exploded. Boos from the pro-development side echoed off the high ceiling, drowning out the shouts from the anti-development people.

Tom marched over to Rachel, his face tight with anger and frustration. "Rachel, what are you doing? You're just making matters worse."

"I'm sorry, but I can't sit here and listen—"

The noise cut her off as both sides hurled insults and threats. People streamed from the bleachers and onto the gym floor, headed for a clash.

"Will you please go home?" Tom yelled at Rachel. "I've got a job to do. I can't protect you."

Joanna gripped Rachel's arm and shouted in her ear, "Let's get out of here."

Rachel, Joanna, and Holly edged through the swarming bodies and made it to the exit. Pushing open the door, Rachel gulped fresh, cool air.

Joanna, grim-faced, didn't speak until the door closed behind them. She stuffed her fists into her jacket pockets and hunched her shoulders. "What am I going to do? How am I going to stop this?"

"You'll stop it by saying no," Rachel told her.

"That's right," Holly said. "Nobody can force you to sell your land."

"Not directly." A gust of wind blew Joanna's hair across her face, but she didn't bother to push it aside. "It's obvious what they're doing. They think if they get everybody mad at me, they'll scare me into selling. I'm going to need a stiff backbone to stand up to them."

"The Joanna I know has plenty of backbone," Rachel told her.

The gymnasium door burst open and a dozen people poured out. Rachel, Holly and Joanna hurried ahead of them into the parking lot.

After they'd gone ten yards, the men and women coming up behind suddenly surrounded them, pressing close. A muscular young man jostled Joanna and almost knocked her off her feet. Rachel grabbed her arm to steady her.

"Hey!" Joanna lunged and caught the back of the man's jacket as he passed. "Do you need a lesson in manners?"

Without breaking stride or looking around, the man jerked his jacket free. The wind carried his mocking laughter back to them.

A heavy middle-aged woman bumped her shoulder against Rachel's. When Rachel saw a man moving in on Holly, she pointed a finger at him and warned, "If you touch any of us again my husband will arrest you for assault."

The man stepped back, raising his hands and making a show of mock terror. "Ooh, I'm scaaaard of the sheriff's wife."

"You should be." Rachel linked arms with Joanna and Holly and they walked on. How strange it felt to be protecting Joanna. The other way around felt more natural.

As they walked up to Joanna's green Cherokee, her face crumpled like paper in a fist. "God damn it. Will you look at that?"

Somebody had painted SELFISH BITCH on the rear of the SUV with white paint, so fresh it still dripped onto the pavement.

"That's not all they did." Rachel pointed at the rear tires. Both bore long, ragged slashes and were already halfway to flat.

Holly darted around to the front of the vehicle to take a look. "These are cut, too."

"I'll drive you back to the horse farm," Rachel told Joanna. "You can send a couple of your men over to deal with this."

Joanna nodded, but for a moment she didn't move. Staring at her damaged Cherokee, she said in a quiet voice, "I'm lucky, I guess. I've pissed off a lot of people. I could've ended up like Lincoln and Marie."

Rachel didn't say it aloud, but the first thought that came to mind was, *You still could.*

Chapter Sixteen

The crowd shoved and shouted, lobbing insults and threats, and a couple of scuffles broke out, but Tom and the deputies managed to steer everybody out the door to the parking lot without bloodshed. Tom was damned glad he'd banned guns at the meeting.

Lawrence Archer, Robert McClure, and the seven county supervisors had formed a protective circle around the scale model of the proposed resort while the room was being cleared. Archer's smirk of amusement never faded.

After deputies escorted the last of the audience from the gym, Tom strode over to the men. "I'd advise you to wait a few minutes for people to leave before you take all this out." He gestured at the display and the podium. "So you don't start the whole shouting match all over again in the parking lot."

Archer's grin broadened. "You and your men are very efficient," he said to Tom. "That looked about as easy as herding cats."

God, what an idiot. "This project's pushing a lot of hot buttons with these people. I hope you've gotten some idea of how divisive it is."

Tom saw McClure and the commissioners stiffen, getting ready to cut him off if they had to.

Archer waved a hand dismissively. "I'm used to it. We go through a version of this everywhere we build. There's always somebody who thinks any kind of development's a bad idea.

But the majority's usually in favor. We've never had to drop our plans."

"Is that right? Have you ever caused a murder before?"

"Now hold on, Bridger—" McClure started.

"Murder?" Somehow Archer managed to frown without losing his general air of condescending amusement. "Are you saying we're responsible for somebody being murdered?"

"Ask Mr. McClure." Tom flicked a hand in the banker's direction. "He can tell you all about it. He was nearby when it happened."

McClure shook his head. "You can't blame the Kellys' deaths on this project. Do your job and find out the real reason they were killed, and stop throwing around wild accusations."

"I don't have to be told to do my job," Tom said. "I hope it turns out the motive was personal. I hope the Kelly shooting was an isolated crime, and when we make an arrest that'll be the end of it. But I'm starting to think it was just the beginning of something a lot worse."

"That's just...that's absurd," McClure sputtered.

Ellis O'Toole, the county board chairman, glared at Tom from behind his thick bifocals. "That is an irresponsible statement, Sheriff Bridger, completely unfounded, and I don't want to hear that you're spreading that kind of negative opinion around."

"We can't ignore what's going on here," Tom said. "This is stirring up a lot of anger and resentment on both sides. A couple who refused to sell their land were murdered yesterday, and I'm worried about what's going to happen next. Some people are so damned determined to force others off their land and see this deal go through, I don't think they'll stop with words."

Archer made a gesture of innocent helplessness, palms up. "Maybe Packard should just pull the plug on this project right now."

You son of a bitch, Tom thought. The guy wasn't capable of straight talk. The minute he'd met Archer, he'd known what kind of man he was: slick and slippery, always polite and ingratiating, phony enough to turn any clear-eyed person's stomach. McClure and the supervisors had dollar signs flashing in their eyes, and they weren't seeing anything clearly.

O'Toole rushed to reassure Archer. "Our sheriff is imagining things. The government of this county supports growth and development and new jobs for our residents." He fixed a cold look on Tom. "Do your job and leave the business matters to us. And find a way to control that wife of yours."

Tom bristled. He was going to give Rachel hell when he saw at her home, but he wouldn't put up with the likes of Ellis O'Toole criticizing her. "My wife is a grown woman with her own opinions. The county board doesn't tell her what to think."

Tilting his head upward, O'Toole squinted at Tom through the bottom of his bifocals. Then he grasped Tom's arm and led him a few feet away from the other men. Startled, Tom didn't resist.

O'Toole kept his voice low but masked none of his anger. "There's one thing the board can do, and if you're smart you'll keep it in mind. An election put you in office, but if you give us cause, the board will find a way to remove you."

"Will you go in with me?" Joanna asked as Rachel pulled her Range Rover into the driveway. "Maybe they'll act like civilized people if you're there."

"I have to go pick up Simon. He's spending a few days with us. Besides, what influence would I have on the Kellys' son and daughter? I'm a stranger to them."

"Exactly. They might tone it down in front of somebody they don't know." Joanna unbuckled her seat belt. "Please, honey, just come in for a minute."

Rachel wasn't keen to walk into another verbal brawl, but she had to admit she was curious about Ronan and Sheila Kelly. Ronan had stayed at Joanna's house overnight. Sheila had arrived that morning, and according to Joanna they'd started bickering the second they landed in the same room. On the drive back from the meeting, Joanna voiced a fervent wish that one or both would be gone by now, but two cars Rachel had never seen before sat on the farm road in front of the house.

"Please," Joanna repeated. "I've had all the screaming I can take for one day."

With great reluctance, Rachel killed the engine and climbed out.

The second Joanna swung the front door open, her golden retriever, Nan, and her little mutt, Riley, bounded out, followed by the Kellys' dog, Bonnie. Rachel was afraid Bonnie would take off for home, but she seemed content to stay in the yard with the other two.

"It's half mine," Ronan Kelly was saying as Joanna and Rachel walked into the living room. "I have as much control as you do."

"Oh, for God's sake," Sheila said. "Can't you at least wait until they've been buried? We have a funeral to plan. Not to mention helping Tom find out who killed them. I'm not going to talk about property and money right now, and that's final."

Joanna raised her voice to be heard over their continuing argument. "Can y'all stop fighting long enough to meet my guest?"

Startled, they snapped their heads toward Joanna and Rachel.

Tall and attractive, both sister and brother had the same olive skin tone and coal-black hair that gave Tom and Holly their distinctive appearance. These were among the few people Rachel had come across in Mason County who were recognizable as Melungeon.

Joanna introduced Rachel.

Sheila stepped forward and offered a hand. "Hi, I'm Sheila Hayes, Lincoln and Marie Kelly's daughter."

When they shook, Rachel noted that Sheila looked exhausted and puffy-eyed from crying. She appeared calmer than her brother, though. Ronan gave Rachel a moist, jerky handshake and regarded her as if she were an unwelcome interruption.

"I'm sorry about your mother and father," Rachel said. "They were good people."

Both murmured their thanks, then stood for a moment in awkward silence. Rachel expected them to say something about the horror of losing both parents to murder, but neither spoke.

"I have their rabbits," Rachel said. "I can bring them to you anytime you—"

"No," they said in unison.

"You don't want them?"

"I can't take a couple of rabbits home with me," Ronan said, with no further explanation.

Sheila added, "I couldn't possibly take them either. My husband and I are both attorneys. We work eighteen-hour days. We don't have time for pets."

"Oh, really?" Joanna said. "And what are you going to do about that dog that doesn't have a home now? Linc and Marie doted on her. They'd want her taken care of."

Sheila and Ronan exchanged a glance, as if each was waiting for the other to do the right thing.

Joanna threw up her hands. "All right, if that's the way it is. I guess I just acquired another dog."

"And what do you want me to do with the rabbits?" Rachel asked.

Ronan gave a couldn't-care-less shrug and Sheila said, "Does it matter, really? I mean, they're just rabbits. Maybe you could turn them loose in a field somewhere?"

These two, Rachel thought, must have been dropped into the wrong nest when the stork made his rounds. They couldn't be more different from their gentle, animal-loving parents.

Obviously reacting to the expression on Rachel's face, Sheila hastened to correct herself. "No, no, of course you couldn't do that, it wouldn't be humane. Maybe the Jones sisters might like to have them. They have quite a menagerie over there."

"They're vegetarians, so at least they won't cook them for dinner," Ronan said, grinning as if he'd made a joke.

"I'll ask." Rachel didn't trust herself to say more.

"So how did the meeting go?" Ronan stuffed his fists into his pants pockets. "Did it turn into a free-for-all?"

"More or less." Joanna peeled off her barn jacket and flung it across the back of the sofa. "A lot of shouting. Somebody vandalized my Cherokee, and now I have to get it towed back here."

"Oh, that's too bad," Sheila murmured.

"You know," Ronan said, "you really ought to start thinking about taking that offer from—"

"For God's sake," Sheila snapped, "can't you give it a rest?"

"I'm just saying it's a hell of a lot of money. An offer like that won't come along again."

Her face flushed with anger, Joanna crossed her arms and fixed a steely glare on Ronan. He seemed reluctant to meet her eyes, his gaze jumping from one spot to another. Rachel wondered if she could escape and go home without any of them noticing. But Joanna would probably strangle her if she tried.

"This isn't the time or place, Ronan," Sheila said.

"She ought to know that everybody around her is selling."

"Do you think she doesn't know that? She lives here, for God's sake. And I thought I made it clear that you're not going to pressure me either."

"Why the hell should we wait? The property's in trust. It's already ours. We can sell it today if we want to."

"I'm not going to make a decision now, Ronan. How many times do I have to tell you that?"

Ronan reached toward his sister with open hands, and for a second Rachel feared he was going to grab her. But he curled his hands into fists again and jammed them back into his pockets. A muscle in his cheek twitched. "You don't have any use for the place. You're not going to come back here to visit now that Mom and Dad are gone. You'll never set foot in Mason County again."

"That's not the point."

"No, it's not, is it?" Ronan's voice rose to a near shout. "Sticking it to me, that's your point. Anything you can do to drag me under, I can count on you doing it."

"Oh, please. You sound like a five-year-old."

In the space of a second Ronan pulled a fist from a pocket and aimed it at his sister. Rachel and Joanna both stepped closer to intervene, but Sheila stood her ground, unfazed.

At the last instant, Ronan uncurled a finger and stuck it in her face. "You've talked to me like that for the last time. I'll force you to sell."

"Try it."

"Count on it! Joanna, thank you for letting me stay here last night. I've already put my things in the car. I'm moving over to the farm. Then I'm going to see their lawyer." Ronan turned and stalked out of the room and out of the house.

"Hey, Ronan, it's Saturday," Sheila called after him, but he didn't seem to hear. She shook her head and said with a little smile, "He'll probably track the poor man down at home. When we hear an explosion in the distance, we'll know my brother's just found out where things really stand. He's about to get the shock of his life."

Through the front window Rachel watched Ronan cross the yard to his car. Bonnie, who lay in the grass with the other dogs, jumped up, tail wagging, when Ronan approached, but he strode past her without so much as a glance. Her tail drooped and she dropped onto her belly.

"Is this something that's going to shock me, too?" Joanna asked Sheila. "I don't like surprises."

Curious, Rachel turned back to the two women.

Sheila shrugged. "I might as well tell you. I've already told Tom, and it'll all come out soon. Ronan thinks he has an equal share in the trust, but he doesn't. My parents loaned him a lot of money over the years, money they couldn't afford to lose, and he threw it away on his business schemes. He never repaid a cent of it. He's only getting a quarter of their estate."

"And they never told him?" Joanna sounded more curious than shocked.

"Why should they? He was driving them crazy as it was, always trying to wheedle more money out of them. If they'd told him about changing the trust, he would've hounded them for the rest of—" Sheila broke off, squeezed her eyes shut, and swallowed hard. "The rest of their lives," she finished in a whisper.

Joanna placed a consoling hand on Sheila's shoulder, but Rachel could see in Joanna's distracted, anxious expression that only one thought, one question, burned in her mind.

Rachel decided to ask the question herself. "Are you going to sell your parents' farm to Packard?"

Sheila sighed and pushed a loose strand of black hair off her cheek. "I have to plan a funeral before I make any decisions about the farm." As if she had no idea she was torturing Joanna, Sheila asked her, "Will you help me with the arrangements? And do you mind if I stay here?"

Joanna hesitated before answering. "Sure. You're welcome to stay here. I can see why you wouldn't want to stay at home. At your parents' house."

"I think I could handle knowing what happened there. It's not that so much as...to tell you the truth, I don't want to be alone with Ronan after he finds out about the trust. I'm afraid of him."

Chapter Seventeen

Tom's boots on the old floorboards sounded like an elephant crossing the quiet squad room, but Dennis was so engrossed in what he saw on his computer screen that he didn't look up until Tom stood before his desk.

The dozen other desks lining the walls were empty. Tom had left the deputies to make sure everybody was safely off the school property so he could get back to the murder investigation.

"What have you found?" he asked.

"His sister was right." Dennis sat back in his chair, nudging his wire-rimmed glasses snug against the bridge of his nose. "Ronan Kelly's got major money trouble. I found a lot online, and I'll probably come up with more on Monday when everybody's back at work. I've got a ton of stuff here that I printed out, and I tried to come up with a rough figure for his outstanding debt."

Dennis peeled a single sheet off the inch-high stack of printouts on his desk and handed it to Tom.

Tom scanned the figures. "Oh man. Almost a million? You're sure?"

"That's a conservative estimate. And those are bank loans, and money from investors. It doesn't include the money his parents loaned him. The losses really add up when you try to start a business and fail, and Ronan failed in a big way. Hired a lot of high-priced people, took a lease on a fancy office suite, took out ads in business magazines. I was just reading a business column about some of his former employees threatening to sue for unpaid wages."

"What kind of services was he offering? He's a bridge engineer, isn't he?"

Dennis straightened the edges of the paper stack. "I've learned more about building bridges in the last couple hours than I ever wanted to know. You'd be amazed at the opportunities out there."

"You can amaze me some other time. Just tell me what happened with Ronan Kelly's business plans." Tom handed the paper back to Dennis, then stripped off his uniform jacket and tossed it onto a nearby desk.

"He had this idea—it sounds crazy, but a couple of other companies were already doing the same kind of thing—they were taking old flatbed railroad cars and salvaging the materials to make small bridges for community parks, golf courses, places like that. Bridges for walking, not vehicles."

"Hunh." Tom moved to the window next to the desk. Through the dirt-streaked glass he watched a dry poplar leaf as big as a dinner plate tumble across the parking lot in the wind and disappear under his cruiser. He faced Dennis again. "It does sound a little crazy, but I guess it makes sense. They got contracts for projects like that?"

Dennis shrugged. "Not enough, obviously. Like I said, a couple of other companies got there first, and it's not that big a market. I guess Ronan was a copycat, not an innovator."

"He hasn't filed for bankruptcy?"

"I couldn't find any record of it. He's got to be hurting bad, but he probably wants to salvage his credit rating by coming up with the money to pay off his debts."

Leaning on the windowsill, Tom summed up the situation, speaking more to himself than Dennis. "This is the perfect time for both his parents to die, with Packard standing by and holding out a fat check for their land. Ronan still believes he's going to get half of that money. And what he believes, and whether he acted on it, that's all that matters."

"If he hired somebody to kill them," Dennis said, "he would have been smart to get somebody from out of the area. Somebody who could just drive away afterwards and disappear."

"That's what I'd expect. But we've got other suspects closer to home." Tom repeated what Mrs. Turner had told him about Tavia Richardson.

"I remember that tractor accident," Dennis said. "Nine, ten years ago? The department didn't investigate it. I never heard your dad or Sheriff Willingham say there was anything suspicious about it. You know, a lot of people thought it was a good thing, Sam Richardson dying. His wife got the insurance money and the farm, and she could stop worrying about him beating her to death someday."

In the brief silence that followed, Tom wondered if he and Dennis were thinking the same thing: Tom's father, who had been chief deputy and lead investigator for the Sheriff's Department at the time, wouldn't think twice about letting the death of a vicious, widely hated man go uninvestigated if it looked like an accident and the outcome was an undeniable blessing to his wife. Tom knew Dennis would never speak that thought aloud, any more than he would.

"Well, it's an interesting theory Mrs. Turner has," Tom said, "about Tavia killing the Kellys in a way that nobody would associate with her. It's just crazy enough to be true. But I also think Jake Hollinger could've done it, or they could have done it together. Jake and Tavia want that Packard money pretty badly."

"And now we know Ronan *needs* the money to stay afloat, and he believes he's going to get it, or half of it anyway."

Tom pulled his notebook from his shirt pocket. Flipping through the pages, he found the notation he'd made of Ronan Kelly's cell number. He reached for the desk phone. "I'd better track him down and find out what he's up to."

◇◇◇

The raw ugliness of the community meeting and the display of hostility between the Kelly siblings left Rachel in a foul mood, but her spirits lifted the instant she turned into Grady and Darla

Duncan's driveway and saw Tom's young nephew coming down the front steps to greet her. She smiled as he hit the yard and broke into a run. Simon seldom did anything slowly.

While she unbuckled her seat belt, he rounded the front of her Range Rover. As soon as her feet touched the ground, he threw his arms around her. "Hey, Rachel!"

"Hey, sweetie, it's so good to see you." Rachel hugged him tightly and planted a kiss on his unruly black hair. Ten years old now, he'd started growing so fast that he seemed taller every time she saw him. Soon he would probably decide he was too big to be hugged this way. She'd better enjoy it while she could. "It seems like it's been forever."

Laughing at her, Simon pulled away. "It was just last weekend. That's not forever."

"Well, it's too long. I miss you, and so does Uncle Tom. We're going to have a lot of fun while we've got you all to ourselves."

His grandmother, Darla, stepped out onto the porch of the big Victorian house, and as Simon's gaze shifted to her the light dimmed behind his smile. Rachel caught a momentary glimpse of the fear and worry he was trying so hard to hide, but he swiftly banished every trace of anxiety from his expression and broadened his smile again. Pity and sadness washed through Rachel as she watched this little boy mask his own emotions for the sake of the adults in his life.

Rachel had to hide her own feelings behind a cheerful greeting. Darla looked awful. In the three months since she'd been diagnosed with lymphoma, she had lost twenty pounds and her skin had taken on a dull cast. Her brown hair, generously streaked with silver, no longer shone, and although she hadn't lost all of it, she had noticeable thin patches. Like Rachel and Simon, though, she shoved reality aside and put on a happy face, smiling as the two mounted the steps to the porch.

"You think you can manage this little ruffian for a few days? Tom must have his hands full right now, so you're probably going to be doing it all."

"I can't wait. You know I only married Tom so I could spend more time with Simon."

"I suspected as much."

Simon grinned with pure childish delight, and his olive skin couldn't hide a flush of pleasure.

"You go get your stuff now," Darla told him. "But let Rachel get Mr. Piggles. His cage is too big for you to carry."

The boy took off at his usual top speed, the glass storm door slamming after him. From the porch Rachel and Darla watched him pound up the stairs.

Darla waited until he was out of sight. "Thank you, Rachel. I know if he's with you and Tom he'll always be okay."

Darla wasn't usually a hugger, and she startled Rachel by suddenly pulling her into an embrace.

Closing her arms around the older woman, Rachel could feel Darla's ribs through her loose cotton shirt. "We both love that little boy. We'd do anything for him." Tears burned Rachel's eyes. *Don't cry. For God's sake, don't cry.* "And we're right here to help you anytime you need us. You're going to beat this, you know."

Pulling away, Darla blinked tears from her own eyes and forced a smile. "That's what I'm planning on. I feel like crap, but the doctor thinks the treatment's working. I guess I'll find out Monday."

"You're getting the best of care." Rachel still wished Darla would see a specialist at one of the Washington, D.C., medical centers, but she had never voiced that opinion because she recognized it as personal bias. Now she reminded herself, once again, that the University of Virginia in Charlottesville had an excellent medical school and hospital with specialists as skilled as any at George Washington or Georgetown. She was immensely relieved that neither Darla nor her husband, a deputy who worked with Tom, had ever considered sticking with a doctor in Mason County.

The storm door flew open and Simon thumped onto the porch, dragging a duffle bag. The backpack he wore bulged with schoolbooks.

Darla laughed and shook her head. "I think you packed everything you own. Are you sure you're planning to come back?"

"Aw, Grandma, I need my stuff."

Rachel hefted the duffle, exaggerating the effort required. "Darla, you'd better check on Grady's coin collection. I think Simon might be making off with it."

They stashed Simon's belongings in the Range Rover, then carried out the roomy cage housing his guinea pig, Mr. Piggles. The little brown and white animal squeaked in protest at the movement but seemed mollified by Simon's gift of three big peanuts.

Darla kissed Simon's forehead, told him to be good, and buckled him into his seat. She walked around to the driver's side with Rachel. "You be careful, okay?"

"Careful? Driving, you mean? I always am."

Darla crossed her arms and hunched her shoulders as if suddenly realizing she shouldn't have come out without a jacket. "No, that's not what I mean. With all this nonsense going on about that resort, everybody taking sides and turning against each other— I know how much Simon loves the horses, but so many people are mad at Joanna McKendrick right now, maybe you shouldn't take him over there tomorrow."

Darla's words stung, not because the advice was unnecessary but because it hadn't occurred to Rachel—despite the vandalism to Joanna's vehicle and the open hostility to her at the community meeting, despite the murder of Joanna's closest neighbors—that Simon might not be safe at the McKendrick horse farm. What was wrong with her?

"I won't," she promised. "Don't give it another thought. You have enough on your mind."

Darla smiled. "Thanks. I know our boy's in good hands. I'll see you in a few days."

Simon smiled and waved at his grandmother as Rachel backed out of the driveway. As soon as they were on the road and beyond Darla's sight, his smile faded and his young face tightened with fear and anxiety.

Rachel reached over to touch his thick black hair, which felt so much like Tom's. God, she loved this kid. He had already suffered the unimaginable loss of both his parents, in the road accident that also killed his beloved Bridger grandparents and almost killed Tom, who had been driving, and Simon himself. Now the comforting world his maternal grandparents had created for him was threatened by Darla's illness.

"She's going to be all right, Simon. I wouldn't say that if I didn't really believe it."

He nodded and tried to smile, and Rachel hated herself for lying to him.

◇◇◇

What the hell was the man doing? Tom had a fist raised to knock on the front door of the Kellys' farmhouse when he caught sight of Ronan through the living room window.

Ronan pawed through the drawer of a writing table, sending envelopes and papers flying in every direction. Apparently frustrated at not finding what he wanted, he yanked the drawer free, carried it to the coffee table and dumped out its contents. He flung the drawer aside, and it crashed into the fireplace screen and dropped to the hearth. Leaning over the coffee table, he searched through the papers, dropping one after another on the floor.

Tom knocked and saw Ronan snap his head up, then stride toward the door, which led directly into the living room.

Ronan didn't issue a greeting or an invitation to enter but left the main door standing ajar as he returned to his task.

Pulling the storm door open, Tom stepped into the chaotic scene. Sofa cushions lay askew. The doors of a cabinet under the TV set stood open and a couple dozen DVDs littered the rug in front of it.

"What's going on here, Ronan?" The room smelled of hamburger and fried potatoes, and Tom noticed a crumpled fast food carryout bag half-buried under the drawer's contents on the coffee table. "Did you lose something?"

"I'm trying to find—" He broke off as if afraid to say too much, and when he spoke again his tone sounded accusatory. "Did you take anything out of here? Any papers?"

Tom folded his arms across his chest. "Why? What do you think is missing?"

Ronan threw up his hands in exasperation. "Just *tell* me, will you? Did you take anything?"

Tom suspected Ronan was looking for something in writing from Packard that would indicate how much the company would pay for this land. The Packard proposal Tom had found in the kitchen, fixed to the tabletop with the sharp point of a knife blade, now rested on a shelf in the evidence room at headquarters. "If you think something's missing, you'll have to be specific. I can't play a guessing game."

Ronan sank onto the sofa, or tried to, but he landed on an unsupported corner of a crooked cushion and had to scramble to keep from landing on the floor. Face flaming, he shoved the cushion back into place and sat on it, his head in his hands. His voice came out strained and rough, as if he were holding back tears. "I just want all this to be over."

Tom sat in a padded rocking chair facing Ronan. "Have you and Sheila made any plans for the funeral?"

"No."

"Maybe that ought to be your first priority. You should be able to have the funeral and burial next week. I know your parents weren't church-goers, so you might want a simple service at the funeral home. That's easy enough to arrange."

Ronan didn't respond.

"Are you listening to me?" Tom prodded.

"Yes, damn it, I'm listening. I've got other things to think about."

Things that were more important than burying his murdered parents? More important than finding their killer? Most relatives would be demanding to know why no one had been arrested yet. Ronan didn't seem to have a single question about the investigation.

"You going to be around for the next week?"

"I don't know if I can take that much time off work." Ronan gripped his head as if trying to hold it together. His hair, soot-black and thick, stuck out at odd angles, as if he'd been grabbing it by the fistful and yanking on it in frustration. Fatigue had painted bruised half-circles under his eyes. "I've got things scheduled, places I'm supposed to be. I'll have to see what I can work out on Monday."

"Where are you working these days?" What employer wouldn't give a man a few days off after both parents had died?

"I'm with VDOT." He gave the information grudgingly, as if he felt ashamed of working for the state's Department of Transportation. "I spend my time doing inspections and recommending repairs."

"I heard you'd set up your own business."

Ronan expelled a bitter little laugh. "That didn't work out."

"Building small bridges out of recycled materials, right? What's involved in that?"

"It's technical. You wouldn't understand." Ronan rose from the sofa before Tom could respond to the put-down. "You said on the phone you had some questions for me. Is that it? If there's nothing else, I've got things to do."

Tom stayed in his chair. "Sit down. I'm not done."

With an elaborate sigh, Ronan flopped onto the sofa again. He spread his hands, inviting Tom to continue, but his expression mixed impatience and contempt.

"Did your mother say anything to you recently about Tavia Richardson?"

Ronan frowned. "No. Why? Has something happened to her?"

"How about Jake Hollinger? Aside from the disagreement over the fence, I mean."

"Well, yeah, Mom said he wanted them to sell the land. Didn't we talk about that yesterday?"

"Did your mother mention any specific incidents? Did she feel like she was being harassed?"

Tom saw the precise moment when Ronan realized he'd been handed an opportunity. He straightened and put on a serious expression. "Yeah, now that you mention it. She said Hollinger was getting intense about it. Pressuring her." He paused briefly, then embroidered the story. "He told her she ought to put Dad away somewhere and let professionals look after him. She'd have enough money to settle down close by, so she could visit him whenever she wanted to."

Tom wondered if that was Hollinger's suggestion or Ronan's. At the moment, he didn't want to press Ronan about his own motive for getting his parents out of the way. He wanted the Kellys' son to stick around while the investigation played out. "That's good to know. If you remember anything, be sure to tell me about it. I need all the information I can get, even if it doesn't seem important to you."

"Yeah, sure. Of course I will."

"Will your sister be staying here at the farm with you?"

"I don't know what Sheila's going to do. I just want to dispose of this place and move on."

"You mean sell it? This soon?"

Ronan threw a belligerent look at Tom but instantly caught himself and transformed his expression into a bland mask. "No reason to wait and let it sit here empty. We can sell it legally. Everything was in trust. It passed to Sheila and me as soon as our parents—when they died. Sheila lives hundreds of miles away and I know she doesn't want to drag things out and keep coming back here to tie up loose ends. I wanted to talk to the lawyer who drew up the trust, but he's gone away for the weekend. I'll see him first thing Monday."

Ronan had no inkling yet that his parents' deaths wouldn't save him from financial ruin. Tom wanted to keep him in the dark until the time seemed right, and that would require Sheila's cooperation. She'd be wise to hold off and let the lawyer tell him. If she decided to do it herself, Tom hoped she would drop the bombshell in a safe place with other people around.

Chapter Eighteen

Rachel paused in dinner preparations to lean against the counter and watch Tom and Simon trying to figure out how to set the kitchen table.

"The forks go on the right side," Tom said. "No, wait, that looks wrong. Here, they go on the left. The knife goes on the right."

Simon frowned at the arrangement. "Why don't they all go together on one side?"

"Don't ask me, buddy. As long as they're somewhere I can reach them, that's all that matters to me."

Grinning at their exchange, Rachel grabbed a couple of oven mitts from the counter to remove a macaroni and cheese casserole—Simon's favorite—from the oven. Tom and Simon were so much alike they could be father and son, rather than uncle and nephew. Each time she saw them together, she knew she was getting a preview of what their life might be like if she and Tom had kids of their own.

Rachel knew how much Tom wanted children, and she felt guilty for thinking in terms of *if* instead of *when*. Sometimes she shared his longing, and managed to stifle her doubts and believe she had the qualities that made a good mother, even though she'd never had a positive role model when she was growing up. In a burst of enthusiasm and confidence, she'd stopped taking birth control pills. But deeply engrained self-doubt had made her hesitant to tell Tom. Soon enough, the old familiar fears had overwhelmed her again. What if she could be no better a mother than her own, her real mother, had been? Worse, what if she had absorbed so much poison from Judith, the imposter, the criminal who raised her and her sister, that she couldn't keep it from leaking into her relationship with a child of her own? She had almost decided to go back on the pills.

She lifted the casserole out and set it on top of the range while she turned off the oven.

"Yay!" Simon scrambled into a chair. "Mac and cheese! I'm ready to eat."

Rachel smiled, relieved to be distracted from her dark thoughts. "You have to eat your veggies too."

He screwed up his face in disgust. "Okay, if I have to."

Why did she feel so at ease with Simon? Was it because he had no connection to her own twisted family? She believed she could be a good mother to him. But it wasn't hard to be confident about something that would never happen.

If Darla's cancer progressed, though—if, God forbid, she didn't make it…

Rachel froze, her mitt-covered hands on the casserole dish. How could she think such a thing? Simon wasn't a prize they might win if his grandmother died.

"Hey," Tom said. "You okay?"

"Yes, of course." Rachel carried the casserole to the table and set it on a trivet. Unsure how much emotion showed on her face, she avoided Tom's gaze.

As they ate they focused on Simon, and Tom appeared totally relaxed, with all thoughts of the murder investigation and the raucous community meeting banished from his mind. When they were alone later, though, he would probably have plenty to say to her about her impromptu role in the uproar. Maybe she'd get lucky and the edge of his irritation with her would wear off before they got around to speaking privately.

◇◇◇

Rachel was turning down their bed when Tom came in and closed the bedroom door. "He finally drifted off to sleep. He's really worried about his grandmother."

"I know. He's trying so hard to be brave. It breaks my heart."

Tom said nothing as he removed his shoes and unbuttoned his shirt. Rachel knew he wouldn't let the day end without a discussion of her behavior at the meeting, and she decided to bring it up first and get it out of the way.

"I'm sorry I made things harder for you today," she said, "but I couldn't sit there and keep my mouth shut while that man lied to all those people. Somebody has to inject a little truth into this fairy tale he's putting out."

"That somebody doesn't have to be you."

Rachel sighed and sat down on her side of the bed, facing away from him. "I'm the sheriff's wife now, so I can't ever say what I think? I'm sorry, but I'm having a little trouble adjusting to that idea."

She couldn't see Tom's face, but his voice sounded tight when he answered. "This is a dangerous situation. And it's going to get worse. I don't like having to worry about you all the time. Stay out of it and let other people fight this battle."

"I didn't hear anybody else asking the questions I did."

Tom came to sit beside her, but he left a foot of space between them. He didn't speak at once, and the silence grew more and more uncomfortable as it stretched out. She'd rather have anger than this uneasy quiet.

When he spoke at last, he sounded tired, resigned, rather than irritated. "You really hate this place, don't you?"

"No." Her answer was automatic. "Of course I don't hate it."

He looked at her, and his solemn, sad expression brought a stab of alarm. She had pushed him too far. Was he wondering if he'd made a mistake in marrying her?

What he said next startled her, only because neither of them had ever spoken the truth so baldly before. "I know I'm the only reason you stay here. You'd be long gone if it wasn't for me. That's one reason you took a while to say yes when I asked you to marry me. You couldn't decide if I was worth staying here for."

Rachel hesitated, choosing her words and resisting the urge to drown him in reassurance. "All right, yes, I'd probably be gone by now if it weren't for you. But you are absolutely worth staying here for. I love you. I want to be wherever you are. And you have to admit that you aren't here willingly either. You told me as much."

"I came back because of Simon. You know that. I owe it to him to be here if he needs me."

"I understand that. I always have. But if the accident had never happened, you'd still be a detective with the Richmond police."

Tom reached for her hand, and the warmth of his skin made Rachel realize that she felt icy, through and through.

"If I'd stayed in Richmond, I never would have met you."

And would you be better off? "Oh, we might have met, one way or another, when you came here for a visit with some other woman as your wife."

He enclosed her hand in both of his, as if trying to warm her. "Then I would've had to get a divorce so I could be with you. You drive me crazy sometimes, but you're the best thing that ever happened to me."

A rush of relief made Rachel's breath catch in her throat. She smiled and laid a hand against his cheek. "In case you have any doubt, the feeling is mutual."

"Which part? The driving me crazy part or the best thing part?"

"Both." She leaned into him, needing his arms around her. What strange and twisted roads had brought them to this point. And how easily this fragile happiness might be lost.

The telephone rang, a jarring intrusion in the quiet room.

Tom groaned and pulled away from Rachel. "What now?"

Nothing but bad news ever came in a call this late in the evening. Somebody hurt. Somebody dead. As Tom walked around the bed to answer the landline phone on his night table, Rachel waited with growing apprehension.

Tom listened for a moment, then said, "No, it's okay, you were right to call me. I'll go out there now."

"What's happened?" Rachel asked when he hung up.

"Joanna called for help and the dispatcher thought I'd want to know about it."

Rachel jumped to her feet. "Joanna? What—"

"Joanna's fine, nothing's happened to her, but Ronan's over at her place raising hell, and she's holding a gun on him to keep him away from his sister."

Chapter Nineteen

Deputy Kevin Blackwood, assigned to night patrol, had reached Joanna's house ahead of Tom, and his cruiser sat on the farm road with its light strip flashing red and blue. Tom trotted across the lawn from the driveway and mounted the steps to the porch.

The main door stood open, and with only the glass storm door to muffle them, the raised voices inside carried into the quiet night. Through the living room window on the left, he saw Sheila Kelly standing with her arms crossed, her face hard and unyielding. Ronan stalked around the room, glaring and yanking on his hair. The deputy, a tall blond man in his twenties, looked on without interfering.

Tom found Joanna, in robe and slippers, standing in the center hallway outside the living room, her shotgun propped on the floor and her fingers gripping the barrel. "They've been at it for a while now," she told Tom, "and it's getting worse, not better."

"You can't do a thing about it," Sheila was shouting at her brother, "so just suck it up and move on."

"Like hell I will!"

"You brought it on yourself. Don't you dare blame me!"

Tom upped the volume of his own voice so Joanna could hear him above the barrage of shouted insults between Ronan and Sheila. "Why did you let him in the house?"

"She let him in. I was in bed asleep, and the racket woke me up." With her free hand Joanna swept her tousled red-gold hair off her forehead. "He was pushing her around, threatening her."

Ronan spun to face them. In one hand he gripped several crumpled sheets of paper. "I didn't do a damn thing to her. She's the one who screwed me over."

"If I hadn't come down here with a gun and stopped you," Joanna said, "God only knows what you would've done. You're acting like a crazy man."

"I thought he was going to break my arm." Sheila held her left arm against her body and clutched it with her right hand.

"Your parents would be ashamed of you," Joanna told Ronan.

"Aw, to hell with this." He started toward the door.

Kevin Blackwood stepped into his path, hands raised. "Stay right where you are."

"Get out of my way."

Tom added his own body to the barricade. When he moved closer, he caught a whiff of sour whiskey coming off Ronan. "You're not going anywhere until you explain what you're doing here."

"My sister's the one who has some explaining to do." Ronan shook the crushed papers in his fist. "I want her to tell me how she pulled this off."

"Pulled what off?" Tom asked, although he had a good idea.

With clumsy motions Ronan tried to smooth out the papers. Tom took them from him and looked them over. Exactly what he'd expected. Ronan had dug up a copy of his parents' trust.

Ronan focused on his sister again. "This is your doing. You can't tell me they decided this on their own. What kind of lies did you tell them? How did you make them turn against their only son, their oldest child?"

Tears ran down Sheila's cheeks, but she looked furious. "You did that all by yourself. You took advantage of them, you milked them for every cent you could get when you knew they couldn't afford it, and you wasted it all. They would have been justified if they'd left you absolutely nothing. They were disgusted with you, they'd had enough—"

"Shut up, you bitch!" Before Tom realized what was happening, Ronan took a long stride toward his sister and whacked her across the face with the back of his hand.

Sheila cried out and staggered backward. Ronan went after her, fist raised, but Tom and Kevin grabbed his arms and pulled him away from her.

Joanna rushed to Sheila's side and wrapped an arm around her.

"I'll make you pay for this!" Ronan twisted, trying to jerk free, but Tom and Kevin held on and forced his hands behind his back.

"What the hell do you think you're doing?" Tom said. "Settle down."

Sheila pressed both hands to her cheek and jaw. Blood dripped from her lower lip and streaked the front of her white terrycloth robe. "Keep him away from me. I'm afraid of what he'll do to me."

"Oh, boo hoo," Ronan said. "Poor Sheila. That's how you did it, playing the sweet little daughter while you cut me off at the knees." He jerked again, trying to throw off Tom and the deputy. "Goddamn it, let me go!"

They pressed on his shoulders, forcing him to his knees, then facedown on the carpet. Tom unhooked a pair of handcuffs from the back of his utility belt and snapped them on Ronan's wrists. "You're under arrest for assault."

"Damn it, Bridger, you can't do this." Writhing like a snake, Ronan kicked his feet up and out, trying to connect with Tom's legs.

Tom placed a knee on the man's back and leaned his weight on it.

Ronan raised his head and let out a high-pitched wail. "My back, oh fuck, my back—"

Tom eased up on the pressure. "You ready to behave yourself?"

Panting like a dog, Ronan went limp and dropped his head.

Together Tom and Kevin pulled him to his feet. Still breathing hard, Ronan blinked tears from his eyes as they propelled him toward the door. "You're not getting away with this, Sheila," he threw over his shoulder. "You hear me? This isn't over."

◇◇◇

An hour later, Ronan Kelly sat on a bunk in the county jail, bent over with his head in his hands. He still had traces of fingerprint ink on his fingers, and he'd transferred black smudges to his forehead, temples, and nose.

Tom stood outside the cell. "That was quite a performance at Joanna's house."

Without looking up, Ronan mumbled, "I had a couple of drinks before I went over there. I wasn't myself."

"Oh, is that right? Then who were you? Where did all that rage come from, if it didn't come from you?"

Ronan sat silent and motionless.

"Do you really think your sister could talk your parents into cutting your share of the estate if they didn't want to? If they didn't have any reason to?"

Ronan dropped his hands and raised his head, but he stared at the wall in front of him and didn't look at Tom. "That's exactly what I think. She's been working on them, trying to turn them against me."

"Why would she do that?"

"You know why."

"No, I don't. Enlighten me."

Ronan drew a deep breath, squeezed his eyes shut for a moment, and said, "She's always resented me. Been jealous of me. She knew I was Dad's favorite, and she couldn't stand it. Then when his mind started to go, she grabbed her chance."

"Are you telling me this is all about sibling rivalry? At this late date?"

Abruptly Ronan rose and stepped over to the bars. "It's about money. She knew they'd be rich if they sold to Packard. She wanted it all, or as much as she could get her hands on. And she made sure she'd end up with it. Well, she's not getting away with this. I'll go to court and get the trust invalidated because Dad wasn't mentally competent to sign it."

"I thought your parents were holding out, like Joanna. They weren't going to sell."

"They would have. Or Mom would have. But she needed to get Dad declared incompetent first, so she could do it on her own."

"Are you just speculating, or was your mother really planning to do that?"

Ronan gripped the bars with both hands and leaned against them as if he were exhausted and needed the support. "She wanted to do it. She told me so. She was just waiting to see what Joanna decided."

"I can tell you that Joanna's not budging."

Ronan's words were barely audible. "Damn stubborn woman. Standing in everybody's way."

And we've seen what happens, Tom thought, when you think somebody's standing in *your* way. "Even if your parents had sold, it wouldn't have done you any good, not as long as they were alive."

Ronan dropped his hands and took a step back from the bars. "What do you mean?"

Tom shrugged. "The money would be theirs, not yours. Even if you'd been in line to inherit everything, you wouldn't have got it until both your parents died. But you need money *now*."

"What the hell do you know about my financial situation?"

"It's not a secret. I know you're up to your ears in debt. You must have thought a lot of your problems would be solved if both your parents were out of the way."

His fists opening and closing at his sides, Ronan stared at Tom for a long moment. Dawning comprehension showed in his widening eyes and slack jaw. At last he said, "I'm not talking to you anymore without a lawyer."

Chapter Twenty

When Tom found Jake Hollinger's truck parked in Tavia Richardson's driveway Sunday morning, he almost turned around and drove off. He wanted to talk to both, but separately. After sitting on the road in his cruiser thinking about it for a couple of minutes, though, he parked and got out. Seeing these two together might tell him something about their relationship and how far they would go to be together.

Tavia answered the door in bare feet, wearing a blue robe that hung open over a lacy nightgown. Through the sheer fabric of the gown, one nipple and the dark triangle of her pubic hair were clearly visible. Startled, Tom averted his eyes.

Tavia laughed softly, mocking him, as she drew her robe closed and tied it. "Look who's here again. What can I do for you this time?"

"I have a few more questions." Glancing beyond her into the living room, Tom saw Jake buttoning his plaid shirt. He met Tom's gaze for a second before turning away and disappearing into another room. "Is this a bad time?"

Tavia shrugged. "Is there ever a good time to be questioned by the police? Come right in, Sheriff, but we'll have to talk in the kitchen. I haven't had enough coffee yet."

The living room they passed through looked as neglected as the outside of the house, with magazines in a sliding stack on an end table, several whitish moisture rings on the coffee table, the green upholstery worn thin on the couch and chairs. In the dining room, dust lay so thick on the table that Tom assumed the space hadn't been used in months, perhaps years. He wondered what family dinners had been like when Tavia and her abusive husband, Ron, and their four terrified children had gathered around the table. Not much happy chatter, he supposed.

Jake was in the kitchen, his shirt now buttoned and tucked into his jeans. He didn't meet Tom's eyes as he took a mug from a cabinet, set it in an empty spot on the round wooden table and filled it with coffee from a glass pot. Their breakfast, scrambled eggs on one plate and fried eggs and bacon on another, sat half-finished.

As he pulled out a chair, Tom noticed an enormous orange tabby curled in a cat bed in a corner, fast asleep and oblivious to his arrival. Its food dish, next to the bed, contained only traces of its breakfast. Before Tom left home that morning, he'd asked Rachel what she thought of Tavia, and her only comment was, "She overfeeds her cat." Tom had taken that as a condemnation.

Tavia sat in the chair closest to the cat, drained her coffee mug, then used her fingers as a comb to neaten her short dark curls, so she looked a little less like someone who'd just rolled out of bed. "Were you looking for Jake too, or is it just me you want to talk to?"

Tom glanced across the table at Jake, who now seemed intent on polishing off his eggs and bacon in record time. "Both of you."

"Honey," Tavia said to Jake, "you're going to give yourself indigestion, shoveling your food in like that."

A flush mottled Jake's neck and cheeks. He laid his fork on his plate and gulped coffee. His words, directed at Tom, came out loud and angry. "What do you want now?"

In its bed, the cat stirred in reaction to Jake's raised voice, made a low grumbling sound, and clamped a paw over its eyes.

"I've been hearing some things that don't match what the two of you told me," Tom said.

Tavia pushed her plate aside with her thumb and sat forward, arms folded on the table. "And of course you believe the gossip instead of us."

"I don't know what to believe yet. I'm just asking questions and hoping somebody will give me honest answers."

"Exactly what are you talking about?" Jake sat with his back rigid, his jaw tight. "What are you accusing us of?"

Tom turned his full attention to Jake. "You claimed you were at the lumber mill when the Kellys were shot, but now it looks like that's not true."

"What the hell? Did my son tell you that? Is he claiming I wasn't at the mill?"

"Does he have any reason to lie about it?"

"No, damn it, he—"

"So whatever he told me would be the truth."

"He—" Jake broke off and made a visible effort to calm down. "Look, I was at the mill most of the morning, and if my son says otherwise he's just got the time confused. I didn't see him before I left, but I saw a couple of other people, talked to them. I came home, saw the fence down and started working on getting it back up. The first I knew about the shooting was when you showed up asking questions."

A loud snort erupted from the orange cat. Tavia extended a leg, poked him with her toe. "Tater, turn over. You're snoring. I swear, you're worse than a man." Without opening his eyes, the animal stretched his hind legs and rolled onto his other side. Tavia turned back to Tom. "And what am I supposed to be lying about?"

"You told me you hadn't put any pressure on the Kellys to sell their land, but I hear you were over there quite a bit, trying to talk Marie into it. Badgering her."

Tavia dismissed the complaint with an airy wave of a hand. "Oh, that. Yes, I spoke to her. Tried to persuade her. I wouldn't say I *badgered* her."

"Who told you that?" Anger coloring his face again, Jake scraped his chair back and rose. "We've got a right to know who's accusing us."

"As if he's going to tell us." Tavia refilled her coffee mug.

"You're right." Tom nodded to Tavia, "I'm not going to tell you. What matters is that I believe what that person says."

Jake leaned toward Tom, his rough hands splayed on the tabletop. "There's no way *that person* could know what was said between us and the Kellys without being there. And I didn't notice anybody else hanging around. If there's somebody claiming the Kellys told them that, well, good luck proving it."

"Isn't that called hearsay?" Tavia asked between sips of coffee.

They had a point, one that Tom wasn't interested in arguing. He shifted gears. "Does either of you own a thirty-aught-six deer rifle?"

Tavia's gaze met Jake's, and for a second Tom saw a tiny crease of worry between her eyes.

"Hell," Jake said, "who doesn't own one? If that's the kind of gun that killed the Kellys—"

"Ballistics will tell us whether or not a particular rifle fired the shots. If there's no match, you won't have a problem." Tom asked Tavia, "Do you own one?"

"I've got a bunch of Ron's old guns, but I couldn't tell you if one of them's a thirty-aught-whatever. I don't know a thing about guns." Tavia shrugged, but her casual response wasn't convincing. She reached for her coffee but changed her mind. Her hand, Tom noticed, was trembling. "They're still right where he left them. I haven't even opened the cabinet in years."

"Can I take a look?"

"You need a warrant for that," Jake said.

"Not if I have the owner's okay." Tom repeated his request to Tavia.

She hesitated, frowning at Jake as if he were sending her a silent message and she couldn't quite make it out. Finally, she pushed back her chair and stood. "Why not? I don't have anything to hide."

Jake remained silent, and he didn't accompany them when they left the kitchen.

In her bare feet, Tavia led Tom to the back hallway off the kitchen and opened the door into the basement. As she reached for the light switch, she looked back as if wondering why Jake wasn't with them.

Tom followed her down the stairs. The basement, finished for use as a rec room, looked dusty and unused, like the dining room. Over the shabby couch, the mounted heads of three bucks with impressive antlers stared with blind glass eyes.

Tavia walked to a tall, wide steel cabinet in a corner. "Ron got most of these guns from the Jones sisters after their dad died. They didn't want them around—they're scared of firearms. I think Ron took advantage of them, paid them next to nothing and got them to throw in the cabinet too." Standing on tiptoes, she felt around atop the cabinet and retrieved a key. She gave Tom a wry smile. "Some security system, huh?"

She opened the cabinet door and stood aside. "Look all you want."

Before he touched anything, Tom pulled latex gloves from his back pocket. As he put them on, he heard footsteps overhead, then what he thought was the sound of a door slamming.

"Jake's making his escape," Tavia said with a grin. "Don't you want to go chasing after him?"

"I'll catch up with him later." Tom heard a vehicle starting outside. Even if Jake had nothing to do with the murders, he might rush home and conceal a rifle of the same type as the weapon used on Lincoln and Marie Kelly. That didn't matter much at the moment, since Tom had no basis for a warrant to search Jake's house or land.

He counted eleven guns racked upright in the cabinet, eight of them rifles and the rest shotguns. Why in God's name, he wondered, did anybody need that many hunting guns? He checked each of the rifles and found one, an old Winchester, that could have fired the bullets that killed the Kellys. "Will you give me permission to take this rifle for testing? I'll need you to sign some paperwork."

"Sure, if it's going to clear me." Tavia's defensive mask fell away and her expression softened into genuine sadness. "I didn't kill those people, Tom. First of all, I wouldn't know how to use that gun if I had to. And Linc and Marie were always good to me. I didn't like them holding out on the land sale, but I never would have done anything to hurt them."

The heavy rifle in one hand, Tom started to close the cabinet. Tavia grabbed the door to stop him. "Wait a minute. This doesn't look right."

"What do you mean?"

Tapping the air with her index finger, she counted the rifles and shotguns. "And that's eleven." She pointed to the one Tom held. "There's supposed to be twelve in here."

"You sure?"

"Positive. I counted them right after Ron died, when I was looking for stuff I might be able to sell if I needed money. There were twelve. One of them's missing."

Chapter Twenty-one

Sheila Kelly rose from the bench in the lobby at headquarters when Tom walked in. "What is that?" She pointed to the plastic-wrapped rifle he held.

Phil, the retired deputy who manned the reception desk, glanced up from his copy of the Roanoke newspaper, saluted Tom with a little wave, then returned to his reading and his coffee.

"I'm sending it to the lab for testing." Sheila's lip, Tom noticed, was swollen and bruised, but the blow from her brother the night before hadn't done any major damage. She wore no makeup, so she wasn't hiding anything. She looked exhausted, though, and he doubted she'd slept much. "Thanks for coming in. I'll need a few minutes to do some paperwork, then—"

"Do you think that's the gun that killed my parents?" Sheila stared at it with pure revulsion. "Who does it belong to? Where did you get it?"

"Whoa, whoa." Tom raised his free hand. "I doubt it has any connection. I just want to rule it out."

"You mean you want to rule out the owner. Who is it?"

"Wait for me here while I take care of this. Then we can talk about it."

Tom took the rifle to the evidence room and logged it in. On Monday morning he would assign a deputy to drive it to the crime lab in Roanoke. A waste of time, almost certainly, but he didn't want to make assumptions.

Sheila wasn't waiting in the lobby when Tom went to collect her. "Restroom," Phil said without looking up from his paper. Tom found her pacing the hallway outside his office.

"I want to get my brother out of jail," Sheila said. "I'm not going to press charges, so you can let him go."

What the heck had brought this on? "Sheila, I witnessed the assault, remember? It's not your word against his. Why would I drop the charges?"

"Okay, if you insist, then I'll bail him out. It's a misdemeanor, right? He's entitled to bail. Can I do that before we talk?"

"Why do you want to help him? Let him call a lawyer and make arrangements with a bondsman."

Sheila shook her head. "He doesn't have any money for a lawyer or a bondsman. And nobody else is going to help him."

"What about his wife? She ought to be told he's in jail, in any case."

Sheila sighed and leaned her back against the wall, knocking a big framed photo askew with her shoulder. "Oh, for fuck's sake," she muttered, grabbing the frame to straighten it. "I'm so damned clumsy."

The photo, a shot of the squat cinderblock building that housed the Sheriff's Department on the day it opened decades before, still looked crooked after she repositioned it. "Forget the picture, it doesn't matter. What about Ronan's wife?"

With both hands Sheila pushed her thick black hair off her cheeks and anchored it behind her ears. "His wife is in Boston. With the kids. She walked out on Ronan two months ago."

"Hunh." That was one bit of intelligence Dennis hadn't picked up on the Internet. "Did she leave because of his money problems?"

"That's what Mom thought. She told me about it. Ronan would never confide in me. I'm sure he's mortified by it."

"Sheila…" Tom took her arm and nudged her toward the open door of his office. "Let's talk about this before you do anything."

She went with him willingly, but as he closed the door she said, "You can't change my mind. I'm the only one Ronan has left. I'm not going to let him sit in jail."

Tom sat on a corner of his desk and folded his arms. "Even though you're the one he assaulted? He's mad as hell at you. What makes you think he won't come after you again?"

"He knows he'll get in trouble if he does it again. I'll be fine."

To Tom she sounded like all the abused wives and girlfriends he'd ever dealt with after the men in their lives used them as punching bags. But Ronan was her brother, not her husband or boyfriend. "Has he done this before? Hit you during an argument?"

Sheila wrapped her arms around her waist and hunched her shoulders, defensive body language Tom recognized. "A time or two, back when we were younger. He's always had a terrible temper. But Dad knew how to deal with him."

"You don't have anybody to act as a buffer now. Ronan's desperate. He needs money. He was counting on getting half of your parents' estate. And he blames you for him losing out."

Tom paused, but she didn't respond. Staring at the floor, she traced the swirling pattern in the vinyl tiles with the toe of her shoe.

"Tell me what you're thinking," Tom said.

She jerked her head up, her expression angry, defiant, confused. "He couldn't have killed them. He wasn't here. He was in Richmond, at work."

"That doesn't mean he wasn't respons—"

"They were his mother and father! I can't believe—" Sheila broke off, blinking back tears.

Tom waited while she pulled herself together. But he didn't soften his voice. "If you think there's any chance he killed your parents, you can't protect him. But you need to protect yourself. You could be next."

Squeezing her eyes shut, she pulled in a deep breath and let it out. "He has a right to be angry at me. I *did* push them to cut him off. They planned to leave him half, but I kept after them until they changed the terms of the trust."

"But he didn't know that. He still believed he was going to inherit half interest in a valuable piece of property. That's motive for murder. And it's not your fault."

She chewed on a thumbnail, her face screwed up by conflicting emotions. At last she squared her shoulders and spoke with no doubt in her voice. "My brother isn't the greatest guy in the world, and believe me, I don't like being hit in the face, but I've thought about it and thought about it, and I just can't believe he killed our parents. I want him released now."

◇◇◇

Simon was awfully quiet in the back seat of the Range Rover. Rachel wanted to hear his usual mile-a-minute commentary on everything they passed. She wanted him to be himself. He wasn't a child who sulked, but he'd been unable to hide his disappointment that morning when she told him they couldn't go riding at Joanna's place, and he'd hardly spoken as they ate an early lunch. Glancing in the rearview mirror, she saw the sad, lost expression that settled over his face when he didn't realize anyone was watching.

He kept one hand on the carrier that contained the two rabbits, holding it steady so it wouldn't slide around when the vehicle hit a pothole or rounded a curve. Simon wanted the rabbits the Kellys had left behind. He'd begged Rachel not to give them to the Jones sisters. But she couldn't predict what his grandmother's health would be like in the coming months, and she couldn't place another burden, however small, on Darla. She wanted to promise Simon he could have a rabbit of his own, or maybe a dog, when life got back to normal, but she had no right to promise him anything. He wasn't her child. She didn't control his future. And she knew the odds were high that life in his grandparents' household would never be normal again.

"I'm sorry we couldn't go riding," she said, not for the first time that day. "There are things going on—well, I told you that already. It's just not a good time."

"That's okay." Simon spoke so softly she barely heard him.

If they were on horseback, climbing the hilly trails on Joanna's property, he would be distracted, he would be pointing out hawks and ravens in the treetops and squirrels foraging in the leaf litter. He would be happy, for at least a few hours.

"Hey, I was thinking we could go out to the river and see the ducks and geese," Rachel said. "We'll stop by the house first and pick up Billy Bob. How does that sound?"

In the mirror she saw Simon's eyes light up. That big grin Rachel loved spread over his face. "That'd be fun."

"Okay then. Let's go see the Jones ladies, then we'll have the whole afternoon to ourselves."

A few minutes later, as she approached the Jones sisters' house, a vague anxiety tugged at Rachel's mind. She didn't know what to expect. Just how eccentric were they? Was it wise to bring Simon along instead of leaving him with Tom's aunt and uncle?

She knew the Joneses and their cats—one for each sister— from their visits to the animal hospital, but she'd never been to their house before. The thought of the never-married sisters still living together in the family home, conjured up images of room after room overflowing with junk they'd hoarded for decades. Tom had assured her they were ordinary older women whose greatest vice was a love of gossip, but she would wait and make her own assessment. If she detected anything troubling about the household, she would hustle Simon away and she wouldn't hand over the orphaned rabbits to the sisters.

As soon as she turned into the driveway, most of her fears evaporated. The Colonial house and its yard practically shone from loving attention and made a pretty picture that could have graced a magazine cover.

The oldest sister, Winter, waved from the front steps. This white-haired woman might be an old maid, a senior citizen, whatever society chose to call her, but her body looked strong and fit in dark slacks and a sweater, and in her movements Rachel saw the physical assurance of a woman who was still active and intended to stay that way.

"The poor little things," Winter crooned as Rachel approached with the carrier containing the rabbits. "They must be so confused and frightened by all this moving around." She smiled at Simon, who carried a bag containing the rabbits' dry kibble and their dishes. "Hello there, Simon. I'm sure you don't remember meeting me when you were a baby, but I taught both of your parents—and your uncle Tom—in high school."

Simon's face brightened with eager curiosity. "You were my mom and dad's teacher?"

"I was. They were excellent students, I'm happy to tell you. The kind that every teacher loves to have in her classroom."

Simon beamed, and he looked up at Rachel to share his pleasure with her.

She squeezed his shoulder, but restrained herself from a caress that might embarrass him. "Simon's pretty sharp himself. We're all proud of him, and I'm sure his parents would be, too."

"They certainly would be. Now let's get the bunnies inside out of this chilly breeze." Winter clucked her tongue as she shepherded them into a pleasant, neat living room. "What a shame Lincoln and Marie's son and daughter can't be bothered to care for their parents' pets. Too much trouble, I suppose? It would interfere with their schedules?"

That was a clear invitation to discuss Ronan and Sheila, and Rachel was surprised Winter had brought it up in front of Simon. "They both live some distance away, and they'd rather not put the rabbits through the stress of traveling. Or the dog. Bonnie's happy with Joanna and her dogs." Before Winter could comment, Rachel added, "I appreciate your willingness to do this, and I'm sure the Kellys would be grateful."

Winter pursed her lips and shook her head but said no more about the dead couple's disappointing offspring.

Three cats—black, gray tabby, and seal point Siamese—marched into the living room single file, forming an advance guard for the other sisters, Spring and Summer. Simon laughed as the cats circled his legs, and he dropped to his knees to pet them.

All three sisters fussed over him, remarking on his way with animals, telling him how much he looked like his father, explaining their personal connections to his family—Spring had also taught Simon's parents, and Summer had worked with his grandmother, Anne Bridger, at the hospital. Rachel wanted to gather them in a hug for putting a real smile on Simon's face.

"The sunroom is all set up for the rabbits," Summer said. "Simon, do you want to see where they're going to live?" When Rachel had last seen the youngest Jones sister, she'd been in tears over the Kelly murders, but today she was calm and smiling. Her pink blouse and cardigan complemented the rosy glow of her complexion and made her look younger than her age.

Summer and Simon led the way, but the three cats hustled to get in front of them, single file again, and seemed to know exactly where they were headed. The procession of humans and animals crossed through the dining room and kitchen on their way to the sunroom at the rear of the house.

The house was spotless, Rachel noted. No clutter, no dust on anything. In the kitchen, pots and pans with gleaming copper bottoms hung from a ceiling rack, and the white appliances shone as if they'd been waxed. If anything, these women went overboard on tidiness. She could imagine them spending most of their time perfecting a house that few people besides themselves would ever see. That was the kind of household Rachel had grown up in, and she pushed the unwelcome memory aside with an inward shudder.

"Summer's been making some of her specialties," Spring said as they walked through the kitchen. She gestured at a plate piled with delicate pastries, all drizzled with chocolate, under a glass cover. "You and Simon will have to stay long enough for a snack."

"Yeah!" Simon said over his shoulder, making all of them laugh.

The sunroom was a cozy space filled with hanging plants and potted plants on tables. More than a dozen orchids of various sizes and colors sat on long tables. Needlepoint throw pillows had been arranged invitingly on a white wicker settee and matching chairs. "We've moved all the plants out of reach," Summer said, "so the bunnies can be free and we won't have to worry about them eating something harmful."

"Wow," Rachel said. "You've gone to so much trouble. I can't thank you enough."

When she set down the carrier, all three cats pressed close to see what was inside. The black one, Maggie, jumped back in surprise, hissing and growling. Belle, the gray tabby, took a look, quickly lost interest, and sauntered away. Tootles, the Siamese who belonged to Spring, hooked claws over the grille that formed the carrier's door and tried to pull it open. Failing in that, she stuck her nose through the grille. The male rabbit moved closer and touched his nose to the cat's, and the female rabbit followed.

"See there?" Winter said. "They'll be just fine. Don't mind Maggie. She's set in her ways and always resists change, but she'll come around. Tootles is the boss in this little trio. If she likes our new residents, Maggie and Belle will follow her lead." Barely pausing between subjects and no change in tone, Winter went on, "Is Tom making any progress on finding the person who killed Lincoln and Marie?"

Startled, Rachel took a moment to answer. This was the second time Winter had mentioned something they shouldn't discuss in front of Simon. "I don't really know much." *And I wouldn't tell you if I did.* "I'm sure Tom will get to the bottom of it. He always does."

"Yes," Winter murmured, almost absent-mindedly. "He does have a perfect solve rate, doesn't it? This killer will have to be very clever to avoid being found out."

The sisters stood in silence for a moment, and Rachel felt an odd thrumming sensation, an undercurrent among them. Fortunately, Simon seemed engrossed in the interaction of the rabbits and cats and wasn't paying attention to the adult conversation. Rachel tried to cut Winter's speculation short before the boy heard too much. "Why don't we let them out so they can explore their new quarters?"

"Can I do it?" Simon reached for the latch on the wire mesh door.

Summer smiled at Simon. "Of course you may. Will you help us keep the cats from overwhelming them?"

"Sure!" With a flourish Simon pulled the door open.

The rabbits twitched their noses but didn't move. Tootles, the Siamese, sat down a couple feet away and issued a string of the guttural sounds that constituted Siamese speech. Rachel thought she sounded encouraging. After a moment of hesitation and a lot of nose wiggling, the rabbits took their first cautious steps out of the carrier.

Without preamble, Spring asked, "Do you believe we should be worried about our safety?"

Simon, engrossed in the rabbit-cat encounter that was underway, seemed to be paying no attention to the adults, but Rachel nodded in his direction. "Do you mind if we don't talk about this right now?"

Rachel didn't know how to make her concern any clearer, but Spring continued as if she hadn't heard. "After all, we do live in a rural area with no neighbors close enough to see our house. If someone wanted to hurt us, we'd be totally vulnerable."

"But why would anyone want to hurt us?" Summer asked.

"Oh, for heaven's sake, you know exactly why," Winter said. "If we don't come to an agreement among ourselves soon about selling to Packard, we'll have both sides mad at us. Heaven knows what could happen in the dead of night when we're asleep in our beds."

Simon looked up at Rachel with a troubled frown. What on earth was wrong with these women? She spoke to them in a low voice. "I sympathize with you, but could we please not talk about it in front of a child?"

"Oh, of course," Spring said. "You're absolutely right."

"I'm sorry," Summer added. "We're being thoughtless."

Rachel expected them to stop discussing the murders altogether, but instead Winter and Spring both took her by the arm, steered her a few feet farther away from Simon, and picked up where they'd left off.

"We heard that Lincoln and Marie changed their minds and decided to sell," Winter said, keeping her voice to a near-whisper. "Well, it would have been Marie's decision, with Lincoln in such a poor mental state. That must have been the reason behind the murders."

Rachel despaired of her chances of making them shut up. All she could do was get Simon out of here. He was on the floor, petting both rabbits and cats, but his expression had turned solemn as the sisters talked on.

As Rachel started to make an excuse to leave, Spring said, "I wouldn't be surprised if the murders were purely personal. Lincoln and Marie were more than a bit on the self-righteous side—"

"Sister, please," Summer broke in.

Spring threw a peevish glance at Summer and continued, addressing her comments to Rachel. "They were always trying to tell other people how to live. Would you believe Lincoln went around looking in people's trash on collection day? To see who was committing recycling sins."

"Oh, don't tell that story," Summer pleaded.

Spring ignored her. "He came to our door once with an empty toilet paper roll he'd fished out of our trash. He had to open a trash bag and root around to even find the thing. There he was at our door, holding it up like a trophy, as if it were evidence of the worst behavior he'd ever witnessed, and he proceeded to lecture me about the proper recycling of cardboard. I shut the door in his face."

Under any other circumstances, Rachel might have been amused as she imagined the scene, but at the moment she didn't find it funny. "I'm afraid we have to go. We have plans—"

"A fervor for recycling is not a motive for double murder." Winter drowned out Rachel's words. "The only person the Kellys had any serious trouble with was Jake Hollinger."

Summer's sharp intake of breath made Rachel glance her way. The woman bit her lower lip in an oddly girlish way and lowered her head.

"I don't really know Mr. Hollinger," Rachel said.

Winter snorted. "Well, you're one of the few. A great many women in this county are *closely* acquainted with him."

"Winter, please!" Summer exclaimed.

"You know it's true," Spring put in. "The man has always been a womanizer."

Oh my God. Rachel glanced at Simon and found him grinning at the way the cats and rabbits were sniffing each other. Maybe he wasn't listening after all, or the women were speaking so quietly he couldn't make out what they were saying.

"Our father started hearing stories about Jake and his women early on," Winter continued, "after he sold that piece of land to him and Sue Ellen. There were even rumors about him and Marie Kelly at one point in those early years. Our father didn't approve at all. He wanted to be rid of Jake. He even tried to buy the land back. The way Jake carried on with Tavia Richardson while his wife was dying—" Winter shook her head. "Well, I'm glad our father wasn't around to see *that.*"

Summer stood with her arms wrapped around her waist, a deep flush coloring her cheeks. She seemed more than embarrassed by her sisters' gossiping. She looked furious.

Winter wasn't finished. "As for whether Jake killed Lincoln and Marie—"

"Would you like to try my pastry now, Dr. Goddard?" Summer cut in. "They're fresh, I made them this morning. Don't you think Simon would like a treat?"

"Oh. I—" Rachel saw the plea in Summer's eyes. The woman had listened to as much vitriolic gossip from her sisters as she could take. Rachel felt guilty for wanting to run out on her. "Thank you. We'd love to have something, then we really will have to go."

Summer hurried into the kitchen, and after a moment Winter followed. To prevent Spring from starting the gossip again, Rachel knelt next to Simon to watch the cats and rabbits interact.

Summer brought out dessert plates holding cream-filled pastries, each topped with a drizzle of chocolate. As Rachel had hoped, the conversation was constrained by Simon's presence as they ate, and they let him chatter about the rabbits, the cats, Billy Bob and Frank, the pileated woodpecker pair he'd seen on Tom and Rachel's farm that morning. Summer remained silent, never looking up as she nibbled on tiny bites of her pastry.

The encounter had been interesting, to say the least, but Rachel was so tense that the rich pastry made her slightly queasy. To avoid hurting Summer's feelings, she forced all of it down. She was enormously relieved when they could finally get the hell out of there.

She let out a long breath as she drove away.

"Let's get Billy Bob and go to the river," Simon said.

Rachel smiled. "You got it."

The queasy feeling wasn't going away. The pastry had been too rich. She didn't normally eat anything with so much fat and sugar. "Do you feel okay?" she asked Simon. "That pastry's not making you sick, is it?"

"Nope. It was real good." He looked at her with wide, concerned eyes. "Did it make you sick?"

"Oh, it's nothing." She wasn't going to disappoint him by bailing on him when he was looking forward to an excursion to the river. She wasn't sure they had any antacid at home, but they had ginger ale, which would work as well.

A spurt of acid rose in her throat, and she tasted the sourness at the back of her mouth. Swallowing hard, she concentrated on driving. Just get home. Drink some ginger ale. She'd be fine.

A wave of nausea roiled her stomach and she knew she couldn't hold it back. She wrenched the steering wheel to the right and pulled onto the shoulder of the road. Slamming the gearshift into park, she flung open the door and scrambled out. Hanging onto the door for support, she leaned over and surrendered to the sickness.

Chapter Twenty-two

Tom suspected that Raymond Morton, Mason County's prosecutor, had suggested they meet over lunch on Sunday because he knew Brandon Connolly's parents were sending over sandwiches for Tom, Brandon, and Dennis. Morton, a thin, balding man of seventy, dug into a bag labeled "Connolly's Fresh Deli" and came up with a fat sandwich before he took a seat at the conference room table.

"I couldn't talk Sheila out of paying Ronan's bail." Tom pulled out a chair across from Morton and Dennis. He took a sandwich for himself. Brandon, sitting next to Tom, had already emptied a bag of oven-baked chips into a bowl in the center of the table. The rustle of waxed paper filled the room as they settled down to eat. "And she didn't want a deputy to drive him back to Joanna's place to pick up his car. She insisted on doing it herself."

"I thought she was afraid to be alone with him," Dennis said. "What changed her mind? Is she feeling guilty because she's getting most of the estate?"

"Yeah, I think that's exactly what's going on." Watching them leave together, Ronan disheveled and unshaven and scowling, Tom had hoped he wasn't seeing the prelude to a disaster.

"You still think the Kelly boy could have hired out the killings?" Morton sank his teeth into a roast beef sandwich.

"He's got the motive. But Jake Hollinger's just as likely a suspect."

"And it would have been easier for Hollinger to pull off." Brandon popped a chip into his mouth and crunched on it.

"We need to pin Hollinger down about his movements that day," Tom told Morton. "He claims he didn't see the Kellys, but we've got the Jones sisters saying he was arguing with Lincoln at the fence. And his own son didn't back up his alibi. I got the strong feeling from Mark Hollinger that his father told him to lie, but he made a mess of it."

"You think he'd be stupid enough to go after Joanna McKendrick now?" Brandon asked. "I mean, if it's obvious the only people getting hurt are the ones holding out on the land sale, Hollinger's gotta know we'll come after him."

Morton swallowed a bite of sandwich. "If you don't have the evidence, you can't touch him. Don't bring me a case I can't prosecute. Tom, you think we've got reason to worry about Joanna?"

"You're damned right I do. We've got the Jones sisters to think about, too. They say they're undecided about selling, but I think they're just divided. Winter wants to sell, and Spring might, too, but Summer doesn't want to uproot herself. If they don't all agree, they won't be going anywhere."

Dennis pushed aside his half-finished sandwich and reached for a bag of cookies. "Could they have some financial problems that we don't know about? A reason why Winter wants to sell?"

Morton wiped a bit of mustard from his bottom lip with a paper napkin. "It would have to be serious to force them to sell out and leave. They've had some bad times in that house—it's not exactly your normal family—but it's the only home they've ever known. Regardless of what Winter says, if Joanna stands her ground, I believe the sisters will stand with her. And that's going to make them targets, too."

"The killer could be somebody we haven't looked at yet," Tom pointed out. "Somebody we haven't even thought about. A lot of people feel like they've got a personal stake in that resort development." His worst fear was that while he was trying to find evidence against the obvious suspects, the real killer was operating under the radar, free to strike again at any time.

They all fell silent as they ate. After a couple of minutes, Morton popped the last of his sandwich into his mouth and said, "Brandon, give your mom and dad my compliments. They make the best sandwiches I've ever tasted. They saved me from having to eat pasta salad with my wife and her sisters."

In mid-afternoon, Tom and Brandon headed out to the Hollinger farm. Jake's truck sat in the driveway, but Tom's pounding on the front door brought no response. As they'd done on the day of the murders, he and Brandon set out to locate Jake. Thinking he might still be working on the fence Lincoln Kelly had knocked down, they went there first.

The fence was back up, and a row of crows perched on it, preening their feathers in the sun and carrying on a quiet conversation among themselves. The small herd of white and chocolate-colored Merino sheep grazed on late season meadow grass, and goldfinches chattered as they foraged among wildflowers gone to seed. Jake was nowhere in sight.

"I doubt he's in the cornfields," Tom said. "He's probably already plowed them under for winter. Let's head over to the barn."

As they walked, Tom caught sight a couple of times of the barn's faded red roof, but the rolling landscape and several massive old pecan trees obscured most of the building. Jake hadn't harvested the fallen nuts, and squirrels pawed through the leaf litter to collect them and carry them off to store for winter.

They were crossing a low spot, with no view ahead, when a gunshot rang out.

The birds took wing and the squirrels scattered.

"Aw, no," Tom groaned. It could mean nothing. It could be something harmless. But he knew it wasn't. "God damn it."

His heart pounding, he took off toward the barn with Brandon beside him. When they crested a slope, the weathered old barn loomed before them, a couple hundred feet away. And Jake Hollinger was running from it, streaking toward a stand of evergreens.

"Tavia!" Jake cried. "Tavia!"

Tom changed course and, with Brandon on his heels, raced after Jake.

He heard Jake screaming before he saw what had happened. "Oh God, oh God. Tavia, Tavia!"

By the time Tom and Brandon reached him, Jake was on his knees in the grass, rocking back and forth and clasping Tavia Richardson's limp body to his chest.

Tom was still trying to pull Jake away from the body when Brandon returned from his pursuit. Bending over, hands on his thighs, Brandon gasped, "Nothing. Didn't see anybody. But I found the weapon. Hunting rifle."

"Jake, come on now." Tom tugged on the sobbing man's arm. He had been gentle up to this point, but he wanted Jake under control before the EMT unit showed up. Not that they could do anything for Tavia. As Jake held onto her, Tom had felt her neck and wrists for a pulse and found none. He couldn't see the entry wound because of the way Jake held her, but he saw the hole the round had blasted open in her back on its way out. One of Jake's hands covered part of the wound, and her blood drenched his skin and the cuff of his plaid shirt.

Brandon moved to the other side of the two, grasped Jake's arm and helped Tom pull him upward. Jake held onto the body, dragging it with him.

"Let her go," Tom told him. "You hear me? Let Tavia go. Put her down."

They needed several more minutes to pry Jake's arms off the body and return it to the grass. As two emergency techs charged toward them, equipment bags banging against their legs, Tom led the still weeping Jake back to the barn.

Inside, Tom steered Jake to a bench along one wall. His sobs echoed in the dim and nearly empty space. A tractor and a long rack of hand tools took up one corner. No animals were inside at the moment, but a mixture of odors familiar to Tom, sheep manure and lanolin, permeated the building.

Tom stood over Jake and tried to break through his grief. "Did you see anybody? Did you see who did it? Come on, Jake, I need you to talk to me."

Jake shook his head. "No. Nobody."

"Was anybody here with you and Tavia? What happened here?"

Jake took a shuddering breath and swiped his shirtsleeve across his nose. "There wasn't anybody else here. She was going to walk home. She likes to walk." He choked up again. "I was still in the barn when I heard the shot."

"Damn it." Tom scraped his fingers through his hair.

"I left the rifle where it was," Brandon said. "Want me to go get it?"

"Show me where it is." Tom told Jake, "Stay right here until I get back. I don't want you to move. All right?"

Jake nodded. As they walked out, Tom heard his sobs start up again.

On their way to the wooded patch, Tom stopped to look at Tavia's body. The emergency techs knelt on either side of her, but they weren't working on her. One of them, a middle-aged woman named Janice, looked up at Tom. "Nothing we could do. You don't want us to transport her yet, do you?"

"No. I've got deputies on the way, and I told dispatch to get Dr. Lauter out here. It'll probably be about an hour before you can take her."

One of them, Tom noticed, had closed Tavia's eyes. Except for the wound in her chest and the smears of blood on her cheeks, she looked peaceful.

The rifle lay on a springy bed of pine needles among the trees. Tom stooped to take a closer look without moving it.

"Why do you think the shooter left it behind?" Brandon asked. "Stumbled and dropped it, maybe?"

"Maybe. We might get prints. Even if we don't, we've got the weapon."

"This is our break, right?"

Tom looked up at Brandon. "The only problem is, this rifle doesn't fire the same caliber ammo that killed the Kellys. This isn't the same gun."

Chapter Twenty-three

"We have to start looking at this from a different angle." Tom stood with Dennis and Brandon near the barn, watching the medics place Tavia Richardson in a body bag and zip it closed. Dr. Lauter had been there and gone, releasing the body for immediate transport to the medical examiner's office in Roanoke. "One thing we know for sure is that Jake Hollinger didn't kill Tavia. And she'd already agreed to sell her land, so she wasn't standing in the way of the development. But I can't believe this killing, three days after the Kelly murders, is a coincidence."

"Maybe the other side's hitting back, retaliating for the Kelly murders." Dennis cradled his digital camera in the crook of his arm. "Somebody on the anti-development side could have shot Mrs. Richardson."

"Aw, God, that's the last thing we need, an all-out feud with both sides taking shots at each other." Tom raked his fingers through his hair. He wondered briefly what Rachel and Simon were doing at the moment. She'd told Tom she might take Simon to the river this afternoon, and he'd felt a pang of disappointment that he couldn't go with them.

The medics lifted the body bag onto a gurney. They had driven the ambulance into the field and it waited nearby, its rear doors standing open.

"How many people would be so set against the development that they'd do something like this?" Dennis asked.

The thought of Joanna McKendrick sprang up, unbidden, in Tom's mind, and for a long moment he forced himself to face it. Joanna had turned a shotgun on Robert McClure because he showed up at her place to make another pitch for her land. An unloaded shotgun, or so Joanna claimed. Rachel had been present when it happened, but she'd brushed off Tom's questions about it, insisting that Joanna would never hurt anybody. He could tell, though, that Rachel had been shaken by the incident. He should have pursued the matter, at least talked to Joanna about it.

Tom watched the medics roll the gurney to the ambulance. Did he believe that Joanna, a woman he'd known all his life, could have committed this cold-blooded killing? No, he thought. An instant later he warned himself: *Don't assume anything.*

"The shooter must have known she was here with Hollinger," Dennis said. "Or followed her over here."

The medics collapsed the gurney and lifted it into the ambulance. They slammed the doors.

"Maybe Hollinger was the original target," Brandon suggested. "Maybe the killer was on his way to shoot Hollinger and he panicked when he saw Tavia coming his way."

"If he panicked," Tom said, "he sure was neat about it. He didn't even disturb the pine needles on the ground, much less leave footprints. I'm betting we won't find any prints on the rifle and cartridge either." He kept saying *he*, as if he believed, as if he knew, the killer was a man. But wouldn't a woman, smaller and lighter, be more likely to come and go without disturbing the ground or leaving footprints?

"I don't understand how the shooter got away," Brandon said. "We didn't see anybody, we didn't hear a car driving off. Whoever it was, they just vanished."

Joanna, Tom thought, could have cut across the fields to her own property. She was strong, in good shape. It would have been a quick walk for her.

The two medics raised their hands in farewell salutes and climbed into the cab of the ambulance. In a couple of minutes they would be on the road to Roanoke.

Dennis took the rifle and shell casing with him when he left to return to headquarters. A deputy would take them, along with the rifle Tom had confiscated from Tavia's house, to the crime lab the next morning.

Tom and Brandon walked across the field to Jake Hollinger's house, where Tom had told him to wait. The back door stood open, and Tom saw him inside the kitchen, sitting at the table with his head in his hands.

Jake didn't look up when Tom and Brandon came in, but he said, "This is the third time."

"The third time for what?" Tom asked.

"Third time somebody's died on this land. Isaac Jones falling out of the barn loft. Autumn Jones going crazy after her daddy died and coming over here to hang herself in the barn." Jake pulled in a shaky breath. "Now Tavia. This place has got a curse on it. It's poisoned."

"Jake, listen to me." Tom pulled out a chair and sat across from him. Brandon remained standing, leaning in the doorway. "Is there anything I need to know? Anything you haven't told me about? Has somebody been threatening you or Mrs. Richardson?"

Jake pushed his chair back and stepped over to an under-counter cabinet. He yanked open the top drawer, scooped out a handful of envelopes, and tossed them on the table in front of Tom. "You think we've been pressuring Joanna and the Kellys? Take a look at that shit."

Tom pulled latex gloves from his jacket pocket and drew them on before he touched the scattered items. Brandon moved closer to look over his shoulder. Some of the envelopes had been addressed with a computer printer and sent through the mail. Others were blank. All of them contained folded sheets of paper printed with similar messages. "TRAITOR. SELL-OUT. ALL YOU CARE ABOUT IS MONEY. YOU'RE HELPING PACKARD DESTROY OUR LAND AND OUR PEACE AND QUIET."

"They look like all of them could have been sent by the same person," Brandon said.

Tom gathered them into a bundle to take with him. "Do you have any idea who sent them?"

Jake, slumped against the counter with his arms folded, shook his head. "Tavia got some, too. She just threw them away or burned them. We both got some phone calls, but we just started hanging up, we didn't even listen anymore. Neither of us ever thought—" His voice caught on a sob, and he hung his head while he pulled himself together. "We didn't think it would come to this."

"Why didn't you report that you were being harassed?" Tom was always amazed at the things people held back from the police even when their own safety was at stake.

"I told you, we never expected it would lead to anything. We thought somebody was just blowing off steam."

"I want to know if you get any more letters or phone calls," Tom said. "And I want to know immediately."

Jake nodded.

"I'll have to let her children know what's happened." Tom got to his feet. "I guess I'll find their phone numbers at her house."

"I doubt that. She doesn't—didn't—know where they are. She hasn't heard from any of them in years."

Tom wasn't surprised by that. "Did she have any idea what states they're living in?"

Jake shook his head.

"We'll have to track them down. I might find something at the house to point me in the right direction. Whether they care or not, they need to know she's died. And unless she made some other arrangements, they'll have to decide what to do about her estate."

As Tom and Brandon stepped onto the back porch, Jake said, "I'm coming, too. I'll be right behind you."

"No, you're not coming." Tom held the door open to speak to Jake. "You don't have any business over there."

"I have to get her cat and bring him back here. He knows me. It's what Tavia would want."

Tom sighed. "All right. But you need to stay out of our way. Lock up this house before you leave. I don't want you to come back here and find somebody waiting for you with a gun."

Tom opened Tavia's front door with a key from the ring he'd taken off her body. While Brandon helped Jake gather up all the cat's food, bowls, and bedding, Tom searched the small desk in a corner of the living room. The cheap, black-covered address book he pulled from the top drawer had only a few entries scattered through it. He looked for the names of her four children and found them—first names only, with no indication of whether the two daughters were now using married names. In each case, the address and phone number under the name had been crossed out and Tavia had written MOVED next to them.

Feeling a mixture of pity and anger, Tom slid the address book into one of the plastic evidence bags he'd brought in from the car. Maybe Dennis could do one of his Internet searches and track down at least one of the younger Richardsons. Why, he wondered, had they deserted their mother? By all accounts, she was more of a victim of their father's violence than they were, sometimes deflecting their father's rage from them and focusing it on herself. Did they see her as weak? Did they blame her for staying with him, not rescuing herself and them? For waiting until they were all gone and scattered before she killed him?

He slammed the desk drawer shut. A sudden high-pitched *"Rowwrrr!"* from the kitchen told him that Jake was forcing Tater into the hated cat carrier. Jake hurried through the living room and out the front door with the fat orange tabby clawing the metal grill door of the carrier and screeching nonstop.

Chapter Twenty-four

Rachel unscrewed the bottle cap and gulped down more ginger ale. She wasn't being much fun, but Simon didn't seem to mind. He was exploring the river bank, watching a flotilla of black ducks on the water and hawks flying overhead, and trying to keep Billy Bob away from the flock of Canada geese resting in the grass a hundred feet away.

Rachel leaned against a tree, keeping an eye on the boy and the dog. The nausea hadn't completely gone away, but it no longer threatened to overwhelm her. She'd thrown up again at home, behind the closed bathroom door while Simon was in the yard with Billy Bob. Apparently she'd put on a convincing act with Simon and he believed she was okay now.

What had made her sick? The pastry was so rich, so sweet, that she'd had enough after three or four bites, but she'd finished it to be polite. Maybe she was paying a price for her good manners. Observation of Simon during the time she'd known him told her he had a cast iron stomach, so she wasn't surprised the pastry didn't bother him. Maybe the evil Jones sisters had tried to poison her just for the fun of it.

That thought brought to mind the cackling witches in a Disney movie and made her laugh aloud.

Simon pivoted in her direction and waved. Rachel waved back, her laughter subsiding to a soft smile. She loved watching him, loved knowing he would always be part of her life with Tom.

Her mind kept circling a thought that thrilled her and terrified her in equal measure: Could she possibly be pregnant? Morning sickness didn't always come in the morning. She should do a pregnancy test. But first she would wait and see if the nausea persisted.

Lost in thought, she jumped when her cell phone rang. She dug it out of her shirt pocket and answered Tom's call. "Hi. What's up?"

His brief silence, followed by a weary sigh, told her something had happened and he hated having to tell her.

Rachel pushed away from the tree, her fingers tightening around the phone.

"There's been another shooting," Tom said.

"Please don't tell me it's Joanna." Nausea roiled her stomach. A mixture of ginger ale and bile rose in her throat. "Please."

"No, no, it's not Joanna."

Rachel went limp and reached out for the tree trunk to brace herself.

"It's Tavia Richardson," Tom went on. "She was killed on Jake Hollinger's farm. I wanted to let you know I'll be tied up for a while, I can't say when I'll be home."

"Tavia Richardson? But why her? She's not opposing the resort development." Rachel wished she could feel more than the usual sadness for a victim, but she'd barely known the woman and hadn't particularly liked her. Rather than grief or pity, Rachel felt a clutch of fear for what this death might mean and what might follow it.

"We've got a lot of unanswered questions," Tom said. "Where are you right now?"

"At the river with Simon and Billy Bob."

"Look, I want you to be careful, okay? Pay attention to anybody who's around you, any car that's behind you on the road." He hesitated. "Maybe you ought to head home. Find a way to keep Simon indoors the rest of the day, without letting him know anything's wrong. I don't know what the hell's going to happen next."

◇◇◇

Tom and Brandon had searched Tavia's house with little expectation of finding anything useful. All they took away with them was a locked fireproof box Brandon had found on the floor in her bedroom closet behind a jumble of shoes and boots, plus a set of small keys Tom found in a desk drawer. The storage box or Tavia's safe deposit box might contain something that would point to her children's whereabouts.

With the box secured in the trunk of the cruiser, Tom drove over to Joanna's horse farm. In the passenger seat beside him, Brandon sat rigid, his hands clutching his knees and his boyish face grave with tension. Tom, used to his deputy's enthusiastic theorizing, felt grateful for Brandon's silence now. Questioning Joanna about a murder was going to be one of the hardest things Tom had ever done as a cop.

Although the Richardson farm abutted Joanna's property in the rear, the route from one front door to the other in a car involved two turns and two roads. The McKendrick horse farm had never belonged to Isaac Jones, but the swath of meadows and farm fields that wrapped around it in an L shape had all been his property before he sold off parcels decades ago to the Kellys, Hollingers, and Richardsons. Tom had never before had reason to consider how easy it was to walk between the farms without using a road. And without being seen.

Ronan Kelly's car was no longer parked outside the McKendrick house, but Sheila Kelly's rental sat in the driveway behind Joanna's Cherokee.

Sheila answered the door, a humorless half-smile twisting her lips. She held the storm door open. "Come to check up on me already? Well, I'm still alive and kicking, as you can see. Ronan got in his car and left after I drove him over here—he didn't stick around. The only assault my brother has committed against me today was verbal." She cocked her head to look past Tom and nod a greeting at Brandon.

Tom could imagine the barbs and accusations that passed between brother and sister during the drive from jail to Joanna's house, and he wasn't interested in hearing her repeat any of it. "I'm glad to see you're okay, but I came to talk to Joanna."

"She's not here right now. She's off somewhere, working." Sheila indicated the whole of the farm with a vague wave of one hand.

"When did she leave?" If Sheila placed Joanna at the house when Tavia was shot, Tom could get back in the car and drive away, a heavy burden lifted.

"I haven't seen her since lunch. Around twelve-thirty. You could call her on her cell phone and come in and wait."

"We'll catch up with her. There aren't too many places she could be."

As he and Brandon started down the steps, Sheila said, "Tom?"

He looked around, but gestured for Brandon to continue to the cruiser. "Yeah?"

"Was that a gunshot I heard a while ago?"

"Yes, it was. Where were you when you heard it?"

"Sitting out here on the porch. Thinking. Trying to figure out a few things. Who was shooting? What happened?"

"Was anybody with you?"

"No, I was by myself." Her expression of concern deepened into alarm. "Just tell me what happened, for God's sake. Has somebody else been shot, or was it just a hunter?"

"Tavia Richardson was murdered on Jake Hollinger's farm."

Sheila's hand flew to her mouth. "Oh my God." Then her eyes widened in outrage and she dropped her hand. "Were you asking if I had an alibi?"

"Something like that."

"Well, I didn't have the slightest reason to hurt Tavia Rich—"

"I'll take your word. Now I need to find Joanna."

For a long moment Sheila's eyes held his, and Tom expected her to launch a defense of Joanna, a protest against the idea that she could kill anyone. Instead, she nodded, her face solemn, then stepped back and closed the door.

"Her brother probably doesn't have an alibi either," Brandon said in the cruiser

"He also had no reason I can see to kill Tavia Richardson." Tom shifted into drive and started down the farm lane. "They were on the same side, and her death is going to slow down the sale of her land. Besides, Ronan doesn't have much to gain anymore. The land sale would help him, but it won't save him."

Beyond the wood frame house where the farm manager and his wife lived, the meadows and horse paddocks stretched out for almost a mile on both sides of the paved lane. Elegant American Saddlebred horses in a variety of colors grazed in small groups, their sleek coats gleaming. Farther on, the barn and the cavernous stable faced each other. At the far end of the pavement sat the small cottage where Rachel had lived for more than two years after she bought Mountainview Animal Hospital and moved to Mason County. At any other time, the sight of the cottage in the distance would be enough to make Tom smile. But even pleasant memories couldn't lighten his mood today.

Brandon broke the silence. "You think anybody working this far out could've heard the shot?"

"Maybe, maybe not. Joanna's house isn't too far from Jake's barn, straight across the fields. But out here, this is a long way from where Tavia was shot."

"There's Mrs. McKendrick." Brandon pointed to the paddock on the right up ahead. "With that devil horse."

Joanna stood in the grass, rubbing the long nose of a big chestnut mare named Marcella. The horse lowered her head and nuzzled Joanna's neck. The three dogs, Joanna's two and the one orphaned by the Kellys, dozed in the sunshine just outside the fence. The Kellys' dog, Tom noticed, wore a leash that was looped over a post. It might be a while before she could be trusted not to run off toward home in search of her owners.

"The only other person who can handle that horse is Holly," Brandon said, with a touch of pride. "I've seen Marcella run to Holly like a puppy, practically begging for attention."

As Tom pulled to the side of the lane, Joanna gave the horse a last pat and walked over to meet them at the fence. She crossed her arms along the top rail. She wore jeans, boots, and a sweater, and her strawberry blond hair was gathered in a wide gold clasp at the back of her neck. "Hey, boys. What can I do for you?"

Tom slammed his door and joined her at the fence, Brandon following him. "I guess you haven't heard the news."

The same alarm and dread he'd seen on Sheila's face spread over Joanna's. "Oh, good God. Now what?"

Genuine apprehension? Or was she fearful because he had sought her out so soon after the killing? He told her what had happened.

Joanna lowered her head to her folded arms and stood that way, her shoulders rising and falling with her rapid breaths. Glancing at Brandon, Tom found the deputy watching her warily, as if he was afraid she might erupt with an extreme reaction at any second. Tom wavered between concern for Joanna's own safety and the reluctant recognition that she could be the person who waited in the woods and fired one expertly placed round through Tavia's chest.

Drawing a deep breath, Joanna lifted her head and swiped at her eyes with the back of one hand.

"You and Tavia weren't close, were you?" Tom asked.

"No. We didn't like each other. But does that mean I can't be upset that somebody murdered her?"

Tom gave a noncommittal grunt. "So you didn't hear the shot?"

Joanna shook her head. "I wouldn't expect to, with all the hills and trees between here and there. Who would do this? Do you have any idea?"

How long, Tom wondered, would it take a woman Joanna's age, in good shape, to run between the Hollinger farm and this end of the horse farm? "Somebody opposed to the resort development. That could be totally off-base, but it's my first thought. Do you know anybody who feels that strongly about it? You've all been getting together, haven't you, to talk about stopping Packard?"

Joanna stared at him for a long moment, her expression gradually turning cold and guarded. She pulled her arms from the rail and folded them across her chest. "I'm not giving you a list of possible suspects, if that's what you're after."

"I don't expect you to do that. But I do expect you to give me any information you've got that could help stop these killings."

Another long, silent stare before she spoke. "I don't know anything that could help you."

Tom nodded. He looked around and saw none of the farm hands. One person who had been here with her, just one…that was all he needed. "Where is everybody?"

"It's Sunday, Tom. Nobody works all day on Sunday. You know that. A couple of the guys will be back to help me get the animals inside before dark."

"Have you been out here all afternoon? Just yourself?"

Her gaze, cold and defiant, held his. "And the dogs. Too bad they can't talk. They can't give me an alibi."

"People are dying," Tom said. "I'm trying to put a stop to it. I can't be worried about anybody's feelings right now."

Joanna's eyes shifted from Tom to Brandon. "Pay attention," she told him. "Tom's going to teach you how to lose every friend you've got in the world."

"I'm doing my job," Tom said.

"Well, I don't have to prove anything to you. You're the one who has to come up with proof. Now I want you to leave. I have things to do, and I don't have anything left to tell you."

Joanna turned and walked off toward the stable, her gait barely short of a jog. The horse, Marcella, snorted and trotted after her.

◇◇◇

During dinner Tom commented that Rachel wasn't eating and asked if she felt okay. She was fine, she told him. Just not hungry. She avoided making eye contact for the rest of the meal. No point in telling him about upchucking the offending pastry, at least not while he was trying to eat.

Later, when they were getting into bed, Tom studied Rachel's face. "You look a little green around the gills."

"Oh, thanks." She smiled as she drew back the covers and slid into bed. Her stomach lurched, but the spasm of nausea was mild and quickly passed. "You say the sweetest things."

He got into bed beside her and propped himself on an elbow. Running a finger along her jaw line, he said, "Seriously, do you feel all right?"

"I'm fine. Really. The Jones sisters tried to poison me today, but I'll survive."

"What?" Tom sat up straight, looking horrified.

Rachel laughed. "Kidding, kidding. They gave me some pastry that didn't agree with me, but I'm perfectly all right now. Come on, let's get some sleep. We both have busy days tomorrow, and we have to get Simon off to school early."

Tom lay down, stretching out his legs. He kissed her goodnight, and gave her a last look, his brow creased with stubborn concern, before he turned off the lamp.

Chapter Twenty-five

Rachel's nausea had faded overnight, but the sight of Lawrence Archer in her clinic threatened to bring it on again. The casual way the Packard Resorts official leaned on the reception desk irritated her. Smug, condescending, insensitive, mercenary—she could exhaust her supply of negatives without fully expressing her dislike for this man.

If she had a choice, she would duck into the back hallway and avoid him, but she had a patient to check out, and that required delivering the chart to the front desk so Shannon could give the kitten's owner a bill and take her payment.

When Rachel approached, Archer's smile widened, the perfect complement to his impeccably creased gray slacks, his blue silk open-necked shirt, and a light suede jacket that looked soft as butter. Not her type—he was no more than a high-end huckster who thought everybody was for sale because he was—but plenty of women would let his good looks and surface charm sway their decisions.

"Hello there," he said. "I've been going around to all the businesses in town to introduce myself, and I wanted to stop by and say hello to you and your staff."

"We're all busy. I'm afraid I can't interrupt everybody's work to introduce you." Rachel handed Shannon the chart with the current day's charge sheet clipped to it. She smiled at the client, a middle-aged woman named Eileen Pearce, and said, "Pepper's a beautiful kitten. I'm going to enjoy watching her grow up. Thank you for giving her a good home."

Archer leaned down to peer into the small carrier Mrs. Pearce held. He wiggled a finger through the metal grill door and cooed, "You're a cute little thing, aren't you?"

The gray tabby kitten let out a bloodcurdling screech and raked her claws down his finger.

"Ow!" Archer jerked his hand away. "Damn it! Shit!" Blood dripped from his finger.

Rachel bit her lip to keep from laughing.

"I'm sorry she scratched you," Mrs. Pearce said, "but you should have more sense than to stick your finger in an animal's face when she doesn't know you. She was already upset about being at the vet's. And I don't appreciate your language, by the way."

Archer forced a smile as he pulled a pristine white handkerchief from his pants pocket and wrapped it around the finger. "You're absolutely right. I just couldn't resist her, she's so cute. I apologize for swearing."

"I'll clean that and put a bandage on it," Rachel told him. She glanced past Archer, through the clinic's glass door. No wonder he was wandering around town instead of staying put in his office across the street. A couple dozen protesters carrying signs milled around outside the store front Packard Resorts had leased. Although Joanna wasn't visible at the moment, Rachel knew she was somewhere in that crowd. Joanna had organized the protest and tried to talk Rachel into joining it.

"Oh, it's just a little scratch, it's fine," Archer said. "I don't want to put you to any trouble."

"Come with me." Rachel motioned for him to follow and didn't wait for a response. She led him down the hall to an empty exam room.

Rachel pulled disposable gloves from a box on the counter and stretched them on. Standing across the exam table from her and looking sheepish, Archer presented the finger for inspection. When she wiped it with alcohol, he reacted to the sting with a gasp. "I'll admit I've always been a coward about anything medical."

Rachel stripped the wrapper off an adhesive bandage. "Yeah, well, you really should be more careful around strange animals."

"Right. Lesson learned."

She wrapped the bandage around his finger and tossed the bloodied alcohol wipe into the hazmat trashcan. "All set. Now, if you'll excuse me, I have to get back to work."

"Could I have just a minute of your time? I won't take long."

"All right, but just a minute. I have patients waiting. What is it?"

"In the short time I've been here," Archer said, "I've come to realize that you're one of the opinion makers in Mason County. Someone other people listen to."

Again Rachel had to clamp down on the urge to laugh. "Oh, really? I can't say I've ever seen myself that way."

Archer smiled. "You're too modest. You're one of the county's most prominent citizens."

Where did he come up with this stuff? Rachel might be married to Tom, but if she lived here until she was a hundred years old, the natives would always consider her an outsider. "What do you want from me, Mr. Archer?"

"Call me Larry, please. And I hope I can call you Rachel?"

"I need to get back to work, Mr. Archer."

He put on a wounded expression that lacked any trace of sincerity. "Work is what I'm here to talk to you about. I'd like to hire you."

"What?"

"Our resort will allow people to bring their pets with them. I'd like to put you on retainer as our official veterinarian, so our guests will know they always have access to the best of care for their pets while they're here, away from home. We'll feature you in our brochure."

Was he for real? "Aren't you getting a little ahead of yourself? You don't even know for sure that you can build a resort here."

"We always think positively. We believe it will all work out in the end. So, can we count on you to look after our guests' pets? I can draw up a contract and offer you an advance on the retainer."

"You want to give me money now, before you've even bought the land?"

"Some of our employees will be coming here during the development stage, and they might want to bring their families with them, including their pets."

"Well, if that happens, and they need a vet, all they have to do is call here and make an appointment, like everybody else. I don't want Packard's money."

He looked at her for a long moment, a half-smile on his face, his gaze speculative. "You're a very direct person, Dr. Goddard."

"I try to be. I don't see much point in anything else."

"Then I'll be direct, too. We *are* going to build this resort. I'd like to have you on our side." He paused. "And I'm not sure you realize the consequences of opposing us."

Rachel stared at him. His tone of voice hadn't changed. His smarmy little smile hadn't faltered. He didn't have an evil maniacal gleam in his eyes. But his message came across clearly. He was threatening her.

"Exactly what consequences are you talking about?"

He sighed and shook his head. "Gosh, I hate to be spreading tales, but—"

"Go right ahead. I promise I won't think less of you." As if it were possible to think any less of him than she already did.

"Well…" He screwed up his face as if it pained him to say what he was about to tell her. "The powers-that-be around here aren't too happy about your opposition to this project."

Was that all? She was relieved, but at the same time she wondered why she'd expected him to say anything she didn't already know. "I'm sure they aren't. But I have a right to my opinion."

Archer nodded with fake solemnity. "Of course. It's just a question of how much you're willing to sacrifice for the sake of your opinion. How much you're willing to hurt the most important person in your life."

"I beg your pardon?" She felt the heat of outrage flooding her face, and she hated knowing he could see her fury.

He raised his hands as if trying to calm her. "I overheard something on Saturday, after the meeting, that worried me, and I wanted to be sure you're aware of it. Maybe your husband's told you all about it, and I'm totally out of line for bringing it up, but I had to make sure."

She had no idea what he was talking about. But she'd be damned if she would admit that to him.

When she didn't respond, Archer leaned against the exam table, hands in his pants pockets, looking as if they were engaged in a friendly exchange. "You know, we've been in situations like this quite a few times, when a community's divided over the whole question of development. We've always found a way around the opposition. If we weren't able to reach an agreement with property owners, the local elected officials have been willing to help bring it about."

"They can't force people to sell private property."

"Oh, you'd be surprised what can be done. Rezoning, increases in property tax rates—and most property owners have no idea how much latitude the courts have given to local government to exercise public domain, if the commercial development is vital for the community's economic survival. Wouldn't you say Mason County's economy is on its last legs? In desperate need of a boost?"

Archer's words chilled Rachel. Was it possible? Could the county take Joanna's land away from her if she refused to sell? She wondered if Tom knew such a thing could happen. "Is that what you overheard on Saturday? The county commissioners plotting to steal people's land and give it to Packard?"

He waved away her question. "No, no. It was something that affects you much more personally. I just thought you should be aware of it, for your sake and your husband's."

"Then why don't you just tell me so I can get back to work." Rachel glanced at her watch, trying to mask her growing anxiety with a show of irritation.

"All right then." He gave her an apologetic little smile. "The local officials have informed your husband in no uncertain terms that if he doesn't control you—I believe that was the expression that was used—if you continue to publicly oppose the development, your husband will suffer the consequences. There are ways, it seems, that an elected sheriff can be removed from office."

Rachel's first impulse was to dismiss this as nonsense. The voters had elected Tom sheriff. The commissioners couldn't take the job away from him. Or could they? She had been a Mason County resident long enough to know that almost anything, from the absurd to the outrageous to the downright illegal, was possible in this insular little mountain community.

If the commissioners had threatened Tom with the loss of his job—threatened him because of her—why had he kept it from her?

That was between her and Tom. Right now the only thing she wanted was to get Archer and his smarmy grin out of her sight. She yanked open the door. "You've delivered your message, loud and clear. Goodbye, Mr. Archer."

"Finally." Tom tossed a handful of business envelopes onto the conference room table. Dennis had been waiting for him to return from the courthouse next door. They'd found only old photographs of Tavia's children in the fireproof box, which was just as well because the prosecutor wasn't happy they'd removed the box from the house and opened it without getting a warrant to make sure all the technicalities were covered. He had ordered Tom to get warrants to open Tavia's safe deposit box and to authorize further searches of the house. "I had to wait for court to recess before I could get the judge's signature."

"Probably not worth the trouble." Dennis took a seat at the table. "If she didn't have her kids' contact information in her address book, and we didn't find anything in the lock box, how likely is it we'll find it in her safe deposit box?"

"I still want to see what she considered worth keeping locked up. There's not much of it, just these envelopes and this." Tom pulled a small plastic bag containing a blue velvet ring box from his jacket pocket and dropped it on the table. "Have you heard anything from Brandon?"

"Yeah, he called a few minutes ago. The pro-development people have started showing up and it's getting noisy, so I sent over a couple more men."

Tom removed his jacket and tossed it over the back of a chair. Taking a seat across from Dennis, he reached for the first envelope on the small stack. "All we need is a brawl in the middle of Main Street. But I'd rather have them fighting in public than shooting each other."

"It doesn't seem to be an either-or question. They're doing both. We've got two killers out there."

Tom didn't answer. He was afraid Dennis was right, and he felt a mounting frustration with their lack of progress in the investigation. Using a finger, he broke the seal on the envelope.

Dennis picked up the bag containing the ring box. "Her wedding ring?"

"Yeah. I doubt she's worn it since her husband died."

"You know, I can understand her, and her kids too, being glad to get rid of the son of a bitch, but I don't understand her kids breaking their ties with their mother. What did she do to deserve that?"

"She reminds them of what their lives were like growing up. And my guess is that they put a lot of blame on her for not getting them away from their father. It's not fair, but that's the way people think." Inside the envelope, Tom found a sheet with Tavia's bank account and credit card numbers and a list of three investment accounts. He set that aside and opened a business envelope with a local law firm's return address in the upper left corner. "Here's her will, or a copy of it."

"She's probably left everything to them. It'll be up to her executor to track them down and find out what they want to do with the property."

"I don't think there's much doubt about what they'll want to do." Tom scanned the first page of the document and raised his eyebrows in surprise. "This will is less than a month old."

"Hunh. Do you think she updated it because she believed she'd be coming into some money from the sale to Packard?"

"Could be," Tom murmured, reading on. Writing a will seemed like a grisly thing to do in the midst of life. He didn't have one himself, although he knew it would be sensible to draw one up now that he and Rachel were married.

"What does it say about her sons and daughters?" Dennis asked.

Tom looked up. "This specifically cuts out her children. She spells it out—they don't get anything."

"Well, I guess the hard feelings went both ways."

Tom's eyes landed on a name in the document. "Damn him."

"What? Who?"

"Jake Hollinger is her sole beneficiary, and he's also the executor."

Dennis shrugged. "Make sense, doesn't it? Weren't they planning to get married?"

"I don't know if marriage was part of the deal. They were planning to live together somewhere else—if they sold to Packard. Everything depended on that. Well, if the deal goes through, Jake Hollinger's going to be twice as rich. He must know about this will, but when I told him I needed to reach her children because they'd have to handle the estate, he didn't say a damned word about it."

"Maybe he was afraid to, because it might make him look guilty," Dennis said. "This inheritance gives him a motive for killing her. But you and Brandon saw him right after the shot was fired. Wasn't he too far away? You're sure he couldn't have killed her, aren't you?"

"Yeah, I'm sure." Tom tapped his fingers on the will. "If we believe she was murdered because she wanted to sell to Packard, the killer could be almost anybody. And Hollinger, maybe the Jones sisters, too, could be in danger. But I still think there's a good chance Hollinger was the target and Tavia was in the wrong place at the wrong time."

"So who would benefit from Jake Hollinger's death?" Dennis asked. "His son?"

"That's assuming his son is his heir. Jake might have changed his will, too, and made Tavia the beneficiary. So if Jake had died instead of Tavia, his property would have gone to her."

"Which would've made Jake's son damned mad, if he knew—" Dennis broke off when his cell phone chimed. He pulled it from his shirt pocket and looked at the display. "Brandon."

"Let me talk to him."

Dennis slid the phone across the table.

"Hey, Brandon, it's me," Tom said. "How's it going?"

"You need to get over here right now." Brandon sounded breathless, frantic. "All hell's breaking loose."

Chapter Twenty-six

Tom saw the commotion from three blocks away, as soon as he turned onto Main Street, and when he powered down his window he heard people screaming insults and threats at each other.

Damn Joanna. What made her think she could stage a protest march without attracting a mob from the other side? What had begun with a dozen men and women marching back and forth on the sidewalk had grown to at least fifty people spilling into the street, yelling, shoving, playing tug-of-war with protest signs.

The Main Street office of Packard Resorts was in easy walking distance of Sheriff's Department headquarters, but Tom had decided to drive over in his cruiser so he'd have a place to stash anybody he arrested. Dennis would follow with the van they used for transporting more than one prisoner at a time.

Tom parked in the middle of the street and waded into the melee in search of his deputies. Opponents parted, stepping back from their confrontations to let him pass, then closed behind him to pick up where they'd left off. He found Keith Blackwood and yanked on his arm to claim his attention. "Get on the outside," he shouted over the racket of the crowd. "Don't stand here in the middle of it." He located Keith's twin, Kevin, and gave him the same order.

Brandon was trying to force two men apart, but the heftier of the two leaned around the deputy and threw a punch at a slight, bespectacled man carrying a protest sign. The second man's glasses flew off and his nose spurted blood. Dropping his sign, he covered his nose with both hands.

Tom grabbed the attacker's arms, jerked them behind his back, and handcuffed him before he realized what was happening. "What the hell?" the man sputtered, craning his neck to see Tom behind him.

"Shut up and settle down," Tom told him.

Brandon was holding back the people around them as the other man, one hand over his bleeding nose, groped for his glasses on the pavement. With the toe of his boot, Brandon nudged them into their nearsighted owner's grasp.

"Put this one in my car, then stay on the outside of the crowd," Tom told Brandon. He foisted the handcuffed man on the deputy.

"Aw, shit," the man groaned as Brandon hustled him away.

Where was Joanna? She'd started this, and now Tom was going to make her help him get it under control. With the advantage of being over six feet, he skimmed his gaze over the heads in the jostling crowd, looking for Joanna's distinctive strawberry blond hair. He spotted her on the sidewalk in front of the plate glass window of the Packard office, and started toward her. The crowd shifted and he lost sight of her again.

The sound of shattering glass abruptly silenced the crowd. All heads turned toward the big window. A jagged hole gaped in its center, with cracks snaking outward on all sides. A cheer went up from some in the street, but most stayed silent.

Swearing under his breath, Tom pushed to the front, where Joanna and another woman peered in through the hole. They seemed not to notice that big shards of glass at the top of the window were loosening as horizontal cracks formed. Tom grabbed both women by the arm and hauled them backward just as the glass broke free and, piece by piece, dropped with a crash to the sidewalk. In seconds, a layer of splintered glass covered the concrete at their feet.

"What the hell do you think you're doing?" Tom demanded. He hadn't seen Joanna break the window, but she'd been the one in the best position to do it. "What do you think you'll accomplish with vandalism?"

Joanna drew back, indignant. "I didn't do this. I was as surprised as anybody else."

"All right, then who did? You were standing right here. You must have seen what happened."

Joanna hesitated, opened her mouth, closed it again, as if debating what tack to take. She decided on defiance. Folding her arms, she returned his angry gaze with a stony stare. "I didn't see a thing."

Tom looked at Maureen McCoy, the other woman he'd pulled out of harm's way. She was in her late thirties but looked younger, with her makeup-free face covered in freckles and her dark hair hanging in a braid down her back. "Did you do this?" Tom asked.

Her gaze darted to Joanna, back to Tom. "No."

"Did you see who did it?"

"No."

Tom turned to the crowd. "Can anybody tell me who broke this window?"

Some of them glared at him. Some dropped their gaze, refusing to meet his eyes.

Tom glanced around, spotted Brandon, and motioned him over. "We're taking both of them in."

"What?" Joanna and Maureen cried in unison.

"Do you want to go peacefully, or do you want us to cuff both of you?"

"You're such a disappointment to me." Joanna shook her head. "Whose side are you on? This is your home. Do you want to see it destroyed by a greedy corporation—?"

"We're not talking about this on the street."

A sudden buzz ran through the crowd, and a man yelled, "Look who's decided to show up."

The drama with Tom and the two women lost everybody's attention as they turned to watch Lawrence Archer approach, ambling up the sidewalk as if he were out for a casual stroll. The crowd was getting worked up again, some of them jeering at Archer and promptly being shouted down in return.

Tom faced them and raised his voice to drown out theirs. "I want everybody off this street in two minutes, or I'll charge all of you with disturbing the peace. We've had enough violence. We don't need you stirring up more."

They hesitated, shuffled around without moving far, waiting with keen curiosity for Archer's reaction to the destruction.

The man stood before the hole that had been a window, scanned the shattered glass on the sidewalk, and looked up at Tom with a wry smile. "I don't suppose you could recommend a skilled glazier?"

"You're on your own, pal."

Tom and Brandon escorted Joanna and Maureen to the van that now sat behind Tom's cruiser in the street. Brandon helped Maureen mount the steps into the back of the vehicle, but Joanna shook off Tom's hand and climbed in unaided. A couple of doors down, the manager and waitresses at The Mountaineer had come outside to observe the fracas.

As he closed the door on the woman who had been a friend to him all his life, he looked across the street to the animal hospital. Rachel stood at her office window, watching, too far away for Tom to read her expression.

Chapter Twenty-seven

The side door leading to the jail opened and Joanna strode into the Sheriff's Department lobby, looking disheveled and angry. Rachel rose from the bench to greet her, braced for an outpouring of fury.

Joanna halted when she saw Rachel. "Don't tell me you bailed me out."

"You didn't need bail. Tom isn't charging you with anything. He let Maureen go too, but I guess you know that already. Her husband just picked her up."

"He's not charging me? Are you kidding?"

Rachel reminded herself that the distrust on Joanna's face and the hostility in her voice weren't aimed at her. For three years Joanna had been a steadfast friend, someone she could lean on, and she believed Joanna regarded her the same way. "He didn't see you do anything. He's not going to hold you responsible without any evidence."

"Well, isn't that magnanimous of him." Joanna raked her tangled hair back from her face and yanked the hem of her jacket to straighten it. "He didn't think twice about dragging us over here and locking us up. You'll have to excuse me if I don't feel grateful right now."

"Joanna—"

"What are you doing here, anyway?"

"I wanted to make sure you're okay."

"I'm fine. Don't concern yourself."

That stung. Rachel stifled her impatience and kept her tone mild. "Of course I'm concerned. I care about you."

Joanna answered with a contemptuous grunt and started for the door.

Rachel fell in step beside her. "Is that so hard to believe? We're friends, aren't we?"

Joanna rounded on her, fixing her with a cold glare. "Your husband came to my farm yesterday and accused me of shooting Tavia Richardson. Has he told you that? If I didn't have you and Robert McClure to give me an alibi, he'd probably think I killed Lincoln and Marie, too."

For a second Rachel could only stare at Joanna, then she fumbled for words. "I'm sorry, I— I didn't know about that."

"Sounds like you and Tom haven't been talking much lately."

That was true enough. What else was he keeping from her? "Listen—"

Deputies Keith and Kevin Blackwood came through the front door, and Rachel moved out of their way. The lanky young men, identical blond twins, nodded in greeting to Rachel, then Joanna, and hurried past as if they wanted to avoid any verbal exchange.

"Listen to me." Rachel stepped closer to Joanna. "You know I don't believe you killed anybody. And I doubt that Tom does. Will you please talk to him? You might be able to help him solve these murders. You knew the victims, you know everybody connected to them. He's desperate to keep anybody else from getting hurt, and you could probably tell him a lot that would help."

"Did he tell you to come over here and waylay me and talk me into cooperating?"

Rachel resisted the impulse to throw back an answer in the same harsh tone. This wasn't the Joanna she knew. This was a woman who felt she was under attack and couldn't help lashing out. "He didn't tell me to do anything and he doesn't know I'm here. I meant what I said. I think you might be able to help the investigation if you sat down with Tom and talked to him."

"Until he tells me to my face that I'm not a murder suspect, I'm not saying a word to him about anything."

All Rachel could do was let her go, and as she watched Joanna shove the door open and storm out, she felt she was letting go of a friendship she had cherished.

Jake Hollinger slumped in a chair in the conference room, his hands laid limp and flat on the tabletop. He had come in willingly at Tom's request but seemed removed from the situation, his mind elsewhere, his eyes dull and unfocused. His rumpled shirt and pants looked as if he'd slept in them, and he had a two-day growth of white stubble.

Tom switched on the tape recorder that lay in the middle of the table and gave his and Jake's names and the date and time. Jake remained indifferent.

"We haven't been able to locate any of Mrs. Richardson's children," Tom said. "Can you remember anything she said that might help us find them?"

Jake shook his head, the slow movement of someone too exhausted to put any effort into it. "She didn't know where they were. All she had were old addresses. They abandoned her years ago. Decades." Tears welled in his eyes. "I was the only person in the world who gave a damn about her."

"How's her cat doing?"

"How do you think? He hates being in a strange place. He wants to go home. He wants Tavia." Jake's voice choked up on the last words.

"He'll settle down after a while. Call Dr. Goddard if you need any help with him."

Jake didn't respond.

"Why didn't you tell me that she wrote a new will and made you her sole beneficiary?"

Jake released a long, weary sigh. "Because I knew as soon as you found out you'd get me in here and throw a lot of questions at me. And here I sit."

"I know you didn't shoot her. I was there, remember?"

"That won't stop you. You probably think I hired a hit man or something."

Tom let that go unanswered. "Did you change your will too and make her the beneficiary?"

He took the slight dip of Jake's head as an affirmative nod.

"Your sole beneficiary?"

"Except the lumber mill."

"Does the mill go to your son Mark?"

Another barely perceptible nod.

"But Tavia would have inherited your land?"

"What does it matter now? She's dead. Why are you asking me about this?"

"How many people knew you changed your will?"

Jake hesitated for a second before he said, "The lawyer. Tavia. I guess the secretary who typed it. And Mark."

"How did Mark feel about it?"

Jake stirred at last, shifting in his chair, sitting a little straighter. "I didn't want him to find out. But he heard Tavia and I went to see the lawyer together. You know how it is. You can't take a piss in this county without fifty people passing around the news."

"Was he angry?"

"Hell, yeah. He hates Tavia. Hated her. He couldn't stand the thought of her getting anything of mine. He thinks he's *entitled* to it all, and I don't have any right to decide who gets it. No right to spend any of it making life easier for myself in my old age. It's all for him and his kids after him. I think he'd be happy if I dropped dead and got out of his way."

Tom stayed silent a moment, waiting to see if Jake would retract what he'd said. He didn't. "That's a strong accusation against your own son."

"It's true." Jake's voice had dropped to an angry mutter. "I didn't know what a selfish little shit he is until that offer from Packard fell in my lap. Then all of a sudden it was gimme gimme gimme."

"What did he say about Tavia when he found out you'd rewritten your will in her favor?"

Before answering, Jake scrubbed his hands over his haggard face and flexed his shoulders. "I caught him at the house, going through my papers. He—"

"When was this?"

"Two, three weeks ago, not long after we saw the lawyer. Mark went in the house while I was in town, and I came home and found him pawing through the file cabinet where I keep financial records."

"He still has keys to your house?"

"He did up to then." Jake rubbed the back of his neck as if trying to loosen the tension there. "I changed the locks after that, he made me so damned mad."

"To get back to my question, what did he say about Tavia when he realized you'd changed your will?"

"Called her a slut, a whore, a schemer, every name you can think of. Said she didn't have any right to the family assets. Those are the words he used, the family assets, like we were some kind of aristocrats with a big estate that had to be passed down to the son."

"It will be a big estate if you sell to Packard."

Jake leaned his arms on the table and hunched his shoulders. "If that happens, it'll be *my* money. And he won't get his hands on a damn penny of it."

"I don't know much about the estate laws, but if you die without changing your will again, won't your son get everything? Now that Tavia Richardson is out of the picture."

"That's probably what Mark's counting on. But I called the lawyer first thing this morning, and I've got an appointment tomorrow. I'll have a new will done and signed by the end of the day." Jake paused, his lips twisting in a bitter little smile. "Provided I live that long."

"What are you telling me? You think your son might have shot Mrs. Richardson? You think he'll come after you next?"

Jake took a long moment to answer, clenching and unclenching his fists. "I'm just saying I'll be sleeping with a gun next to me tonight."

Chapter Twenty-eight

The mother, holding a tiny black and brown terrier, rolled her eyes as her young son and daughter continued their argument at the front desk over the puppy's name.

"It's not a problem." Rachel handed Shannon the billing sheet for the dog's exam and vaccinations. "We can call her 'Puppy' on her file for now and change it when you decide on a name."

"No!" the girl, a freckled eight-year-old named Annabelle, cried. "She needs a name *now*. I want to call her Cindy."

The little terrier yipped.

"See?" The boy, ten-year-old Maverick, looked triumphant. "She doesn't like it either. Her name oughta be Cinder, 'cause she's mostly black."

"Compromise, children," a familiar voice said.

Rachel turned. Winter Jones stood behind her, an imperious figure in a long black coat.

"Call your puppy Deeder," Winter declared.

"Huh?" the boy said.

What was the woman doing here? She didn't have an appointment, and she didn't appear to have a cat with her.

"D-y-d-e-r," Winter spelled out, in the patient but emphatic tone that marked her as a longtime teacher. "A combination of the endings of Cindy and Cinder, pronounced as Deeder."

"I like it," the mother said, a note of desperation in her voice. "Thanks, Miss Jones. How about it, kids?"

The brother and sister held a silent consultation, their gazes locked for a long moment. "Okay!" they cried in unison.

With that, the matter was settled. The family departed and Rachel turned her attention to Winter Jones.

"Were you waiting to see me? Are the rabbits okay?"

"Oh, yes, yes, they're thriving." Winter waved away the question. "I know you're busy and have patients waiting, but I wanted to make sure…" She paused, glanced around in a furtive manner. "Could we speak somewhere more private?"

Rachel wasn't about to take Winter into her office or an exam room. She was afraid she would never get rid of her. "I only have a minute to spare. Why don't we step over here?"

Without waiting for a response, Rachel led Winter to the wall of shelves that held pet toys, beds, and other items for sale.

Her brow creased with concern, Winter spoke in a near-whisper. "I wanted to ask how you're feeling. Are you all right?"

Did she know Rachel had been sick after visiting the Joneses the day before? How was that possible? She recalled joking with Tom about the sisters trying to poison her. But that was only a joke. She didn't believe it. "Why do you ask? Why wouldn't I be feeling okay?"

"Well… Oh, dear. This is simply mortifying."

Winter did appear embarrassed, an emotional reaction Rachel would never have expected to see from her.

Rachel waited for her to continue.

"It appears an ingredient in the pastry we served yesterday was tainted." Winter met Rachel's gaze with earnest, apologetic eyes. "My sisters and I all fell ill shortly after you left, and we could only assume that you and Simon suffered the same digestive upset."

That made sense to Rachel, except for one thing. "Yes, I felt sick, but Simon was fine. He never showed the slightest sign of having an upset stomach."

Relief washed over Winter's face, and she pressed a hand over her heart. "Oh, that is so good to hear. That sweet child—we would all feel terrible if he had suffered any discomfort as a result of his visit with us. And of course we're so very sorry that you were taken ill."

Why would the pastry make four adults sick and leave a child unaffected? "You think the pastry was tainted? How? With what?"

"I'm very much afraid that Beulah is to blame."

"Beulah?"

"Oh, of course, you don't treat livestock, so you don't know Beulah. She's our milk cow. And the source of the cream that was in the pastry. Now and then a noxious weed springs up in our pasture, and we don't realize Beulah has been nibbling on something unhealthy until it turns up in her milk and makes all of us ill."

"Ah. I see." Rachel could believe that. She'd heard stories of people suffering severe allergic reactions and internal inflammation after drinking milk from a field-grazing cow. But still—why didn't Simon get sick, too? Was Winter telling the truth about all three of the sisters getting sick? If she'd concocted the story, that meant only Rachel was affected, and she had no idea how to explain it. "Well, no real harm done. I'm fine now. Have you found the plant?"

"Not yet, but we are on the case." Winter's tone had turned jaunty. "It will be found and extirpated."

"Good. Thank you for letting me know what caused my nausea. I was wondering." Wondering if she could be pregnant. Now that she knew she probably wasn't, she felt an undeniable pang of loss and disappointment. "I'm sorry to rush, but I have a client waiting with her pet."

As Rachel started to walk away, Winter touched her arm lightly to detain her. "Could I take just another second of your time? My sisters and I were so distraught to hear what happened to Octavia Richardson."

Really? Rachel could have sworn they felt only contempt for the woman.

"We can't help wondering who's going to be next," Winter went on. "And we have no way to defend ourselves. We haven't had any firearms in the house since our father died. We feel so terribly vulnerable."

Of course. Rachel should have known Winter's distress has less to do with Mrs. Richardson's death than with the possibility that they were in the crosshairs, too. She couldn't think harshly of them for that. Anybody in their position would be terrified. "I don't know what to tell you, except that it's probably not a good time for all of you to be out searching your pastures."

"Searching our pastures?" Winter looked puzzled.

"For the plant your cow ate."

"Oh! Oh, of course. You'll have to forgive me. I seem to be having more than my share of senior moments these days. You're right, we will have to be more careful. We won't breathe easy until this is over. Is Tom any closer to catching the murderer? Does he have any suspects?"

"I'm afraid I don't know anything I could tell you." Nothing I'm willing to tell you. "Just be careful."

"Yes, dear, we will. Thank you for your concern." Winter gave Rachel's arm a light pat. "And I hope you'll give Joanna McKendrick the same advice."

◇◇◇

"Doesn't look like anybody's been here," Tom said as he pulled into Tavia Richardson's driveway. The yellow crime scene ribbon he and Brandon had stretched across the door, forming a giant X from top corners to bottom, remained in place.

"At least not through the front door," Brandon said.

Tom wanted to collect the guns from Tavia Richardson's basement before somebody walked away with all of them. The tape in itself wouldn't keep looters out, but three murders in the area might be enough to scare them off.

He and Brandon walked around to the back door and found the tape there undisturbed as well. Tom ripped it loose from the top of the door frame and unlocked the door with the dead woman's key.

The kitchen looked much the same as it had the day before, when Tom had disturbed Tavia and Jake's breakfast, but it had the stillness of an abandoned place and felt empty and unused despite the clutter of dirty dishes on the counter by the sink and the green sweater hanging on the back of a chair. The cat's bed and dishes had gone with the cat to the Hollinger house, but a small catnip mouse toy, made of an unnatural red fabric, lay forgotten in a corner.

Tom led the way down the basement steps. They had done a cursory search of the first and second floors following Tavia's death on Sunday, and they hadn't come down to the basement at all. "Let's take a good look around. Make sure there's nothing down here that could help us find her family."

"Does it matter anymore?" Brandon asked. "I mean, she didn't have anything to do with them and didn't leave them anything."

"Don't you think her children ought to know she's dead? Regardless of whether they've been in touch, she was still their mother."

Most of the basement had been used as a recreation room and contained no cabinets or storage boxes that might yield information. Part of the space had been walled off, though, and when Tom opened the door he found it served as furnace room, laundry room, and storage. An old wooden table in the middle held an assortment of tools jumbled together.

"Grab one and start looking." Tom gestured at a stack of eight file boxes next to the gas furnace.

They worked in silence, flipping through old bank statements and tax returns dating back more than thirty years. Only one box held anything promising: a cache of old handwritten letters addressed to Tavia. Tom read a couple with postmarks from Pittsburgh and another Pennsylvania town he'd never heard of. "These sound like they're from relatives. They're old, but we might find somebody who still lives at the same address. Take the whole box out to the car, then come back and help me with the guns."

Feeling around on top of the metal gun cabinet, Tom found the key Tavia had used the day before. He swung the door open and reached for two of the rifles. Then he realized he wasn't looking at the same collection of rifles and shotguns Tavia had shown him.

She'd said one gun was missing. Eleven had been left in the cabinet, and Tom had taken one with her permission. Now only six remained.

He felt like kicking himself. Since yesterday morning, somebody had walked off with four more guns, and because he hadn't checked the cabinet immediately after Tavia's death, Tom had no idea when the theft occurred.

Chapter Twenty-nine

Rachel took a deep breath, grabbed her medical bag from the passenger seat, and hopped out of her Range Rover onto Joanna's driveway. Maybe Joanna had forgotten that they'd rescheduled Rachel's visit to vaccinate the dogs after the Kelly murders sidetracked them on Saturday afternoon. But Rachel had carved time out of her day for this appointment, and nothing short of a door slammed in her face would keep her from doing her job. The dogs needed their vaccines. And Rachel needed to heal the rift in her friendship with Joanna.

As she walked over to them, the three dogs rose from the spot on the front lawn where they'd lain basking in the mellow sunlight. The Kellys' dog, Bonnie, wasn't on a tie-out. She must have settled in enough that Joanna was sure she wouldn't take off.

"Hey, guys, how are you doing?" Rachel crouched and set down her bag so she could devote both hands to scratches and pats. The little mongrel, Riley, stood up with her paws on Rachel's knee and licked her face with excessive enthusiasm. Bonnie still looked a little sad, and when Rachel hugged her she pressed her head into Rachel's neck. Nan, Joanna's aging golden retriever, accepted attention with her usual dignity.

The front door of the house opened and closed again, but Rachel didn't look around. She braced herself for an angry outburst.

That didn't come, but Joanna's voice sounded harsh when she said, "They don't know you're about to stick needles in them."

Rachel glanced her way. Joanna stood on the porch with her arms crossed like a sentry ready to deny admission to the house.

"They know, but they forgive." Rachel rose and picked up her bag.

"Well, I guess there's something to be said for that attitude." Joanna sounded grudging, but her rigid posture loosened a bit and she unfolded her arms. "You want to do this on the porch or inside?"

"The porch is fine. I'm going to include Bonnie. She's due." Marie Kelly had made an appointment to bring the dog to the clinic for a routine visit later in the week. Shannon had called it to Rachel's attention that morning and canceled the visit.

The dogs escorted her across the yard and up the steps. For the next few minutes Rachel focused on the animals, kneeling on the porch to administer vaccines, listen to hearts and lungs, peer into eyes and ears, fend off Riley's slobbering kisses. Joanna, sitting in a wicker chair, answered her questions about the dogs' behavior, diet, and activity in a cool, impersonal tone.

Rachel waited until she was zipping up her medical bag to say, "I need to talk to you about something. I want your opinion."

She saw Joanna tense again as a protective wall went up between them. "Oh?" Joanna said. "What would that be? My opinion doesn't seem to have much value these days."

Sighing, Rachel took the chair next to Joanna's without being invited to sit. "You know, this marriage thing takes some getting used to. All of a sudden we're a unit, not two individuals. I have to answer for what Tom does, even when I don't know he's done it. Even when I don't agree with him."

Joanna grunted. "He's your husband. I'd expect you to go along with him."

"I thought you knew by now how stubborn I am." Rachel grinned. Softly, softly. She didn't want to provoke another outburst by flatly telling Joanna that her assumptions were both wrong and hurtful. "Tom's pretty much given up trying to tell me what to do. And God knows I'd never get away with telling him how to do his job."

For a second Joanna looked as if she might cry, as her eyes filled and her chin trembled. But true to form, she instantly banished all signs of weakness, and the tough, stubborn woman Rachel knew took charge again. "I've known Tom all his life. I've never been so disappointed by anybody. How could he accuse me of murder?"

Rachel doubted Tom had made a bald accusation, but she let it go. It had felt that way to Joanna, and at the moment that was what mattered. "He hasn't discussed it with me. I really don't know what's going on. But I certainly don't think you killed Tavia Richardson."

"Well, I wish you'd tell him that."

"I will. He won't like me interfering, but I will. You know, some people are holding him responsible for my behavior too. I'm sure his life was a lot easier before he married me."

That piqued Joanna's interest and made her swivel her head toward Rachel. She was silent a moment, and Rachel knew she was wrestling with her curiosity as she tried to maintain her chilly aloofness. "Is Tom in some kind of trouble because you spoke out against the resort development?"

"Yeah. Apparently the county supervisors expect him to keep me on a leash. Lawrence Archer stopped by this morning to tell me they've threatened to remove Tom from office if I side with the opposition."

"Oh, for God's sake." Joanna's invisible wall collapsed in the face of her outrage. "Lawrence Archer is a snake oil salesman. You're giving him way too much credit if you believe a word he says."

"I'm afraid it's true, though. They'll invent something they can use under the law to take Tom's job away from him."

"Honey, listen to me. Those bozos on the county board don't have as much power as they pretend they do. And you have a right to your opinion. Don't you ever let anybody take that away from you. Not Tom or anybody else."

Rachel wished it were as easy as holding onto her principles, with no regard for the way her actions affected others. The anxiety she'd held at bay since Archer's visit gripped her now, as all her fears burst from their hiding places like monsters ambushing her from behind doors. She would hurt Tom. She would cost him something he valued. She would never fit in here and would always be a liability. But those were minor worries, dwarfed by her deepest and darkest fear.

"People are getting killed over this, Joanna. If somebody thinks the sheriff is on the wrong side, just because I mouthed off at a meeting—"

"Stop that." Joanna reached over to squeeze her arm. "Don't let yourself think that way."

Rachel searched her friend's face and found, despite Joanna's bravado, an echo of her own terror. "You're scared too, aren't you?"

Joanna pulled in a sharp breath and raised both hands to her face. "Oh, God. I try not to think about it. I try to go about my business, do what I normally do."

"But it's there in the back of your mind."

Joanna dropped her hands to her lap and clasped them tightly. "Always. Every second since Lincoln and Marie—and then Tavia, for no earthly reason. She was on the other side. It's crazy. I don't know what's going on, so how can I protect myself against it? I'm always thinking I could be next."

Rachel nodded. "Winter Jones said pretty much the same thing today. I think she and her sisters feel like sitting ducks."

Joanna's abrupt laugh startled Rachel. "I wouldn't worry too much about them. They hardly ever leave their house, and they can defend themselves if somebody tries to get in."

"Defend themselves how? Winter told me they haven't had any guns in the house since their father died."

"Well, I remember them selling a whole collection of shotguns and rifles to Sam Richardson, but I just assumed they'd kept one for protection."

"Would they know what to do with it?" Rachel couldn't picture any of the Jones sisters wielding a firearm.

"Are you kidding? Isaac Jones made sure all his daughters knew how to use a gun. Somebody told me that when they were kids, he forced them to go hunting with him, and he wouldn't let them come home until every one of them killed something. They'd come back bawling, carrying all these dead squirrels and rabbits, then he'd make them skin the animals and cook them and eat the meat. No wonder they became vegetarians."

"And no wonder they never got married, with that kind of father representing the male gender in their lives." The thought of any child being forced to kill an animal appalled Rachel. "He sounds like a sadistic bastard."

"No, I'm afraid he was just a typical father for these parts. You'd be amazed how many ten-year-olds are out trying to kill some innocent animal to please dear old dad. You know, now that I think about it, I guess it makes sense that they got rid of all their father's guns. But they ought to have one now, just to be on the safe side. In fact, I think I'll tell them exactly that."

Rachel had come here intending to ask Joanna's opinion about the strange pastry incident, but now she felt so sorry for the sisters that she hesitated to say anything accusatory. Winter had explained Rachel's sickness. Simon was lucky enough not to have a sensitivity to the toxic plant the cow had eaten.

The thought of Simon brought her to her feet. "I have to pick up Simon before I go home. Tom's aunt and uncle are keeping him after school while Tom and I are both at work."

Joanna rose to see her off. "When are Darla and Grady coming back?"

"Tomorrow or Wednesday, if the news is good. If it's not, they might stay a little longer while the doctors work out a new treatment regimen."

"Well, let's hope for the best. We've seen enough tragedy lately to last us a while." Joanna startled Rachel by stepping closer and pulling her into a tight hug. "You be careful, okay? Don't go out walking or running alone, and keep Simon close to home. Remember there's a nutcase running around loose with a gun."

Chapter Thirty

The tangy smell of raw pine, pleasant enough when Tom split kindling for the fireplace, stung his nostrils when he crossed a lot where thousands of boards lay bound into pallets. The whine of high-speed saws inside the lumber mill drowned out every other sound in the yard.

The mill looked like what it was, a relic of the early twentieth century, a big wooden building so weathered that no trace of exterior paint remained. It sat on a strip of flat land between steep hills, bordered by the paved road on one side and railroad tracks on the other.

A man using a forklift to load pallets on a flatbed truck paused his work to let Tom pass in front of him, and Tom threw up a hand to thank him.

One side of the building stood open, the metal door of the bay rolled up. Half a dozen men in hard hats and thick plastic ear muffs moved around the cutting floor, shepherding logs along the conveyers to saws that sliced off the bark, then cut the wood into narrow boards.

Wishing he had a pair of earplugs, Tom pulled open a door marked OFFICE. The large room he entered had a counter along the front and three desks, none of them occupied, spaced out farther back. Tracked-in sawdust and bark slivers littered the floor, and a fine film coated the counter. Somewhere a phone was ringing, barely competing with the noise from the mill's saws, but Tom didn't see it and couldn't pin down its location. The small brass bell on the counter almost made him laugh. Was he supposed to tap on that little thing to get somebody's attention? He'd have better luck using telepathy.

A door at the side of the room opened, and the decibel level rose enough to make Tom's ears ring. Mark Hollinger strode in, wearing a hard hat and ear muffs, and closed the door on the worst of the noise. He started when he saw Tom on the other side of the counter. Knowing the other man couldn't hear him, Tom lifted a hand in greeting.

Mark lifted his hard hat and slid the ear muffs' metal band off his hair and down around his neck. He fixed his strange silvery blue eyes on Tom as he approached. "What can I do for you?"

Tom raised his voice to answer. "I need to talk to you."

"I'm busy." The phone rang again, and Mark reached under the counter and came up with the receiver. "Hollinger Lumber," he said, loudly enough to be heard over the background noise.

What was it like, Tom wondered, to spend every working day, all day long, shouting?

"Yes, sir," Mark was saying. "We're loading it right now. It'll be on the road at daylight, ought to reach you by midday tomorrow. Yes, sir. Thank you for the business."

The receiver disappeared under the counter again. Mark frowned at Tom as if annoyed that he was still there. "I'm busy," he repeated.

"I need to talk to you. Is there anyplace quiet?"

Mark let his shoulders slump and screwed up his face in a peevish expression. Without speaking, he rounded the corner and stalked out, not bothering to hold the door. Tom caught it before it could slam shut.

Outside, Tom took the lead, gesturing for Mark to follow him to the cruiser parked outside the high chain link fence.

Once there, Mark balked at getting into the car for their chat. "We can talk standing right here. What's this about?"

Tom leaned against the front fender and crossed his arms. "I want to talk to you about your father's will. And Tavia Richardson's murder."

"That's got nothing to do with me."

"I heard you weren't happy about your father leaving everything to Mrs. Richardson."

Mark fidgeted, adjusting the position of his hat. "He wasn't going to leave her everything. I'd still get the mill."

"But his land, and all the money from selling it to Packard—provided he does sell—all that would have gone to her."

Hot color flooded Mark's face. He stared past Tom, his jaw set in a hard line.

Tom persisted. "Did you know your father was planning to move away with Mrs. Richardson if they sold their land to Packard?"

"He doesn't talk to me about his so-called love life."

Tom allowed the anger underlying Mark's bitten-off words to build for a few seconds before going on. "It must have been hard on you, all the rumors about the two of them while your mother was dying."

"It's not like she was the first. He had other women. I don't know how my mother put up with it."

"He must have cared about Tavia Richardson, to make her his beneficiary. He says he loved her."

The ugly sound Mark spat out sounded like a cross between laughter and strangulation. "Like he knows the meaning of the word. He wasn't thinking about her. He was thinking about me, how he could slap me down, teach me a lesson."

Tom kept his voice neutral. "I know a lot of fathers and sons that don't get along, but I'm having trouble understanding why your dad would want to cut you off, especially since you're a hard worker and he's leaving the mill to you."

Too wound up to keep still, Mark paced back and forth beside the car, flinging his hands around in broad gestures as he spoke. "He knows I don't respect him. I'll never forgive him for what he did to my mother. So he wants me to fail. He doesn't give a damn what happens to the business when he's gone. If he did, he'd be investing in it, bringing it into the goddamn twenty-first century. Other mills have got computers running the machines, but we're still operating like it's 1950. We'll be lucky if we get any business from the resort development."

"Now that Tavia Richardson's gone, maybe your father will change his mind."

Mark shook his head. "That'll be the day. He'd leave everything to that woman's cat before he'd leave it to me."

If Mark believed he had no chance of inheriting anything but the lumber mill from his father, he had no financial motive to kill Tavia or Jake. But hatred was always a stronger motive than money. Mark had no reason to kill the Kellys, though, unless his motive was so deeply concealed that Tom hadn't caught a glimmer of it. "Was your father really here on Friday? Did he ask you to lie for him?"

"Soon as you left his place that day, after he fed you that story, he called me and told me what to say when you got around to asking. He made some promises if I'd go along, but I found out soon enough he didn't mean a word of it."

Tom nodded. That kept Jake in the picture for the Kelly murders. But he hadn't killed Tavia. "He told me he's changing his will again, to make sure there's no loophole that'll let you inherit. So Mrs. Richardson's murder hasn't done anything for you. Unless you hated her so much that just knowing she's dead gives you satisfaction."

Still pacing, Mark stumbled over a rock half-hidden in weeds and swore under his breath. He delivered a swift, hard kick that sent it sailing through the air. It banged into the chain link fence and dropped to the ground. Mark stood with his hands on his hips, shaking his head, anger and frustration mixing on his face. "When I first heard she was dead, I was glad. But it doesn't change anything. It doesn't change what the two of them put my poor mother through."

"Where were you yesterday afternoon?"

He took a minute to answer. "Hiking. Trying to think, figure some things out."

"By yourself? Can anybody back that up? Did anybody else see you?"

Mark raised bleak eyes to Tom's. "Not a soul."

Chapter Thirty-one

Tom dropped the faxed ballistics report, a single sheet, onto his desk after reading it. Leaning back in his chair, he rubbed his tired eyes. "We've got nothing," he said to Dennis and Brandon. "We can't seem to get off square one."

Brandon leaned against the window sill, the darkening sky at his back. "You think the gun that killed Tavia Richardson was stolen from her house?"

"Maybe," Tom said. "But maybe not. We don't have any way of knowing for sure what she had and what's missing. Whoever got into her house must have had a key, and was smart enough not to leave fingerprints. Hollinger swears it wasn't him, for whatever that's worth."

Dennis, slouched in a chair facing the desk, said, "At least we know the gun we found at the scene is the one that killed her."

"But it wasn't used to kill the Kellys. And the rifle I took from her house wasn't either."

"So what does all this tell us?" Dennis asked. "Two killers? One killer using different guns?"

"But remember that the Kellys and Mrs. Richardson were on opposite sides of the development fight," Brandon reminded them.

"We know Jake Hollinger didn't shoot Tavia." Tom picked up a pencil and tapped it absentmindedly against the edge of the desktop. "But he *could* have shot the Kellys. He lied about his whereabouts and told his son to back him up."

"And his son could have killed Tavia," Brandon said. "Mark had plenty of motive."

"Father and son killers?" Tom shook his head. "It's possible, but how likely is it?"

"Well, greed does seem to run in families," Dennis said.

"Speaking of greed, what's Ronan Kelly been up to?"

"He's still at his parents' house. I had guys go by there a couple of times to check. And Sheila's been busy making funeral arrangements. I've been doing as much as I can by phone, checking on their movements, and neither of them was anywhere near Mason County when their folks were killed. You still think Ronan could've paid somebody to do it because he thought he was going to get half their assets?"

"Yeah, I think he's capable of it. Proving it is something else." Tom dropped the pencil and sat forward. "We've got a whole county that's divided over the Packard project. A whole county full of suspects. And not an ounce of solid evidence against anybody."

"What about Joanna McKendrick?" Brandon said. "She's got an alibi for the Kellys, but not Tavia Richardson."

For a long moment they were all silent, the only sound in the room the scrape of Brandon's boot soles on the floor as he shifted position. Tom couldn't forget the way Joanna had looked at him when he'd questioned her at the horse farm. Her sad disappointment had cut more deeply than her anger. If they came out the other side of this crisis with somebody else in custody, would she ever forgive him for believing her capable of lying in wait and murdering a defenseless woman in cold blood? Did he believe that?

Tom thought anybody was capable of anything if pushed hard enough. And Joanna had gone off the rails. She hadn't been herself since the Packard proposal was announced and the company had started pressuring her to sell her land. Even so, he saw her as a more likely victim than a killer.

"Tom?" Dennis broke into his thoughts.

"I'm not ruling anybody out. Maybe we've got people on both sides who are willing to commit murder to get what they want. Maybe we're making a mistake to keep looking at their families, the people close to them. There might be an angle we haven't even considered, some connection between these murders that we're not seeing."

"Then we'll keep digging until we unearth it," Dennis said.

Tom blew out a sigh and glanced at the window. The lights in the parking lot had blinked on while they'd been talking, as the sky faded from deep blue to black. "Let's all go home and get some rest. If anything happens overnight, short of another shooting, the Blackwood twins can handle it. Maybe tomorrow's the day we'll catch a break."

"Tom's home!" Simon slid off the stool and barreled out of the kitchen and down the hall with Billy Bob trotting behind.

Rachel, cutting up vegetables at the counter, paused to listen to Simon's chatter and Tom's responses. Without seeing them, she knew they stood by the open door of the hall closet while Tom stripped off his equipment belt and holstered pistol and stashed them out of Simon's reach at the back of the shelf. Their words were indistinct, but the rhythm of their voices made her smile. She could imagine this scene playing out every night, a child—or children—of their own running to greet Tom. Someday, Rachel thought. But the part of her that still couldn't believe in her happiness added its insidious whisper: *If we ever learn to trust each other completely.*

"I'm starving," Tom said as he came into the kitchen with Simon and Billy Bob in tow. He kissed Rachel and patted Frank the cat, who had been napping on a chair. "Let me get out of my uniform and Simon and I will take care of setting the table."

Simon followed him out, eager to share his teacher's astonishing revelations that day about the inner workings of volcanoes. "Can you *believe* that?" Rachel heard him say as they started up the stairs.

The telephone rang. Still smiling at Simon's excitement, Rachel grabbed the receiver of the wall-mounted phone. Her smile faded when she heard the strained voice of Simon's grand-mother, Darla Duncan.

"What's wrong?" Rachel gripped the coiled phone cord in her fist, winding it around and around her hand.

"Can Simon hear you?" Darla's voice broke on the last word, and Rachel heard her husband, Grady, murmuring in the back-ground. "No, I'll tell her myself," Darla said to him, her voice muffled as if she'd placed a hand over the mouthpiece.

Rachel freed her fingers from the twisted cord and leaned her palm and forehead against the wall. "Simon's upstairs with Tom." She tried to keep her voice level, but it sounded like a hoarse croak to her own ears. "But he'll be back in a minute."

Darla drew an audible breath. Her voice had turned brisk when she spoke again. "We wanted to let you know we have to stay another couple of days. Maybe until the end of the week. Can you manage Simon that long?"

Sudden tears burned Rachel's eyes and her throat closed up. She forced her words out. "Of course we can. We love having him. Darla, what's—what did the doctors say?"

"It's not too bad, not really. They want to do another test or two, get another doctor's opinion. I'll give you all the gory details when we come home."

It's spreading, Rachel thought. It's not going away. "Don't worry about Simon. We'll take good care of him."

"I know you will, honey. He couldn't be in better hands."

Rachel heard Simon's cheerful voice then, and the *thump thump thump* of his footsteps on the stairs. She wonder, irrel-evantly, how one small boy could make as much noise as a herd of hoofed stock. Blinking to clear her eyes, she told Darla, "Simon's coming down. Do you and Grady want to talk to him?"

While Simon spoke with his grandparents, Rachel held Tom's gaze, and without words they shared their fear and sadness and their determination to keep up a good front for the boy's sake. Whatever Darla and Grady told Simon must have been reassur-ing, because he hung up with a smile on his face and launched into a description of the great book about dinosaurs his grand-parents had found for him.

By the time they got Simon to bed, Rachel felt drained, exhausted by the effort of pretense during dinner and early evening. In the privacy of their bedroom, she and Tom put their arms around each other.

"Darla's tough," Tom said. "Let's hope for the best."

"I feel terrible for her and Grady." Rachel's voice was muffled against his shoulder. "And Simon. That poor little boy has so lost so much already."

"He hasn't lost us, and he's not going to."

No, he wouldn't. Tom would always be here for Simon, and so would she. Suddenly she didn't know why she'd cared about Tom keeping the county officials' threats from her. Even his suspicion of her good friend Joanna seemed unimportant. It would work out. Tom would arrest the real killer, and Joanna would eventually concede that he had simply been doing his job.

They showered and went to bed. Tom fell asleep quickly, but Rachel lay awake, staring at shadows on the ceiling and trying not to think, not to let her mind wander to the unknowable future. She was still awake when the telephone rang a few minutes past two a.m.

The sound didn't surprise her. This call, whatever it might be, felt like something she'd been expecting, dreading. Tom stirred as she reached across him in the dark to grab the receiver.

The young female dispatcher blurted an urgent summons. She added, "I know the sheriff didn't want to be called tonight, but I figured this is too important—"

Tom pushed himself upright and switched on the lamp.

Rachel handed him the receiver. "Somebody set fire to Joanna's stable."

Chapter Thirty-two

Tom jumped out of his cruiser and sprinted toward the chaos.

Fire roared from a hole in the stable's roof, spewing burning cinders into the air. Whipped by the wind, the flames lit up the night sky and cast a reddish glow over a towering cloud of smoke. A Mason County fire truck sat sideways on the road, its headlights and flasher illuminating the ground around the stable. Two firefighters held a hose, alternately directing a stream of water at the blaze and dousing the red-hot cinders that threatened the undamaged part of the roof.

In the paddock next to the stable, terrified horses crowded together, snorting and whinnying and stamping, their eyes reflecting the fire's glow. Joanna and two of her ranch hands moved among the horses, stroking their necks and patting their sides.

Sheila Kelly stood outside the paddock in semi-darkness, her arms folded and shoulders hunched against the chill wind. Tom joined her and called Joanna's name.

Joanna left the horses and ran to the fence. "Marcella's still in there!" she cried. The firelight threw flickering red and orange shadows across her face. "They wouldn't let me go in and get her."

"Let the fire chief and his men get her out," Sheila pleaded. "You can't go in a burning building."

"But they can't manage her. She's going to die in there."

A strong gust of wind blew smoke and ash their way and made all of them cough.

"Just hang on," Tom said. "They'll get her out. What the hell happened here anyway?"

"It was arson. Somebody deliberately set fire to a building that had twenty horses in it." Never taking her eyes off the stable, Joanna raked her disheveled hair off her face with both hands. In the poor light, her hair looked wet, and so did her jeans and sweatshirt, but she didn't seem to care about being drenched in the cold night air. "Some little shit called me, woke me up, said I'd better get my horses out before they burned to death. Then he laughed, can you believe that? And I heard somebody else laughing in the background. There were two of them."

"Boys? Men?" Tom asked.

"They sounded like kids. Teenagers."

"Did their number show up on your Caller ID?"

She shook her head. "It was blocked."

"We can still get it. We'll find out who did this."

"Right now all I care about is Marcella." She bounced up and down on her toes. "God, what's taking so long in there? I've got to go in and get her myself." She started to move away from the fence.

Tom reached over the rail and caught her arm. "No, Joanna. It's too dangerous, and the firemen shouldn't have to worry about you and the horse both."

"Please listen to Tom," Sheila said. "You know he's right."

Joanna yanked her arm free of Tom's grip, but instead of bolting she leaned on the fence and buried her face in her folded arms. Sheila patted her shoulder.

After a moment Joanna raised her head and swiped at her eyes with the back of a hand. "Thank God for the sprinkler system. But part of the roof was already falling in by the time I got here. If I'd been a few minutes later I couldn't have got half of them out."

"So that phone call saved their lives," Tom said.

"But I left Marcella in there, way in the back where the fire is. I'll never forgive myself. Why didn't I get her out?" She covered her face with hands.

"You did all you could." Tom added, hoping it would help, "Rachel's coming any minute. She had to wait for my aunt and uncle to come over to the house and stay with Simon. She'll be here if Marcella needs her." Time seemed to be crawling by although he knew he'd only been there a few minutes. How long could it take to get one horse out, even a cranky one like Marcella? For a second he considered going in to help, but he knew he'd be ordered out when the fire chief spotted him.

"Look!" Sheila grabbed Tom's sleeve and shook it. She pointed toward the front of the stable. "They've got her."

Joanna was already running that way. Tom jogged after her.

Light spilled from the barn directly across the narrow farm road and fell on the scene in the wide stable doorway. The fire chief, his coat and hard hat dripping water, was backing out and pulling the furious chestnut mare by her halter. Marcella tossed her head, snorted and reared, forcing the chief to let go. She slammed her front hooves down, barely missing the man's head and shoulder.

Joanna approached the mare, crooning, "Marcella, Marcella, come on, girl, it's me, Marcella. Calm down, girl, calm down, you're okay now."

The horse whinnied and shook her head again, sending drops of water flying in every direction. A smattering hit Tom's face, and he wiped the water away with his sleeve as he moved in to help Joanna.

Two firefighters behind the horse tried to push her all the way out, but she bucked and kicked backwards. Tom heard one man let out a loud "Oof!" and guessed Marcella had landed a punch in his stomach.

Joanna grabbed one side of the halter and Tom the other, and together they guided Marcella into the paddock. A haze of smoke hung in the air, and Tom heard a timber crack as more of the stable roof collapsed. The fire, though, was dying down under the relentless stream of water pumped up from Joanna's well and fed through the fire hose.

Rachel appeared, marching out of the darkness with her medical bag, and followed them into the enclosure. "Are they all safe?" she asked Joanna.

"Yes, thank God, but Marcella was in there the longest."

Rachel dropped her bag on the ground, unzipped it, and pulled out a flashlight. "Hold her still if you can. Let me check her for burns and cuts."

The horse didn't want to stand still. She wanted to spin in circles, complaining and kicking up clods of grass and dirt. Together Tom and Joanna kept her from breaking free, and Rachel moved with her, playing the light over her body from neck to flanks.

"She has a burn on her right flank," Rachel reported.

"Oh, no," Joanna groaned.

"Don't panic. It's not bad. But she won't like me cleaning it, so hold on tight."

Easier said than done, Tom thought, bracing himself for a kick or a bite. The sharp odor of alcohol cut through the stench of smoke and horse sweat as Rachel prepared a gauze swab. Tom and Joanna both threw arms around Marcella's neck, gripping the halter with their free hands. Tom leaned his weight against the horse to steady her. When Rachel dabbed the burn with alcohol, Marcella whinnied and jerked, trying to turn her head toward the source of the pain. The ripple of her powerful muscles sent a tremor through Tom's body.

"Good girl," Rachel crooned. "Now I'll put on something to make it stop hurting."

Tom noticed that the other horses were calming down, growing quieter, as Joanna's employees moved from one to another, touching them and talking to them. Marcella finally stopped struggling and stood still while Rachel applied medication and a bandage. The fire was dying down, and when Tom glanced at the sky, he saw the nearly full moon through a break in the cloud of smoke.

"Now what?" Joanna said when they let the horse go. "Where am I going to put twenty horses? I'd better see if any of the stable's usable."

"Let me go talk to the chief first," Tom told her. "Hang on for a couple minutes."

The fire chief stood in the undamaged front section of the stable, shining a handheld spotlight into the interior. He and Tom walked down the wide center aisle, inspecting every stall and the ceiling above it.

"No damage past the back end," the chief reported. "Aside from everything being wet, I'd say seventy-five percent of the structure's sound."

"You think it was arson?"

"Oh, yeah, no doubt about it. Looks like somebody threw a fire bomb, maybe more than one, on the roof at the rear. A lot of accelerant. I could smell kerosene when we first got here. It burned right through the roof to the rafters."

"Joanna said some kid called her and told her the stable was on fire. Laughing about it."

The chief grunted. "Let's hope the little s.o.b. was dumb enough to use his own phone. I sure would like to get my hands on him for about five minutes."

The same thought had crossed Tom's mind. "I guess Joanna can't put the horses back in here tonight."

"Not till it's cleaned up and aired out. She'd better make other arrangements, at least for tonight."

Tom nodded. "I'll call the State Police and ask for a crime scene unit to go over the ground out back. Come see me tomorrow, after you work up a report. When I catch these kids, I want to throw everything I can at them."

Outside, he discovered Winter Jones, Jake Hollinger, and Ronan Kelly had arrived while he was in the stable with the chief. Jake had left his truck's headlights on, and he stood in the glare with Winter, Ronan, and Sheila, all of them clustered around Joanna. Rachel had joined them and seemed to be arguing with Jake.

"I don't think that's a good idea," she said. "They've been stressed enough without being loaded in a trailer and moved to a strange place in the middle of the night."

"They'll be fine," Jake said. "My barn's big enough for half of them."

Tom interrupted to give Joanna the fire chief's assessment of the stable's condition.

After thinking it over, she said, "Thank you, Jake, I appreciate the offer, but they can all stay in my barn until morning. They'll be a little crowded, but they'll be okay and out of the night air. By the end of the day tomorrow my men can have the hole in the roof covered and the inside cleaned up. Thank you all for coming over. Now go on home and get back to bed."

"We need to talk about this right now," Jake protested. "I'm afraid something like this is going to happen again. I don't know about the rest of you, but I've been getting threatening letters. I already gave them to Tom. Tavia got some too."

"I found some letters at Mom and Dad's house tonight," Ronan said. "Unsigned. Full of crazy threats."

"Oh my God," Sheila said. "Death threats?"

"Yeah. And they sure as hell weren't idle threats, were they?"

"I want to see those letters," Tom said. "I'll come and get them in the morning. Don't handle them any more than you have to. Miss Jones, what about you and your sisters? Has anybody been threatening you?"

"Well, we have had some very nasty phone calls lately." Winter pulled her long black coat closer around her. "My sisters and I don't feel safe at all. We're so afraid someone is going to attack us on our own property. In our own house."

So why the hell didn't you tell me you're getting threats? "You should have told me this earlier. We can find out where the calls originated. I'll be over to see you in the morning, too, and I want you to try to remember everything—what was said, what the voices sounded like. Everything, all right?"

"Yes, of course, Thomas." Winter sounded chastened, a first in Tom's memory.

Tom turned to Joanna. "Did anybody threaten you before this happened?"

She sighed, sounding and looking exhausted. "I got some letters. Just garbage full of misspelled words and foul language, telling me I'd be sorry if I didn't get out of the way and sell my

land to Packard. Nothing about burning down my barn and killing my horses. If I'd thought something like that might happen,
I would have had somebody guarding the stable all night."

"We could all be at risk," Jake said. "It could be one of our
houses set on fire next time."

"You and Joanna are on opposite sides of the land sale issue,"
Tom pointed out. "If somebody's trying to drive Joanna out,
why would they bother you, when you've already decided to
sell to Packard?"

"Retaliation. Getting back at the other side. We've got our
own little civil war going on here, haven't you noticed? And it's
escalating."

"We're doing our best to get things under control."

"Well, we can see how that's going." Jake flung an arm in the
stable's direction. "And you still don't seem to have any idea who
killed Linc and Marie. Now Tavia's dead. When's it going to end?"

Rachel opened her mouth to shoot back an answer, but Tom
shook his head and she stayed silent. Reining in his temper, he
managed to keep his voice level. "I'm not denying we've got a
bad situation here. But we'll find out who's behind the murders,
and sooner or later we'll find out who set this fire."

"Tom," Sheila said, "do you think the person who started the
fire is the same one who killed Mom and Dad? Since they were
on the same side of the resort issue as Joanna."

Joanna shook her head. "I think kids set my stable on fire.
Vandals. Not cold-blooded killers."

"I think you're probably right," Tom said. "But I'm not ruling
anything out."

"I've got a pretty strong suspicion about who killed my parents," Ronan said. He glared at Jake Hollinger.

"What the hell are you looking at me for?" Jake demanded.

Tom raised his hands. "Stop it, both of you." What brought
this on? The first time Tom had suggested Jake Hollinger as a
suspect, Ronan dismissed the idea. "Ronan, if you've got something to say, then say it to me. Don't throw out accusations in
the middle of the night when everybody's worn out."

"I'm going to take care of my horses," Joanna said. "If you all want to fight, please do it somewhere else."

As Joanna rejoined her employees in the paddock, Tom told the others, "Let's all go home. The fire chief has to finish his inspection and Joanna has to get her horses settled for the rest of the night, and they don't need anybody else underfoot."

Jake shot another venomous look at Ronan, then climbed into his truck. He made a tight U-turn on the narrow pavement and sped off, tires screeching.

Tom blinked, trying to adjust to the sudden absence of Jake's headlights. Ronan, his sister, and Winter lingered, as if each was waiting for the others to leave.

"Ready to go?" Rachel asked Tom.

"Yeah, I am." Tom looked from Winter to Ronan. "I'll talk to both of you in the morning. Go home now and get some sleep."

Sheila tugged her brother's arm. "Come on, Ronan. You can give me a ride back to Joanna's house."

He shook off her hand and spoke to Tom. "There's something you need to see. Besides the letters, I mean."

"What? Is it something to do with your parents' deaths?"

Ronan threw a wary glance at Winter as if reluctant to say more in front of her. "I think it might. It could, anyway. I don't know. I can't be sure. You need to see it and figure out what it means." He shook his head. "I don't know what to make of it. It might not mean anything."

Why didn't Ronan come right out and tell him what it was? Why didn't he want to spell it out in front of Winter? "You want to show it to me now?"

"Oh, Ronan, for heaven's sake," Sheila said. "Can't it wait until morning? These people want to go home and get back to sleep. Come on. Let's go."

Ronan hesitated, then gave in. "Yeah, yeah, it can wait a few hours." As his sister pulled him away, he said over his shoulder, "You'll come to the house in the morning?"

"I'll be there." Tom was beginning to think he'd spend the whole day in this neighborhood.

"What do you suppose that's about?" Rachel asked, watching Ronan and Sheila go.

"God only knows. Miss Jones, can I walk you to your car?"

"Oh, thank you, Thomas. My eyesight isn't very good in this poor light." She looped her arm around his. "I'm getting to the age when I'm always afraid of stumbling and falling."

With Rachel on her other side, they accompanied her down the road, past Tom's cruiser and then Rachel's Range Rover. A little farther along, car doors slammed and Ronan's headlights flashed on. The three of them moved out of the way so he could turn around. As the car passed, Sheila waved from the passenger seat.

When they resumed walking, Winter said, "I confess I'm terribly curious about what it is Ronan wants to show you. He sounded so urgent. Thomas, what do you suppose it is?"

"I have no idea."

"Could it relate to Lincoln and Marie's deaths?"

Could I get that lucky? Tom wondered. He'd be willing to bet it would be nothing. The threatening letters interested him more. "I can't even begin to guess."

"He's such a hotheaded boy," Winter said as they reached her old station wagon. "He always has been. But do you think he was insinuating that Jacob Hollinger was the one who killed Lincoln and Marie?"

"I'm afraid I can't discuss that with you." Tom opened the car door for her. "I'll come by tomorrow and we'll talk about ways to make you and your sisters feel safer."

"Thank you, Thomas. But I do wonder—"

"Good night, Miss Jones." Tom took Rachel's arm and set off toward their vehicles at a brisk pace.

"Nice try," Rachel said, "but don't think you're going to stop her from gossiping about all this."

"At least I didn't feed her any extra tidbits. God, I can't wait to get back in bed. I have a feeling tomorrow's going to be a hell of a day."

Chapter Thirty-three

Under a clear morning sky and a bright sun, the stable and barn area looked much the same as always to Rachel—except for the dark streaks down the side of the stable and the gaping, black-rimmed hole in its roof. Horses draped with blankets grazed in the surrounding paddocks as if their night hadn't been interrupted by a terrifying fire.

Rachel found Joanna inside the stable, using a push broom to clear sodden straw out of a stall.

When she saw Rachel, Joanna gestured at the mess around her. "Welcome to my own personal disaster area."

Rachel could tell she'd never gone back to bed. Exhaustion had turned her skin pasty and darkened the half-circles under her eyes. She'd changed out of her wet clothes from the night before, but her fresh jeans were already splattered with grime up to her knees.

"It's really not as bad as I expected," Rachel said. "Most of it's still usable, right?"

"Yes, thank God. After we get it cleaned up and dried out."

The four men Joanna employed wielded brooms, pitchforks, and shovels, cleaning the two rows of stalls and loading the detritus into wheelbarrows. The stench of smoke stung Rachel's nose and throat even now, hours after the fire. No one had touched the rear of the building, where chunks of charred wood covered the floor and a fallen timber had demolished the door and one wall of a stall. Sunlight streamed through the hole in the roof and glinted off a pool of filthy water in the center aisle.

Rachel returned the men's greetings, but she couldn't muster a smile for them. The sight of the damage, and the thought of the malice behind it, sickened her.

Joanna leaned on the broom handle, looking toward the rear. "We need to get that hole covered, but we have to wait until the guy from the insurance company takes a look at it."

"Is he coming today?"

"Later this morning. Then I've got a builder coming after lunch to give me the bad news about the cost of repairs. God, this makes me want to organize a lynching party. All of my horses could've died last night."

"Tom's going to get the phone records," Rachel said. "He seems sure he can find out who called you. Maybe by the end of the day the kids who did this will be in jail."

"They'd damn well better pay a price for it. This ought to teach their parents a lesson. Kids hear mom and dad talking about me like I'm the devil incarnate because I won't knuckle under, and they get the idea I'm fair game."

"I'm sure you're right about that." And organizing a protest and getting arrested had made Joanna an even more inviting target. Yet how could anyone tell her she was wrong to fight back against the people trying to force her off her land?

Joanna went on, "The crazy thing is, Packard wants my stable so they wouldn't have to build one. They'd take my horses too if I'd sell them. So whoever set the fire wasn't doing the developers any favors." She propped the broom against a stall door. "Come on, I'll make Marcella behave while you check on her. I've got a pocketful of sugar."

The chestnut mare proved more cooperative than she'd been during the night. While Joanna fed her sugar cubes, Rachel examined the burn on Marcella's flank, getting a better look than she'd had during the night. "It should heal without any problems." She placed a fresh bandage over the injury. "By the way, where's Sheila this morning?"

"Over at their parents' house with Ronan. She's curious about what he wants to show Tom."

"He didn't tell her last night?" Rachel was curious too, and she'd hoped that Joanna had ferreted out the information by now.

"No, she couldn't pry it out of him." They walked to the paddock gate and Joanna swung the latch up. "I didn't tell Sheila this, but I've got an inkling what he found over there."

"Really?" Rachel stopped outside the gate and turned to Joanna. "What? Is it something that'll help Tom?"

"I doubt it. But I'm sure Ronan's in shock, and Sheila will be too."

"Oh, now you have to tell me. Come on, spill it."

Joanna grinned and leaned back against the paddock fence. "I hate to disappoint you, but it's not all that exciting. It just seems sordid and sad to me. You know Jake Hollinger's got a reputation as a womanizer? Well-deserved, I might add. He made a pass at me once—groped me in my own kitchen—but I threatened to neuter him with my shotgun if he ever touched me again. I never had any trouble with him after that."

Rachel laughed. "I'm sure you didn't. He seems like an ordinary older man to me, but I guess he was attractive when he was young. Winter Jones made him sound like the local Casanova."

Joanna snorted. "Like she has any right to be sanctimonious."

Startled, Rachel said, "What? Don't tell me she—"

"No, no, not her, for heaven's sake. Can you imagine Winter Jones rolling around naked in the hay with Jake?"

The image was so ludicrous and unlikely that Rachel burst out laughing. "Yeah, that's a stretch. So who—one of the other sisters?"

"Autumn, the youngest one," Joanna said. "That was pretty low, even for Jake. She was just a kid. Nineteen, I think, and Jake was a married man in his thirties. He took advantage of that poor girl."

"Winter was gossiping about other women, but she forgot to mention that her own sister was involved with Hollinger."

"They don't talk about Autumn. They've got her picture on the mantel, but aside from that it's like she never existed. She killed herself, you know."

"Don't tell me she did it because of Jake Hollinger. Good grief, he couldn't have been *that* special even in his heyday."

Joanna shook her head. "No, I think it was her mother's death that tipped her over the edge. Then her father died in that freak accident not long afterward. But I doubt that being involved with Jake did the girl any good. From what I hear, she was pretty messed up emotionally."

"All of them seem a little…" Rachel couldn't come up with the right label for the Jones sisters.

"Odd? Spacey?" Joanna grinned. "Downright weird? Am I getting close?"

"Well, eccentric is a kinder word. Winter comes across as very strong and capable when I deal with her, but you should have seen the little old lady act she put on for Tom last night. Summer really does seem fragile, though. She got upset when Winter was talking about Hollinger and his affairs. Now I understand why."

"Yeah, bad memories. I think she and Autumn were pretty close. The older two are hard as nails, but Summer's sweet-natured, and Autumn was the same way. I wouldn't advise you to eat anything Summer cooks, though."

Jolted, Rachel asked, "Why do you say that?"

"She's got some awfully strange things growing in her garden. She likes to experiment, and you never know when you're going to be her guinea pig. I learned a long time ago it was safer just to say no."

Why had Winter told Rachel that tainted milk had made her sick? Made all of them sick—except Simon. No real harm was done, but Rachel felt uneasy about the differing stories.

She pulled her mind back to the original question. "So what do you think Ronan found in the house?"

"Pictures. Lincoln Kelly had some pictures he took of Marie with Jake, decades ago, back when they were all young. From the way Ronan was looking at Jake last night, I've got a feeling he found those pictures of Jake and his mother. I don't know what else it could be."

My God, it's true. Marie Kelly, a warm and unpretentious Earth Mother type who'd seemed devoted to her husband, had fallen prey to Hollinger's charms. "Wow. Winter mentioned the rumors that they had an affair, but I didn't believe her. Are you saying Lincoln spied on his wife and took pictures of her with her lover?"

"Oh, they weren't pictures of them having sex. But it's pretty clear something was going on between them. You know, kissing, touching. The way they looked at each other."

"How do you know all this? Have you seen the pictures?"

Marcella had ambled over to the fence and now laid her chin on Joanna's shoulder. Joanna rubbed the horse's muzzle up and down. "I wish to God I hadn't, but Linc showed them to me. Just recently, about three weeks ago."

"Why?"

Joanna hesitated. "It was pitiful. It just broke my heart. You know Linc had Alzheimer's?"

"Yes."

"His short-term memory was just about gone. So he began confusing past with present. When he came across those old pictures, he thought they were new. It didn't matter that Jake and Marie looked so young in them. He seemed to believe *he* was young too. He thought everything was happening right now."

"Oh my God. How did you get involved?"

"He came over here crying like his heart was breaking, and he begged me to help him get his wife back. But he hadn't lost her. Marie never left him and the kids. Jake never left Sue Ellen. I don't know how Marie coped with Lincoln. She had a lot more resilience than I would under those circumstances."

While telling the story, Joanna had stopped petting the horse, and now Marcella lifted her head and caught the end of Joanna's ponytail in her teeth. "Hey, whoa, girl! You can't eat my hair." Joanna tugged on the ponytail but the horse held on.

"Maybe she wants more sugar," Rachel suggested.

Dipping into her barn jacket's pocket, Joanna found a couple more sugar cubes to offer the mare. Marcella let go of the ponytail, scooped the cubes off Joanna's palm, and moved off to resume grazing. Joanna fussed with her ponytail, which the horse had pulled askew.

Rachel nudged her back to the subject. "Are you sure Marie didn't destroy the pictures? That's what she should have done."

"She told me she was going to, if she could get them away from Linc, but she never told me whether she did. I didn't bring it up because she was so embarrassed that I'd seen them and I figured she wanted to pretend it never happened. But I'll bet you anything Ronan found them. He's been over there tearing that house apart."

"Do you think Ronan believes Jake Hollinger killed his parents?"

"I'm afraid that's exactly what he believes." Joanna shook her head. "But Jake didn't kill Linc and Marie. He's got his faults, but I don't believe for a minute that he's capable of that. He knew Linc was sick and harmless."

"Those pictures weren't harmless."

"Oh, I don't know about that. Marie was embarrassed that Linc was bringing it up again, but I don't think Jake cared. His wife is gone, she can't be hurt by it now. And God knows Tavia never had any illusions about him."

"Tell Tom all this when he comes by later," Rachel said. "He'll want to know."

"Honey, what's the point? It just confuses the issue. He doesn't need to go off on a tangent while people are getting killed and buildings are being firebombed. This is about the resort development. It's big business, big money."

"But who would kill over it?" Tom's own frustration, so deep and intense it was palpable, was infecting Rachel. "If everybody in the county's a suspect, how is Tom ever going to find the killer?"

"He doesn't have to look too far. And no, I'm not going to tell you who I'm talking about. But I'll point Tom in the right direction. I'm not going to let him waste any more time thinking I could have killed Tavia, when it's obvious as the nose on his face who had a reason to want her dead."

Chapter Thirty-four

Tom, accompanied by Brandon, pulled into the driveway at the Kellys' small farmhouse and parked behind Sheila's blue rental. Ronan's black sedan sat in front of his sister's car. "Looks like we'll have to deal with both of them at the same time."

"Can I just hide in the car?" Brandon asked.

Tom laughed. "Not a chance. If these two start throwing punches and heavy objects at each other, it'll take both of us to separate them."

They heard the shouting before they'd made it as far as the front porch. Tom exchanged a look of commiseration with Brandon and banged on the door, hoping the battling siblings could hear over their own racket.

Ronan yanked the door open and glared at Tom and Brandon.

"You wanted me to come this morning," Tom reminded him. "If you've changed your mind, we can leave."

"No, come in." Ronan made the invitation sound like a threat. He moved aside, raking his fingers through his already messy black hair. "Sheila's here."

"Yeah, we heard," Brandon said.

Sheila stood in front of the fireplace, arms folded and face flushed with anger. "Don't do this, Ronan," she said as they walked into the living room. "It's private. Don't you have any respect for our parents?"

"Why won't you listen to me?" Ronan's exasperation matched his sister's barely controlled fury. "How many times do I have to tell you? This means something, I can feel it in my gut. It could be a motive."

Sheila raised her eyes heavenward as if silently pleading for patience. "After all these years? It doesn't make any sense."

Tom held up his hands. "Hold on. I don't even know what you two are talking about, but if it's anything that could be connected to your parents' deaths—"

"It's not," Sheila said.

"Let me decide that. What is it?"

Ronan reached around Sheila and grabbed a shoebox off the mantel. She snatched at it, gripping one end. Ronan didn't let go, and they stood there playing tug-of-war with the box.

Tom heard a choking noise from Brandon as the deputy stifled a laugh.

Tom wasn't in the mood to find it funny. "Come on, you two, that's enough."

Ronan shifted his attention to Tom, and Sheila took advantage of his distraction to yank hard on the box. The top peeled off in her hands. The bottom slipped from Ronan's grasp and tumbled to the floor, spilling dozens of photographs as it went.

The brother and sister yelled recriminations at each other while Tom and Brandon scooped pictures off the floor by the handful. After a quick look at some of them, they exchanged a glance. The photos weren't explicit, but Tom didn't have to see people in the raw act to know they had a sexual relationship. He would need some time, though, to absorb and understand what he was seeing here.

Tom stuffed the last of the photos back in the shoebox, replaced the lid and stood. "Where did you find these?"

"Inside the basement ceiling," Ronan said, "on top of those removable tiles."

Tom frowned. "Why were you searching inside the basement ceiling?"

Before her brother could answer, Sheila said, "Yeah, did you think you'd find a secret stash of money you could make off with?"

Ronan's face reddened. "Fuck off, Sheila. Mom told me Dad was always hiding things the last couple of years. We can't sell this place without making sure we've found everything that's here."

"What makes you think these old photos have some connection to your parents' deaths?" Tom asked. "They're just old pictures of Jake Hollinger with different women."

"A bunch of women," Brandon added.

"Right." Ronan nodded with the eagerness of someone sharing a revelation. "Dad must have taken these. If he showed them to Hollinger, that gives Hollinger a personal motive—"

"You're accusing our father of blackmail." Sheila was almost shouting. "I'm not going to stand here and listen to it."

"Then leave, damn it!" Ronan flung out an arm toward the door, making Brandon duck to avoid a blow to the head.

"No," Sheila said. "You're the one who's going to leave. I own the majority share of this property, and I want you out of here today."

"You can't—"

Tom held up a hand. "Stop arguing for a minute, will you? This isn't getting you anywhere, and it's wasting our time. Ronan, what are you saying? These pictures are old. Hollinger's wife is dead, and some of the women in the pictures are dead too. There's no leverage for blackmail here. And no motive for murder."

Ronan pulled on his hair again, creating random spikes. Tearing his hair out, Tom thought. He'd never before seen anybody literally trying to do it.

"I know there's a connection," Ronan insisted, his voice tight with frustration. "Why did Dad keep those pictures all this time? Why the hell did he take them in the first place if he didn't have any use for them?"

Something occurred to Tom, but he hesitated, reluctant to provoke a storm of anger aimed at him personally. He had to ask, though. "Is your mother in any of these pictures?"

"No!" Ronan and Sheila exclaimed in unison.

"How can you even suggest such a thing?" Sheila demanded.

"Just covering all the possibilities."

"Well, you can forget about that one," Ronan said. "I looked at every one of those pictures, and Mom's not in any of them."

"Did you expect her to be? Were you looking for her?"

"Hell, no. You're twisting my words."

"Okay, then. We'll take these and look at them more carefully. I doubt they'll be any help, but you never know."

"We need the letters," Brandon reminded him.

"Right. Ronan?"

"Here they are." Scowling at his sister as if daring her to stop him this time, Ronan retrieved a plastic food bag from the mantel and handed it to Tom. "That's everything I found. Nine of them."

"They're outrageous," Sheila said. "They sound like they were written by an illiterate moron. Which they probably were."

"So you read them too. And handled them." Tom suppressed his irritation before it could turn into a lecture. Too late now for it to do any good.

"Of course I read them. I want to understand what happened to Mom and Dad. What they were going through the last few weeks of—" Sheila suddenly ran out of breath. She pressed a hand to her lips as her composure crumbled and her eyes brimmed with tears.

Rolling his eyes, Ronan turned his back on his sister.

Nice, Tom thought. "I want both of you to let me know right away if anything else happens—threatening phone calls, more letters, any vandalism on the property. Try not to be out in the open, exposed, any more than you have to be."

"You think somebody'll come after us, too?" Ronan's contemptuous expression vanished as fear flooded in.

"I'm just telling you to take commonsense precautions. And do everybody a favor and stay away from Jake Hollinger."

Chapter Thirty-five

Rachel flung the pen down. It bounced off her desk and hit the floor with a sharp *thwack*.

She couldn't concentrate. She hated the paperwork associated with owning a small business, and she tended to let it accumulate until she needed a whole day to plow through it. Today had been set aside for the chore, but she couldn't keep her restless mind on budget figures and supply orders and insurance renewal forms. Despite her best efforts, her attention kept circling back to her conversation with Joanna, to the unwelcome image of Marie Kelly and Jake Hollinger meeting in the woods for a tryst, to the memory of Joanna's stable ablaze in the night.

She swung her chair around to the window and checked the progress of repairs on the Packard company's plate glass window across the street. The two workmen had the new glass in place, and Lawrence Archer watched from the sidewalk as they applied putty inside and out.

The phone rang. Rachel swiveled around again and saw it was an outside call transferred from the desk. She reached for the receiver, expecting to hear a distraught owner with a question about a pet that didn't seem well or had swallowed something potentially harmful. "Hello. This is Dr. Goddard."

The voice on the other end sounded muffled, as if the caller had covered the telephone with a cloth. "If you don't change your tune, your animal hospital's gonna be next."

A hot flash of anger jolted her. "What kind of coward threatens a woman on the telephone? Afraid to say it to my face? Afraid I might hurt you?"

The man didn't answer.

Rachel waited.

"Or maybe that little boy'll be next."

A gasp escaped her before she could stop it.

"You can't watch him every minute," the caller said. Then he hung up.

Paralyzed, Rachel gripped the phone in her trembling hand and listened to the drone of the dial tone and her own rasping breath, in and out, in and out. Simon's in school, she told herself. He's safe. For now.

She slammed down the receiver and snatched her address book from the top drawer of her desk. Flipping through it, catching too many pages in her fumbling fingers, backtracking, she found the school's number.

The woman who answered told her the principal wasn't in her office, she was elsewhere in the building. "Let me take your number and she'll call you back."

"I have to talk to her right now. This is urgent."

"I can't leave the desk," the woman protested. "There's nobody to—"

"This can't wait. Find her and bring her to the phone or give me her cell number."

"I can't give out her private—"

"Listen to me. Somebody has threatened to hurt Sheriff Bridger's nephew, Simon. If anything happens to him because you wouldn't let me talk to the principal—"

"All right, all right. Hold on."

An interminable time seemed to pass before the principal, a Mrs. Rogers, came on the line. "Dr. Goddard? Maggie said somebody threatened little Simon. My goodness, this is terrible. What can we do to help?"

Thank God, thank God for sensible people. "Don't let him leave the school with anybody except me, or my husband's aunt or uncle, or my husband himself. If you see anybody strange hanging around the school, call the Sheriff's Department right away."

"Oh, absolutely. It's just shameful, the things that have been going on around here lately. You have my word that Simon is safe here with us."

After hanging up, Rachel sat at her desk, her face buried in her hands, until her heartbeat slowed. "He's okay," she whispered. "He's okay."

When she thought she could speak calmly, she picked up the receiver again and punched in Tom's cell number, hoping he was in an area with reception.

He answered quickly. "Hey, what's up?"

"I got an anonymous call a few minutes ago. A man. He threatened to hurt Simon if I didn't stop opposing the resort development."

"Aw, Christ—"

"I called the school and told the principal about it. They'll make sure he's safe while he's there. But I knew you'd want to know."

"I'm on the road right now. I'll call Uncle Paul and ask him to go keep an eye on the school until classes are out. I don't think we ought to pull Simon out of class."

"No, no, I agree. That would scare him." Rachel's pulse was pounding in her temples again, and she pulled in a shuddering breath to calm herself.

"He'll be all right," Tom said. "Remember Uncle Paul's a retired deputy. He knows what he's doing, and he cares about Simon. We'll find out where that call came from. Did it come in on your landline or cell?"

"Landline. The office number."

"You've got Caller ID there, don't you? Check it for me."

Excited by the hope that it really would turn out to be that easy, Rachel hurried out to the desk. Her spirits plummeted when she looked at the incoming call record and found not a number but the word UNAVAILABLE. She returned to her office to let Tom know.

"I'm not surprised," he said. "I'll tell Dennis to get a warrant for the records. Don't worry about Simon, okay?"

"I'll try not to." *But if he gets hurt because of me...*

She squelched the thought. None of this was her fault. She had to keep telling herself that. Drowning herself in guilt was nothing more than self-indulgence.

After she hung up, she rose and walked out, telling Shannon as she passed the front desk, "I'll be back in a couple of minutes." When she pushed open the front door, the chilly wind whipped her white coat around her body and lifted her hair off her neck. Ignoring the cold, she marched ahead, cutting through the parking lot and crossing the street.

Archer seemed startled when she walked up beside him, but he quickly produced a broad smile. "Dr. Goddard, it's always a pleasure to see you."

You smarmy bastard. "How's your finger? Any sign of infection?"

Still smiling, he held up the bandaged finger. "I think I'll survive."

"I'm beginning to wonder if Mason County will survive."

Archer's smile faded a bit but he hung onto it. He didn't respond to her statement.

"Somebody set Joanna McKendrick's stable on fire last night," Rachel added.

"I heard about that." His smile vanished and he put on an unconvincing expression of concern. "The horses are all okay, aren't they?"

"It's pure luck that they survived. I think we'll see more incidents like that, more damage to property. And attacks on people. Somebody just called me and threatened to hurt my husband's little nephew."

Archer frowned, and now his concern appeared genuine. "I'm sorry. That's despicable."

The two glaziers, outside and in, had stopped working to listen to their exchange.

"None of this would be happening if it weren't for you and the company you work for."

"That's not fair, Dr. Goddard. We're here to conduct business—and our business will benefit this community in more ways than you can imagine."

"Why can't you take no for an answer? Joanna McKendrick is never going to sell you her land. So stop pushing and look somewhere else."

"But that property is—"

"As long as you keep telling people that's the only property you'll consider, it's Joanna's land or nothing, this county is going to be a war zone. But you don't give a damn, do you? No matter how it turns out, no matter who gets hurt, you'll just walk away from it and move on to the next place. I don't know how you sleep at night."

"I have no trouble sleeping." Archer's tone was mild, but his eyes had turned cold and hard. "I'm helping to bring jobs to this community. I don't apologize for that."

"Oh, that's right. How silly of me. I was appealing to your conscience, and I forgot that you don't have one."

Rachel turned and walked back to the animal hospital, tugging her white coat closed and hunching her shoulders against the wind.

◇◇◇

Tom paced Jake Hollinger's driveway, cell phone to his ear. He'd caught Dennis Murray as he was leaving headquarters for the courthouse next door in search of a judge to sign warrants for Joanna's and the Jones sisters' phone records.

As Dennis returned to his desk to write up another warrant for the animal hospital's records, he reeled off a list of complaints called in to the Sheriff's Department so far that morning. Mailboxes knocked down. Threatening messages painted on houses in the dead of night. Cow dung dumped on front porches. "The targets are all people who oppose the resort development. I've sent four guys out to take victim statements and collect any evidence they can find."

"I guess we ought to feel lucky our firebugs didn't go on a spree last night." Ending the call, Tom shook his head and told

Brandon what he'd heard. "This is going to be normal until the resort issue's settled."

"It probably won't stop even then," Brandon said. "The losing side's not going to give up easily."

Jake opened his front door and called, "Y'all coming in, or you gonna stand on my driveway all day?"

The house felt stuffy, too warm, and the living room, with its dust-coated tables and unlit lamps, looked as if it hadn't been used in a long time. Jake led them through it without stopping, then through the small dining room into the kitchen, where the aroma of fresh coffee mingled with the fishy odor of cat food. His shirttail hung out over his khaki pants, he hadn't shaved yet, and his silver hair looked as if he'd combed it with his fingers. Going downhill fast, Tom thought, without Tavia around.

"Want some coffee?" Jake asked. "I just made it." When Tom and Brandon both declined, he motioned at the table. "Sit down. I don't know what you're here for, though. I don't have any more letters to give you."

Brandon took a seat at the table, but Tom stooped next to the cat bed where Tavia's pet lay curled up. "What's his name again? Spud?"

"Tater."

"Hey, Tater." Tom rubbed his knuckles over the cat's head. "How're you doing?"

The cat looked up at him with sad eyes and didn't lift his head.

"He's still down in the dumps, but he ate his breakfast this morning." Jake pulled out a chair and sat across from Brandon, mug in hand. "There's not much that can come between that cat and his food."

"Be sure and call Rachel if he doesn't adjust. She can help." Tom joined them at the table.

Jake nodded, watching the cat. "They mourn, you know. Animals. They mourn like people do."

"Yeah, I know." Jake's own grief for Tavia had deepened the lines around his eyes and mouth, and for the first time Tom had the conscious thought: *This is an old man.* An old man who

230 Sandra Parshall

would grow older alone, without the woman he'd loved, alienated from his only child. But that wasn't Tom's concern today. "Was everything quiet here overnight?"

Jake scrubbed a hand over his chin, and Tom could hear the scrape of stiff gray bristle against his palm. "Quiet as a tomb. I don't expect it to last, though. Like I said last night, both sides are going to retaliate. One side set Joanna's stable on fire, so I won't be surprised if the other side torches my barn. Or my house."

"You still planning to change your will today?"

"You bet I am. I've got an appointment with the lawyer. I need to shave and get out of here soon or I'll be late." Jake paused, then added, "My son might not be losing out on a fortune after all. With Tavia gone, I don't care about the Packard money. I might as well stay put."

"That'll make a lot of people mad," Brandon said.

"I don't give a shit who gets mad. Tavia's dead. Nothing else that happens can be any worse than that."

"That just leaves the Kelly property and the Jones property in doubt," Tom said. "Ronan's hot to sell, but it's hard to tell which way Sheila's leaning. We just came from the Kelly house, by the way."

Jake shoved his chair back, scraping the linoleum, and moved to the sink as if he had an urgent task to perform there. But all he did was grip the edge of the counter, his head down. "What did Ronan find that he thought was so important?"

"It was interesting. I don't know how important it is." Tom noticed something on the floor then, something caught and dragged by a leg of Jake's chair. It looked like a knitted scarf. Pink, light and soft.

Jake didn't speak for a long moment, but when Tom didn't go on, he blurted, "Something to do with me?"

"What makes you think that?"

Jake pivoted, his face contorted by anger and frustration. "God damn it, will you just come right out and say it? You're acting like a cop on some damned TV show. What are you here for, if it hasn't got anything to do with me?"

"Ronan found some pictures with you in them."

Jake slumped against the counter, shaking his head. "That's what I figured, from the way he was acting at Joanna's. Damn. We searched everywhere and we couldn't find all of them. Where were they? Where did Linc hide them?"

"We?" Brandon said. "Who do you mean?"

"Marie and me. We searched every inch of that house a couple weeks ago, and the wood shed, even the damned chicken house, and they just weren't there."

"Did you look inside the ceiling in the basement?" Tom asked.

Jake slapped a palm to his forehead in an almost comical show of self-reproach. "Aw, shit. The one place—"

"Why did Marie want to find the pictures?"

Jake raised his eyebrows. "Have you looked at them?"

"Not thoroughly, but we've seen them."

"Then you ought to know why she wanted to find them. She was going to burn them, and the negatives too if she could get her hands on them. She never wanted her kids to see those pictures."

Brandon shook his head. "Why would the pictures bother Ronan and Sheila? I mean, except for them making their dad seem like a perv."

Because their mother is in them? Tom wondered. But in his quick glimpses of the photos, he hadn't seen Marie Kelly. When Sheila objected to Ronan turning them over, her only concern seemed to be the implication that their father was a stalker and a blackmailer. Tom waited to hear what Jake would say.

Obviously puzzled by the question, Jake hesitated, glanced from Brandon to Tom. "I thought…" He shook his head. "Never mind. It doesn't matter."

"You thought what?" Tom rose and faced Jake. "Are there some other pictures we don't know about?"

Jake ignored the question. "Why did you come to see me? What does it matter now if Linc liked to spy on me? It hasn't got a damn thing to do with the murders."

"Was he blackmailing you?"

Jake's burst of laughter startled Tom. "Is that your theory? You think Linc was blackmailing me with pictures he took thirty-some years ago, and I killed him over it? Killed him *and* Marie?"

"I'm trying to find out what was going on between the two of you the last few weeks before the murders. What were you talking about when you said Marie wouldn't want her son and daughter to see the pictures? Did Lincoln have photos of you and Marie together?"

His amusement fading, Jake said, "Linc was sick at the end, his memory was scrambled. I didn't hold him responsible for anything he did. Forget it. You're on the wrong track."

"I don't think so. I want to know what happened. What made you and Marie suddenly decide you had to find the pictures and burn them, after so much time had passed?"

"It was personal, Tom. It didn't matter to me, but it mattered to Marie. For the last time, this hasn't got anything to do with the murders. You must have better things to do than badger me about old pictures. So why don't you go do your job and leave me in peace? I'm not answering any more questions."

But there was a connection between the old photos and the murders—suddenly Tom was as sure of that as Ronan Kelly was. How were they connected? What the hell am I missing here? Tom had the feeling something important was just out of reach, lurking at the edge of his awareness. He'd had that feeling before, in other investigations, and he'd learned to trust it. "All right. But I doubt this will be our last conversation about the pictures."

"I didn't think I could get that lucky," Jake muttered.

Tom leaned to scoop up the pink scarf, pulling it free of the chair leg. He held it out to Jake. "You dropped something. Was this Tavia's?"

"God damn it." Jake snatched the scarf from Tom's hand and flung it onto the table, where it landed in a soft heap of pink fluff. "She did that deliberately."

"Who? Did what?"

"Summer. She left that here on purpose, so she'd have an excuse to come back."

Tom frowned. "Summer Jones?"

"What other Summer do you know? She's been over here four times since Tavia died, fussing over me, bringing me food. Like I'd eat anything she cooked, after what happened with Sue Ellen." Rachel's voice echoed in Tom's mind: *The Jones sisters tried to poison me.* Joking, she'd claimed. "What happened with Sue Ellen?"

"The chemo made her so damn sick she couldn't raise her head off her pillow without throwing up. If it wasn't for Marie supplying her with marijuana, she wouldn't have been able to cope. So what does Summer do? She brings over some of her special custard, says it's full of natural ingredients, herbs and stuff, to give Sue Ellen more energy. That slop damn near killed her."

"Do you think it was deliberate? Was she trying to hurt Sue Ellen?"

Jake was already backing away from his anger. "Aw, I didn't mean it to sound like that. They're harmless enough, all three of them. They just don't seem to know when they're interfering. Summer was a nurse, she'd never hurt anybody deliberately. She wants to take care of people, but she's a damned nuisance." He grabbed the pink scarf off the table and thrust it at Tom. "If you're going over there, give that to her. Then she won't have any reason to come back here."

Chapter Thirty-six

"It was Mark Hollinger." Joanna spoke with absolute conviction, but kept her voice low, as if she thought the men working across the road in the stable might overhear her talking to Tom and Brandon in the barn. "If you weren't so convinced I killed Tavia, you'd see I'm making perfect sense."

"I'm not convinced that you—" Tom broke off, deciding it was better to bypass that point for the moment. "What makes you think Mark is guilty? I'm listening. I'll take anything you say seriously."

The stiff wind streaming through the open double-wide door chilled the back of his neck but didn't dilute the odor of horse manure in the shadowy interior. Joanna's farm hands, busy getting the stable ready to house the horses again, hadn't yet cleaned up what the animals had left behind during their half a night in the barn.

"Mark despised Tavia," Joanna said. "He'll tell you that himself, he never made a secret of it. He knew Jake was involved with her while his mother was dying. He hated her and he hates his father for taking up with her. I believe he killed the Kellys too. If you're thinking there are two killers, I'd bet anything I own that you're wrong. It was Mark, nobody else."

"Why would he kill the Kellys?" Tom asked.

"To get them out of the way, of course, so their land could be sold. Everybody knows he wants to modernize the lumber mill. He's obsessed with it, it's all he talks about. He's thinking about his own kids, giving them a reason to stay here instead of moving away to find work when they're grown. But he needs money. He wanted to get a bank loan, but Jake still owns the mill and he wouldn't take on the debt. That offer from Packard must look like money falling from heaven to Mark."

Joanna's thinking was in line with Tom's own. He still considered Mark a solid suspect. He'd realized that morning that although he'd broken Jake's alibi, persuaded Mark to admit his father hadn't been at the lumber mill when the Kellys were gunned down, he hadn't verified where Mark himself was at the time. Mark had no provable alibi for the time when Tavia Richardson was shot, and it was possible he didn't have one for the Kelly murders.

Brandon asked, "Did he have any reason to think Sheila and Ronan would sell the land to Packard?"

"Well, it makes sense, doesn't it? Neither one of them wants to move back here. What use do they have for a little farm in the mountains? Mark figured they'd inherit, and they'd turn around and sell it to Packard."

"But he knew he'd been cut out of his own father's will," Tom said.

"Exactly. So he killed Tavia, Jake's only heir. Mark's capable of it, Tom, I know he is."

"Believe it or not, all this has occurred to me."

"Well, I'm glad to hear that. I don't like being accused of a murder I didn't commit."

"I said it's occurred to me. A lot of possibilities have occurred to me. I've got suspects. What I need is evidence."

"You have to trap Mark into saying something incriminating. Get him to confess."

"Thanks for the advice," Tom said with a wry smile.

"I'm not trying to tell you how to do your job."

"Yes, you are. Look, if you come across anything that could pass for evidence, bring it to me. But I'm already looking at everybody involved, and hoping we'll find some physical evidence."

"If you don't stop him, he'll kill his father, and he'll come after me next. Then only the Jones sisters will be left. I told Winter they need to get a gun. I offered to lend them one."

"Did she take you up on that offer?"

Joanna shook her head. "She said she won't allow any guns in the house. But they all know how to shoot, and they ought to have some protection."

"I wouldn't encourage them to arm themselves, especially when they haven't fired a gun in years. That's asking for trouble."

"We all have to protect ourselves, Tom. You can't be out here looking after us every minute. I'm a woman living alone. The Jones sisters are three women without any kind of protection. We might as well have targets painted on our backs."

Tom couldn't argue against her fears. But he doubted that having a gun would protect them from a killer who might shoot from cover or take them by surprise. "I wish I could do something to make you feel safer, but all I can tell you is to be careful."

With her fingers interlocked and pressed to her lips, Joanna paced in a tight circle. Her boots landed in manure, releasing a strong odor. "There's another reason Mark hated the Kellys." She faced Tom. "Lincoln had pictures of Jake with Marie. They had a fling a long time ago, and Lincoln followed them around and took pictures."

Exactly what Tom had suspected. "How do you know? Have you seen the pictures?"

"I didn't know until recently, and I'm pretty sure Mark didn't either. Is that what Ronan found last night? I thought it might be."

"How do the pictures connect Mark to the murders?" Tom asked.

She told them about Lincoln's mental confusion and memory loss, and his belief that events long ago were happening currently. "Linc brought the pictures over here to show me. He wanted me to help him talk Marie out of leaving him, and he said he was going to confront Jake. Well, I couldn't stop him physically, so after he left here—he was on foot—I called Marie. We both went over to Jake's place to head Linc off."

"But you were too late," Brandon guessed.

"Yes." The word came out on a sigh. "It was awful. Mark was there. Linc was yelling and throwing the pictures in Jake's face, and Mark was picking them up and looking at them. He turned on his father, they were shoving each other around and I thought they were going to have a real knock-down, drag-out fight. Marie and I were trying to get Linc to go home, and when we finally got him walking in the right direction, Mark started shouting insults at Marie. Calling her a whore, among other things."

"Where are those pictures now?" Tom asked.

Joanna gave him a quizzical look. "Isn't that what Ronan found at the house?"

"He found *some* pictures."

"But not the ones with Marie?"

"Right. Do you know what happened to those? I'm guessing there were more copies, not just the ones Linc took to Hollinger's place."

"Oh, yes, Linc claimed there were multiple copies, and they were hidden where Marie wouldn't find them. But maybe she did. I hope she burned them. But my point is, Mark saw the proof that his father and Marie had a relationship. He must have known what kind of man Jake was, he must have heard the gossip the whole time he was growing up, but he'd never seen the proof before. And he was enraged—that's not too strong a word. I don't have a doubt in my mind that he killed the Kellys and Tavia."

Chapter Thirty-seven

Holly, surrounded by dogs, waved to Rachel from the big fenced play yard. "Hey, what are you doin' here?"

The dogs, large and small, yipped and jumped with excitement when they saw Rachel coming. She leaned over the four-foot chain link fence and patted as many bobbing heads as she could reach. "I couldn't stand it anymore. I had to get away from the paperwork." The niggling worry about Simon wasn't so easy to escape.

Adopting a mock stern expression, Holly shook her head. "I knew I shouldn't have took time off. I ought to have been there to stand over you and make you keep at it till you got done." She was dressed for a day at the animal sanctuary, in a sweatshirt and fleece jacket over baggy jeans. Her straight black hair hung in a long ponytail.

"It just proves that I can't get along without you."

Holly knew her all too well. Already she was studying Rachel's face with the keen perception that mixed so disconcertingly with her gentle innocence. "What's wrong? Is Joanna okay? I heard about the fire at the stable."

Rachel was always amazed at how rapidly news spread in this sparsely populated rural county. In this case, the fire provided a convenient explanation for her glum mood. Holly adored Simon, and Rachel didn't want to tell her about the threat to him and upset her unnecessarily. "I don't know how Joanna is, to be honest. I don't think this controversy over the resort development is going to end well for anybody. I hate what's happening. It makes me sick that people have been killed over something like that."

"I worry a lot about Joanna, about her standin' up for herself. I sure do admire her, but there's people that'll knock her down just to put her in her place."

Rachel continued patting any canine head that pushed against her hands. Simon loved coming out here and playing with the dogs. She would have to bring him again soon. When they were all safe again. "It's hard to see ahead. I can't even imagine where things will stand six months or a year from now."

"You'll still be here," Holly said. "And Tom. And Brandon and Grandma and me."

"Yeah. That's about all I'm sure of." Rachel straightened, withdrawing her attention from the eager dogs. She hadn't driven out here for a gripe session with Holly. "Your grandmother's here, isn't she? Her car's on the driveway. I need to talk to her."

"She's in the house. We're about to sit down to lunch. Come on in and eat with us."

Rachel had planned to speak with Mrs. Turner privately, but she saw no harm in letting Holly hear their conversation.

The three dogs that lived in the house sprang up from the kitchen floor and surrounded Rachel as soon as she walked in. She dropped to her knees to pet them.

Mrs. Turner, wearing an apron and working at the range, looked around with the moderately pleased expression that Rachel recognized as wholehearted approval. "I'm makin' grilled cheese sandwiches, to go with my homemade tomato soup. That suit you?"

"Oh, yes, thank you. I love your soup." Rachel got to her feet and brushed dog hair off her jacket and pants. "I'll get the recipe out of you one of these days."

"Tell you what, maybe I'll think about leavin' it to you in my will."

"You're a hard woman, Mrs. Turner."

"Oh, hush. Go wash your hands, both of you. Get the dog spit off before you eat."

Only when they were all seated with food before them did Mrs. Turner ask, "So what brings you out here? Always glad to see you, but I've got a feelin' there's somethin' you mean to talk about."

Rachel swallowed a bite of her sandwich and took a sip of iced tea. "Do you mind if I ask you some questions about the Kellys? I know Marie was your friend, and I don't want to offend you."

Mrs. Turner drew back and regarded her with wary eyes. She's going to tell me to get lost, Rachel thought. What right did she have, after all, to pry into the Kellys' personal lives?

After a moment, though, the older woman's expression softened. "You can ask. If I get offended, I'll let you know."

Rachel had no doubt about that. "I've heard stories about them, and I don't know what to believe."

The wariness was back in Mrs. Turner's eyes. "What stories?"

How could she say this without making Mrs. Turner shut down? "I heard that in the last few weeks before they died, Lincoln Kelly was so confused he thought things that happened a long time ago were happening now, in the present."

"Oh my gosh," Holly said. After a sharp glance from her grandmother, she grinned and ducked her head. "Sorry. I'll be real quiet while you two grownups talk."

"Don't you sass me," Mrs. Turner said. She shifted her attention back to Rachel. "That's the way it happens, you know. Alzheimer's, they call it now. Poor Marie. It broke her heart. He was just gone, the man she married. His body was still there, but *he* wasn't."

"It's devastating," Rachel said. "I don't know how anybody copes with it. It seems even worse than losing someone you love to cancer or heart disease."

Mrs. Turner nodded. "Marie told me she'd a whole lot rather see him drop dead of a heart attack, it would be easier on both of them."

"Was he worse in the last few weeks?"

"Oh, lord, ever since Robert McClure started comin' around, tryin' to get them to sell their land, Lincoln was worked up all the time. He thought somebody was gonna throw them out of their house, off their land. He was scared to death, and he got a lot worse real fast. Marie couldn't get through to him. Then he started bringin' up stuff that happened all those years ago. It was like he reached way deep down in his mind and pulled all that rotten garbage up into the daylight. Things Marie thought they'd buried and put behind them."

Holly glanced from her grandmother to Rachel with wide eyes, looking as if she might burst with curiosity. Instead of continuing her tale, Mrs. Turner bit into her sandwich, chewed and swallowed, then spooned up tomato soup. Rachel did the same, deciding to wait until Mrs. Turner was ready to say more.

"*Grandma*," Holly exclaimed. "What *kind* of things?"

Mrs. Turner threw an admonishing look her way. Holly blew out a long sigh of frustration.

Wiping butter from her sandwich off her fingers, Rachel got to the point. "I heard that Lincoln had some old pictures, and he seemed to think they meant Marie was going to leave him for another man."

"Oh, lord." Mrs. Turner patted her lips and tucked her napkin under the edge of her plate. "He took those pictures more than thirty years ago and they're still stirrin' up trouble. Marie let that Jake Hollinger turn her head when she was havin' a rough time, and she regretted it every day for the rest of her life."

"Do you know who Lincoln showed the pictures to?" Rachel asked. "Recently, I mean. Not back then."

"People that didn't have no business seein' them. Joanna McKendrick, and Hollinger's son, and that Richardson woman, the one Hollinger wanted to run off with. But Marie finally got hold of them, and the negatives too, and she burned them." Mrs. Turner paused and sighed. "But he had some more hid somewhere, and he showed some of them to those crazy Jones women."

"Who was in those pictures?" Rachel wanted to see if Mrs. Turner would give her the same story she'd heard from Joanna.

"Hollinger with their baby sister. Autumn was her name. Pretty little thing, and so young. Lincoln plumb forgot she was dead, he thought she was still alive and carryin' on with Hollinger, and he thought her sisters ought to put a stop to it. You know about Autumn and Hollinger, I guess."

"I've heard that people gossiped about them having a relationship."

"It was way more than gossip. She was all by herself, stuck in that house takin' care of her poor dyin' mother every day and not gettin' any help from her daddy or her sisters. Jake Hollinger was like some animal that hunts, he was always on the prowl for a woman with a weak spot. It was just a game to him, but Autumn Jones was crazy enough to think he was gonna leave his wife for her."

Holly was agog, her mouth hanging open as she listened.

"Why did she commit suicide?" Again, Rachel wanted verification of Joanna's story. "Was it grief for her parents? Or because she finally realized Jake wasn't going to get a divorce?"

"I don't know all of what happened. Just what little I heard from Marie, and I know she didn't tell me everything. Besides, you know how secondhand tales can get things twisted around. I don't want to speak ill of the dead."

"You can't hurt the dead. Is there some big secret about Autumn Jones that nobody knows?"

"Oh, I expect a few people know every little detail. I bet Hollinger does, for one, no matter what he claims. And the other Jones sisters. But I don't know it all, and I'm not gonna say somethin' that might not be true. I already feel embarrassed because I was so sure Tavia Richardson and Jake Hollinger killed Lincoln and Marie. I even told Sheriff Bridger that. But I was wrong. I learned my lesson."

"If you heard it from Marie, it was probably accurate," Rachel said. "She lived close to them. Didn't she know what was going on with Autumn?"

"Well…" Mrs. Turner drew her spoon back and forth in the remaining inch of blood-red soup. "I always did trust Marie to tell the truth. And it's not the kind of thing she'd make up. She wouldn't have any reason to."

Holly almost vibrated with impatience, leaning toward her grandmother as if afraid she would miss something, but she bit her lip and stayed silent.

Rachel felt equally curious and impatient, and she was going to be sorely disappointed if Mrs. Turner didn't produce something worth waiting for. "What did Marie tell you about Autumn Jones?"

Mrs. Turner took a deep breath and released it. "Marie thought it was all Lincoln's fault, because he followed Jake Hollinger around and took pictures of him. He'd been doin' it for a while, since Marie got involved with Jake. So Lincoln had some pictures of Hollinger and Autumn Jones, and he went and showed them to Autumn's daddy. Everybody knowed what he was like when it come to his girls, never wanted any man gettin' near them, and there was Lincoln, showin' him a bunch of pictures of his baby carryin' on with a married man."

Mrs. Turner reached for her tea and took a sip.

"What did he do?" Holly asked. "Old man Jones?"

"All I know is, Isaac Jones ended up dead on the ground in front of Hollinger's barn. Hollinger put out a story about him buyin' a bushel of oats from Hollinger for the horse he kept, and losin' his balance when he was tryin' to get it down out of the loft. Broke his neck, died on the spot. And there wasn't a soul that saw it, nobody that could say it didn't happen the way Hollinger claimed."

"Do you think Mr. Hollinger killed him?" Rachel asked.

"Now don't put words in my mouth. I told you, I don't know the whole story. And that's all I've got to say about it." She fell silent and concentrated on finishing her tea.

Rachel found the story Mrs. Turner told tragic and terrible. But did it really have anything to do with the murders of Lincoln and Marie Kelly and Tavia Richardson?

Chapter Thirty-eight

Tom pulled onto the shoulder of the road a hundred yards beyond Joanna's gate, flattening the brown stalks of Queen Anne's Lace and wild aster left over from summer. "I want to get a better look at those pictures before we talk to the Jones sisters."

"I'll get them." Brandon opened his door. "Pop the lid for me."

They had stowed the box of photos, inside a plastic evidence bag, in the trunk along with the anonymous letters they'd collected from Ronan and Joanna.

When Brandon returned, Tom slit the seal on the clear, oversized bag with his pocket knife and slid out the box that held the pictures. He scooped out half the photos. "Grab the rest," he told Brandon. "Look for any with Marie Kelly in them, or—hell, I don't know what we're looking for. Let's hope we'll know it when we see it."

For a couple of minutes they worked in silence. The only sounds were the hum of the cruiser's engine and the whisper of photos sliding off stacks and dropping back into the box balanced on the console atop Summer's soft pink scarf. Tom's glimpse of the pictures at the Kelly house had left him with the impression that Lincoln Kelly photographed Jake with dozens of women, but now that he examined them closely he saw only five. Each appeared in numerous pictures, in different clothes, in different locations. Passionate embraces on a blanket in the summer woods. Kisses in a parked car on a narrow dirt trail.

Half-clothed groping in a secluded riverside spot. Twilight made some photos fuzzy and dimmed the colors, but most had been snapped in daylight.

Tom recognized all the women. Two had died in recent years of heart disease and cancer. The other three still lived in the county, their hair graying and their faces etched with wrinkles as old age overtook them. He recalled seeing a couple of the women in church with their husbands and children every Sunday when he was growing up.

"Whoa." Brandon held out a picture for Tom to see. "This is the first one I've come across that's X-rated."

The picture showed Jake and a woman having sex on a blanket, surrounded by woods. The woman's face was hidden below Jake's shoulder, but her blond hair was visible. Tom couldn't identify her, but he knew she wasn't the raven-haired young Marie. "I guess Lincoln developed these himself. I seem to remember him having a darkroom a long time ago, but I didn't see any sign of it when we went through the house."

"I'm starting to wonder if he got off on this stuff," Brandon said, "sneaking around and taking pictures of Hollinger and his women."

Tom glanced at the back of one picture. "No date stamp. But he spied on Jake for a lot of years. Look at the hair." He held up two pictures. In one Jake appeared to be in his thirties, with dark hair, in the other he was older, with silver streaks at his temples.

"The whole thing's pretty sad," Brandon said.

Tom tried to summon a cool indifference to what he was seeing, but didn't succeed. Although none of these people meant anything to him personally, and he didn't think he had a right to judge, he felt disappointed in them because they'd taken stupid risks that could have cost them their families. Lincoln Kelly was the biggest disappointment. He'd been a kind and generous man, quick to smile and easy to like. And apparently he'd been a stalker and a voyeur.

"Hey, look." Brandon passed a picture to Tom. "Autumn Jones?"

Tom studied the pretty young woman in the photo. She wore a blue dress and her glossy brown hair hung loose to her shoulders. She faced the camera, and Jake's arms circled her waist from behind, holding her close. The expression on her face as he nuzzled her neck was one of pure bliss. As if she were in the arms of the most beloved person in her life. Dappled sunlight fell in streaks of brilliance on the tree trunks and foliage around them, and a gap in the undergrowth revealed the river's glittering surface.

"Yeah, that's her." She was the only one of Jake's women who had never grown older.

"There's more." Brandon handed the pictures to Tom one by one.

Jake and Autumn in different settings, different seasons.

"It wasn't short term. It went on for months. I wonder if her sisters knew." Tom dropped all the pictures into the box. "No pictures of Marie Kelly."

"She must have found them and got rid of them."

Tom shifted the car into drive. "Well, we've established that Jake's a real dog, but we're no closer to finding our shooter."

As they drove off, Brandon slid the box of photos back into the evidence bag. He gestured at Summer's pink scarf on the console. "That's kind of pathetic, isn't it? Her hanging around Hollinger. You think she's trying to get something started with him?"

"God, I hope not. I can't see that ending well."

Although the Jones farm was adjacent to Jake Hollinger's, Tom had detoured to see Joanna first and now doubled back to visit the sisters. Rolling along the rising and dipping road, he didn't see the two young men at the end of the Jones driveway until he was barely a hundred feet away.

"What the hell are they up to?" He hit the gas pedal hard to speed up.

Brandon leaned forward, peering ahead. "Looks like they put something in the mailbox."

As the cruiser approached the two spun around, and Tom saw they weren't grown men but teenage boys. He thought he recognized one of them.

The boys sprinted for an SUV parked on the shoulder of the road nearby. Tom floored the gas. By the time the boys were in their vehicle he was pulling up so close to it that the driver had no room to maneuver the bulky SUV onto the pavement. He parked the cruiser at an angle, its nose pressed against the rear door of the larger vehicle.

Tom killed his engine and jumped out. The young driver tried pulling the SUV ahead, but it was pinned in place. Tom positioned himself in front of it.

The boy's head swiveled as he sought an escape route, and his companion in the passenger seat gestured wildly, urging the driver to back up. Brandon was already standing behind the SUV when the boy began inching it backward and to the left. The vehicle jolted to a stop when one rear tire slid into the drainage ditch.

Tom heard the engine die. The driver lowered his head and banged it against the steering wheel.

The passenger door opened and the other boy tumbled out into the ditch. He took off past the rear of the SUV and leapt onto the pavement. Brandon was waiting for him. The boy stopped short of a collision with the deputy, stumbled backward, and fell flat on his back in the ditch.

Tom stepped into the ditch and hauled the boy to his feet. The surly-faced kid, his brown hair spilling over his forehead, didn't stop struggling until Tom slammed him against the side of the cruiser.

"You're Robert McClure's kid, aren't you?" Tom kept a hand on the boy's back as he checked his pockets for weapons. He found none. "Answer me."

The boy's face was pressed against the roof of the car and his voice came out muffled. "Go to hell."

"What did you say?" Tom grabbed his jacket collar and shook him. "You want to say that to me again? See where it gets you?"

The boy didn't speak.

"Get the other one out," Tom told Brandon.

A couple minutes later both boys stood against the cruiser, heads down. Now that Tom had a good look at the driver, he recognized him as the grandson of the county's Board of Supervisors chairman. His last name was O'Toole, but Tom couldn't recall his first, if he'd ever known it. He and the McClure kid were high school students, juniors or seniors. "Why aren't you guys in school?" Tom asked.

O'Toole looked so terrified that Tom almost expected him to wet his pants right there on the road. He gulped and mumbled, "Teachers' conference."

Tom folded his arms and examined them head to toe. Well-dressed, in shoes, jeans and jackets that had an expensive look to them. That late-model SUV wasn't a standard teen ride. Both had rock singer hair, combed down over their foreheads to their eyebrows. "So you decided to spend your time off hanging around the home of three elderly women? What are you doing here? What did you leave in their mailbox?"

No answer.

"Don't let them move an inch," Tom told Brandon. He walked back to the post-mounted mailbox, a fanciful little replica of a Swiss chalet. As he was about to flip open its door, both the boys shouted at once. "No! Don't open it!"

Tom jerked his hand away. "What's in here?" When they didn't answer, he strode back to them. "Look at me. Stop looking at your damned feet."

Both raised their heads just enough to show him their eyes.

"What did you do? Did you rig a pipe bomb in there?"

"It's not a big one," the driver said, his voice high-pitched and shaking. "It's just like, you know, a few BB pellets mixed in some red paint. It wouldn't hurt anybody."

Tom swore under his breath, imagining one of the Jones sisters opening the mailbox and getting a spray of paint and lead pellets in her face, in her eyes. "You're both under arrest."

Their heads jerked up. "You can't do that," the McClure boy protested. "My dad—"

"Don't say it." Tom pointed a finger in the boy's face. "You don't want to tell the sheriff that your dad won't allow me to arrest you."

The boy responded with a self-confident glare. He still expected to come out the winner.

"We'll book you for trespassing and vandalism, and the U.S. Attorney will probably be bringing charges too. In case you didn't know, putting a bomb in a mailbox is a federal crime."

O'Toole went pale and slumped as if he'd been socked in the gut. The McClure kid's face flushed scarlet.

Tom called the dispatcher and ordered a car to pick up the boys, then called the State Police and requested a tech to disarm the explosive in the mailbox.

Almost an hour passed before the boys were gone, accompanied by Brandon, and the State Police tech arrived. In all that time, Tom had seen no sign of the Jones sisters. That seemed more than odd, considering how nosey they were and how promptly Winter had shown up at Joanna's place when the stable was on fire.

He left the tech to his work and pulled into the driveway, parking behind the ancient station wagon the sisters used to get around. Halfway up the walk to the front door, he remembered Summer's scarf and had to go back for it. He rolled it tightly and stuck it in his jacket pocket. For more reasons than one, he wanted to see Summer's reaction when he returned it to her.

Chapter Thirty-nine

All the draperies in the front of the house were closed, as if the sisters hadn't awakened yet. Tom knocked on the door anyway, and the sharp rap of the brass knocker startled sparrows from an evergreen foundation shrub. The edge of the living room drapery flicked aside. Winter Jones peered out between curtain and window frame.

Tom raised a hand in greeting, and the drapery dropped back into place.

Winter opened the door. "Oh, Thomas, hello."

Instead of swinging it wide to invite him in, she cracked it about six inches, just enough to look out at him. Enough for Tom to see that her white hair, usually wound into a neat knot at the back of her head, hung in untidy wisps around her face, and the hem of her green blouse had come untucked from the waistband of her black skirt on one side.

Tom had never seen her when she appeared less than immaculately groomed and self-possessed. "Are you ladies okay?"

"Oh, yes, yes, we're fine, thank you." Winter's gaze slid sideways, as if drawn to something or someone in the living room. "Of course, we are concerned about the goings-on down there in the road."

Yet they hadn't come out to investigate. "There hasn't been any damage, but some kids put a pipe bomb in your mailbox. You'll probably be getting a visit from a federal agent at some point."

"Oh, dear lord." Winter pressed a hand over her heart, and her eyes shifted to look beyond him, down the gentle hill to the road.

"Like I said, they didn't do any damage, and an explosives expert from the State Police is down there right now, disarming it. The boys are in custody, so you don't have to worry about them coming back."

"Who are they? Do we know them?"

He told her.

Winter shook her head. "That's terrible. Simply terrible."

Why was she keeping him at the door? "May I come in? I wanted to talk to you about the phone calls you've been getting."

Winter hesitated, her reluctance obvious. After a moment, though, she opened the door wider and moved aside. "Of course. You'll have to forgive my rudeness. We're all very much on edge."

Tom stepped inside. "That's understandable. I think everybody's a little—" He broke off, stunned by the sight of the living room.

The sofa and chairs sat undisturbed, their plump throw cushions perfectly placed, but they were islands of order in a wash of destruction. Two ceramic end table lamps lay in pieces on the floor, their shades bent. Shards of china and glass littered the coffee table and the rug around it. A long streak of what looked and smelled like coffee trailed down one wall and pooled around a framed painting on the floor. Heavy splatter on the country landscape and a tear in the canvas told Tom the painting had been the point of impact. A mop leaned against the wall. Evidently Tom had interrupted Winter's cleanup effort.

"What's going on here?" he asked. "Did somebody break in? Why didn't you report it?"

"It wasn't a break-in," Spring said. "I did it."

She had appeared in the doorway between the living room and dining room, looking as disheveled as her older sister, her bright gold hair a mess, her purple blouse wrinkled. Most startling was Spring's total lack of makeup. Tom wasn't sure he would have recognized her without the garishly dyed hair.

"You did it?" Tom said. "What are you talking about?"

"Oh, dear, this is so embarrassing." Spring fluttered a hand before her face. "We've all been under so much stress, the constant tension and worry. Winter has been a rock, but I simply reached my breaking point. I snapped, as they say."

"And you…" Tom looked around. "You started throwing things?"

"Yes, I suppose that's it in a nutshell." She pressed her hands to her flaming cheeks. "I'm so ashamed of myself. I can't imagine what you must think of me."

Tom wasn't sure what to think.

Winter had regained her composure, and she seemed eager to cut off discussion of Spring's meltdown. "You wanted to ask about the phone calls. What can we tell you? We want to help in any way we can."

Neither Winter nor Spring had suggested that they sit down, another oddity for these women. The air in the room seemed to thrum with a disturbing vibration. And where was Summer? At the thought of the youngest living sister, his eyes were drawn to the mantel, to the photograph of Autumn. She smiled, forever fresh and pretty, from a gilded frame. But a crack ran diagonally through the glass over the picture, from upper left to lower right.

Dragging his attention back to Winter, Tom said, "That's right. We're getting your phone records. With any luck, we'll find out who made the calls. Was it always a man?"

"Oh, yes." Winter began tucking strands of hair behind her ears. "Always the same man, as far as I could tell. His voice was rather muffled, as if he had something covering the mouthpiece. So I'm not at all sure what his natural voice would be like. He was trying very hard to make himself sound menacing."

"What exactly did he say?"

"It was classic bullying," Winter said. "If we didn't sell our land and make way for the resort, we would be sorry, that sort of thing. Once he threatened to burn down our house while we were sleeping, if that was what it took to force us out."

A strangled cry pulled Tom's attention back to Spring. She slumped against the door frame. "You never told us that."

Winter sighed. "I didn't want to provoke the kind of hysteria you're demonstrating at the moment."

"Did you always answer the phone?" Tom asked her.

"Yes, I do tend to be the one who takes calls. What few we receive."

"Why haven't I heard about this before?"

"It was weeks ago," Winter said. "Before Lincoln and Marie died. And the Richardson woman. As I explained, it sounded like typical bullying to me. Remember that I taught high school for many years. I've known boys—and a good many girls, I might add—to make far worse threats than those to their unfortunate victims. But the worst that ever materialized was a scuffle or minor hair-pulling. I believed our caller was also engaging in bluster, nothing more."

"Now that three of your neighbors have been murdered, I hope you're taking this whole situation more seriously." Tom doubted that their anonymous caller had anything to do with the shootings, but it ticked him off that they hadn't reported the threats. How could citizens expect the police to protect them if they withheld potentially vital information?

The color had risen in Winter's pallid cheeks, but it looked more like a flush of irritation or anger than a blush of embarrassment. "Of course we take it seriously, Thomas," she said, in that tight, admonishing tone he remembered from high school. Miss Winter Jones never lost her temper, but she could freeze a student into submission with her frosty voice and eyes. She waved a hand at the mess on the floor. "You can see the toll it's taking."

"From now on I'll expect all of you to let me know about anything and everything out of the ordinary that happens around here."

"We will," Winter said. "I promise you that."

A thud overhead drew Tom's gaze upward. "Is Summer upstairs? I need to see her."

"Oh, she's suffering from one of her migraines," Winter said. "She needs to rest. Those headaches are a plague."

Tom heard the unmistakable creak of a floorboard directly above him. "Sounds like she's up. Would you ask her to come down for a minute? I want to talk to all three of you at the same time." When Winter hesitated, he added, "I won't keep her long, but I want to see her."

With a sigh, Winter walked past him to the stairs. As she mounted the steps out of sight, Tom heard a clinking noise that sounded like a ring of keys pulled from a pocket. For a second he wondered if Summer might be locked in her bedroom, but that seemed so crazy and unlikely that he dismissed the thought.

Spring remained in the doorway from the dining room, but when a Siamese cat appeared beside her and seemed about to venture into the living room where broken glass and china posed a hazard, she shooed it away.

Tom turned when he heard footsteps on the stairs. At the sight of Summer, he almost regretted forcing her to leave her room. Her normally rosy complexion had paled to a grayish cast, her uncombed brown hair fell over one eye, her sweater and slacks were wrinkled, disarranged, as if she'd been lying down in them. Winter gripped her arm to steady her.

"You'll have to excuse my appearance." Summer pulled her arm from Winter's grasp and brushed her hair off her face. Her pink sweater, Tom noticed, matched the scarf that created a bulge in his jacket pocket. "I'm not having a good day, to put it mildly."

"I'm sorry to disturb you," Tom said. "I'll let you go in a minute. I have a couple of questions that I want to ask with all of you here."

"What questions could you possibly have," Winter said, "that we haven't already answered?"

He hesitated, wondering how to phrase it, and decided to get straight to the point. "Did Lincoln Kelly come to see you recently with some pictures he took a long time ago? Pictures of Jake Hollinger and your sister Autumn?"

Outrage flooded Winter's face. "What on earth does our poor little sister have to do with your work? Why are you prying into our personal business?"

"I'm just trying to make sense of—"

Summer's hand darted out and grabbed at Tom's jacket. Startled, he caught her arm and forced it back. The pink scarf slid from his pocket, unfurling from the edge she gripped in her fingers.

They all stared at the length of fluffy knitted wool.

"Why do you have my scarf?" Summer demanded, sounding like a child whose belongings had been pilfered.

"Jake gave it to me. He wanted me to bring it to you, so you won't have to go back to his house for it."

"You see?" Winter said. "I told you he didn't want you over there."

Summer lunged at her. For a second Tom was too astonished to act, then he got an arm between them and forced Summer to back off. Her face contorted with fury, she spun away. The pink scarf trailed from her hand as she ran from the room and up the stairs.

In the quiet moment that followed, all Tom heard was raspy breathing, in and out, and he couldn't separate the sound of his own from that of the two women remaining in the room. "You all right?" he asked Winter.

Winter cleared her throat and said, "I'm perfectly all right. We're all overwrought. We have cooperated with your investigation, Thomas, but we never expected you to open up the terrible wound of our sister's…indiscretion."

"I'm sorry about that," Tom said, "but I need to know whether Lincoln Kelly came over here recently with those pictures."

"All right, if you must know, if you must have your curiosity satisfied, yes, Lincoln brought his shameful pictures here again, three weeks ago." Winter shook her head, anger and defeat mixing in her expression. "I have done my very best to protect this family in the way our father would have wished. To preserve our family's reputation so that we can live here and hold our heads up without shame. I believed that…that incident was behind us. Marie promised us years ago that she would destroy those pictures, but here Lincoln was, throwing them in our faces."

"Why now? Why bring it up again after all this time?"

"The man was sick. He thought Autumn was still alive. He thought our father was still alive, and he demanded to see him. He'd completely forgotten that he drove our sister to suicide, that our father would not have died the way he did if he hadn't seen those pictures and gone looking for Jake Hollinger to confront him."

Tom's mind was racing, making connections, throwing up more questions. "I thought your father's death was an accident."

"It *was* an accident. But Father wouldn't have been over there at all if he hadn't found out that Jake Hollinger had seduced our sister."

"I see," Tom said. "And I can understand it must have been a shock when Lincoln brought it up again. How did you handle it?"

"We made allowances for his condition because Marie begged us to. But in my opinion, Lincoln was always mentally unbalanced. What kind of man follows another man around with a camera, hoping to take pictures and use them to humiliate others? He took pictures of his own wife with Jake. Can you imagine such a despicable thing?"

"Did he show you the pictures of Marie and Jake when he came over here recently?"

Winter shook her head. "No, we were spared that experience. Marie told us about them, as if it would make us feel better to know we weren't the only ones he tormented. She said she had confiscated those and destroyed them, and she promised yet again to destroy the pictures of Autumn. Despite her failure in the past, we had no choice but to trust her to do that. But now you've seen them, and God only knows who else. Our trust was once again sadly misplaced."

Listening to her, Tom realized he had waded into a swamp of bad memories and festering grief and inflicted still more pain on this sad trio of aging sisters.

That didn't stop him from adding Winter Jones to his list of suspects.

"Do you have a gun in the house?" he asked.

Winter drew herself up, shoulders back, and gave him the glare of a disappointed and disapproving teacher. "No, Thomas. Look around, if you don't believe me. Search high and low, but you will not find a firearm anywhere inside this house. Now I would appreciate it if you would leave and let us try to deal with the damage you've done."

Tom held her gaze for a long moment, and in her eyes he saw no fear, no uncertainty, only the rock-hard defiance of a guard who would never let him breach their walls again.

Chapter Forty

Back in her office, Rachel struggled to focus on her paperwork, but she angled her chair toward the window so she wouldn't miss Tom's cruiser when it passed on the street. She had to talk to him face to face. A quick phone conversation while he was busy elsewhere wouldn't do.

How likely was it that Mrs. Turner's story about the Kellys, Jake Hollinger, and the Joneses had any bearing on the recent murders? Not very. The twisted relationship among those people had existed for decades before anyone ever heard the corporate name of Packard, and they'd never gone after each other with guns. Jake Hollinger had continued to live next door to both the Kellys and the Jones sisters, his presence tolerated if not welcomed. All that personal turmoil was a sideshow, stirred to life again in a sick man's mind by the fight over the resort development.

Rachel told herself that the Kellys and Tavia Richardson had been murdered because of their positions regarding the resort development.

Why, then, did she feel such urgency about talking to Tom, repeating what Mrs. Turner had told her? Why couldn't she reason away the sick knot in her stomach, the dread that something terrible lurked just ahead, around a blind corner?

When a brown Sheriff's Department car came into view, she jumped up to get a better look. Brandon sat in the passenger seat up front, but the car didn't have SHERIFF printed above the department's seal on the door. She couldn't see who was driving, but through the tinted window she thought she saw a couple of people in the back seat. Where was Tom? Why wasn't Brandon still with him?

She returned to her chair, working for thirty seconds at a time between glances out the window. Tom's aunt called to report that her husband had fetched Simon from school and the boy would be waiting, safe and sound, for Rachel to pick him up on her way home. One enormous weight was lifted, at least temporarily.

Another hour passed before she saw Tom drive by. She stripped off her white coat and pulled on her jacket. The walk to Sheriff's Department headquarters a few blocks up the street would give her time to compose her thoughts and Tom time to check in with Dennis Murray, his chief deputy.

She didn't see Lawrence Archer until she pushed open the front door of the animal hospital. Striding through the parking lot at a brisk clip, he raised a hand in greeting when Rachel stepped outside.

She kept going. "I'm on my way somewhere. I don't have time to talk."

"I'll walk with you," he said, falling in beside her.

She wanted to swat him away like a pesky insect. "I'm not looking for company."

Without acknowledging her statement, he kept pace with her as she crossed the two-lane Main Street. She continued past small shops toward the courthouse, an ornate relic of an earlier time that loomed over the downtown area from its own little hilltop. The Sheriff's Department and the jail were tacked onto the rear of the courthouse.

Rachel tried to pretend Archer wasn't at her side. What the hell did he want? Was he ever going to tell her?

At last he said, "I called your friend Mrs. McKendrick and invited her to sit down with me and talk, just the two of us face to face."

"I'm sure she was overjoyed to hear from you," Rachel said.

"I tried to tell her how sorry I am about the damage to her stable, and assure her that Packard had nothing to do with it and doesn't condone criminal acts. She hung up on me."

"And you're telling me about it why, exactly?"

"I was hoping you could persuade her to meet with me."

Rachel stopped and faced him. She let a couple of women pass them on the sidewalk and waited until they were out of earshot. "What does it take to get through to you? Joanna will never sell you her property. If the county tries to take it against her will, she'll fight them every inch of the way. She'll tie it up in court so long that you'll grow old and gray waiting to get your construction crew onto that land."

Archer held up both hands, not in surrender but in an effort to stop the words spilling out of her. "I've got a new proposal for her," he said. "It'll let her keep some of her land and continue her horse breeding operation, but—"

"Joanna wants to keep *all* of her land. She's funny that way."

He sighed and, hands on hips, bowed his head for a moment as if summoning patience to deal with Rachel's stubbornness.

She started walking again, faster now. Another couple of blocks and she'd be with Tom.

Caught off-guard, Archer hustled to keep up. "Don't you think she should make up her own mind? You can't speak for her. She might like this proposal."

"Fine. Go talk to her and find out. Why are you coming to me?"

"I told you that she… Look, will you ask her to hear me out? This could be a good compromise. Good for everybody."

"I don't work for you, Mr. Archer. I'm not your intermediary. I'm not anything to you." *Except, perhaps, a thorn in your side. I hope so, anyway.* "Don't ask me to do your job for you. It's never going to happen."

He threw up his arms in a sudden gesture that made Rachel flinch. She stopped and stared at him.

"You're right," he said. "None of this is ever going to happen."

"Is that a promise?"

"You people are impossible, you know that? I'm sick of trying to get through to you."

"Then stop. Please. Just give up and go away."

Rachel walked on alone, fighting a powerful urge to look back and check the expression on his face. At the foot of Courthouse Hill, where wide stone steps led up to the building, she did look back. Archer was walking briskly in the opposite direction, returning to his office.

Rachel veered to the left and followed the driveway around the courthouse to the rear. She crossed the parking lot to the Sheriff's Department headquarters.

The sound of a raised voice inside made her hesitate before swinging the door open. She couldn't tell who was yelling. Cracking the door a few inches, she peeked inside.

At the front desk, where the middle-aged female receptionist looked on with amusement, Tom stood straight and solemn as a totem pole while a red-faced Robert McClure flung his hands about in broad gestures and shouted in Tom's face. "This is outrageous! If you don't bring my son to me this minute, you're going to face serious consequences."

Tom regarded him silently.

"Well, why are you just standing there?" McClure demanded. "Go get my son. And I warn you, if he has a scratch on him, you'll be facing criminal charges."

Rachel pushed the door open a little farther, madly curious about the situation. Why was McClure's son at the Sheriff's Department? Sounded like he'd been arrested.

Tom let a second pass in silence before he asked McClure, "Are you finished?"

McClure blew out a noisy breath. "I want an explanation of your behavior. But first I want my son out here, where I can see that he hasn't been harmed."

"Don't worry about your son's health," Tom said. "You ought to be more worried about the people he's harassing."

"Harassing? What are you talking about?"

"Deputy Connolly and I caught him and a friend in the act of placing a bomb in the Jones sisters' mailbox."

A strangled laugh sputtered from McClure's throat. "A bomb? Is this your idea of a joke?"

"No, but it seems to be your son's idea of one. We caught them in the act, Mr. McClure. Your son William and his friend James, Supervisor O'Toole's grandson. We've notified Todd's parents. They'll be here shortly."

McClure's face faded from blazing red to chalk white. "You've made a mistake. This isn't possible. My son would never do such a thing."

"Like I said, I'm an eyewitness, and so is Deputy Connolly. We'll see how the prosecutor and the judge feel about it. The prosecutor's in court right now, so we'll have to wait for him to get over here at the end of the day. We can probably arraign your son and his friend sometime tomorrow—"

"*Tomorrow?* You can't keep my son in jail overnight."

"We can and we will. Before the judge can set bail, we have to find out how the U.S. Attorney for this district wants to handle the federal aspect of the case."

"Federal… What do you mean?"

"As I explained to the boys, tampering with a mailbox is a federal offense. Putting a bomb in a mailbox is generally frowned on."

Rachel stepped inside and quietly closed the door behind her. She didn't know whether to be horrified by what she was hearing—a bomb in the Jones sisters' mailbox?—or amused at seeing McClure thrown for a loop and momentarily speechless. Tom glanced at her with the barest hint of a smile.

"Oh, and one more thing I want to ask you about," he said to McClure. For the first time Rachel noticed the papers Tom held in one hand. He brought them up now, held them out for McClure to see.

"What is that?" McClure blustered. "Am I supposed to guess what it means?"

"Telephone records," Tom said. "I just walked in the door a couple minutes before you did and got these from Captain

Murray. I haven't had a chance to go over them thoroughly, but it appears that a call was made to Joanna McKendrick shortly after one a.m. last night from your cell phone."

"What? Are you out of your mind? I was in bed asleep at one in the morning."

"I didn't say you made the call. In fact, I'd be amazed if you had, so thanks for confirming it wasn't you. Somebody used your cell phone last night to call Mrs. McKendrick and tell her that her stable was on fire. It sounded like a boy's voice, she said. And she heard another boy laughing in the background."

McClure took a wobbly step backward.

"Hey, watch it." Tom grabbed McClure's arm to steady him. "Don't pass out on me."

"I can't believe this," McClure said, his voice losing volume with each word, ending his sentence in a breathless near-whisper.

"Believe it. Your boy and his friend are in a lot of trouble. Now if you want to sit down on the bench over there and wait for Todd's parents, somebody will take all of you back to see your sons. But those boys aren't going anywhere tonight." Without waiting for a response, Tom gestured for Rachel to follow him.

Amazed, amused, and gratified, Rachel had trouble holding back her words as she and Tom walked down the hall. Inside his office with the door closed, she exclaimed, "Robert McClure's baby boy? He set fire to Joanna's stable?"

Tom dropped into his chair with a sigh. "I hope that phone call is enough to get a confession out of him. Even if he won't admit it, I'm going to charge him with arson. Maybe he'll break down and implicate the O'Toole boy. We've got them on the bomb charge, in any case."

"Oh my God, this blows my mind." Hands pressed to her cheeks, Rachel paced the room, too keyed up to sit. "Is the McClure boy the one who called me today?"

"Probably. And he and his friend probably made some of the other calls too. We found a whole collection of disposable cell phones in the O'Toole kid's SUV."

"Good grief," Rachel said. "Well, I guess now McClure and O'Toole and the rest of them won't dare try to push you out of your job."

"What? What are you talking about?"

She stopped to look at him. "Oh, I never got around to telling you, did I? Lawrence Archer came to see me. He said if I didn't behave myself and stop opposing the resort development, the Board of Supervisors would find a way to fire you. He said it would be my fault if you lost your job."

"That goddamned son of a—" Tom jumped to his feet, sending his chair crashing into the wall behind him. "Where the hell does he get off, telling you something like that? I ought to—"

"Calm down, calm down." Rachel moved around the desk to lay placating hands on his chest. "No harm done. I think those boys have wiped out any advantage the powers-that-be thought they had."

Tom was making a visible effort to rein in his temper. "I'd still like to take Archer's head off, just on general principle."

"Well, I can't argue with that. Be sure to include me if you decide to do it."

They both laughed.

"Come here," Tom said, pulling her into his arms. "I haven't kissed you since this morning, and I really need to."

He did, more than once.

She pulled away at last, reluctantly, and said, "I came over here to tell you about something. I don't know if it'll help your investigation at all, but I thought I should tell you just in case."

"Okay. What is it?"

To avoid the distraction of his closeness, Rachel went to sit in one of the visitor chairs facing his desk. He sat again, and she recounted everything Mrs. Turner had told her.

"If it's all true," she finished, "there's something very fishy about the way Isaac Jones died. And it all happened because of those pictures Lincoln Kelly took."

Tom didn't respond. He sat with a grim expression on his face.

"Tom?" she said. "What are you thinking? Does it mean anything?"

He roused himself, focused on her. "I'm not sure yet. Is that everything Mrs. Turner told you?"

"Yes."

"Okay. Thanks. It could be useful."

He stood, and she knew he wanted her to leave so he could get back to work.

"All right then," she said, getting to her feet. "I guess I'll see you at home later."

He walked her to the door and kissed her. Feeling a little let down, she left the building, ignoring Robert McClure on the bench in the lobby. In the parking lot, she saw a woman in casual clothes and a man in a business suit get out of a silver Lexus and rush toward the building. The O'Toole boy's parents, she guessed. At least one piece of the puzzle had fallen neatly into place.

Had the information she relayed stirred something in Tom's mind, or was she imagining things? She would have to wait and see whether anything came of it.

She was walking back down Main Street to the animal hospital when her cell phone rang in her shirt pocket. Jake Hollinger was calling.

"I hope you don't mind me calling this number," he said. "The girl at the animal hospital gave it to me."

"No, no, it's fine. What can I do for you?"

"Well, it's Tater, Tavia Richardson's cat. You know I've got him here with me now."

"Yes, I know. How is he?"

"I thought he was okay. But I'm getting a little worried. He ate this morning, but now he's acting like he feels bad. He threw up a little while ago, and he seems a little warm to me, like he might have a fever."

"Oh, I'm sorry to hear that. Animals are like people. The stress of major changes can lower their resistance to infection. Look, I have time to run out there and see him if you want me to. Or you can bring him in."

"Would you mind coming out? I'd really appreciate it. I hate to haul him into the animal hospital on top of everything else he's been through."

"Let me get some things together and I'll be right out. I'll see you in a while."

Chapter Forty-one

"They're positive about that?" Tom asked Dennis between bites of his roast beef sandwich. He hadn't realized how hungry he was until a late lunch, in the form of sandwiches made by Brandon's mother at the family shop, arrived along with a small basket of donuts.

"Yep." Dennis sat next to Brandon in one of the visitors' chairs, an ankle crossed over a bony knee. Pushing his perpetually slipping wire-rimmed glasses back up his nose, he added, "The Blackwoods managed to talk to three different employees at the lumber mill before Mark Hollinger even realized they were there. Everybody said the same thing. At the time the Kellys were shot, Mark was at the mill, running a saw himself, getting a special order of pine ready for a builder in Fairfax County. It's going to be used for rustic ceilings in rec rooms, in case you're interested."

"He still could've killed Tavia Richardson," Brandon said, "and he sure as heck had motive." He popped the last of a frosted donut into his mouth and licked chocolate off his fingers.

"I'm not ready to give up on the idea of a single shooter." Tom looked to Dennis again. "You haven't found anything pointing to Ronan Kelly?"

Dennis shook his head. "If he's got the money to hire a hit man to kill his parents, I don't know where it came from. He's so deep in debt he's living on credit cards. One credit card, anyway. He was using four, and three of them have been blocked for non-payment."

"If a single shooter killed the Kellys and Mrs. Richardson," Brandon said, "then it's got to be somebody who's not even on our radar. The whole county's mad about the development, but they're taking sides, for it and against it. Who would kill a couple who didn't want to sell, then turn around and kill a woman who did want to sell?"

"Those letters you brought in won't help us," Dennis said. "They could've been written by half a dozen different people. Some of them are just words cut out of magazines and pasted on sheets of paper. Most of them came off computer printers, no handwriting at all. When we do have handwriting to look at, there's not much they have in common, except for three that I think could've been written by the same person. Somebody who's practically illiterate, or wants us to think he is. It's just garbage, no real serious threats. Bullying."

Classic bullying, Winter had said of the calls that came to the Jones house. Tom swallowed the last bite of his sandwich as he shuffled the printouts of telephone records. "Did you get the log for the Jones sisters' home phone?"

"It's in there somewhere," Dennis said. "I was about to mention it earlier, then McClure showed up and interrupted us. Except for one from Rachel's cell last weekend and one from Joanna McKendrick yesterday, they all came from untraceable cell phones. I think those two boys were responsible. I mean, you caught them putting a bomb in the Jones sisters' mailbox, so making a few nasty phone calls wouldn't be hard to believe."

"All right, we've got some of this cleared up, at least."

"The little stuff," Dennis said with a wry grin.

"Right." Tom dropped the phone records onto his desk and pushed them aside. Some aspects of the situation were starting to come clear, but others remained stubbornly out of focus. "Let me talk this through. Let's say the murders aren't directly connected with the development, not in a straight cause-and-effect way. I think when Packard came in here and started pressuring the owners to sell that whole section of land, it stirred up memories people thought they'd put to rest a long time ago. And that's where we'll find the motive for the killings."

"How so?" Dennis asked.

Brandon leaned forward, frowning, elbows on his knees. "It all comes back to Lincoln Kelly, right?"

"Yeah, I think so," Tom said. "He didn't have much short-term memory. I can't even imagine what it was like inside his mind, with all those burned out connections, but we know he was confused, and probably scared about losing control. When Robert McClure started coming around, talking about them selling their property to make way for the resort, Linc got it in his head that they were about to be thrown off their farm, the only place that felt familiar and safe to him."

Dennis and Brandon both nodded.

"That threw him into a tailspin," Tom went on. "It took him back to another time when he felt threatened—when he found out Marie was having an affair with Hollinger, and he thought he was losing her. So he did the same thing he did the first time around, he set out to make as much trouble for Jake Hollinger as he could."

"He dug up those old pictures and started showing them around like they were new," Brandon said. "He must've shocked the heck out of everybody."

"That's putting it mildly," Tom said. "We know he went to Hollinger with his pictures of Jake and Marie. Mark was there, and he saw the pictures too. We know Lincoln went to Joanna, begging her to help stop Marie from leaving him. And Winter Jones says he showed up there with pictures of Jake and Autumn, demanding to see their father so he could tell the old man what was going on. It was a replay of what happened all those years ago, when Isaac Jones and Autumn both ended up dead on Hollinger's property."

"The girl committed suicide, but Isaac's death was an accident, wasn't it?" Dennis said.

Tom rubbed the back of his neck, trying to loosen the tension in the muscles. "That's what most people believe, because that's what Hollinger said at the time. He claimed Isaac bought a bag of grain from him and he lost his balance and fell out of the loft while he was getting it out on the pulley. But now Winter and Mrs. Turner are both telling a different story. Winter told me the same thing Mrs. Turner told Rachel—that Lincoln showed Isaac pictures of his youngest daughter with Hollinger, and Isaac went over there to confront Hollinger. That's why he was in the barn that day, not because he needed some grain."

"Ah." Dennis tapped his fingers on the arm of his chair. "Yeah, that makes sense. So how did he really die? I mean, he did fall out of the loft, didn't he?"

"I think Jake was working in the loft and Isaac went up there after him. They got into a fight and—what? I don't know." Tom threw up his hands. "Jake pushed Isaac? Or Isaac really did lose his balance and fall?"

"Can we prove any of this?" Dennis asked.

Tom blew out a sigh. "No. It's all hearsay. If it's true, though, it gives Hollinger a motive for killing the Kellys. Just a few days ago, I thought a stupid fight over a fence line was enough to drive Jake to murder. But if Lincoln and Marie knew the real reason Isaac was in Jake's barn the day he died, and Lincoln was dragging it all out in the open, well, that sure as hell beats the fence line as a motive."

"Yeah, for killing the Kellys," Dennis said. "But what about Tavia Richardson? Why was she murdered?"

Tom shook his head. "I still can't answer that. All I know is that Jake didn't shoot her."

Chapter Forty-two

As Rachel drove out to Jake Hollinger's farm on the quiet country road, she wondered how much probing she could get away with, how many prying questions she dared throw at him.

None, she decided. This situation was too serious, too dangerous, for her to risk angering any of the people involved. She would stay out of things that didn't concern her and let Tom do his job without interference.

But she knew that every second she was in Hollinger's presence, she would be thinking about the past, about the man he once was and the young woman whose affair with him ended in her father's death and her own suicide.

She was about halfway to her destination when her cell phone rang. With no other vehicles in sight, she slowed to a crawl as she dug the phone from her shirt pocket and answered.

"Hello, this is Rachel Goddard."

"Dr. Goddard—Dr. Goddard?" The woman's voice sounded breathless, high-pitched, familiar but so distraught that Rachel couldn't put a name to it.

"Yes, this is Dr. Goddard. Who's calling, please?"

"You have to promise me—" The voice rose toward hysteria.

Alarmed now, Rachel steered the Range Rover onto the weedy shoulder of the road. "Who is this? Tell me who's calling."

The name came out on a trembling exhalation. "Summer. Summer Jones."

"What's wrong, Miss Jones? Has something happened?"

"You have to promise me—" Summer paused, drew a couple of gasping breaths, and when she spoke again she sounded calmer. "Please promise that you'll take care of the cats. Please don't put them to sleep. They haven't done anything to deserve that. And the rabbits. Don't forget the rabbits."

Full-blown panic seized Rachel. "What are you talking about? What's happening?"

"Do you promise? I want you to promise."

"Yes, yes, I promise. What's happening? Miss Jones? Summer? Answer me!"

Dead air. She had disconnected.

"Oh my God," Rachel said in the sudden silence.

She checked the screen to make sure Summer had truly disconnected, then with trembling fingers punched the speed dial button for Tom's cell number. Before he could say hello, she blurted, "Something's wrong at the Jones house. I got a strange call from Summer. Send somebody over there, please. Now."

"What do you mean, a strange call?"

"Don't ask me questions I can't answer. Just send somebody."

A moment of silence.

"Tom!"

"Okay, all right. I'll head out there myself. Talk to you later."

"Thank you, thank you," she whispered after he'd disconnected.

She leaned her forehead against the steering wheel and took several long, deep breaths, in and out, in and out, until she felt her heartbeat slow, felt the band of tension around her throat loosen. Probably nothing, she told herself. The Jones sisters were odd women with a sad history, and Summer seemed the most fragile of the three, the one most likely to bow under the weight of their history and the fear generated by the murders of their closest neighbors.

Rachel eased her Range Rover back onto the road. She had an appointment to keep with Jake Hollinger and his sick cat.

And that would take her near the Jones house, so maybe she'd be able to find out what was happening there.

Tom and Brandon jumped into Tom's cruiser and tore out of the lot.

"What do you think?" Brandon asked. "You think Winter's done something to her sisters?"

"I don't know. I don't want to guess. But I'll tell you, nothing can surprise me at this point."

"They don't have any guns, do they?"

Winter's angry words earlier in the day came back to Tom, but this time he heard a different meaning in them. "Winter told me I could search and I wouldn't find any guns *anywhere inside the house.*"

"But you think she's got some stashed—"

The dispatch radio crackled to life, cutting Brandon off. The department's young dispatcher sounded like a frightened child. "Sheriff Bridger? Are you there?"

Brandon pulled the mike from its hook and held it up for Tom. "This is Sheriff Bridger. Go ahead."

"Joanna McKendrick called and said she heard gunshots, then right after that Jake Hollinger called and said the same thing. They both thought the shots were coming from the Jones sisters' house."

"We're on our way," Tom said as he sped past the Mountainview city limits. "Get all our men over there. On duty and off. And send an ambulance."

Rachel was tempted to drive on past Jake Hollinger's driveway to the Jones house, but she forced herself to turn in. Tom didn't need her underfoot.

But what on earth was going on over there?

Put it out of your mind. Concentrate. Do your job. Let Tom do his.

Medical bag in hand, she walked to the front door of the brown-shingled house.

Jake didn't answer her knock.

She knocked again, harder, and tapped her foot as she waited. "Come on, come on," she muttered. She strained to pick up sounds in the distance but heard nothing. Even the birds had gone silent.

When she got no response to her knock, she retraced her steps to the driveway, then cut around the side of the house to the back. He might be in the yard, unable to hear her knock on the front door.

She didn't see Jake out back, so she mounted the steps to the porch. Despite the chilly autumn air, the main door into the kitchen stood open and the storm door wasn't fully closed. Not good. She would have to warn him about the danger of the cat pushing his way outside and getting lost. Tater wasn't exactly equipped to cope with the great outdoors.

Shading her eyes, she leaned into the glass in the storm door and peered inside. The fat orange tabby was there in the kitchen, sitting up in his bed and looking alert. When he saw Rachel, he meowed.

She pulled the storm door open and stepped inside. "Mr. Hollinger? Are you here?"

She thought she heard movement, somewhere to her right.

"Mr. Hollinger?" she called again. "It's Rachel Goddard."

She walked over to the doorway that opened off one side of the kitchen. It appeared to lead to a hallway that ran alongside the stairs.

Turning left into the hallway, she found her face inches from the barrel of a rifle.

She yelped, staggered backward, and dropped her bag. Her back slammed against the door frame. Dragging her eyes upward, away from the black hole at the end of the barrel, she saw the tear-streaked face of Summer Jones.

"What are you doing here?" Summer cried. She sounded grievously disappointed with Rachel. "You shouldn't be here."

"What—What's—" Rachel couldn't catch her breath.

"It will all be over soon." Summer sounded as if she wanted to reassure and calm Rachel. "I'm the last one left, and I'll be gone soon. Then it will be over."

"Where's—" *Breathe, breathe. Stay calm, stay calm.* "Where's Mr. Hollinger?"

A faint smile curled her lips. "In the basement. He fell down the stairs."

Chapter Forty-three

Tom pulled off the road and parked in a spot where several evergreens would hide them from anyone looking out of the Jones house. He and Brandon didn't speak as they pulled Kevlar vests from the trunk and fitted them over their jackets.

Ten or fifteen minutes at a minimum would pass before backup arrived. Tom didn't think they could afford to wait. They had to go in now.

He met Brandon's eyes, knowing he didn't have to speak the question aloud. The young deputy nodded. He was ready.

His pistol drawn, Tom crossed the drainage ditch and moved into the small patch of evergreens to take a good look at the house. The afternoon sun sat low in the sky, its glare reflecting off the house's front windows and making any glimpse of the interior impossible.

Tom signaled for Brandon to move to the left. At the same moment, they both broke cover and ran for the nearest trees. Tom didn't breathe again until he pressed his back against an ancient, gnarled maple. Brandon, shielded by another maple, looked to Tom for direction.

Tom listened, heard nothing. He took a quick glance around the tree trunk. From this angle, the windows looked blank, all the curtains drawn, no one in sight. Wind shook the tree branches overhead.

He gave Brandon a hand signal and they peeled away from their tree cover, Brandon to the left, Tom to the right, and bolted for the house. When they reached opposite corners, too close for anyone inside to see them or get off a good shot, Tom indicated that Brandon should stay put and watch the front door.

Tom moved around the house, staying close, ducking under windows. When he rounded the corner to the rear, he saw Winter Jones sprawled face down at the bottom of the back steps, a bloody wound between her shoulders.

"Aw, Christ," Tom said under his breath. He'd expected Winter to be the one with the gun, not a victim.

The shooter could still be in the house, or concealed somewhere nearby. Tom's gaze darted from the tool shed to the hen house, both a good fifty yards from the house. He saw no one, no movement.

Did he dare go to Winter? Could he do anything for her if he risked his own life to reach her?

Hugging the wall of the house, he edged toward the porch. He stopped next to a basement window and glanced in sideways without exposing himself. He saw only dark space. The window into the main floor of the house was elevated, and the best he could do was peer in over the sill. A light fixture glowed in the kitchen ceiling, but he couldn't see much of the room.

Abandoning the safety of the wall, Tom rounded the side of the porch and took the steps as quietly as he could. The main door stood open, but the storm door, with glass in the top half, was closed. With his back to the wall next to the door, he angled his head to look in.

Spring Jones lay on her side on the kitchen floor, a pool of blood spreading below her ribcage.

With her back pressed against the door frame, Rachel remained perfectly still and let Summer talk.

"Someone was knocking on the front door—I didn't know it was you—and I was afraid he would call out and you'd hear him, but he just backed away from me, and then down he went, without making a sound." Summer's eyes appeared unfocused, almost dreamy, but her steady grip on the rifle never faltered.

"Father didn't either. It's so strange, that they both died without crying out. Just fell, down and down and down."

Rachel stayed silent, her eyes fixed on the rifle barrel. Where was Tom now? She had sent him to the Jones house. He had no idea she was in Jake Hollinger's house. Would he see her Range Rover when he passed the driveway? Was it parked too far up, obscured by trees between the house and the road? Would Tom even glance this way as he drove by?

"It was Lincoln Kelly's fault," Summer was saying, "with those dreadful pictures he took. And Jake, seducing our poor little sister. Those two men played with her life, they made her do things she would never have done otherwise. It was their fault that our father died, you know. Not ours. We may have pushed him, but Lincoln Kelly and Jake Hollinger were to blame." Now Summer focused on Rachel. "You see that, don't you?"

Summer stared at her, expecting an answer. What was she supposed to say? "Yes, I think so—but I don't really understand what happened."

Summer blew out an impatient sigh. "I just told you what happened. Lincoln showed Father those pictures and told him Autumn was in the barn with Jake at that very moment. Father went over there with a gun. If I hadn't gone after him, if Autumn and I hadn't stopped him, he would have killed Jake, and then what would have happened to all of us? We were trying to prevent anyone from getting hurt. We were doing the right thing."

"Yes, you were doing the right thing." Rachel focused on keeping Summer calm. "So you…you pushed your father, to keep him away from Jake? I don't see how you could have done anything else. You had no choice."

"Yes, yes, that's right, there was nothing else we could have done." Summer's head bobbed up and down several times. "But he fell, and—well, he died. And Jake took charge and made us leave and take the gun with us, and he told us never to let anyone know we'd been there."

"But your sister—" Rachel bit off her words. She couldn't ask about Autumn's suicide. That would only provoke Summer.

Summer's eyes had filled with tears. "It didn't bother me that we pushed Father and made him fall. I was glad he was dead. He was always so mean to us, and he was even worse after Mother died. But Autumn was too sensitive. She felt guilty, and she couldn't live with it. She thought she'd done something wrong. But those men, Lincoln and Jake, they were the cause of it all. And they never gave her another thought after she was dead and buried. They simply went on with their lives, as if she'd never lived. How could they do that?"

Again Summer seemed to demand an answer. Rachel shook her head. "I don't know."

"She was so very dear to me. We were very close, you know. When we were little, she always wanted to pretend we were twins." Summer's brief smile faded into sorrow. "Spring and Winter were jealous of us. None of us had any friends—Father wouldn't allow it—but Autumn and I had each other. When she died, I lost the only friend I've ever had. And I've felt like a prisoner all these years, with Winter and Spring constantly telling me what to do. They're as bad as Father was. Worse."

"I'm sorry." How long, Rachel wondered, had she been standing here, frozen, listening to the ramblings of a crazy woman? Half an hour? Longer? No one was coming to rescue her. She had to find a way to get out of this alive. "It must have been terrible for you when Lincoln dug out those old pictures and started showing them to people."

"Oh, you can't imagine. You can't imagine the pain it caused me. Winter told me I had to put it out of my mind, I had to be strong, I couldn't let it hurt me. But how could I simply brush it aside?" The rifle barrel bobbed in her hands, moving downward, away from Rachel. "Jake didn't care either. He was going to move away with that awful Tavia Richardson and start a new life. He was going to be *happy.*"

"Is that why—"

"Yes," Summer broke in. "Now he knows how it feels to lose someone dear to him. He didn't care when his wife died. He had Tavia waiting for him. But now he knows what grief feels like. And I shot her with one of my father's guns that I took from her house. You know, she never locked her back door. I simply walked in while she was out and helped myself to as many guns as I wanted. I knew it would confuse the police if I used different guns."

Rachel's cell phone rang, a loud buzz from her shirt pocket. Hope flared inside her as she grabbed for it.

"No!" Instantly Summer's sad, dreamy mood vanished and she was alert to Rachel's movements. "Don't do that, Dr. Goddard. I like you, and I'm sorry that you've involved yourself in this, but I can't let you talk to anyone."

The ringtone stopped, and the flame of hope died.

Tom stood on the Jones sisters' back porch, cell phone to his ear, and listened to Rachel's recorded voice asking him to leave a message. "Where the hell are you?" he said. "I hope you're not headed over here. Call me back."

In the yard, the medics moved Winter Jones onto a gurney. She was alive, drifting in and out of consciousness. Spring was dead. Tom and Brandon had searched the house, and now other deputies were searching the property. They had found a stash of rifles and ammunition in the tool shed, but they hadn't found Summer.

Tom called the animal hospital and spoke to Shannon, the receptionist. "Where's Rachel? Is she there? She's not answering her cell phone."

"Oh, no, she's not here," Shannon said. "She picked up her bag and some antibiotics and went out to Jake Hollinger's house to take care of a sick cat."

Tater had left his bed and waddled over to rub against Rachel's legs. "Mr. Hollinger thought the cat was sick," Rachel told Summer. "But he seems to feel better. He's probably hungry. Maybe I should put down something for—"

"He cared more about that woman's cat than he cared about my sister. He was an evil man. You know that, don't you?"

"I know that he hurt your family."

"I wanted to make him suffer. I wanted him to die slowly and painfully. But he wouldn't eat anything I brought him. I think he threw all of it in the trash." Summer seemed outraged that Hollinger hadn't cooperated in her effort to poison him. Her gaze connected with Rachel's again. "I didn't mean to make you sick. I hope you don't think that was deliberate. That was Winter's fault. She knew I was angry with her, and she thought she was being so clever, switching the pastries around when I wasn't looking. I was furious. She had no right to make you sick that way."

I have got to get out of here, Rachel thought. Summer was coming apart in front of her, and the longer she stood here doing nothing, the more likely the woman was to turn on her. She was casting about desperately for something to say or do when she saw a movement down the hall, ten feet behind Summer.

Jake Hollinger had appeared in a doorway, one side of his face covered in blood from a gash on his forehead. Pressing his back to the wall, he inched forward.

Rachel caught his eye but quickly shifted her gaze before Summer could notice and wonder what she was looking at. *Talk*, Rachel told herself. *Say something.*

"You wanted me to take care of the cats. And the rabbits. I promise I will. But your sisters—"

Summer gave a sharp laugh that veered toward hysteria. "They won't mind. They won't be here, you see."

"Oh." Dear God. What had Summer done to them?

Tater moved away from Rachel, meowing, and hustled past Summer, headed for Jake.

Distracted by the cat's cries, Summer looked down. "Where is he going?" She turned and saw Jake. "*No!*" she screamed. "You're supposed to be dead!" She swung the rifle up and aimed it at him.

Rachel sprang forward, threw both arms around Summer from behind and yanked her backward, forcing the gun toward the ceiling. Summer lost her balance a split-second before her finger pressed the trigger. The blast of the shot rang in Rachel's ears. A light fixture shattered and shards of glass rained down on them.

"Let me go!" Summer bucked and twisted in Rachel's grasp. Rachel held on, and they tumbled to the floor together. The rifle flew out of Summer's hands, hit the floor and slid down the hall. Jake scooped it up.

"Get that damned thing out of here," Rachel yelled at him. She was on top of Summer, fighting to hold the struggling woman down. "Do it! Throw it outside!"

◇◇◇

Tom heard the shot as he scrambled out of his car in Jake Hollinger's driveway. The gunfire came from inside the house. He sprinted for the front door, halted when he thought he heard a voice, someone shouting. Rachel? Where? He swung around and ran for the back of the house.

Jake stumbled out the back door, his face bloodied, a rifle in one hand.

Tom drew his pistol and aimed it. "Put it down. Put down the gun."

"It's okay." Jake's voice wavered, fading to a whisper. "It's all right."

He leaned down, laid the rifle on the porch, and kept on going, falling unconscious beside the weapon.

Chapter Forty-four

Two days later, Tom and Rachel stood in Grady and Darla Duncan's front yard at dusk, Simon between them, to welcome the boy's grandparents home.

Darla threw her door open before Grady brought the car to a complete stop.

"Grandma!" Simon cried, barreling toward her.

She held her arms wide and Simon flung himself into her embrace.

Rachel blinked back tears, looked at Tom, and saw he was doing the same. Grady slammed his door and smiled across the roof of the car at the boy and his grandmother. "I guess you didn't miss your old grandpa at all, huh?"

Simon broke away from Darla, charged around the car and hurled himself at Grady.

When Rachel hugged Darla, she felt an answering warmth rather than the awkwardness she expected.

"Listen," Darla said as they stepped apart. "I want you to hear this too, Tom. I think I've got some good news."

"Oh?" Tom said. "You mean—"

"I had some more tests." Darla dashed tears from her eyes with an impatient swipe with the back of her hand. "Got that second opinion. That's why we stayed over. I didn't want to say anything on the phone the other night because I didn't want to get anybody's hopes up. I guess I didn't want to get *my* hopes up. I figured the news could just as easily be bad as good. But it's starting to look like I might beat this thing."

"Oh, Darla." Rachel hugged her again. "That's fantastic. That's incredible."

"Hey, now." Darla extricated herself. "You're going to have to help me with our little shared responsibility there." She nodded toward Simon. "I've still got some chemo ahead, and you know how that wears me out."

"She thinks I can't manage this little guy on my own," Grady said. He kept his arm around Simon's shoulders and the boy leaned into his grandfather as they joined the rest of the family.

"You spoil him rotten," Darla said. "Anyway, when I need some peace and quiet, this won't be any place for a whirling dervish like him. I want him to be where he can run around and make all the noise he wants to."

"He can stay with us anytime, you know that," Tom said.

"Of course he can," Rachel said. "We love having him."

"Well, all right then." Darla looked around at all of them. "I don't know about the rest of you, but I'm hungry."

"I thought you'd probably want an early dinner," Rachel said. "It'll be ready soon. I'm not as good a cook as you are, but it's edible."

"Anything I didn't have to cook is fine with me."

After the meal, after the apple pie dessert provided by Brandon Connolly's parents, Simon took Billy Bob into the backyard and the adults moved to the living room with their coffee. Tom lit a fire in the grate, and as the aroma of hickory wood filled the room, the conversation turned at last to the recent events they didn't want to discuss in front of Simon.

"I can't believe Packard's just pulling the plug and getting out," Grady said.

"They've done it before," Tom said. "They don't like to admit it, but they've given up in a couple of places, where the opposition was so strong they decided it wasn't worth the fight. And they didn't want any association with a string of murders."

"Besides, they could see they'd never get the land they wanted," Rachel said. "Joanna won't sell, and now Jake Hollinger's inheriting Tavia Richardson's land, and he's decided not to sell either parcel. I don't know what Sheila and Ronan Kelly will do, or Winter Jones. All I care about is that Packard decided to look elsewhere."

"I heard they had a backup plan all along," Tom said. "Somewhere nearby, I'm not sure where. Maybe some of the Mason County people who want those minimum wage jobs with no benefits will be able to commute."

They were all silent a moment, then Grady heaved a sigh. "It's hard to say what the right thing is when people are hurting and can't find work. But taking Joanna's land away from her, that wouldn't be right, not by my measure."

Rachel couldn't extinguish the twinge of guilt she felt when she considered all the potential jobs that local people had lost. But neither could she believe that a predatory company like Packard taking over the county's work force and government would help anyone in the long run.

"Well, that Packard man certainly stirred up a hornet's nest in the time he was here," Darla said. "What I can't get over is Summer Jones. My lord. I always thought she was the sane one in that family. You should've seen us in our motel room, listening to the news on the Charlottesville station. Our mouths dropped all the way to the floor when we heard your name, Rachel."

Oh, good grief. Rachel hadn't realized she'd been in the news. "It's a sad situation. I feel terrible about all of it."

Grady reached over to pat Rachel's hand. "We're just grateful you're all right. You're the one that matters to us."

"Didn't her sisters know what she was up to?" Darla asked. "She was running around shooting people, and they didn't do a thing to stop her?"

"I honestly don't believe they knew until the last day," Tom told her. "I've talked to Winter at the hospital, and she's still having a hard time believing what happened. She keeps making excuses for Summer. If she ever suspected anything, she must have blocked it out, refused to let herself face it."

"I think she's done that with a lot of things in her family's history," Rachel said. She knew from her own experience that the need to believe a lie, to preserve the calm surface of a false world, was sometimes strong enough to overwhelm reason and reality. She also knew that self-deception couldn't last forever. Eventually the truth would shatter the most lovingly constructed fantasy. "I feel sorry for her. I feel sorry for everybody involved."

Rachel thought she was prepared to leave Simon behind with his grandparents, and she was annoyed with herself when his good-bye hug at the door brought hot tears to her eyes. She blinked the tears away before she straightened and allowed the boy to see her face. "We'll pick you up Saturday morning to go riding, okay?"

"Yeah." Simon smiled up at Rachel, but he was reaching out for his grandmother, slipping a hand into hers. "It's been like forever. The horses probably forgot who I am already."

Tom ruffled Simon's thick black hair. "Nobody could forget you, pal. You go easy on your grandmother and let her get some rest. We'll see you in a couple of days. And don't forget about Thanksgiving next week."

As they left the house and walked down the driveway with Billy Bob trotting ahead, Tom slipped an arm around Rachel's waist and pulled her close. She leaned into him, glad of his warmth against the cold night air.

"He still needs us, you know," Tom said. "He always will."

"I know."

"Maybe it's time we started thinking seriously about…" His voice trailed off as he aimed the electronic key and the SUV's locks popped open. He hefted the short-legged Billy Bob into the back, then held the passenger door open for Rachel.

When they were both seated with their seat belts in place and the engine running, Tom finally spoke again, without facing her. "I don't want to pressure you, but maybe it's time."

Rachel didn't answer. She sat and waited for him to look at her. When he did, she knew that in the glow from the dashboard he could see her smiling.

"What?" His own smile spread but still seemed tentative. "You're okay with it? You're saying you're ready?"

Rachel laughed. "I'm saying that you are way behind the curve. I've known since yesterday, and I've just been waiting for the right time to tell you." She leaned over and kissed him. "Congratulations, Dad."